Psychologist **Vicky Newham** grew up in West Sussex and taught in East London for many years, before moving to Whitstable in Kent. She studied for an MA in Creative Writing at Kingston University. *Turn a Blind Eye* is her debut novel. She is currently working on the next book in the series.

Turn a Blind Eye

Vicky Newham

ONE PLACE. MANY STORIES

HQ
An imprint of HarperCollins*Publishers* Ltd
1 London Bridge Street
London SE1 9GF

This edition 2018

1

First published in Great Britain by
HQ, an imprint of HarperCollins*Publishers* Ltd 2018

Vicky Newham asserts the moral right to be
identified as the author of this work.
A catalogue record for this book is
available from the British Library.

ISBN: HB: 978-0-00-824067-7
TPB: 978-0-00-824079-0

MIX
Paper from
responsible sources
FSC
www.fsc.org
FSC™ C007454

This book is produced from independently certified FSC™ paper
to ensure responsible forest management.

For more information visit: www.harpercollins.co.uk/green

Printed and bound in Great Britain by
CPI Group (UK) Ltd, Croydon, CR0 4YY

For my father, who believed in kindness.

'You may choose to look the other way but you can never say again that you did not know.'

— WILLIAM WILBERFORCE (1791)

Kala Uddin Mosque, Sylhet, Bangladesh Thursday, 21 December 2017 – Maya

No amount of crime scenes and post-mortems could have prepared me for seeing my brother's charred remains, wrapped in a shroud in the mosque prayer room. Out of the casket, and on a trolley, his contorted limbs poked at the white cloth like twigs in a cotton bag.

Since receiving the news of Sabbir's death, I'd teetered on the water's edge of grief. Imprinted on my mind were images of him burning alive in his own body fat, skin peeling away from his flesh. I imagined the flames using his petrol-doused clothes as a wick. And here, now, beneath the camphor and perfumes of the washing rituals, undertones of burned flesh and bone lingered.

In the dim light, surrounded by *Qur'an* excerpts, it was as though the walls were leaning in. My legs buckled and I folded to the ground, knees smashing on the concrete beneath the prayer room carpet. Tears bled into my eyes, and my *hijab* fell forwards. All I wanted was to curl into a ball on the floor and stay there forever because my kind, sensitive brother was nothing more than a bag of bones and a handful of teeth.

Burned alive in his flat in Sylhet.

My sister was beside me now on the floor, kneeling. 'Get up,' Jasmina muttered in my ear. 'Remember what the *imam* said.' She slotted her arm through mine. Hauled me to my feet and turned me to face the *mihrab* for prayers.

'In the name of Allah and in the faith of the Messenger of Allah,' said the *imam*.

His words rang out like bells from a far-off village.

In front of us, his back filled my view. I had a sudden image of standing behind white robes at the hospital in London twenty years ago when thugs beat Sabbir into a coma. Hadn't that started it all? Sent him scuttling back to Bangladesh?

I scanned the room for an anchor. Took in the bulging bookcases, and the carved wooden screen which separated my sister and me from the four local men who'd carried in the casket. It was the medicinal smell of camphor that returned me to familiarity: when we were children, and had a cold, Mum would put a few drops on our pillow. Yet, despite the memories, Bangladesh hadn't been my home for over thirty years.

The *imam* was asking for Sabbir to be forgiven and I felt the storm of anger swell.

'Sssh,' Jasmina hissed into my hair. 'Maya. Look at me.' She straightened my *hijab* and pinned it back in place. Licked her thumb and dabbed at my tear-streaked face.

But he hasn't done anything wrong, I wanted to yell.

Five minutes later, and despite the humidity, it was a relief to be in the open air of the cemetery. How tiny the grave looked for my big brother.

The *imam*'s face was tight, and his cheek twitched with the misgivings he'd relayed to us over the phone. It will mean a *woman* positioning the bones in the grave, he'd said.

I removed my shoes and clambered down the rope ladder into the pit. The sweet smell of freshly dug soil filled my nostrils. It squished, soft and yielding beneath my toes, cold on my skin.

From above, Jasmina passed me Sabbir's shrouded remains.

The *imam*'s cough was urgent.

I'd forgotten the dedication.

'In the name of . . .' I couldn't say it.

He took over. 'In the name of Allah, and by the way of the Messenger Allah . . .'

I carefully positioned my brother's bones on the soil.

Femur.

Pelvis.

Laid his skull on its right cheek to face Mecca, the way the *imam* had shown me.

Then, in my periphery, something small scampered across the mud, brushing my foot. The scream was out of my mouth before I could muffle it and I hurled myself at the ladder. A man appeared at the graveside. In one swoop he raised a spade and sliced it down into the pit, on top of the animal and inches from my feet. Spats of fresh blood speckled the white shroud and my bare toes.

The *imam* raised his hands to either side of his head. 'Allahu Akbar,' he chanted. Then recited quietly, 'You alone we worship. Send blessings to Mohammed.'

I imagined Sabbir's clothes pulling more and more of his body fat into the orange, red and yellow flames as he burned alive.

'Allahu Akbar. Forgive him. Pardon him. Cleanse him of his transgressions and take him to Paradise.'

His muscles drying out and contracting, teasing his limbs into greasy, branch-like contortions.

The *imam* gave the signal for the wooden planks to be placed on top of the shroud. Then the soil.

Beside the grave now, I pushed damp feet into my shoes. Took out the poem and, with Jasmina's arm round my waist, read it aloud. Sabbir's favourite: about the boy who waits for his preoccupied father to come and give him a hug before bed.

As the words of the poem echoed through me, I felt my brother's suffering as though it were my own. I saw, more clearly than ever, how kind Sabbir had always been to others and how events over the years had eroded his faith that the *unkindness* that others had shown him would stop.

I closed the paperback and held it between my palms.

3

Dignified sorrow, the teachings stipulated.

And three days to grieve.

Yet Sabbir had endured a lifetime of anguish and was gone forever.

Wednesday, 3 January 2018 – Steve

Steve sat back in the plastic chair, squashed between two colleagues. Today was the start of the spring term at Mile End High School and he'd managed to turn up for the first day of his new job with a hangover.

'Good morning, everyone. Welcome back.' Linda Gibson, the petite head teacher, stood at the rostrum and surveyed the hall with an infectious grin. Her blue eyes danced with energy. 'First of all, apologies for the lack of heating. I believe the engineers are fixing the boiler as I speak.' She raised crossed fingers. 'They've promised to perform miracles so we can all get warm and have lunch.'

Laughter ricocheted round the hall where the hundred-strong staff sat in coats and scarves, the room colder than the chilled aisles at the supermarket.

'I hope you all had a lovely holiday,' she continued. 'I'm delighted to share good news: Amir Hussain, the year ten boy who was stabbed on Christmas Eve, is out of intensive care and doing well. In the sixth form, offers of university places have begun to trickle in.' She paused. 'Two final updates. Kevin Hall sadly had a stroke on Boxing Day, and Talcott Lawrence will step in as chair of governors until the end of term. Lastly, OFSTED notification could arrive any day.'

Nervous chatter skittered round the room.

'There's no cause for concern.' Linda quickly raised her hand to reassure. 'The inspectors will quickly see what a brilliant school we are.' She gestured to the awards that hung proudly on the walls of the school hall.

Linda's words floated over Steve's head. All he'd been able to think about since arriving at the school that morning was when he'd be able to get to a shop for some Nurofen – but, despite his befuddled mental state, optimism began to tickle at him for the first time in months. After his last school in sleepy Sussex, he'd longed to escape mud and meadows and return to the vibrancy of East London, where he'd grown up. Hearing Linda speak, he felt sure he'd made the right decision – even though his head was swimming with information and everyone's names were a blur. What an idiot he'd been to start drinking last night. After the long flight home from New York, the plan had been to have an early night. Why the hell hadn't he stuck to it? To add to his regrets this morning, he'd read through his drunken texts to Lucy while he waited for the bus and cringed. What a twat. Hadn't he promised himself he wouldn't plead?

Linda was still talking. 'We were all devastated by the suicide of Haniya Patel last term, and her parents have asked me to convey their thanks for our support.'

Steve's phone vibrated in his pocket. His heart leaped at the thought it might be Lucy replying – and then sank. *That* was never going to happen. He had to focus on getting through today without making a prat of himself. This job was the new start he needed.

'It's a tragedy we're all still coming to terms with.' Linda's voice was solemn. 'In your e-mail you'll find details of her memorial ser—'

A loud click sounded and a cloak of darkness fell on the hall. Stunned, the room was silent for a second, followed by whispered questions and nervous speculation.

'We seem to have hit another problem.' Linda's voice came from the front of the room. 'Can I suggest we all reconvene to the staffroom? I'll find the caretakers.'

*

An hour later, the staffroom resembled the late stages of a student party. Gaping pizza boxes lay empty on every horizontal surface, and the room honked of warm fat. The engineers had got the heating working again, and although the lights were back on, the power cut meant they'd had to order in pizzas for the whole staff.

Most people were still eating chocolate fudge cake when the assistant head, Shari Ahmed, stood up and tapped on her mug with a biro. 'Sorry to disturb you, everyone. Could we have a volunteer to nip along and tell the head we're waiting for her? She must've got held up with the caretakers.'

'I'll go.' Steve's hand shot up. Result. Senior managers delegated everything in schools, which usually pissed Steve off, but it was a chance to get some air. And hopefully a fag.

'Thanks,' said Shari.

From the main corridor, Steve made his way through the ante-room where the head's secretary worked, and approached the door to Linda's office. He knocked and stuck his ear to the opening. Couldn't hear anything. He knocked again, pushed the door open and walked in. 'Mrs Gibson? Are you there?'

The room was in complete darkness. After the brightly lit corridors, he couldn't see a thing. Disorientated, he stumbled into the room, right hand groping ahead for the lights. The tips of his shoes, and his knee caps, butted against a hard vertical surface, propelling him forwards. Arms flailing, he fell, landing on his front on something soft and warm and—

His senses exploded.

Hair was in his mouth and on his tongue. In the black of the room, the smell of human skin filled his nostrils, and he could taste sweat and perfume and – 'Christ.' Adrenaline spiked into his system as he realised it was a person underneath him. His limbs struck out like someone having a seizure, wriggling and writhing. With a push from his legs, he raised his trunk but his arms struggled on the shifting mass beneath him. Soft skin brushed his cheek. Hair forced its way from his tongue into his throat. Instantly his bile-filled guts retched, and his pizza shot over whoever was beneath him. 'Oh my God.' It was a low moan. Propelled by revulsion, his hands scrabbled, finally gained a hold and he heaved his core weight upwards and back onto his feet. Straightened his knees and stood up. His head was spinning.

Whoever it was, they were still warm. And if they weren't dead, every second was critical.

Eyes adapting to the darkness, he made out the door nearby and lurched over, drunk with alarm. One hand landed on the architrave while the other grappled for the lights. Nothing that side. Ah. He flicked the switch.

Squinting in the brightness, he absorbed the scene.

The curtains were shut. An upturned chair. The desk surface was clear and objects littered the carpet. And on her back, on a deep sofa near the door, lay Linda. Her wrists were bound with cloth, and were resting on her belly. Hair – the tangle he'd had in his mouth – lay like a bird's nest over her forehead. Steve's vomit speckled the cream skin of her face and gathered at the nape of her neck. Hold on. Were those marks round her chin or was it the light?

And her eyes . . .

What the hell should he do? He knew nothing about first aid. And schools were sticklers for procedures. He'd have to get Shari.

Steve stumbled through the door into the office and corridor, aware every second counted. He traced his steps back to the staffroom, careering round corners. Relief swept over him when he saw the room was just as he'd left it: pizza boxes and people.

Shari frowned when she saw Steve arrive back alone. She scuttled over to meet him at the door, adjusting the *hijab* round her flushed face as she moved. 'Is everything . . .? Where's Mrs Gibson?'

'Could I have a word?' Steve's stomach was churning. He slid to the floor. No. I can't throw up here. Not in front of everyone.

Slow breaths.

'Yes. Of course.' The older woman's eyes narrowed with concern. She stood over Steve. Waiting.

'It's Mrs Gibson . . . I think she's dead.'

Wednesday – Maya

The sound wrenched me awake. Trilling. Vibrating. Sylhet dreamscape was still swirling, and I had no idea where the noise was coming from. Fumbling for the alarm clock on the bedside table, my clumsy fingers sent objects crashing to the floor.

It was my mobile, not the clock. Why the hell hadn't I switched it off?

'Rahman.' I cleared my throat. My body clock was still adjusting after Sabbir's funeral and a day spent travelling.

A woman's voice came through. 'This is Suzie James from the *Stepney Gazette*. There's been a suspicious death at Mile End High School and —'

'A *what*?' Suzie's name was all too familiar. 'How did you get my number?'

'A suspicious death. It's your old secondary school so I was hoping for a quote for the paper.'

The groan was out before I could catch it. 'Who's dead?' I was wide awake now, synapses firing. I groped for the light on the bedside table.

'It's the head, Linda Gibson. Would you like to comment?'

'No, I *wouldn't*. This is the first I've heard of it.'

'The thing is, I've got parents asking questions and —'

'Okay, okay.' I flung the duvet back and swung my legs over the edge of the bed. A whoosh of cold air hit my skin. Suzie James would always write something, regardless of how much she knew, so it was better to give her the facts. 'Give me twenty minutes. I'll meet you at the school and find out what's going on.'

'Ta.' The line went down.

I threw the phone down on my bed and moved across the room to open the blinds. From the window of my flat, the canal was serene and green in the afternoon light and ducks weaved through the shimmering water. A jogger shuffled along the tow path from Johnson's Lock. In the distance, the skyscrapers of Canary Wharf loomed against a thundery backdrop. I rested my forehead against the glass. What was I doing? I was on compassionate leave until tomorrow. Then I remembered the poem I'd read at Sabbir's funeral; how much my brother had suffered. Wasn't this why I did my job – to bring justice to people who should never have become victims? Nostalgia flooded through me as I recalled my first day at the school in year seven, and how the place quickly became my lifeline. Just as it would be now for other kids like me. There was no way I was going to let the school's reputation nosedive. I had to find out what was going on.

Wednesday – Maya

On the main road, a few minutes later, the traffic was solid in both directions towards Bow. In front of me, a lorry, laden with scaffolding, clattered along behind a dirty red bus, while a shiny black cab sniffed its bumper. Ahead, at Mile End tube station, the carriageway snaked under the Green Bridge, from which school pupil Haniya Patel had hanged herself in the small hours four weeks earlier. Driving under it, I held my breath.

Soon I was off the main drag, and the grey fell away. Yellow brick houses lined the streets in elegant terraces, holly wreaths on their ornate door knockers. In the afternoon light, Christmas fairy lights twinkled in bay windows. They were so pretty. I'd left for Sabbir's funeral in such a hurry I'd not put my own lights up, and it was pointless when I got back. Outside the Morgan Arms, the beautiful red brick pub, smokers and vapers huddled beside the window boxes of purple pansies, sharing the chilly air. Up ahead, flashing blue lights cut through the slate grey sky.

When I pulled up, uniformed officers were struggling to contain members of the public within the outer cordon. Family members scurried about, indiscriminately seeking information and reassurance from anyone who could give it; others stood in huddles, no less anguished, simply shell-shocked and immobilised. The outer cordon covered an enormous area, far bigger than I remembered the school being. Round me, engines droned and vehicle doors slammed.

I'd clocked Suzie as I was parking and told her to wait for me.

I headed over to a uniformed officer who was standing at the main entrance to the school. I'd met PC Li several times.

'Hi, Shen. Who's the SIO?'

'DCI Briscall, but he's not here. DS Maguire's over there.'

'*Who?*'

'He's new. That's him.' She pointed at a man with ginger hair and urgent movements.

'Okay, thanks.' I surveyed the area outside the cordon. 'Could you get me a list of everyone here, and their connection to the school?'

'Sure.' Shen took out her notepad.

I approached the man she'd gestured to. 'DS Maguire?'

He whirled round and I was struck by his milky white skin, all the more pronounced by a crew cut.

'I'm DI Rahman. I was expecting DCI Briscall...'

'He's at a meeting with the Deputy Assistant Commissioner. He's sent me.' His vowels had a twang, and his sentences rose at the end.

I was trying to think of a polite way of asking how he'd got on the team. 'I don't think we've met?'

'I'm a fast-track officer.'

'Ah.'

'Don't worry. I know we aren't popular. I'm all up to speed.' He waved his warrant. 'Done a three-month intensive in West Yorkshire, a sergeant rotation, and passed my exams.' He stopped there. 'Aren't you meant to be on leave?'

'Until tomorrow, but never mind about that.' This was a shock, but now wasn't the time to debate the merits of the Met's fast-track programme. 'I've just had a call from a local reporter. She said the head's dead.' I used my eyes to indicate Suzie, who was holding court with a bunch of parents and locals. 'If she doesn't get some facts soon, she'll make them up. If Briscall's not coming, you'd better fill me in.'

*

Twenty minutes later, I'd dealt with Suzie James and was in the school canteen with the Murder Investigation Team. With its swimming pool acoustics and tortoise-slow broadband, it wasn't ideal as a temporary incident room but it was a vast space with plenty of tables and chairs. Twenty-four hours ago I was on a long-haul flight home, and now I was perching at one of the tables by the serving hatch. The surface was sticky and I longed for a decent chair to sit on, rather than the plastic kiddie seats that were bolted to the floor. Round me, the investigation team was gearing up. Colleagues were installing our technology, setting up the HOLMES connection and erecting partition boards. DC Alexej Hayek stood, muscled arms folded and legs apart, bellowing instructions and gesturing, as though he was directing traffic. His clipped Czech accent lent authority to what he thought should go where. With DS Barnes suspended, and Briscall more interested in hob-nobbing with his seniors than covering my post, I wasn't surprised when he accepted my offer to curtail my leave and appointed me SIO. If any of my colleagues wondered why I was back early from compassionate leave, they knew better than to ask.

I'd been mapping out our main lines of enquiry in my notepad. We were in the golden hour of the investigation, so these were organised round evidence gathering, witness interviews and suspect identification. Our quickest evidence source was going to be social media ring-fencing: once we found out from Facebook and Instagram who was in the school area between 12 noon and 1 p.m., we could target-interview those individuals.

As I surveyed the room, I remembered standing in line at that exact serving hatch, as a nervous eleven-year-old. The room seemed so much bigger then. Now, I imagined the cohorts of hopeful kids who, like I had, came here to learn, their lives ahead of them, their dreams in their hands. They'd be anticipating the first day of school now. For many, that would mean end-of-holiday blues. But not for everyone. I remembered how desperately I'd longed for the gates to open again after the lonely stretch of the holidays. Had any of today's students come from the same part of Bangladesh as us?

On my laptop, I was watching Linda on the school video. I'd met her at a number of community events, and found her warm and engaging.

'At Mile End High School we've achieved something unique.' Linda's eyes shone with pride, and passion radiated in the muscles of her face. 'Since the school opened in 1949, we've made it our mission to welcome *all* pupils from our continually changing community. We value all ethnicities and creeds equally, so you can be confident that your sons and daughters will learn and thrive in an atmosphere of wellbeing and safety.'

'I suspect *that's* going to come back to haunt her.' The Australian accent yanked me back into the present.

I jumped. 'Jeez . . . Do you *always* creep up on people?' I paused the video.

Dan Maguire stood in front of me, holding out a packet of chewing gum. 'Are you *always* this jumpy?'

Touché.

His pale skin and ginger hair were unusual. When he'd joked earlier about not fitting the bronzed Australian stereotype, he wasn't wrong. Irish heritage, he'd said. Hated water and had a sunlight allergy.

I waved the gum away. Recalibrated. 'Sorry. It's this place. Weird being back here after all this time.'

'I've been reading up on Haniya Patel. Doesn't seem *she* felt safe either.'

I heaved in a breath. 'No. Her death was a tragedy but nothing suspicious.' I shivered and pulled my woolly scarf round my neck. 'I don't remember this place being so draughty. Don't they have the heating on?'

Dan's face was blank. 'You think you're cold? I went from summer in Australia to winter in the North of England. Back home my kids are swimming at Coogee Beach every day.' He zipped up the neck of his jumper as if to support his point. 'Dr Clark is downstairs at the crime scene with the CSIs if you're ready to conduct a walk-through. And I've put the teacher, who found the body, in an office.'

14

'Yup.' I got up. Bundled my notebook and pen into my bag. Questions shot through my mind about Dan's appointment but they'd have to wait. 'I'm officially back off leave. I've told Briscall, who was delighted to hand over the SIO baton so, hopefully, we can get cracking.'

'Good.'

I followed Dan across the canteen to the door, pushing down the awkwardness that was circling between us. A few minutes later, we were walking along the main corridor on the ground floor towards Linda Gibson's office. My mobile rang. It was Alexej from the incident room.

'Until we have a media liaison officer, put all press calls through to me,' I replied. 'The last thing we need is a sensational headline splashed on the front page. I'll compile a holding statement.' I rang off. 'So much for sorting Suzie James out,' I said to Dan. 'She's interviewing parents and the national news teams are on their way.'

'It's inevitable.' He shrugged.

It was strange having a new team member. DS Barnes had been careering towards Professional Standards for years, but I'd got used to the way he and Alexej worked.

'Right.' I took a deep breath. 'Let's make a start on this crime scene.'

Outside Linda's office, Dan and I reported to the guard, pulled on forensic clothing and followed the common approach path. It was a large room with floor to ceiling windows, and thick brown curtains pushed to the side. The first thing that hit me was the smell of vomit. Dotted round the room, crime scene investigators were quietly dusting for fingerprints, bagging up evidence, taking measurements, drawing plans and taking photographs. Objects had been knocked over. So, there'd been a struggle.

I headed over to Dougie McLean, the crime scene manager.

A grin darted across his features when he saw me. 'I thought your flight only arrived back last night? You look shattered.' He reached towards me, but he must've caught my frown as he retracted his arm quickly.

'It did. You know me. Can't see my old school in trouble, can I?' I tucked my hair behind my ears and shifted into work mode. 'What've we got?'

'No sign of forced entry.' He gestured to the windows. 'The killer must've walked straight through the door.'

'Prints?'

'Lots. As you'd expect for a school. But a high cross-contamination risk. The guys have found some footprints and are still checking for blood and saliva. There's a good chance of exchange materials, particularly fibres, hair and skin.'

'Have we got a cause of death?'

'Strangulation.'

I cast about. Objects were strewn round the room. The computer monitor, keyboard and telephone were in a tangle of cables on the floor, surrounded by several silver photograph frames. Soil, from a dislodged pot plant, was sprinkled over the cream carpet like brown sugar, and Linda's office chair lay on its side several yards from the desk. It was as though someone had made an angry sweep of the desk surface or even hauled Linda's petite frame over it.

Swarms of photographs adorned the walls: year groups, award ceremonies, openings, school plays, and sports days. Hundreds of lives in one room, all brought together by the school and Linda. What a terrible loss this woman was going to be.

Over by the corpse, the photographer was packing away his equipment.

'Maya?' Dr Clark, the pathologist, signalled for me to come over.

It was my first look at Linda's body. Close up the rancid smell of vomit was more intense. A watery pool of it had collected at the bottom of her neck, with lumps of food speckling the white blouse on her chest. The perky face I'd seen on the video was barely recognisable; her delicate features had already swollen and her skin was blotchy. But it was her eyes that caught my attention, bulging from their sockets, bulbous and staring, the whites bloodshot. Beneath each socket, in a semi-circle, broken veins and congestion were forming dark channels. It was as though the killer had wanted to squeeze the life from her; to squeeze the eyes out of her head while they watched her suffer; to squeeze the last breath from her throat and lungs so she could never utter again.

'Where's the vomit come from?' I was absorbing the scene in front of me.

'Unless it was our killer, my guess is that whoever found her threw up over her.' He moved closer to the body. 'D'you see here?' His gloved finger pointed at the reddish marks that were creeping through the surface of the skin on her neck. 'I'll be able to tell more after the post-mortem but these' he pointed at fingernail gouges beneath her jaw 'are probably defence wounds. The CSIs have taken nail scrapings. It's likely the killer was squeezing her jugular vein and carotid artery, and crushing her windpipe, so she would have been gasping for breath immediately, and probably trying to pull their hands off her.'

Seeing Linda's bloated face, with broken blood vessels and bruising spreading by the second, what struck me was that she would've known she was going to die. And that her last few moments of life *weren't* going to be with her family but with someone who wanted her dead. She would have died while looking into the eyes of her killer.

'You can see the swelling in her neck. Her tongue is engorged and has been bleeding where she's bitten it.' Dr Clark faced me. 'There's a good chance she scratched her killer's face or pulled their hair. Even poked them in the eye.'

'Any signs of sexual assault?'

He shook his head. 'Not that I've seen. She has a small frame. Wouldn't have taken much to overpower her.' He moved closer to the body. 'My guess is there was a struggle over by the desk, and she was killed on the floor or on the sofa, but Dougie's team will know more.'

Had there been an argument and things had escalated? Or was this premeditated? One good thing was that strangulation involved high levels of contact: combined with the struggle, there was a good chance that fibres and hair from the murderer had transferred onto Linda.

On the cushion beneath her head, dark brown hair splayed, ruffled in places. Below her waist, her wrists rested at her solar plexus, bound together with a piece of white cloth. If the killer had simply wanted her dead, why had they tied her wrists?

'Yes, the forearms are interesting.' Dr Clark must've seen me looking. 'She has numerous scars. See, here?' He pointed to Linda's wrists, which had been positioned so that the left one faced upwards and the right one crossed it. On the inside, at angles across the veins, cut marks had healed into white scars, some thinner than others, now almost blended into her pale skin. Others were jagged and thick, raised and pinker in tone.

'The other one's the same.' He raised her hands gently so I could see. The right one had fewer scars, but they were more jagged. 'I would imagine she was right-handed.' Dr Clark placed her arms at rest.

I gulped. The cut marks upset me. Shocked me, even. They seemed unexpected in a head teacher. Or perhaps they were simply at odds with the smiling face I'd seen in the school video. 'How old are those likely to be?'

'Twenty years or so. No new ones. I'd put her as mid-to-late-forties. Extinguished while she was in her prime. Shame. She did well for this school. My brother-in-law is on the board of governors. It was heading for special measures when Mrs Gibson was appointed. He said she was a nice lady.'

As my eyes drifted back to the sofa, I noticed two evidence spots had been marked out. 'What was here?'

'I've checked the exhibits register.' Dan came over. 'One was a Chanel lipstick. The other was a piece of white card, with lettering on it. I've got a photo of it here.' He passed me the image.

'Some sort of ancient writing.' I inspected it more closely. 'And it was left by the body?'

'Correct,' said Dan. 'Her handbag was knocked on the floor. The lipstick probably came from that.'

I studied the image. Passed it back. 'Thanks. I want to know what it means. Can we get a translation ASAP?'

'Sure.'

'Before you head off, Doctor, anything else I need to know?'

Dr Clark took a final glance at the body and let out a long sigh. 'Not really. It's tragic. A scandal of this sort could send the school's reputation plummeting.'

'Not if I can help it. This place will be a source of stability for hundreds of kids.' My attention travelled round the room. 'And Linda clearly cared a lot about it.'

'Ah, yes. I'd forgotten you're a local.' He chuckled. 'Good to see you back. Dougie was worried you'd stay in Bangladesh.' Dr Clark and I weren't too far apart in age but his avuncular manner had become a habit we indulged.

I laughed. 'Doubt that. Dougie knows better than anyone, if *anywhere* is home for me, it's here.' I changed tack. 'When can you do the post-mortem?'

He checked his watch. 'Unlikely I'll get it done this afternoon. I've got two others to do tomorrow morning but I'll bump yours up the queue. I'll call you when I've finished.'

I returned my attention to Linda. On her back on the sofa, her petite frame and height made her resemble a young girl. Slender limbs and tiny hands created an impression of vulnerability that, in the flesh, was at odds with the vitality that exuded from the photographs and the school video.

'Poor woman,' I said to no-one in particular. Protectiveness had begun to stir in me. Who had crept into this woman's office and strangled her while the staff were having lunch? What had Dr Clark said? *Chopped off in her prime.* The only way we could help her now was to find her killer, and try to soften the blow for her family and friends.

By Linda's desk a CSI was documenting the photographs, which had been flung round the room. These were the first hint of Linda Gibson's personal life. They showed her with a man, both swathed in hats, woolly scarves and padded mountaineering jackets, smiling together on a hill, arms round each other.

'Presumably this is her husband?' I turned to Dan. 'How is he?' It wasn't just the greying hair. The man's clothes and mottled skin tone suggested he was a good ten years older than Linda. Next to this was a close-up of the same man. Kindness emanated from his features. Soft, intelligent eyes and a warm demeanour.

'Still in the Royal London Hospital. They're monitoring his heart and blood pressure. He hasn't taken the news well. Not long retired, apparently. Medical grounds.'

I took a closer look at the man in the photographs. Perhaps ill health accounted for him seeming older? It was hard to tell when Linda radiated so much energy and strength.

I was keen to get cracking with the investigation. Lines of enquiry were settling into place in my mind. The writing on the card was likely to be the killer's signature, and it was a good place to start while the forensic data were being processed.

Beside me, Dan was swiping at his smartphone.

'What d'you reckon that writing is?'

'I can tell you.' He enlarged the text and showed it to me. 'It's Pali. Part of a system of ethics. From a set of five ancient Buddhist precepts.' His pale face was alight. 'This one is the second precept and translates as: *I shall abstain from taking the ungiven*, whatever that means.' He screwed up his face, clearly no wiser than me.

Buddhist precepts? Bound wrists and strangulation? It looked like this was a ritualised killing – and rituals always held enormous significance for the murderer. They also involved careful thought and planning.

What was Linda's killer trying to tell us?

Wednesday

The precept says:

adinnadanna veramani sikkhapadam samadyani
I shall abstain from taking the ungiven

A Buddhist would say that where coercion is used, whatever is obtained hasn't been freely given. That includes manipulation and exploitation. Instead, we are encouraged to do the opposite of taking: to give without any desire for thanks or benefit.

I know you *believed* that your role gave you the right to make decisions, but surely someone in your position should have exercised discernment? Shouldn't you have put the needs of the vulnerable before your own selfish desires?

Mile End High School, 1989 – Maya

All summer I've been wondering how this moment would feel. With each step along the corridor the knot in my stomach tightens. Lockers line the walls ahead like a metal tunnel, so much bigger than the ones at primary. All the classroom doors are closed. Everyone else has arrived on time and they've started without me.

A tired ceiling light flickers. The corridor of scuffed linoleum yawns ahead. Today it's the rush and hurry that I feel in the small of my back, pushing me on, but for a moment it reminds me of Heathrow airport, the day we arrived. Of being herded along endless tunnels with the others from our plane, in the wrong season's clothes. Past faceless officials shouting things we couldn't understand, as we left one world behind and were jostled into another.

Muffled voices bring me back to the present.

Giggles ricochet off the metal lockers and excitement bubbles up. New things to learn, new people. But anxiety soon dampens my eagerness: I knew my class at primary school but I'm not going to know anyone here.

Sabbir is a few steps ahead of me, his gangly legs striding forwards. He tugs the arm of my hand-me-down blazer with one hand, carrying my bag in the other.

'Come *on*,' he keeps urging. 'You aren't the only one that's late.'

I'm glad my brother's with me. Not Mum, whose spokesperson I always have to be. Or Jasmina, whose poise and beauty means I may as well be invisible.

'Here we are,' Sabbir announces finally when we arrive outside one of the closed doors. He checks the room number, peers in and hands me my bag. 'I'll meet you at the front entrance at 3.45 p.m. Okay?'

My guts crunch again, and I screw up my face to say *don't leave me*, attempting to swallow down the panic that's creeping into my chest. 'How do I know what subject they're doing?' It's a croak. My throat has dried out on the silent walk to school.

Taller than me, he ruffles my hair with his hand.

'*Don't.*' I dodge out of reach, smoothing the everywhere hair that I'd brushed and brushed this morning to try and get under control.

The classroom door opens inwards, and suddenly a frowning face is in front of us, all lipstick and powdery skin. 'Can I help you?' The woman glances from Sabbir to me and looks me up and down.

She's seen the pins in my skirt. The floor draws my gaze like a magnet.

'Sorry she's late,' Sabbir mumbles. 'Our mother isn't . . .' His voice dies out.

Inside the room I hear chatter swirl. And giddy, first-day-of-term laughter. The sounds are amplified like when we go to the public baths to have our showers.

'And *you* are?' The voice has an accent.

Sabbir nudges me and I raise my head.

She's peering at me, as if she's used to having her questions answered immediately.

And now I wish Jasmina *was* here and then the woman would look at my sister and not me, and ask *her* questions instead of me. I swallow hard. You've practised this. Come on. 'Rahman.' Then louder, 'Maya Rahman.'

'Oh yes.' The frown's still there beneath a thick fringe. 'The Bangladeshi girl. I wasn't sure whether to expect you.' She steps back. 'You'd better come in.' She leads me into the classroom with a swish of her patterned skirt, and Sabbir fades away as I'm swept in front of a cascade of faces, and rows of tables, not like the individual desks at primary school.

Everyone freezes the moment they see me, halting their conversations and their carefree laughter to stare.

'Now, year seven,' the woman announces, with a chirpy lilt, 'this is Maya Rarrrman.' She presents me with a flourish of her hand, like I'm a stage act.

There I stand, weighed down by dread, swamped by my sister's old uniform, with my raggedy hair and my funny surname. And the fear leans in: *you aren't the same as them.*

On the giant pull-down board there's writing. I can't read it. It's not English and it's not Maths.

'We've just started to introduce ourselves in French,' the woman says, as if she read my mind. '*Je suis Madame Bélanger. Bonjour May-a.*' Her pasted smile does little to reassure me, and all I can think about is that everyone's still staring at me and I can't take in a word she's saying and I haven't a clue what she said her name is.

The room smells like stale crisps. I'm searching for a free seat.

'Do you want to sit on the end there, next to Fatima?' The teacher points to a grey table, wagging her finger. 'Fatima, *bougez-vous, s'il vous plaît? Voilà.* You can have my chair.' She picks up her seat, sets it down next to the wall and pats the back rest. 'You can be friends, you two, *n'est-ce pas?*'

I take my bag over and perch.

'*Alors, on continue,*' the woman says as she glides back to her desk and surveys the class.

All the sounds merge together now. My senses swim and I eye the door. I can make it if I run. Throat tight, my eyes fill up. I blink and blink, determined not to dab them, and wipe my nose rather than sniff conspicuously. All the time I'm thinking, it wasn't meant to be like this.

And I'm wondering whether I would feel different if Mum or Dad had come with me.

Wednesday – Dan

As soon as Dan entered Roger Allen's scruffy office, two things struck him: Allen was out of favour, and was at the bottom of the management pecking order. Scuffed walls were crying out for a lick of paint, and two of the ceiling lights were on the blink. It gave a very different impression from the showroom of Linda Gibson's office and the swish reception area.

Steve Rowe cut a dejected figure in a chair behind the desk. Trackie top. A face full of stubble. Mid-to-late twenties. A rookie.

Maya took the lead. 'Mr Rowe? I'm DI Rahman and this is DS Maguire.'

It was a small space and there wasn't much choice about where to stand. On a dusty cork notice board, a newspaper article was two years out of date, and someone had pinned a flyer for a new breakfast club next to a leaflet on pregnancy advice.

The guy was leaning over the desk, a blanket pulled round his shoulders. Dan got a waft of stale booze mixed with tinges of sick. He looked rough. All the staff were in civvies for training day but this guy could've just got out of bed.

'I understand you found Mrs Gibson.' Dan stood back and watched his new colleague at work. Maya's manner was gentle. You wouldn't mess with her, but she cared. That was obvious. 'What made you go into her office? Weren't you all eating lunch?'

'Yes, we were, but I'd finished and I wanted to get some air. Today is my first day here and I was feeling a bit . . .' He hesitated.

'Overwhelmed. When Mrs Ahmed asked for a volunteer to go and fetch Mrs Gibson, I jumped at the chance. Thought I'd nip out for a fag.'

'And why was Mrs Gibson not with you all?'

'I'm not sure. She left the hall when we had the power cut. Said she was going to find the caretakers. I got the impression she was planning to join us in the staffroom straight after. But it took a while for the electricity to come back on and someone suggested ordering pizzas.'

'I see. How well did you know Mrs Gibson?'

Rowe frowned. 'Hardly at all,' he said. 'I met her a few months ago at my interview. Would've been October. Then again when I came into the school for my induction day in December. And obviously today. She kicked off the staff meeting before lunch.'

'What was your impression of her?'

'She seemed friendly. And passionate about the school. I got the feeling the staff liked her.' Rowe took a swig from the mug in front of him. 'Is Mrs Gibson . . .?' His words petered out and he swallowed hard. 'I'm sorry. I'm shattered. I got about an hour's sleep last night and had a couple more drinks than I intended. I keep seeing her eyes. Bulging. And her face was all swollen. She's dead, isn't she?' The words came out in a splutter.

'We can't say at the moment, I'm afraid. There has been a very serious incident. You've had a nasty shock. Have you got someone at home this evening to look after you?'

'I'm staying with my sister. She should be home after work.' His complexion looked pale and clammy.

'You might want to lay off the drink this evening.'

It would've been easy for this to sound patronising but it didn't. And it was true: he looked dreadful.

Rowe blushed. Glanced at Dan in embarrassment. 'I'm sure I come across as a right numpty, getting drunk the night before starting a new job.' He paused, as if he was thinking about what to say. 'I've just got back from visiting my fiancée in New York – she dumped me. My own stupid fault.' His voice trembled and his hands were shaking.

Dan felt sorry for him. It had seemed odd to turn up for a new job with a hangover.

'We all make mistakes,' Maya said, then shifted gear. 'Was it you who vomited — ?'

'Ugh.' Rowe covered his eyes. 'Yes. Sorry.'

'When you went to fetch Mrs Gibson, did you see anyone?'

'No. I walked from the staffroom and along the main corridor. There was no sign of anybody.'

'After you found Mrs Gibson, what did you do?'

'I went straight back to the staffroom and told Mrs Ahmed.'

Maya's phone vibrated. She indicated to Dan to take over the interview and shifted towards the door, reading the message and watching the teacher from the corner of her eye.

Dan moved over and sat in the chair in front of the desk. 'Going back slightly,' he said, 'did you *think* Mrs Gibson was dead?'

Rowe nodded. 'She felt warm. Sort of soft. But she didn't move. I thought dead bodies went stiff?' He shivered in his seat, the unpleasant memory beckoning to him. 'It was the expression in her eyes. Staring.' He covered his mouth, shaking his head. 'Why would someone bind her wrists?'

'That's what we need to find out.'

Maya tucked her mobile in her pocket and hurried back over to the desk. She lowered her voice. 'We need to get back to the incident room. Urgently.' She faced Rowe. 'A uniformed officer will escort you back to the staffroom. All personnel are required to stay on site. Please let us know if you remember anything else you think could help.'

'I will.'

Back in the corridor, Maya filled Dan in. 'The deputy head, Roger Allen, called in sick this morning. Now no-one can get hold of him. Not even his wife.'

Wednesday – Steve

The staffroom atmosphere was completely different when Steve arrived back. The heating was working and everyone had shed their scarves, jumpers and coats. They sat in huddles, wide-eyed and dazed. As he walked in, was he imagining it, or were there a few nudges and stares? Steve scanned the room for somewhere to sit down. Despite the heat, he was still shivering and felt light-headed. The sense of Linda's body kept coming back to him: her softness beneath him; the smell of her skin; her hair in his mouth… how he'd thrown up over her.

He spotted a chair by the window, slunk over and slumped down on it, relieved to be out of the deputy head's office and among other human beings, even if he didn't know any of them yet. He wanted to reflect on the police interview. He'd burbled about Lucy. How embarrassing. Otherwise he thought it had gone okay but he wasn't sure. Was he a suspect? After all, he had found the body.

Near the door, a woman was firing out questions, repeating them hysterically to anyone who was in the vicinity. 'Why is no-one telling us anything? Is Mrs Gibson dead' Her voice trilled out. 'Has she had a heart attack? Oh my God, she hasn't been murdered, has she?'

Her voice grated. Steve felt like snapping at her to shut the fuck up. But this was a new job. He had to be on his best behaviour. Having a row with a colleague on the first day was not the way to go.

Steve could hear the two people nearest to her doing their best to calm the woman down, while a couple of other staff members stared, panicked into inertia and silence. It was as if they had all been plunged into an existence that was cut off from this morning. Set adrift into a new reality that none of them could quite accept.

Then the woman blurted out, '*He* must know.' She pointed at Steve. '*He* found her, didn't he?'

Steve's stomach did a somersault.

'Is she dead?' the woman asked in his direction, staring at him expectantly.

Shit. What should he say? The police had told him not to discuss what happened. He looked away, tried to tune out, and a few of the people nearby shushed her.

His thoughts drifted to Lucy and he wondered how she'd felt after she'd seen him off at the airport. And over the next day. Perhaps she would forgive him if he gave her time? He'd just have to be patient. Except he'd *been* patient over the last few months and it hadn't made any difference. Cheating was the one thing she'd told him she'd never accept in a relationship. And his stupid pride had got in the way. When she'd told him she wanted to go back home to America, he'd reacted childishly. And now he had to suck up the consequences.

Someone coughed and cleared their throat. Neil Sanderson, the school bursar, was standing at the counter by the kitchen area. He wiped his forehead with his palm. 'Could you gather round, folks, please?' His cheeks were mottled, and patches of sweat stained the armpits of his mauve shirt.

Mutterings flew round the room, some of complaint, others of curiosity and dread.

Neil adjusted the rimless glasses on his nose. 'As you all know, there's been a serious incident involving Mrs Gibson. At the moment the police aren't giving out much information. They have a number of teams here carrying out forensic work. We don't know yet whether the school site will be closed tomorrow, but there will be no lessons or students in school.' He reached over to the counter and took a swig of water from a plastic cup.

A few people put their hands up and he gestured them down. He checked his notes. 'Mrs Ahmed and I have been liaising with the police, the LEA and our governors, and we've produced a . . . a . . .' He looked round for Shari.

'Media and community strategy,' she prompted.

'Yes. With a close community such as ours, word travels quickly. We have contacted all parents to inform them there will be no school tomorrow. The police request that you do not tell *anyone* what has happened. Not even close friends and family.' He mopped his forehead again, and faced Shari. 'Is there anything else we need to cover?'

Shari came to his aid. 'It's a bit tricky as parents are already gathering outside the police cordon to find out what's happened. One of our parent governors is here trying to smooth things over.' She scanned the room, as though trying to gauge the mood. 'Everyone needs to stay on site until we dismiss you. Before you leave, we will inform you of the plans for tomorrow. The police are trying to speak to everyone as quickly as possible. Any urgent questions, please ask either Mr Sanderson or myself.'

Voices flared up again as soon as she stopped talking and people darted across the room to join groups of colleagues.

Steve felt disorientated. He surveyed the room and saw similar feelings mirrored in his colleagues' faces. Some were pale and wide-eyed, staring into the distance in a daze. Others were flushed and agitated. On the soft chairs round the coffee tables a group of people surrounded a young woman wearing a silver and black headscarf. Steve recognised Rozina, the head's PA, who was dabbing at her eyes and adjusting the pin on her scarf. When Steve had come for his interview, Rozina had been kind when he'd forgotten to bring his training folder and needed to print out the details from his e-mail. Poor girl. She had black panda rings round her eyes from crying through make-up. Steve could hear snatches of what Rozina was saying. She could have got help for Mrs Gibson if she'd been at her desk. She felt responsible. If Mrs Gibson died it would be all her fault.

'Stop being such a drama queen, Rozina,' said a fierce-looking woman with long white hair, which was parted in the middle so that it hung like two curtains on either side of her face. She was flicking through the latest *Times Educational Supplement*, licking her finger before each page turn.

'Moira, that's not necessary,' said a girl who was sitting next to Rozina. 'We're all extremely concerned and upset.' The gaggle of people surrounding Rozina stared at the woman.

'I was just saying.' Moira spat out the words as though she had bitten on a lemon.

'Well, perhaps it would be helpful if you *didn't* "just say".'

'Suit yourself.' The woman shrugged and flounced away from the group.

Feeling self-conscious with the ambulance rug wrapped round him, Steve pulled it off and got up. He was still shivering so he headed over to the kitchen area and flicked the kettle on to make himself a hot drink. The usual first day of term activities had been eclipsed. The whole day felt unreal, and he wanted to go home. He shuddered, though, at the grilling he was going to get from his sister.

Especially when she found out that, on top of blowing his engagement, he was now a potential suspect in a murder investigation.

Wednesday – Maya

'Let us know when he *is*,' I said to the family liaison officer. She'd rung to inform us that Peter Gibson had been discharged from hospital but still wasn't fit to be interviewed. 'Thank goodness his GP was on the ball.' On top of a serious heart condition, the news of his wife's death could've been fatal.

I crossed the incident room, leaving Dan with a telephone receiver clamped to his ear, and Alexej in front of a large monitor with a laptop screen either side. Uniformed officers were helping with house-to-house enquiries and staff interviews. Minutes later, I was in reception and had begun compiling the victim profile part of the investigation. With a crime like this, I wanted to get a sense of the school.

Photographs hung proudly on the walls, not a speck of dust on any of their frames. The very first one, dated 1949, showed the celebrations that had taken place the day the school opened. In the autumn sunshine, to a background of bunting and post-war jollity, grinning boys stood in long shorts and knee-length socks, while girls folded their hands over calf-length skirts. As I took in the expressions, I wondered, had life been more innocent then? Or was it just different?

There was a gradual progression in the photographs from monochrome to colour. There were changes in the ethnicities of both the children and the staff as increasing numbers of immigrants and asylum seekers arrived. I could see my compatriots in the images, others from Somalia, China, Pakistan, and from a number of African-Caribbean countries. I knew the reasons off by heart. The need to flee war, famine and oppressive regimes. Could quote the statistics from memory. After all, I was part of them, and I'd seen the demographics of Tower Hamlets printed in dozens of reports and booklets over the years. Like so many Bangladeshis in the seventies and eighties, my own family had fled Sylhet in 1982. As we all crammed into unheated one-room lets in Brick Lane, Whitechapel and Stepney, with outside toilets and no baths, it was no wonder the population of Tower Hamlets had burgeoned in the space of forty years.

As the decades progressed, the photographs showed how Mile End High School had acquired buildings to accommodate the increasing numbers of students. Annexes were constructed, including what was now the sports hall. I realised my eyes were searching the walls for a photograph of my year group in 1989. And there I was, in year seven, eyes bulging with fear, swamped in Jasmina's over-sized blazer and the skirt that Sabbir had helped me pin. My sister stood, tall and elegant, with her year nine form.

From the school's reception area, I continued along the main hall, past the science labs and the music rooms, along the corridor past the walls of metal lockers that had seemed like monsters on my first day of school here. I made notes in my pad as I walked; recorded and analysed impressions; took snaps on my phone. The display boards didn't fool me. I knew they were designed to portray a positive image to whoever saw them, but they somehow seemed too perfect. Who were all the smiling faces, and messages of progress and harmony, aimed at? And where was the information for the people who passed the boards the most often? The information for pupils on internet security, bullying and drugs? It all prompted two conflicting impressions: the place *had* clearly benefitted from the stewardship of Linda Gibson, but underneath the cheery faces and camaraderie, *something wasn't right* . . . I could feel Linda's murder reeling me in. Her legacy and achievements were all around me, vying for my attention, but very much at odds with the fact that she was now dead, with parents outside the school, desperate for information about what's happened to the head teacher.

When I returned to the incident room, I hurried over to where I had been working earlier. A few seats along, Dan was hunched over the table, checking off numbers on a printout with a ruler and yellow highlighter. He was facing me but had his head down, engrossed in what he was reading. Through his number one shave, his white scalp was visible.

At that moment, Alexej arrived, a bunch of papers in his hand. 'Shen dropped these off for you.' He handed them to me. 'Still no trace of Roger Allen. And Linda's post-mortem is scheduled for nine a.m. tomorrow.'

I scanned the list of names Shen had brought. I cross-checked these with the information on HOLMES. Rich, the school caretaker, had arrived late this morning after a delayed return flight from Spain. With all the commotion about the power cut and lack of heating, he'd got distracted and forgotten to switch the school's CCTV back on after the electricity was restored. Wait. His name was on the list of people outside the school earlier. If he wasn't in the staffroom with his colleagues, he might've had the opportunity to kill Linda. I scanned the records. Uniform had interviewed Rich after Linda's death but it needed following up.

'Any luck locating CCTV?' I asked Alexej. Without any, we were reliant on eye witnesses and forensics.

'Still trying to establish what's in the school vicinity. I'm heading over there in a minute to have a chat with one of the parent governors, a man named Talcott Lawrence, and re-interview the caretaker, Rich Griffiths. Rich swears no doors were left open this morning and all of them are entry-code protected, but given he forgot to switch on the school's CCTV, I don't know how reliable he is.'

'I was just reading about the caretaker. Can you grill him on where he was when Linda was killed and how he managed to get outside the school? Check his alibis. Also, find out who the heating engineers were and where they went?'

'Will do.' He put his pen in his jacket.

'And ask him why the power went off, can you? Was someone

34

helping the killer, or did the killer switch it off so there would be no lights and no CCTV?' Crime scene photos were scattered over my desk. 'This wasn't a frenzied, spontaneous attack. A strangulation of this sort suggests a quiet rage, don't you think? It was meticulously organised. The killer would've had to print the precept onto card, bring it with them – *and* the cloth for Linda's hands – strangle her, position the body, tie her wrists, then leave.'

'Exactly. That takes planning.' Alexej was shaking his head. 'I've checked the staff register. Only Roger Allen was absent today. Theoretically, Allen and Steve Rowe had the opportunity to kill Linda. *And* Rich, depending on where he was.'

'Yes, they're our obvious suspects. But we also need to consider the possible involvement of Linda's husband – however unlikely – *and* a student with a grievance. Unfortunately, we don't have any motives at the moment.' I added these to the list of suspects on the board. 'I've been reading the interview summaries. No-one has uttered a bad word about Linda. Good at her job. A competent leader. Nice person. Cared about the kids and staff. Passionate about education.' It made me think about the display boards and the school video. 'It always arouses my suspicions when no-one has anything negative to say about a person who's been murdered. No-one is so nice there's *nothing* negative to say. It's the British thing of not wanting to speak badly about someone who's died. And I respect that. But it only takes one person with a grudge.'

After Alexej left, I laid out several images of Linda on the table in front of me, alongside the staff photographs from the school data management system. I was keen to add pictures of Linda's family and friends to get a grasp on the people in her life. I was struggling to get a sense of what Linda's death might be about. In Tower Hamlets, in East London as a whole, it was mainly stabbings, shootings and beatings, and invariably to do with gangs, grudges or honour.

Seconds later Dan was back in front of my desk, clearing his throat. 'The parent delegation is growing and they've assembled next to the reporters.' He was holding out a paper cup of steaming liquid.

I took it. 'Thanks.'

'And your pal, Dougie, has just called. The technicians have given their initial reports. Linda Gibson has been wiping stuff off her computers on a regular basis.'

'You're kidding?'

'I wish I was. The techs are trying to recover the files but they wanted to warn you: she's used a professional programme to overwrite them.'

'What's the programme?'

'PermErase.'

'Argh. That's a pig of a piece of software.' The news sent my thoughts reeling. 'Why's she been doing that? You don't use PermErase to delete a few photographs and draft emails.' I still wasn't sure about Dan – I wasn't used to sharing my investigations with someone so pro-active. But the hot drink was a friendly gesture. I took a swig.

Dan's expression was thoughtful. 'Course, it could just mean that she's extremely organised or security conscious?'

'Until we know what she's deleted, there's no point speculating. But I definitely don't know anyone who uses professional software to overwrite blurry photographs.'

Dan tilted his head but didn't comment. Presumably it was his way of agreeing. 'Is there any chance it could be a school policy? Or a – what d'you call it here? – local government thing?'

'Local education authority. Can you find out? Shari and Neil should know if it's a Tower Hamlets policy.'

He tapped into his phone.

'Has Dougie's team got Linda's mobile phone? I want to know what's on it. Her contacts, texts, photographs. We need her call records, and details of her social media accounts, so we can assess the passive data for gaps and patterns. I want to know who she's been in touch with recently.'

'Already requested these. Her mobile was part of her handbag contents. I've been going through her call records.' He pointed at the printouts on his desk. 'The technicians are running checks on her

36

handset, then we can have it. Once we have her passwords, Alexej can check any Facebook and Twitter accounts she uses.'

'Well done.'

'A few other things. Neil Sanderson has asked if the staff can go home now.'

'Has everyone been interviewed? Got contact details and prints for them all?'

'Almost. Shen is double-checking against the staff lists.'

'In that case, the staff can go. Except the bursar and the other senior manager. I'd like to interview them myself. If there was something going on with Linda, one of them should know, surely?'

He shook his head. 'People can be extremely good at keeping secrets when they need to.'

'True.' I shifted topic. 'When the staff leave, they need to go straight off site. I don't want anyone wandering round the school.'

'Got it. The CSIs have almost finished. The filming's done and the virtual tour, and the inventories are almost complete. They haven't taken her out yet. D'you want them to wait for all the staff to leave first?'

'Yes. We've got no chance of keeping this out of the news with hawk-eyed Suzie James on the case but I'd prefer it if we didn't have an image of Linda Gibson in a body bag on the front page of the *Stepney Gazette, or* on the national news.'

'Of course. I'll see if the ambo guys can take the body out discreetly. There's always someone with a smartphone handy.'

'Thanks. Can you get details of Linda's bank transactions in the last twelve months?'

'Done it. She banks with Barclays. One current account, a joint account, a savings account and an ISA.'

'Good.' He was certainly more pro-active than Barnesy.

'Alexej's requested Linda Gibson's medical records for any reference to her cutting her wrists.'

'Those should yield some leads. Was anyone *not* in the staffroom apart from Roger Allen, Steve Rowe, the engineers and Rich?'

'We're still checking. A couple of staff nipped out and came back.'

'That it?' He was hovering and I couldn't help wondering what was to come.

'Briscall is on the warpath. Two of the school governors are friends of his and something about —'

'Targets?' I rolled my eyes.

'He wants an arrest within twenty-four hours.'

'And how come you know this and I don't?'

Dan had his hands raised in a don't-shoot-the-messenger gesture.

I felt a wave of annoyance. *Twenty-four hours?* If he wanted to help, he could authorise the fast-tracking of the toxicology and forensic results and get over here.' I drew breath and took stock. 'Okay, shall we go through the key staff at the school?' I re-arranged the photographs, placing the two senior managers next to each other. 'There's the assistant head, Shari Ahmed. She's in charge of the sixth form. And the bursar, Neil Sanderson, who's in charge of staff and budgets. Do you think they're involved?'

'Haven't noticed anything to indicate they are.'

I was silent for a moment. 'What about Roger Allen?' I tapped his mugshot. 'He's the deputy head of curriculum. Also part of the school management team.' I shifted his picture underneath Shari's and Neil's. 'How does he fit into things? Where the hell is he today? You'd think unless he was critically ill, he'd have managed to get himself in for the first day of term.'

'It's pretty odd behaviour. Certainly puts him in line as a suspect, but it might be a coincidence. He's the only person we haven't spoken to. And Linda's husband.'

'Which means when all the staff leave here shortly, unless we get to Allen first, he can get the run-down from someone before we speak to him.'

'He's still AWOL.'

'Where on earth has he disappeared to?'

'No idea at the moment. We've tried to track his phone but it's switched off.' He checked his watch. 'I need to go. Neil Sanderson and Shari Ahmed are about to brief the staff and I want to be there to observe. I'll bring Sanderson back with me to interview.' Dan weaved his way round the canteen tables towards the doors.

I rubbed my eyes and rested the palms of my hands on my face for a moment. Frustration was biting. The two people we most needed to interview, we couldn't.

Wednesday – Steve

The staff were still stuck in the staffroom, waiting for news or to be told they could go home. In the kitchen area, a few people were chatting by the fridge when Steve wandered over.

'Anyone want a cuppa?'

'It's Steve, isn't it?' a friendly-faced woman asked.

Steve recognised the person who'd brought him into the staffroom from reception earlier when he arrived.

'You're covering for Zoe, aren't you, teaching psychology? I'm Andrea. In English. I think I saw you at your interview.'

'Hi. Yes.' Steve was relieved to have a distraction. 'Have you worked here long?'

'Oh, years. Nearly seven? Something like that. It's a great school. Sure you'll love it.' She had a Welsh accent and the sort of impish face and choppy, short hair that made her look fun. 'I started on a temporary contract, bit like you, and ended up staying on. The senior managers are decent and we've got a great team of school governors.'

'I'm glad to get back to London. I grew up here.'

A sneering voice interrupted them. 'Hope you're not telling the new boy all our ghastly secrets.' It was Moira, who was still nursing a sour face and had the staffroom copy of the *TES* tucked firmly under her arm. 'He'll be running back to his training supervisor asking for another job.'

Andrea glanced at Steve and, in full view of Moira, rolled her eyes. 'What *secrets*, Moira?' she simpered patronisingly.

But Moira wasn't finished. 'You do know Linda and Roger —'

'Moira – *enough*.' Andrea faced away from the woman and looked at Steve. 'Don't take any notice of her. She delights in winding everyone up. Let's go and sit down.' She pointed at some chairs on the other side of the staffroom. 'You've gone green. Don't want you passing out on your first day, do we?'

But Moira was tailing them, muttering to herself. 'What happened when you went to fetch Linda? Was she —'

'For *goodness'* sake.' Andrea whirled round. 'Do you ever stop?' And to Steve she said, 'C'mon, let's go and sit over there.'

They carried on chatting as they walked over to some seats.

'*Training supervisor*? Have I got a flashing neon L-plate on my forehead saying I'm a newly qualified teacher?'

They were out of Moira's earshot now.

'Don't take any notice of her. She's a nasty piece of work. Always tries to intimidate new staff. She's the staffroom bully and a dreadful gossip.'

'That's good to know, I guess.' Steve managed a tiny laugh.

'Listen. A few of us are going to the Morgan Arms after school if you fancy it. It's the pub on the corner as you walk towards Tredegar Square.'

They sat down.

'What a good idea,' said Steve. 'Talk about a nightmare day.'

'Yes, I don't remember covering "What to do if your head teacher carks it" on my PGCE. Did you?' She grimaced. 'Which is not exactly in good taste. I'm sorry. It's the . . . Oh bugger. I have no idea what to say so I think I should just shut up.'

They both blushed.

'Dreadful thing to happen and she was a really nice lady,' Andrea continued. 'I've been to school social events with her and she was always friendly to everyone and good value. Not hoity-toity and aloof like some heads are. Bizarre to think of someone planning her —'

'Was she married?'

'Yes. Peter. He's a really nice man. Another teacher. Retired now. Something to do with his heart, I gather, and pretty much house-bound. They always seemed really happy. Goodness knows how this is going to affect him. I heard Linda had some kind of a health scare not long ago too. I wonder if she had a heart attack? Shit. Listen to me. I sound like bloody Moira. Shoot me now.' She pretended to hold a gun to her head.

An unsettled feeling overcame Steve as he remembered how Linda had looked: on her back on the sofa, her wrists bound, and her face all puffy. The image certainly didn't suggest that she had a stroke or a heart attack. It occurred to him that the killer could be one of his colleagues. As he surveyed the room, he felt his pulse begin to quicken.

The killer could be in here with them. Not only that, but whoever it was could be watching . . . and waiting to make their next move.

Wednesday – Maya

After the staff briefing, Dan brought Neil Sanderson to the ground-floor room they were using for interviews. Off the stairs and with no natural light or ventilation, the room was cold and dingy. All it contained was an old wooden table, which looked like it had been rejected from all other locations, and four plastic chairs. On the table was an empty tissue box with a lidless biro popping over the edge.

Neil shuffled into the room with his hands in his pockets. His lowered gaze betrayed not hostility so much as frustration and impatience, eyes glancing sideways.

'Have a seat.' I pointed at the chair opposite Dan and watched the man get settled. I introduced myself. 'You're the school bursar. Is that right?'

'Yes.'

'Was Rich Griffiths at the staff briefing you've just had?'

Neil hesitated. 'I'm not sure. I was concentrating on what we needed to tell the staff. Why?' I felt him searching my face for clues.

'Why wasn't he with the rest of the staff at lunchtime?'

'I didn't know he wasn't. He may have helped Linda with the power cut. She said she was going to find the caretakers.'

'Could you tell me where Roger Allen is today?'

'He's not well.' Neil's hairline and forehead were damp, and the sweat under his arms hadn't dried out. 'He rang me this morning.'

'What's the matter with him?'

'Stomach upset.'

'Where was he ringing from?'

'Home, I imagine.'

'A police officer has been round to Roger's house and his wife said she hasn't seen him since yesterday.'

Neil rubbed his chin and was silent for a few moments. 'I don't know anything about that. He just said he wasn't well and wouldn't be in. It was a one-minute conversation.'

'Why did he call *you*?'

'I'm the person staff report absences to. I do the personnel register each day, and the staff cover. Plus, Roger and I are mates.' He glanced down at his hands and examined his palms.

'Was his absence mentioned this morning when you met with Mrs Gibson for your first meeting of the new term?'

'I told her he wasn't well and wouldn't be in today. That was it. We had a lot to get through.'

'I wonder why his wife doesn't know where he is. They've got two children.'

He shrugged. 'No idea.'

'In that meeting this morning, how did Linda seem?'

'Fine. It was the first day of the new term. She was busy, and keen for things to go well. We all were.'

'She didn't seem preoccupied, anxious?'

'Not at all.' Neil leaned forwards in his chair and sighed loudly. 'She was her normal self.'

His sigh made me curious. 'Did Mrs Gibson have any enemies? Any fallouts?' My phone vibrated in my pocket.

'I've worked here for Linda's entire headship. She was a popular and inspiring leader. She regularly had to deal with staff, students and parents who were unhappy, often angry. But she had good people skills. I don't recall any of those occasions getting nasty or being left unresolved.'

I got up and walked across the room. 'Can you run through what you think the school's challenges are? Issues? Anything that might give us an idea why someone might want to harm Mrs Gibson?'

'Well . . . the language and literacy levels of a lot of our students are lower than we'd like. We have many students with English as their second language.'

'But aren't a lot of the kids who come here born here?' I had a feeling I knew what Neil was going to say.

'Yes. But a problem for many of them is their parents don't speak English fluently, and some not at all. At home they speak their mother tongue and they tend to mix with others of their own culture. Understandable, but it can cause difficulties.'

It pained me to hear this. Had things not moved on at *all* since we arrived in the 1980s? Mum popped into my mind, how she would insist on talking to the three of us in Sylheti when Dad wasn't around. Jasmina and I had quickly become fluent in English but Sabbir hadn't. By the time Jaz and I left home, Mum still couldn't speak English and barely could to this day.

'What prevents parents from learning English, do you think?'

'Lack of government funding for language classes for older family members. And parents and grandparents have learned they can get by without having to learn English. When they need a translator, they take one of their children along. We often see it at parents' evenings. We talk to the students, and they relay what we've said to their uncle, dad, grandparents, whoever has come along with them. They do the same for medical appointments and ones with social services.'

'But doesn't the problem stop when the current generation are proficient?'

'It should. But often the kids only develop their English to a certain point.' He looked genuinely upset about this.

Despondent as this information made me, it rang true. Dad had been insistent that we spoke good English. He knew Mum spoke to us in Sylheti. It was something they'd quarrelled about regularly. 'What implications does that have for their education and for the school?'

'The weaker their English, the more difficult the children find learning. You can then see behavioural problems and absenteeism.'

'Any of the students have a grudge towards Mrs Gibson?' With her being strangled, it seemed unlikely but we needed to rule it out.

'A few. It's inevitable. I'll get you a list.'

'Thank you. As soon as you can, please.' My brain was assimilating Neil's information. Was his testimony reliable? I was keen to hear whether Shari would tell us anything different. 'Two last questions for now. I want to make shure we know about everyone with a link to the school. Take me through them all, can you?' He scoffed. 'In a close-knit community such as this, pretty much everyone has been connected with the place at some point. Teachers, kids and parents, obviously. Past *and* present. Governors. Support staff. You name it!'

'And does the school or LEA have any policies around file storage and deletion?'

He frowned. 'Other than the legal requirements of the Data Protection Act, no. Why?'

Wednesday – Steve

Steve had never been good at being told what to do. The paramedic who'd checked him over had suggested an early night, but Steve couldn't resist accompanying Andrea and their colleagues to the Morgan Arms. He was aware this was more to delay his sister's inevitable lecture than it was to extend the time spent with his new work mates, dissecting what might have happened to Linda Gibson.

'What d'you want to drink?' Andrea asked as they entered the busy backstreet gastro-pub. 'I'm having a pint of this.' She pointed at the Bow Bells hand pump.

Steve swallowed down a surge of nausea. The place reeked of warm goat's cheese and garlic. He'd resolved to have a soft drink but his colleagues were all ordering bottles of wine and double vodkas, so he felt a bit of a wimp asking for a Coke. Besides, after the events of the day, and with his hangover lingering, a livener seemed appealing.

'I'll have the same.' He knew how good the local ale was, having sampled it after his interview a few months ago. In the pit of his stomach, dread was bubbling up in anticipation of the grilling his sister was going to give him when she got home. Even if she had already heard what had gone on with Lucy, and how the Christmas holidays had ended, she would insist on knowing *every* detail. And he wasn't looking forward to having to explain quite how spectacularly he'd cocked everything up. He adored Jane but at times she took her big sister role too seriously, and delighted in giving him a hard time when she thought he'd behaved badly.

Steve glanced round the vast, open-plan bar, taking in its trendy décor. After the cultural homogeneity of Midhurst, and his last school, he was still acclimatising to how much East London had changed since his school days here. The contrasts seemed so much more obvious now. They'd just walked past a boarded-up social housing block with a demolition order, and now they were in a gastro-pub that sold packets of cracked pepper flavoured crisps for two quid, and which had a dedicated wine menu with separate pages for white, red, rosé and sparkling wines. In reality, though, with the high bar, made of what was supposed to look like old ship beams bolted together, the trendy music and shabby chic décor, they could be in New York, Hamburg or Liverpool.

Andrea was waiting to order.

'Nice place,' Steve said. 'I wonder what the old East End dock-workers would make of it.' He pointed at the bar, stroked the grain of the wood. 'Bet it's never seen a dock, let alone a ship.'

Andrea laughed. 'It was probably imported from Central Europe.' She waved her twenty-pound note at the barmaid. 'I grew up in Cardiff so this part of London reminds me of home. For years, Tiger Bay – that's where I'm from – exported coal. I gather this area specialised in wool, sugar and rubber. A bit like Cardiff: lots of tight-knit communities, all with their own distinctive cultures and dialects.' She ordered their drinks.

'My grandmother says there's always been a strong community spirit here. And a survival instinct.' He told Andrea that he'd grown up in East London. 'The Luftwaffe bombed the shit out of the docks during the Blitz, and lots of them had to be re-built. My gran was one of the thousands of families who lived in the slums until they were cleared.' Steve thought about the port in NYC that Lucy had taken him to for dinner. Container ships had brought changes there, she'd told him. Apparently, the salt marshes of the estuary had originally been occupied by Native American *Lenape* people but they'd been pushed out when ocean liners and prison ships moved in.

'Yeah. It's such a shame.' Andrea paid the barmaid. 'My dad said the container ships were the end for the London docks. The hulls were too deep. In the sixties, they lost all the trade to ports with deeper water.' She handed Steve his pint. 'It's weird how cyclical it all is. One group of immigrants arrive and move on, and the next wave takes their place. It's the same in Cardiff and Liverpool. Like how there are hardly any Jews in Brick Lane now. They've all moved to North West London and Stoke Newington.'

Scattered round the bar area were tables that had been carefully sanded and waxed to make them look old, legs painted in matt 'barley' and 'seagrass'.

'Shall we join the others?'

Steve remembered the comments and looks he'd got in the staffroom earlier. He picked his way across the busy bar and chose a seat. Several of his colleagues stopped chatting and acknowledged him as they sat down. Everyone had obviously figured out he'd been the one to find Linda because he'd gone to fetch her. What a mistake that was. He'd have to front it out politely. Presumably the police would find out what happened. It was sod's bloody law it was the first day of his new job and none of the staff knew him from Adam. They were bound to be curious and – much as it bugged him – suspicious.

He glanced round the group of teachers; everyone looked as dazed as he felt. One guy was talking loudly, not to anyone in particular, and repeating himself. Moira was nursing a gin and tonic, and was staring into the distance, wide-eyed and catatonic, her curtain hair lodged behind her ears. Hopefully there wouldn't be any more outbursts.

'How are you feeling?' a girl asked. Steve recognised her from the staffroom earlier. She had her arms round raised legs, the way a child sits. 'We were all saying, this time last night, if someone told us what was going to happen today, we wouldn't have believed it.' She laughed nervously and took a swig of her drink.

'It's been a weird one for all of us, that's for sure. And poor Mrs Gibson. I still can't —'

'What the *hell* is he doing here?' Andrea's question made everyone look up.

The room jerked.

A man, in jeans and a thick leather jacket, was weaving his way across the busy bar and heading for their table.

Wednesday – Dan

Dan accompanied Neil to the staffroom and came back with Shari Ahmed, the other deputy head. The Australian education system was very different and he'd used the walk to get Shari to fill him in.

She scuttled into the interview room ahead of him like a frightened animal. Made a dash first for the far chair then changed her mind and returned to the near one, mumbling apologies under her breath. Sweat dampened the headscarf round her forehead and temples, framing anxious eyes.

Maya gave him the signal to commence the interview. He got the feeling she was curious to see him in action.

'Are you left- or right-handed, Mrs Ahmed?' Dan studied her face.

'What?'

'Left or right?'

'Right. Why d'you —'

'Where were you today between twelve noon and one p.m?'

'In the staffroom with the rest of the staff. I've already told your –'

'Was Rich at the meeting you've just had?'

'I have no idea. I didn't notice him.'

'We keep hearing how happy the school is and how popular Mrs Gibson was…' he said.

'Ye-es.' Her manner was jittery.

'Thing is, she's currently in a body bag, heading towards our morgue.'

Shari let out a gasp. Her eyes filled up. She took a tissue from her sleeve and dabbed at them.

Dan felt Maya's disapproving gaze on him. 'Apologies. I'm Australian. I don't have Detective Rahman's British politeness.' He avoided her glance. 'Any trouble with gangs here?'

'We have a couple but Mrs Gibson introduced a number of effective measures to combat them.' Her voice was high and breathy.

'Tell me about the language and literacy issues.'

'They don't apply to any one ethnic group. Many of our British students don't have good literacy levels. Unfortunately, it can result in poor exam results and a low position for the school in league tables.'

'I guess that'd mean reduced funding for the school, right?' He'd been wondering whether money was involved with the head teacher's murder ever since they learned about Linda's deleted computer files.

'Indirectly, yes. If league-table ranking drops too much it affects how many students apply for places here. And that affects funding. It's a vicious cycle.'

'I see.' He tapped his biro on his notepad and sucked his cheeks in. 'Did you get the impression Linda was well off?'

'I've never considered it.'

'And are you left- or right-handed?'

'Right. I've *told y*—'

'Are there any divisions at the school that might have resulted in bad feeling?'

'There are some tensions between staff groups that we've been unable to overcome.' Shari dabbed at her nose with a tissue. 'We employ a lot of local people. Some of our staff aren't happy about this.'

'Why not?' He fixed his eyes on hers. 'Don't they have the skills for the job?'

Shari seemed taken aback. 'Yes, but some people complain that it's positive discrimination. Bumping up minority ethnic quotas and all that nonsense.' She fidgeted in her seat and tugged at her *hijab*.

'Why's it nonsense? Aren't there guidelines about who the school is allowed to employ? In Australia the focus is on skills. That's it.'

'Yes, but guidelines don't change how people *feel*. Linda, Neil, Roger and I all agreed that it's important for our staff composition to reflect the ethnic mix of our students and community. Unfortunately, not everyone shares that view.'

The prejudices that Shari described mirrored many in Sydney. Dan's family fought discrimination every day as a result of his wife's Aboriginal heritage. The girls, at school. Aroona, in her work with the native communities.

'When do these staff tensions arise most?'

Shari picked fluff off her *jilbab* while she thought what to say. 'When we have Muslim speakers, some of the non-Muslim staff object to the hall being gender-segregated. And when we have celebrations, the non-Muslim staff want one thing and —'

'Is that about alcohol?' Dan cut in.

Shari blinked and looked at Maya, as though she were hoping for sympathy. 'Among other things. At Christmas and end of year parties, many of the staff want wine and beer, and to go to the pub afterwards.'

'And the Muslim staff object?'

'Some mind less. But others refuse to go *anywhere* alcohol is available.'

'Simple, surely? Separate it out?'

'It's not that easy. We've tried having non-halal food and alcoholic drinks in one room, and halal food and non-alcoholic drinks in another but we ended up with two separate parties. That defeats the object, to celebrate collective hard work and achievement. We then tried having all the food and drink in the staffroom at opposite ends. That worked better but the staff who don't want to go anywhere where there is alcohol *still* refused to attend. Linda was convinced she'd find a solution but in the end we came to the conclusion that perhaps there is no way of resolving the situation. A case of necessary segregation for certain occasions.'

Dan could see her frustration. He didn't know what the answer was either. But how the hell were these cultural tensions and literacy problems involved with Linda's murder? And how did money come into it? At the back of his mind was a mental image of Linda, eyes bulging, her hands bound. And the Buddhist precept: *I abstain from taking the ungiven.* Was mousey, dithery Shari a fan of Linda's or had she ducked out of the staffroom and squeezed the life out of her senior colleague?

Wednesday – Steve

The arrival of Roger Allen at the Morgan Arms set everyone on edge. Steve sensed that his colleagues, who had just begun to relax and talk freely, resented having to watch what they said in front of the senior manager who had been off sick all day.

After three pints of real ale, jet lag and the mother of all hangovers, when Steve arrived back at his sister's flat, one desire eclipsed all others: to slide under the duvet and stay there. Shaky, and with a crushing pain expanding inside his head, he climbed the two flights of stairs to the top floor of Durkin House. Outside the flat door, he fumbled in his jeans pockets for his keys. Relief swept over him when he hit the dead lock: Jane was out.

Steve closed the flat door behind him. The place was hardly any warmer than outside. Never mind. He'd soon be under the covers. Then his gaze fell on his sister's gym bag in the hall. '

'Ah, bollocks.' He'd left his messenger bag in the Morgan Arms. He'd get it tomorrow. He couldn't face trekking back there now. Carrying a pint of water, he headed straight for the spare room at the end of the landing. This was home for the next few months until he could find a place of his own.

He took his mobile out of his jeans, rang the pub and asked them to hold on to his bag. Then he sat on the edge of the bed. On the floor his rucksack leaned against the wall and his attention fell to the key ring that Lucy had given him, with the letters NYC, when she'd first told him she wanted to return home to the USA.

He felt a dart of pain in his stomach. How long was it going to take until he could think about Lucy, and see things that reminded him of her, and not feel regret?

Just get into bed, you idiot. And stop feeling sorry for yourself. You've only got yourself to blame. Lucy gave you fair warning. Claiming indignation about her going home to the States was never going to cut it, and nursing your pride isn't going to reverse things.

He exhaled, swung his legs up and lay back on the mattress. Within minutes of head and pillow meeting, Steve's breathing slowed and he was snoring. Until –

'*Hey*. Sleeping Beauty.'

The overhead light flicked on.

'Wake up.'

Steve's eyes were dazzled. The abrupt waking jolted him from his boozy sleep.

It was Jane in strident mode, standing over the bed with hands on hips. 'It smells like a pub in here. How much have you had?'

'Oh fuck,' he groaned and pulled the pillow over his face. Dread surged through him along with ripples of nausea. Jane on a rant was bad enough when he was on top form.

'From what I've heard, you already did that. D'you want to explain why I've had a call from Lucy first thing this morning, and then one from some DI Rahman woman about your school?'

'Not really, no.' He might have guessed Lucy would be on the phone to Jane. They'd been close for several years. 'Look, do one, will you? My head hurts. I'm not up to one of your inquisitions.' He replaced the pillow over his eyes.

She yanked the duvet off the bed and onto the floor, leaving Steve naked, except for his boxers and the pillow over his head.

'Piss off. Don't do that.' He lobbed the pillow to one side, reached over to grab hold of the pastel pink duvet cover and pulled it back over him. This was something his sister used to do when they were growing up and it had always infuriated him. As she clearly remembered.

'Well?'

Steve didn't answer. He rolled over and tucked the pink duvet under his chin in case she tried to pull it off again, feeling like he was about six.

'You heard me. What's going on?'

'I'm not talking to you when you're in this mood. The last forty-eight hours have been a pile of crap. Now can you please leave me alone?'

'The detective wanted me to confirm you're staying here.'

'I am, aren't I?'

'She said you've been involved in a serious incident. What's happened?'

'We aren't allowed to talk about it.'

'Bit late for that. It's already on the national news. The head teacher of your new school's been found dead.'

'If you know what's happened, why are you asking?'

'Oh my God, was it *you* who found her?'

'Yeah. Now please leave me alone.'

'So, you aren't interested in Lucy's message then?'

'*What message?*' Curiosity replaced the world-weary, about-to-die tone in his voice. He was facing her now.

'If you're showered and dressed and in the kitchen in ten minutes, I'll tell you.'

Brick Lane, 1990 – Maya

'In here, you two,' Mum calls from the kitchen.

Plunged into darkness, Jasmina and I grope our way out of the lounge to join Mum. Illuminated by the blue light of the gas ring, she's at the stove. Sweet, spicy smells waft round the kitchen, and there's a pot bubbling on the hob.

Outside, even the street lamps have gone off and the whole terrace is in darkness.

'I wonder how long this one will last,' I ask.

Mum has placed a candle on the table. She strikes a match and it fizzes. Smells. The wick catches, casting a ball of light momentarily before shrinking.

'Sit here.' She's pointing to the table. 'And for goodness sake mind your hair on the flame this time, Maya.'

Jaz and I cram round the tiny Formica table where the five of us sit every evening for tea, knees banging, feet jostling for space against Dad's work boots and Sabbir's huge school shoes.

Jasmina and I sit now, side by side on the wooden bench, and the soft light of the candle flickers, casting a spell over the room. Shadows sway around the dingy, smoke-yellowed walls. As the wick waves in the draught, the flame billows and casts looming shapes. Homework forgotten in the excitement, Jaz tickles me and I poke her; we giggle and wriggle in the tiny kitchen.

'Stop it.' Anxiety rattles in Mum's voice. She always gets tense when the electric goes off. And when Dad's late home. 'When your father gets in, he can get some more candles. Jasmina, call upstairs to your brother, will you?'

In the chilly air of the flat, steam trails upwards from the saucepan as Mum stirs it. The walls round the cooker shine with condensation.

A few minutes later Sabbir arrives, with bed-head hair and sleep furrows in his bruised cheek. 'What's for tea?' He glances round the kitchen.

We all know the answer, but each day we hope it might be different. We love Mum's cooking, but after eight years of school dinners, and tea sometimes at friends' houses, we've got used to eating different food. Perhaps Dad will come home with a treat for us all? A bagel each from the shop in Brick Lane, or some red jam to have on sliced bread?

'Rice and curry,' Mum says. She always talks to us in Sylheti, and at home my sister and I speak our mother tongue too. Unless, of course, it's something we don't want Mum to hear.

'It's the second power cut this week, isn't it?' Sabbir is the eldest of the three of us.

Mum serves out the stodgy rice and curry, and passes bowls over one by one. 'Careful. They're hot.' All seated round the table now, Dad's chair sits empty, no bowl on his place mat, just cutlery and an empty water glass. 'We may as well eat. Your father's obviously got held up again.' The words ride a sigh.

My socked feet are cold. I like it when I can rest them on Dad's work boots. Get them off the cold concrete and warm them up.

Just as we're finishing our tea, we hear the front door bang shut downstairs, and a few moments later the grinding sound of a key in the flat door. Dad comes in, bringing a whoosh of bitter winter air and cigarette smoke, and another smell I've noticed before. The draught pulls the candle wick first one way then the other, and Mum jumps up to shield Sabbir from the billowing flame, bashing the table and knocking over her water glass. She uses a tea towel to mop first the water then the gash of wax that's run onto the shiny tablecloth.

'While we've been here with no power, you've been in that pub again. I can smell it.' The reproach is unmistakeable. 'This is the last candle. We need more. The children can't sit in the dark.'

Dad looks at Mum, and then shines his gaze like a torchlight round the table. Pauses.

I'm watching him. Wondering what he's thinking and what's going to happen. I grab Jasmina's hand under the table. He looks over at the hob, then back to the table. The room shimmers with tension and it makes my skin prickle. Every day now, Dad's late and Mum says the same thing. He must be tired and hungry after working all day, but it's as though there's more to him going to the pub than either of them mentions.

Dad lets out a long sigh, like letting air from a balloon while holding on to its neck. In the soft light, his cheek muscles quiver. 'I'll go and get some now.' He and Mum whisper to each other in very fast Sylheti.

My breathing tightens.

As he turns, I get another waft of that smell, the one his clothes so often reek of. 'Won't be long,' he says in English.

I feel a swirl of something in my stomach, pulling at me. I put down my spoon. I don't want Dad to go out again. He's home now and it's cold. I look into his face, with its gentle creases, the dark growth round his face, and his large eyes the colour of conkers.

'Dad?' I can't help saying. I don't know why.

'You children be good for your mother,' he says sternly, and ruffles my hair with his hand. When he stops, he lays his palm flat on the top of my head for a second, and I feel momentarily held in his warmth before he removes it. He gabbles something else to Mum in Sylheti, his voice even lower than usual. A jumble of sounds, noises, tones.

I squeeze Jaz's thumb. Use my eyes to plead with her, but she shrugs and shakes her head.

Before I know it Dad pulls the flat door behind him and the latch clicks shut. He never even took off his coat and now he's gone.

Mum's spoon drops from her hand and clatters on the bowl in

front of her. She closes her eyes, sucks in a long breath and lets it out, at first with a low moan, like an animal in pain, then in a full-throated wail.

'Mum?' She's never made a noise like this before. 'Are you okay?'

Sabbir's chair screeches on the hard kitchen floor as he pushes it back to stand up. 'Okay. Let's all play a game.'

I know something's happened, but have no idea what. 'Dad will be back soon with the candles, won't he? We can finish our homework then. I've got English to do and Jaz —'

'We can play 'til then.' Sabbir looks over at Mum, and I follow his gaze.

She's sniffing, dabbing her nose and fanning herself with her hand. 'I'm fine,' she says, her voice faltering. 'Just give me a minute.'

But I can still hear that moan in my ears and I know we can't leave her.

'How about we get the blankets from our bedrooms and put them on the floor in here?' It's Jasmina. 'If we push the table over, we can make a camp. Mum?'

Excitement bubbles up. I love camps. 'We could sleep down here too.'

'We may have to if the power doesn't come back on soon,' says Mum.

Five minutes later, Jaz, Sabbir and I have fetched our bedding from upstairs. Mum has cleared away the dishes and pushed the table against the wall. On the gas hob a pan is heating for our hot water bottles. We pile cushions onto the eiderdowns and clamber on top. Our bottles filled, Mum joins us, but with her back against the wall and her legs under the covers.

'Tell us about Bangladesh again,' I ask Mum. 'What was it like growing up outside the city?' All three of us love to hear her stories. We'd lived in the city centre of Sylhet so this part of our home country wasn't something we knew well.

Mum speaks slowly as though she's combing through her memories and putting them in place. Hearing her speak in Sylheti feels completely natural. Comforting, somehow. It's like being in our old flat by the river.

'One of my favourite things was the rolling hills. The land often flooded, especially in the monsoons, and lakes formed on the flood plains. Sometimes your grandfather took us into the swamp forests by boat. They're magical places where trees grow out of the water. Their branches join up at the top to form canopies and tunnels.' Mum gestures with her hands.

In the soft candlelight I catch the look on her face, as though the memories bat her back and forth between pleasure and pain.

'Living here in London, in the cold and grey and the dark, I miss life by the river and the lush green colour. After the monsoons, beautiful star-shaped pink water lilies would float on the lakes. Sabbir, d'you remember the migratory birds? You always loved the swamp hens, didn't you?' Her melancholy makes me wonder how she feels about us moving to Britain. 'The tea estates are glorious,' she says, making a sloping gesture with her arms. 'Carpets of green bushes, all trimmed to waist height. My mother and her sisters would pick the tea. I went once to help.' The soft candlelight melts the ache in her features. It warms her voice for the first time this evening. 'My father's family grew rice.' Energy builds in her voice. 'I liked to watch the buffalos treading on the rice hay to dislodge the grains. It's the traditional way of doing it. Afterwards we'd all swim in the Surma, and watch the cattle as they drank in the river. They're —'

The flat buzzer silences her, and we all jump. Wrenched from the vivid colours of Bangladesh back to our dark kitchen.

'Who's that, ringing at this time?' Mum's tense again.

'Perhaps Dad's forgotten his key?' It's all I can think of. 'I'll go.' I get up and feel my way to the hall, my eyes used to the dark. I open the door, expecting Dad to rush in, laden with bags, full of apologies and jokes and stories.

But there's no-one there.

'Who is it, Maya?' Mum shouts through.

'No-one. Someone must've pressed the wrong bell.' I step outside the flat into the hall and, smelling tobacco, I scour the darkness for a glowing cigarette end or the light of a torch. My foot knocks against an object on the ground. There's something beside the doorway. I lean over to feel what it is. A plastic bag rustles in my fingers. In it is something hard, like a cardboard box. I pick up the package and carry it into the flat.

'Someone left a parcel.' I place it on one of the kitchen worktops.

'At the *door*?' That tone is back in Mum's voice. 'For pity's sake, Maya —'

'No-one was there, just this bag.' I point, although it's obvious.

'Give it to me,' says Mum sternly, moving towards the worktop.

But Sabbir has already begun rummaging in it. He looks at us all in turn, his face excited. 'It's candles and . . . you're never going to guess what . . .'

'*Bagels*?' Jasmina and I shout in unison.

Wednesday – Maya

When I got home and closed the front door, relief surged through me. It wasn't my brother's photo in the hall that brought the tears, nor the suitcase I'd parked by the stairs when I arrived home in the early hours. It was that, all day, my attention and energy had been on the investigation when what I wanted was to be alone with my grief. Now, I finally had the chance to gather it up so I could feel close to Sabbir; to wade through all the conflicting emotions about how he'd died – and why.

In the kitchen, I lobbed my keys onto the worktop, followed by the soggy bag of chips I'd half-heartedly collected on the way home. In the cold air, the smell of malt vinegar wafted round the room and the greasy mass was unappealing. I flicked on the heating. Next to the kettle, the message light was flashing on the answerphone. Mum had probably forgotten I'd gone to Bangladesh for the funeral.

Through the patio doors, the light was reflecting on the canal water in the dark. When I was house-hunting, I'd had my heart set on this flat as it reminded me of Sylhet and our apartment there when we were growing up. I remembered how sometimes, when he'd been in a good mood, Dad would sit between Jasmina and me on our balcony there and read us the poems of Nazrul Islam. On those rare occasions, the two of us would lap up the crumbs of Dad's attention, bask in his gentle optimism, oblivious to the stench of booze and tobacco on his breath, and the smell of women on his clothes and skin.

What I remembered most, though, was how yellow his fingertips were; the feel of his cracked, dry skin. And how much I'd loved his burnt-caramel voice.

I headed into the lounge. Last night's array of mementos littered the coffee table, waiting to be stuck into the journal I'd bought from the market in Sylhet. The fire had destroyed most of Sabbir's belongings so Jasmina and I had chosen what we wanted from the bits that were recovered. My eyes fell on the book of Michael Ondaatje poetry. He'd annotated it. On the plane home, I'd read every single poem and pored over all my brother's notes, then wept in the darkness of the cabin. I'd learned more about Sabbir from those poems than all our conversations.

Sometimes the canal outside was soothing. Tonight, although the water was still, I felt it pressing in on me. Unable to shift Linda's death from my mind, I kneeled in front of the wood burner. As I lay kindling on the bed of ash, my thoughts drifted back to the amalgam of conversations from earlier in the day. I was exhausted. A combination of jet lag, lack of sleep and not eating. I was contemplating having a bath when my mobile rang. It was Dougie.

'Hey, how are you?' We'd Skyped several times when I was in Bangladesh but, other than seeing him at the crime scene, I hadn't had the chance to catch up with him since getting back. He was downstairs, so I buzzed him in and went to meet him at the door, pausing briefly to check my appearance in the mirror.

'I was on my way home. Wanted to check you're okay.' He leaned over and his beard growth brushed my cheek as he gave me a kiss.

I drank in the smell I knew so well, and, for a moment, I longed to sink into his arms. 'Shattered, but pleased to see you. Come in.' I began walking away from the door. 'I was going to call you.'

He followed me along the hall and into the kitchen. Pulled the overcoat off his large frame and draped it over a chair back.

'Fancy a beer?' I said.

'If you're having one.'

I took two bottles from the fridge and passed him one.

'You've met the fast-track sergeant, then.' He took a swig of beer.

'Yeah.' I sighed, irritated. 'Briscall must've known about this for a while. Nice of him to mention it.'

Dougie's bushy eyebrows shot up. 'That man's a prick.' He strode over to the window and back. 'Gather this Maguire bloke's an Aussie? What's he like? Have to say, he looks more Scottish than I do.'

'He seems a good cop. Knows his stuff and he's pretty sharp in the interview room. Briscall will never change. I had a lot of time to think when I was in Sylhet and I'm done with letting him wind me up. I joined the police to make a difference, and to help people like Sabbir. I'm fed up with Briscall side-tracking me with his petty crap.'

Dougie had one hand round his beer, the other in his pocket. He was taking in what I was saying. 'How's it going with the school and the Gibsons? It's all over the media.'

'No real leads. We're waiting to interview two key witnesses. One's under medical supervision, the other's gone AWOL.' I groaned with frustration. 'We're still puzzling over the Buddhist precepts. There are five of them. Why the killer has started with the second, we don't know.' The cold had reached my bones today and I needed to warm up. 'Shall we go through? The stove's on.'

In the lounge, Dougie sank into the sofa, his manner quiet and reflective.

'As a murder method, what d'you reckon strangulation says about the killer?'

'I'm not sure.' He paused to think. 'It's quick and doesn't require any weapons. Silent apart from victim protests. Excruciating agony for a few seconds, depending on the pressure, then the victim slips into unconsciousness. Death minutes after that. It's certainly different from stabbings and shootings.'

I was nodding. 'On training courses we're continually told that murder methods are rarely random or coincidence, except in the heat of the moment. Whoever murdered Linda *chose* to strangle her, bind her wrists and leave a message by her body.'

Dougie was stroking his chin. Silent for a few moments. 'It's certainly symbolic. Whoever did it could've simply strangled her and left.'

The material that had been used to bind Linda's wrists wasn't expensive, but Dougie was right: for the killer to bother, it must symbolise something for them. And forethought had gone into what they had chosen to write. It wasn't an impassioned scrawling of 'BITCH' across a mirror in red lipstick, for example.

'The most logical explanation is that the two acts go together.' I held my forearms the way Linda's had been positioned. 'The precept says, *I abstain from taking the ungiven*. If your wrists are tied, so are your hands.'

'Bingo. You can work from there. Although, hang on.' Dougie placed his beer on the coffee table. 'Did you say there are *five* precepts? Do you think the killer's started with the second precept because of its significance? Or do you suppose there's been a murder before this one?'

Wednesday – Dan

The Skype ring tone danced around the small bedroom. 'Pick up, pick up,' Dan urged, as he pictured the early morning scene at home in Sydney: Aroona getting the girls ready for whichever club or friend they were going to today. It was nearly midnight and Dan was wide awake in his Stepney flat-share. Every cell in his body felt as though night-time had been and gone. He lay beneath his crumpled coat, shivering, longing for the unbearable heat of home.

On his phone the pixelated image solidified. 'Daddee,' came Kiara's squeal through the ether, and the video clicked in. She had a huge grin on chubby cheeks, her face still full of sleep.

'Hey, kiddo. How are you?' Dan searched her features for tiny signs of change, drinking up their familiarity. 'I really miss you guys.'

'Is it cold there? Mum said you've got, like, minus twenty or something.'

Dan chuckled. Swallowed the lump in his throat. Her innocent exaggeration was refreshing. 'Not quite. It is cold, though, and we've had a bit of snow.' It was so good to hear her voice. 'Did you go to the beach yesterday?'

Another face bombed the picture. Sharna. All soft curls and gappy teeth. 'Snow? Take some photos.' A gaping mouth loomed in, and she attempted to point at her gums. 'The toof fairy came last night, Daddy.'

'Is that right? What'd she bring?'

'A new toofbrush.'

Both girls dissolved into giggles. It was a typical Aroona present.

Homesickness pinched at Dan. Being apart from his family and missing out on milk teeth and swimming lessons . . . He hoped they'd all be able to join him soon.

'Mum's coming,' said Kiara. 'I got burned today. I'm all scratchy.' She rubbed at her neck and face as though needing to make her point.

He'd only been away four months. Living in Sydney, he was used to hearing an eclectic mix of accents, but the combination was different in East London. The familiar Aussie vernacular was comforting but sounded different from the way it normally did. More distinct.

Feet shuffled across the laminate of their apartment. Aroona peered over the top of the girls' heads, her dark hair a contrast with Sharna's blonde and Kiara's red.

'Hey,' Aroona said. 'How come you're still up?' She was holding a giant tub of mango yoghurt with a spoon in it, and in the background the TV was blaring out the weather in New South Wales.

'Oh, you know. Wanted to speak to my girls.' Around him, magnolia walls were devoid of home touches. On the floor beside his bed, the greasy KFC box reminded him how hungry he was. He brought his wife up to date with Maya's return. 'I'm still trying to find a proper apartment.' He wanted to ask if she'd thought further on when she and the girls would join him, but didn't want to upset the geniality of their conversation. Things were shifting for the Aboriginal communities and he knew how much Aroona cared about helping them. 'I've heard about the tooth fairy. How did the swimming lessons go?'

In front of him the girls squirmed and giggled.

'She did very well and —

Her reply was drowned out by a banging on the flimsy party wall of Dan's room. 'Trying to sleep here, mate!' boomed the voice of the flatmate he'd heard but never met.

'I'd better go,' Dan hurried, irritation bubbling in his throat. 'It's late here. Speak soon, Okay?'

They waved and he cut the call.

Emptiness seeped back into the confines of his tiny room, silence back into the yawning space. And on his phone, from the background image, Aroona and the girls beamed at him.

Thursday – Maya

During the night it had snowed and, when I left the flat at 7 a.m., a dusting of white crystals lay on the path by the canal and on the lock. It was as though the world at the water's edge had been cleaned. From there, my walk to the car took me past the graffiti tags on the bridge at Ben Johnson Road, and the burned-out shell of a warehouse, with its blackened brickwork and boarded-up windows. Overhead, bulging black snow clouds hung over Mile End like baggy trousers.

All night I'd been unable to shift the idea that there may have been a murder before Linda's. I'd emailed the team and asked Alexej to check all suspicious deaths from the last three months, involving calling cards or anything ritualistic.

I was soon in Stepney, outside the block of flats where the Allens lived; an ugly, seventies-built, three-storey building. Paint was flaking off tired metal windows. On both sides of the entrance the recent snow was melting on mud, and discarded fag butts were leaking brown into the white slush. I rang the buzzer. Nearby, a yellow crane was lowering a vast steel structure onto what used to be playing fields, and I had to raise my voice over the drone and beeping of the site JCBs.

'I'm DI Rahman,' I shouted into the intercom.

Roger Allen buzzed me in and met me at the door of his flat. Stale alcohol fumes wafted towards me. I recognised him from the staff photos but hadn't absorbed quite how skinny he was. Speckled stubble growth clung to his face. Shirt tails trailed over his trousers and his jumper was lopsided.

'Did you get the messages to contact us?' It was more of an accusation than a question. 'We came round here yesterday and rang several times.'

A startled look swept over his features. 'Sorry. My wife did tell me. I've been . . .' He broke off; looked over his shoulder into the flat and then back to me.

'I assume you know that Linda Gibson was murdered yesterday?' People who wasted police time really pushed my buttons. It was one of my most regular rants to the team.

Roger opened his mouth to speak and closed it, as if weighing up what to say. 'Yes, I do. But I don't know anything about it, I'm afraid.'

A draught was making its way down my collar. 'May I come in?' I gestured to the flat and moved towards the open door.

Roger glanced at his watch.

'Got to be somewhere?' My patience was withering.

He rubbed his balding head and stepped reluctantly back inside, gesturing for me to enter.

Down the hallway a television was blaring. There was something familiar about the output. In the hall, a holdall stood up against the wall and a man's jacket hung on the bannisters. A pair of pink wellies nestled on the laminate next to an assortment of family shoes. The hall table was cluttered with toys and a toddler's trike had been parked under the hall table. The smell of toast wafted out from the kitchen. So, he was in the middle of his breakfast – but why did he look like he'd spent the night on the sofa?

Roger led me into the lounge where the television was on.

Of course. It was the school video. I pointed at the source of the noise, and raised my voice over it. 'Could you mute that?'

He scanned the room for the remote control and zapped the TV off.

'Do you usually watch the school video before you go to work?'

He jutted his chin in defiance and slid the remote control onto the coffee table. 'Course not. I was just checking something.'

'Checking what?'

'The . . . the sound.'

72

I stared at him in disbelief. 'Alright to sit down?' I perched on an armchair and took out my notepad. I needed to change tack; get Allen off the defensive. Attempting to make my tone of voice less impatient, I said, 'An officer came round here yesterday afternoon. I called round on my way home last night. On both occasions your wife said you were out.' I raised my voice at the end of the sentence, to imply the question rather than state it. He was a bright man. He knew what I wanted to know.

'Yeah, I popped out for some fresh air.' He cocked his head and stared at me.

'Both times? Did you get the messages to call us *urgently*?'

'I . . .' He was standing in front of the fireplace, his attention fixed on his hands, pulling at them as if they were lumps of dough.

In that moment, I felt sorry for him. I tried to imagine this man, in his scruffy clothes, conducting management meetings at school, leading working parties and standing in front of assemblies. I changed the subject. 'Who's off on their travels?'

'Eh?' Roger's eyes darted round the room.

'The bag in the hall?'

'Oh, that.' He waved his hand in the air dismissively. 'We haven't put it away yet. A Christmas trip.' He was fiddling with his wedding ring now, twisting it round his finger as though he were trying it on for size.

That was about as convincing as his account of why he'd been out when the police came round. I surveyed the room.

Family-worn furniture.

Drinks tables.

Several lamps.

Cheap sound system. Nothing out of the ordinary so far.

Large plasma screen. Telly clearly important to the Allen family.

Wait. 'Do you normally clean your teeth in the living room?'

'You what?' He traced my glance to the toothbrush and tube of toothpaste on the table.

That was it. He'd just arrived home. His wife was out. And he'd been having breakfast. 'Where have you *been*, Mr Allen?'

73

He reddened. 'Nowhere,' he snapped. 'I told you, I wasn't well.' He paced the length of the room. Up. Down. Hands in his pockets.

I waited. Let his reply hang in the air, all the while fixing my gaze on him.

'How did you get on with Mrs Gibson?'

His bored shrug came too quickly – more a nervous tic than a genuine *I don't know*. 'I was less of a fan of hers than lots of other people but I never wanted her dead.' There was a weight to his quietly spoken words. 'If you lot did your job properly, you'd find that there are a few people at the school who were keen to get Linda out of the picture.'

My voice came as quiet as an echo, eyes locked on his. 'Like who?'

Thursday – Steve

Steve was still absorbing Lucy's news as he walked to Mile End to catch the bus. She'd met someone. Why hadn't she told him when he was in New York? At least then they could have discussed it. Giving a message to Jane was cowardly. He turned up the collar of his jacket. On the ground, blobs of rain were washing away the recent snow flurry.

At the bus stop, school kids elbowed and shoved their way onto the double-decker bus, before clattering upstairs to claim their position in the pecking order. Steve waited with the workers, the knackered mums with buggies, the pensioners and this week's reject kids. On the ground floor, an élite group of boys stood in a huddle, too cool to bother with the scrum of the top deck, their voices barely broken and their hormones in a spiral. Steve watched them posture and prance as they sniffed round two girls from another school.

Still feeling delicate this morning, he cursed his decision to get the bus. Had he known he would be cooped up with so much perfume and giggling, he would have walked the mile to school and spared his senses the onslaught.

When he alighted the bus at Bow Road tube station, the cool air was a relief, like stepping into the shade on a summer's day. Momentarily, it soothed his lungs and cheeks before starting to bite. It was not fully light, and traffic chugged along Mile End Road, headlights glaring, carrying jangly city dwellers and bulging haulage loads to their destinations.

On parts of broken pavement the rain had collected in dirty puddles. Beside the cash point in the station wall, Steve saw a homeless man sitting in a dirt-slicked sleeping bag. Only a piece of cardboard lay between him and the concrete slabs. Desperation clung to his hollowed cheeks. Lowered eyelids kept his eyes on the ground in front of him, as though he doubted life would ever be good again, and even looking people in the eye required too much energy. In his lap, out of his vision, lay a sign. 'I hope spring comes soon,' it said.

No request for money, for food or a hostel bed.

What a self-pitying prick Steve was being. Yes, his own life was a mess at the moment. Yes, Lucy had a new bloke, but at least he had a job and somewhere warm to sleep. He looked at the guy's thin sleeping bag, his filthy, cold-ravaged fingers in mittens, and Steve knew he wouldn't survive sleeping rough for more than a couple of days. He changed course and strode over. The closer he got, he saw that the man, whose misfortune-bedraggled appearance suggested he was in his thirties, was probably in his early twenties.

'There you go, mate.' Steve dropped three pound coins in the pot. 'I hope spring comes soon too.'

Hearing the chink of change, the man looked up. His eyes were dead but he managed a thumbs-up. A bluey-brown bruise encircled one eye socket and a scabby graze clung to the cheek below.

A few minutes later, Steve was at the pedestrian crossing, waiting for the lights. An empty Red Bull can ricocheted in the wind. On the horizon the skyscrapers of Canary Wharf and the City boasted of wealth and progress. As he crossed the busy road, the unyielding cityscape seemed such a contrast to the sleepy town of Midhurst. There, the lollipop lady steered school kids safely across the high street, with the castle ruins, the River Rother and Cowdray polo fields in the distance. Had he seen any homeless people there? He couldn't remember. Threads of panic rose inside him. What if coming back to East London was a mistake? What if he couldn't settle back into noisy, crowded Tower Hamlets?

Fuck's sake. Get a grip. Give it your best and if it doesn't work, you can re-think things. At least you won't be bored in London. He sucked in a huge breath and hurried in the direction of Mile End High School.

The Bow backstreets, which were quiet yesterday when Steve walked to school, were thrumming with noise. The closer he got, a mêlée of voices floated towards him, increasingly loud. Someone was shouting instructions into a loud speaker. It reminded Steve of a tuition fee rally when he was at university. Over the tops of houses, blue lights sliced through the grey. This was different from yesterday. Something must've happened. The police presence at the school had been stepped up overnight. His pulse quickened and his shattered body galvanised itself.

Metres away now, voices bellowed warnings. Vehicle engines roared and their doors slammed. Ring tones rode the bitter January wind, and through the tree-lined streets, satellite connections transmitted the news of Linda's death into unsuspecting skies.

When Steve neared the school premises, he saw that the cordon had been enlarged. Crime scene tape flapped in the wind. Half a dozen marked cars were positioned at intervals around the area, and several officers huddled round each vehicle, solemn-faced and urgent in their high-visibility jackets. Scattered around the scene were twenty or so other people, some in work suits, others in forensic clothing. Liveried vans had arrived from the BBC and Sky, and people bustled round these hubs, lugging photographic paraphernalia, recording equipment and microphones. A rangy, pale-skinned man with red hair stood in front of a scrum of journalists and reporters. His arms made determined gestures as he tried to silence their questions long enough to be able to speak.

Steve scanned the scene for a colleague, someone he might recognise from yesterday, but saw no-one familiar. Shit. He'd forgotten to check his email this morning. He'd call Andrea. She'd know where they were meant to be. Before he could dial, a woman clocked him and sped over, waving and grinning and calling out. Long tendrils of black hair bobbed as she ran.

Before he had time to escape, she'd pinned him down. 'I'm Suzie

James . . . from the . . . *Stepney Gazette*,' she stammered, out of breath from running but still able to flash her teeth, her head on one side in the sort of coquettish pose that Steve's fifteen-year-old students adopted sometimes when they were late with their homework.

He stifled a groan. This was all he needed. To commit some dreadful *faux pas* to the press just to make his start at the school even better.

'Are you staff?' she simpered.

He got a waft of her minty breath. 'You need to speak to someone from school management or the police.' Steve felt flustered and cornered. 'We've all been asked not to speak to anyone.' He was just about to walk away when –

'So you *are* staff then?'

He'd fallen into that one. 'Sorry,' he said, using his hand to indicate he wanted her to back off. 'I don't want to be rude but . . .' and he accelerated his pace away from her.

Undeterred, she was running alongside him. 'Do you know who found the head teacher?'

'No comment.'

'Do you think this has anything to do with the Pakistani girl who committed suicide last term? Or the boy who was stabbed on Christmas Eve?' She was alongside him, almost running now, and puffing as she moved. 'Thing is . . . if there's a link . . . we have a duty . . . to keep the community . . . informed.'

Steve heaved in a breath. This woman was testing his patience. She was like a dog with a bloody bone. He was desperate for a fag.

'Right, that's *enough*.' He wheeled round to face her. Leaned over so he was at her height and pressed his face near hers. 'I've tried to be polite and you won't take a hint. Now – *piss off*.' He sped away, just catching her say, 'Can I quote you on that?'

He shifted his thoughts to today. And school. He'd been about to ring Andrea.

Suddenly the reporter was at his side again, making him jump. 'Here's my business card. If you decide you want to talk to the paper, give me a bell. Yeah? I can make it worth your while.' She pushed her hand at him.

Freaked out at the arrogance of her renewed approach, Steve stepped backwards and the fancy business card fell to the pavement. 'Oops. Sorry,' he said. 'Clumsy me.' And this time he thought about Lucy with her new boyfriend, and channelled as much menace into his stare as he could summon.

The woman harumphed loudly, flicked her shiny locks and marched back over to the posse of journalists.

He still had his phone in his hand, so he dialled. Andrea answered quickly and he took in the information. 'Okay, I'll walk back to Bow Road tube and meet you.'

As he left Tredegar Square and headed for Mile End Road he remembered Roger Allen turning up at the Morgan Arms yesterday afternoon and how anxious it had made everyone. It was odd behaviour not to come into school because he was ill, yet arrive at the pub a few hours later and down several pints of beer. Steve had the distinct impression he'd come to get the gossip.

Thursday – Maya

Roger Allen still hadn't answered my question so I repeated it. 'Who wanted Mrs Gibson out of the way?'

'I'm not saying.' He spoke to the floor, shrugging. 'I'm not a grass, alright? All I'm saying is that there are other people at Mile End who you should be talking to rather than wasting time with me.'

'Let me be the judge of that, Mr Allen. A close colleague of yours is dead. If you know anything that could help our investigation, we would appreciate your cooperation. As I'm sure would her family and husband.'

Nothing in the witness statements suggested who he might be referring to. 'Where were you yesterday when we called round? And rang?'

His face reddened but something kept his attention fixed to the carpet. 'I went down to the Morgan Arms in the afternoon, didn't I?' He met my eyes now, defiantly, as though what he'd done was no big deal.

The implications of what he said rippled through me. For an intelligent man, his behaviour in the last two days had been ill-judged at best. 'Let me get this straight. You were unable to go into work as you had a stomach upset? Yet you managed to "pop out for some air" twice and were well enough to go down to Bow to have a drink a few hours later?'

The sarcasm wasn't lost on Allen. He was rubbing his nose and shuffling from one foot to the other, as though he wished he could be anywhere but here. 'It's not what you think.'

'You have no idea what I think. And if you're feeling better, are you going to work today?'

'Maybe.' He took a sideways glance at the TV.

I needed a different approach. 'I'll come back to the colleagues who wanted Mrs Gibson out of the way. Given you admit you weren't a fan of hers, what weren't you happy about?'

He was treading the length of the lounge now, and flicking his fingertips nervously.

'Look. I've been in the game a long time. Well before Linda graduated. There's more to running a successful school than introducing a conveyor belt of initiatives and shouting about it from the rooftops.'

Oh please. The wet-behind-the ears line. Was this the green-eyed monster or something else?

'You're going to need to elaborate. It's the details I need rather than generalities.'

He let out a bored sigh, as if it were all obvious and he was fed up with having to explain. He stopped pacing, parked himself on the arm of the sofa and crossed his arms. 'Before Linda was appointed head teacher, the school had received "requires improvement" in its OFSTED inspection. What it needed was effective leadership. Staff morale was low, and absences high. We were struggling to fill places in year seven, and maintain them into the sixth form.'

'But hasn't Linda turned the place round? On the website it says the school was rated "good" in the 2017 inspection.'

Roger faced me now. 'She has been beneficial for Mile End High. But there's more to running a successful school than outward measures might suggest.'

'Such as . . .?' Why couldn't he spit it out? 'You've been honest about not being a fan of Linda's. I'm not getting the reluctance to explain why.' I flicked to a blank page in my pad and started jotting some notes.

He opened his mouth to speak a couple of times and changed his mind. Then, in a quiet voice, 'All this school video business, Facebook page, the obsession over notice boards, it's not what education is about. Some of the changes she's implemented have been constructive. But they're fads. Active learning, assessment for learning, learning styles. A lot of it is mumbo jumbo.' He was bouncing his leg. 'It was something new every bloody term.'

'What did your management colleagues say about the situation?'

'Oh, they went along with her.' He let his breath out all in one go. '*Outwardly*, anyway.'

'Meaning?'

'You'll have to ask them.'

His concerns made sense, and needed investigating, but something else was niggling at the back of my mind. 'I gather you applied for the head's post when it came up.'

Roger rolled his eyes. 'I did.'

'How did you feel about getting knocked back for it and the position going to Linda?'

'Not great. But I got over it. I thought they'd made a mistake, but then I would, wouldn't I?' His words were sing-song-y and dismissive.

'I understand you were an assistant head at the time. It would have been a significant step up for you. Is that correct?'

'Yes, it would have been. But under *different* circumstances. It's not going to make me want to kill Linda. They won't make me – or either of the other two – acting head now. They'll ship in some numpty from another school in the borough.'

I sensed he was right. But I also knew that when it came to murder, events often had little to do with reason and logic. 'I gather you weren't – how shall I put it? – very gracious in your defeat?'

Roger blushed. 'I was slightly unprofessional in the pub afterwards, I admit.' He scratched his chin and was silent for a moment. 'I thought I could do the job well and I was disappointed. I apologised to Linda for my behaviour and she accepted.'

'Other than you wanting the post, what was your objection to Linda getting the job?'

'A head teacher needs experience dealing with pupils, staff *and* parents.'

'Presumably the interview panel thought she was the best person for the job?'

'Evidently.' Allen looked drawn. He had dark circles round his eyes and several days' stubble on his chin. He seemed exhausted and extremely agitated, well beyond a few bad days and a stomach bug.

'Why were you absent yesterday? I'm not buying the gastro explanation.'

'That's confidential.'

'And *this* is a murder investigation.'

'If you must know, I had some personal problems over Christmas. My wife and I . . . she . . . she told me she wanted a divorce.'

I looked away to give him a chance to recover from what he'd said. 'I see. Sorry to hear that. Do your management colleagues know about this?'

'Just Neil. He's the person we report absence to and he's a mate. Well, sort of.' He blushed.

'Did Linda know why you weren't in school yesterday?'

'I don't know whether Neil told her. I asked him not to unless it was absolutely necessary. I was hoping to be able to sort things out with Ruth and get back to school today.'

'And have you?'

'I'm not sure.' He opened his hands, helpless. 'I don't think so.'

'Is this linked to the bag in the hall?'

Roger muttered under his breath and then said, 'She kicked me out.'

'Why?'

'Ruth hates my job. Says I'm obsessed with it.' He stopped. '*And* Linda.'

'And are you?'

83

'I care about the school but I'm not obsessed. We've been married for twenty-four years. We aren't some lovey-dovey couple anymore.'

'Mr Allen – the school video. Can you press play, please?'

He mumbled something and clicked it back on. There was Linda's face, close-up.

'… so you can be confident that your sons and daughters will learn and thrive in an atmosphere of wellbeing and safety,' she was saying.

'Thank you.' I had to shout. 'You can switch it off again now.' I waited. 'Mr Allen, we both know it's highly unusual for a member of senior management to take a day off work because they have marital problems. We will need to speak to your wife.'

'Good luck,' he scoffed. 'You'll have to find her first.' He marched over to the fireplace. 'She's buggered off and taken the kids.'

Thursday – Dan

Around the mortuary laboratory, stainless steel surfaces gleamed under a mass of bright lights. Wash basins and soap dispensers clung to white walls. Dan felt like a dickhead in the gown the doc had made him wear, and his embarrassment levels were made worse by the fact that the synthetic material and warm room combination was making him sweat.

Dr Clark pinned the microphone to his lapel.

Despite the lights and cleanliness, the atmosphere felt heavy, and the room smelled as though it had been a stranger to life and natural air for a long time. Perhaps it was the lack of windows that made it feel so claustrophobic?

Dr Clark cleared his throat and switched on the mic. 'It's nine-ten a.m., fourth of January, two thousand and eighteen. Present: myself, Dr Tim Clark, and DS Daniel Maguire.'

There were four dissection tables, all with hoses that were connected to a drainage channel in the floor. On one table lay Linda Gibson's cadaver. How tiny she looked. And wax-like. At the end of the table, surgical equipment and containers were in rows, and numerous charts and anatomical diagrams were attached to clipboards.

'The deceased is Linda Ann Gibson, a white female, forty-five years of age, small frame, well nourished. There is extensive congestion to the face and neck, and contusion to the jaw and chin and neck.'

Dan put on his hopeful face. 'In English?'

'Swelling and bruising.' The reply was brusque. 'There are abrasions beneath the jaw and on the neck. Many of these are linear scratches consistent with those made by fingernails.'

Dan placed his fingers on his neck, checking the angles, pressure and positioning that would be required to make such marks.

'Examination of the left eye shows petechial haemorrhages to the eyelids, conjunctivae and sclera. The same to the —'

'Which means?'

'Burst blood vessels.' He shot Dan a silencing look. 'Now I'm going to begin dissection with the removal of the skull cap and brain.' He switched his mic off. 'DS Maguire, please step aside and stop asking questions.'

Dan shifted.

Dr Clark re-activated the mic. 'Now for the Y-incision.'

'The what?'

'It gives access to the neck structures, and enables me to dissect the face to assess for deep bruising and bone damage.' He looked up now. Microphone off again. 'That was your last question. You are hampering my movement and distracting me. My office is the second on the left. If you ask my assistant, she will lend you one of our textbooks on pathology. The report will be on file later today.' He returned his attention to the cadaver. 'Although, you might want to pass on to Maya that Linda Gibson has had a caesarean.' He pointed to the long scar on Linda's lower abdomen.

Dan moved closer. 'As in . . .?'

'She's had a baby.'

Thursday – Maya

I closed the flat door and followed the corridor out onto the Stepney backstreet. Allen's revelations had sent my synapses into a flurry of activity. He'd been honest about his reaction to Linda's appointment and non-stop initiatives, and he was an intelligent man. It seemed unlikely he would kill Linda in the belief it would help him secure her position, but the logic of murder often only made sense to the person committing it. Other aspects of his testimony were more worrying. His wife had accused him of being 'obsessed' with the school – with Linda, specifically. Reading between the lines, his wife might not have been the head teacher's biggest fan. But where had Roger's wife gone?

I had numerous voicemails and text messages, so I rang the team and updated them on what Roger Allen had told me. 'We need to find out who he was referring to when he mentioned people wanting Linda out of the way,' I told Alexej. 'Can you make that a priority?' It was frustrating that Allen had clammed up. 'What did Rich Griffiths have to say?'

'He sorted out the power cut and then escorted the heating engineers off-site. He decided to go to the kebab shop over the road to get some lunch and couldn't get back into the school as we'd begun erecting the cordons.'

'Alibis?'

'Yup. Several staff at the kebab shop. He's around five feet tall, and he's got a skinhead haircut. You wouldn't get him mixed up with someone else.'

'He could have strangled Linda sometime between the power going off and him leaving the school. We need to find out if anyone saw Linda alive after Rich left.' I made a mental note. 'What else?'

Alexej brought me up to date. As yet, they'd found no prior murders with calling cards or rituals, and the laboratory was still processing forensics.

'Keep looking. It's possible that Linda's death is an isolated crime, and a coincidence that the precept was the second in a set of a five, but we can't assume that.'

Uniform were speaking to the students listed as having a grievance towards Linda, Alexej said, and national news crews were at the crime scene, filming for television. He told me about Linda's caesarean scar.

'Really? No-one in her family mentioned children. Her husband must've known. Check her medical records, can you? I won't be long.'

Ten minutes later I parked the car at the school, keen to gather the team so we could review priorities. Mile End High was closed today and I knew Shari and Neil were banking on it being open tomorrow. With journalists and reporters pressing for information yesterday afternoon, and desperate to get photographs, I'd instructed all officers to ensure no-one sneaked onto the crime scene. Suzie James' repertoire of tactics was legendary: on one case, she'd hoodwinked a rookie officer into believing she was pregnant. Cushion up her top, she'd emptied her water bottle on the ground and wailed that her waters had broken. While the concerned officer shot off to get paramedics, she'd nipped under the cordon and inside the building.

I released my seat belt. We needed to keep the media on our side and give them something to go on. Press releases were often vague and uninformative, and the Voicebank wasn't updated regularly enough to be of any use. I knew the Sky and the BBC crime correspondents. Neither would breach the guidelines for reporters at crime scenes.

It was then that I caught a few words from the Sky reporter who had positioned herself in front of the floral tributes that lay at the school gates.

'Here we have another dreadful tragedy . . .' She pointed at the bouquets that people were placing for Linda. 'After Haniya Patel's recent suicide . . .' She then gestured to the cards and flowers that had been continually replenished over the last month.

My throat tightened as I absorbed the significance of the two sets of flowers alongside each other. It was a shock for the whole community to have another death so soon after Haniya's, and when things were still so raw for everyone. It was going to be devastating to be reminded of the details and have them broadcast into everyone's living rooms again.

'The police confirmed an hour ago that this is now a murder investigation and they are confident that an arrest is imminent,' the reporter continued.

Where had she got *that* from? It was important to appear confident about an investigation, but not to mislead the public. I strode over to the reporter, got myself in her eye-line and waved my arms. Slightly flustered, she handed back to the television studio and ended her live broadcast.

'Morning, Carly. Sorry to interrupt. It's early days for the investigation. Who released the media statement?'

She tucked her biro behind her ear. 'Hang on.' She flicked through her notepad. 'DCI Bris—'

'And he told you an arrest is imminent?'

She nodded.

'He's exaggerated, I'm afraid.' I paused. Briscall wouldn't like what I was about to do. But what was the use in giving the public inaccurate information if it meant they might not feel the need to come forward? Steeling myself, I added, 'D'you want to do a live update with me?'

She gave me the thumbs up and signalled to her sound engineer.

A jumble of thoughts swirled in my head as I stood in front of the camera and leaned into the microphone. 'I'm Detective Inspector Maya Rahman. As you know from this morning's statement, the death of Linda Gibson is now a murder investigation, and I have been appointed Senior Investigating Officer. We are currently pursuing a number of enquiry lines and are appealing for *anyone* who was in the area of the Mile End High School between twelve noon and one p.m. yesterday to contact us . . .'

'You've heard it from the horse's mouth there,' Carly told her audience. 'From DI Rahman. We will be live with more updates as we get them.' She faced me. 'Thank you.'

'Contact me if you want information.' I gestured to the flowers. 'It's inevitable people will see Linda Gibson's death as even more of a tragedy, given Haniya's was so recent.'

To the left of the steps, I approached the gaggle of parents and family members. A teenager in skinny jeans and a hoodie was shouting into his mobile, oblivious to the dirty looks from the young mum who was holding a baby and had a pushchair at her side. An elderly man held the hand of a young boy while his wife was using a girl to interpret for her. A blonde woman stubbed out a roll-up and joined the throng. They were all jockeying for the attention of the two uniformed officers, demanding information. If I wasn't mistaken, I smelled weed.

'Here comes that female copper,' the blonde woman announced to the group.

As I approached them, out of the corner of my eye, I caught a mane of jet black spirals coming round the corner towards us, bobbing up and down as she walked. Behind Suzie, a man with a shaved head and short legs was struggling to keep up with her. He fitted the description that Alexej had given of Rich Griffiths. What was Rich doing with the local reporter? There was a smirk on Suzie's face, as though the two of them were up to no good. I'd managed to set the national news channels straight, after Briscall's interfering. The last thing we needed was Suzie stirring up more panic. The grin fell from her features when she saw me. She spun on her four-inch heels, flicked her hair, and sped off in the opposite direction, leaving Rich standing there.

'Ladies and gentlemen, *please.*' The uniformed officer's exasperated tone caught my attention. He and his colleague were struggling to contain the growing crowd of parents. People got stabbed daily in the East End, in back alleys and car parks, outside chip shops and in broad daylight. The locals were so used to reading about it in the newspapers, they barely batted an eyelid. But Linda was a public figure and pillar of the community. It was no wonder people were worried.

I returned my attention to where Rich had been moments earlier but he'd disappeared. Damn it. I'd speak to the parents then get Dan to track him down.

As I walked over to address the group, I gathered my thoughts and prepared to repeat a similar message to the one I'd just given the media. Dan's crew cut and pasty skin came into view.

'Y'alright?' He fell in step with me.

There wasn't time to comment. 'How are we doing here, Sanjay?' I recognised one of the uniformed officers from a previous crime scene.

'Morning.' He gave me a sheepish look, as if he'd tried his best with the posse of parents but didn't know what else to say. I felt sorry for him. I wouldn't be able to tell them much more than he had but knew my rank would reassure some of them.

'Ladies and gentleman, gather round please. I'm Detective Inspector Maya Rahman. As you know, there was a serious incident here yesterday. This is now a murder investigation and my sergeant,' I gestured to Dan, 'my team and I are doing our utmost to identify and apprehend the person responsible.' I checked their faces to gauge how my words were being received. 'The investigation is in its early stages. We are doing everything we can to ensure the school is safe and would very much appreciate your support. The best way for you to help is to return home, and work *with* the school and the police, until everything can return to normal. If anyone has any information, however insignificant it might seem, please tell us.' I pushed up my sleeve to check the time. 'I can take a couple of quick questions.'

I studied the blanket of worried faces in front of me. A woman spoke to a teenage boy in Sylheti. I understood the question before the boy opened his mouth. It was the one on everyone's lips: how Linda had been murdered.

I didn't wait for the boy to translate. 'I'm unable to comment at the moment. We may be able to release more information later this morning when we receive the post-mortem report.' I repeated the information in Sylheti to save the boy translating. It felt strange speaking the dialect again so soon after the funeral but at the same time I felt proud. I only had to think back to my own family experiences to understand how hard many from immigrant communities found it to trust services that didn't always treat them fairly, especially when they couldn't speak the language.

'On Facebook, everyone's saying they know how she was murdered.' A woman at the back of the group was scowling, her ponytailed hair pulled back so hard that it tugged at her features. I recognised the blonde woman who'd stubbed out her roll-up. 'Why can't you lot just tell us the bloody truth?' She spat the sentence out angrily, then stuffed a piece of gum into her mouth and started chewing aggressively. 'After what happened with that poor girl what killed herself before Christmas . . . What's going to happen next?'

The last question pulled a groan from me, which I just managed to keep internal. It was the second mention of Haniya in ten minutes. On occasions like this, I felt less like a detective than a politician and a PR manager – there to schmooze. But the pragmatist in me knew that community relations were critical and, whether I liked it or not, it made a difference to parents and carers *who* delivered *what* updates. And we needed to ask the woman where on Facebook she'd seen the comments.

'At the moment we're investigating yesterday's incident. There is no reason to be concerned about what might happen next, and speculation could put lives at risk and jeopardise the investigation.' I looked at the shiny-faced woman with the ponytail, whose friend had now joined her along with the caretaker. Next to them was a familiar-looking Afro-Caribbean man in a navy coat and dark trousers. 'I give you my word I will pass on information *when* we have it and *when* it is safe to do so.' I glanced at the other faces in front of me.

'That's a fob off, if ever I've heard one.' The ponytailed woman faced the gaggle. She strutted, like a peacock, puffed out with importance and trying to catch everyone's eye. 'Anyway,' she pointed at Dan, 'what does *he* know about our community?'

Dan caught the remark and stepped forwards. 'I understand your concern.' His face was grave. 'And my accent can be a bit off-putting, I get that. But my world is no different from yours. I'm Australian, but my relatives were Irish, and where I live in Sydney, there are many parallel issues to here.'

'You're Irish?' The woman screwed up her face.

'In Sydney, property prices have rocketed, just like here. We've got race riots and unemployment. My kids are mixed race. I might not be a native East Londoner but I understand how divided communities feel.'

My mouth was almost as wide open as the woman who'd asked the question. Dan had picked up on her being Irish and the group was now quiet, hanging off his every word.

'Sergeant Maguire is an asset to this investigation, I can *assure* you.' I glanced at the woman.

'DI Rahman is right, Sinead.' It was the Afro-Caribbean man. He stepped away from the group and faced them. 'Everyone is claiming to know what happened and each version of events is different. It's like Chinese whispers. We are *all* here as concerned parents, but it's best for us to leave the police to do their job.'

I smiled gratefully, realising that I recognised him from meetings about the new mosque at Whitechapel. He was Talcott Lawrence, Jamaican, and stood on the Stepney Chamber of Commerce and Mile End High's board of governors.

'Please, everyone, go home.' I gestured to him, acknowledging his contributione. 'Let the police do their job. Thank you.' I turned to Dan. 'Can you ask Sinead where exactly on Facebook she saw the comments?'

'Sure.'

'After that, could you find Rich Griffiths? He's just sloped off.'

Keen to get back to the incident room, I left the crowd of parents and headed for the school entrance. A young man peeled away from the group and followed me.

'Hey. *You.*' It was a snarl.

I turned to see an angry face, body language tight as a knot and jabbing at the air with his finger. With so many people gathered at the school, including police colleagues, I wasn't scared so I stopped walking. I'd seen the guy lurking at the back of the group, chewing the inside of his cheek. A baseball cap partially obscured youthful features. I guessed he was late teens or early twenties.

He made slow, exaggerated claps with his hands. 'Impressive speech back there.' He leered up at me through low lids. The non-verbal signals screamed at me. 'Have you forgotten what these streets are like? There's a killer on the loose.' Contempt burned out of narrowed eyes. 'How do we know we can trust you?'

For a moment I was about to explain. But I was tired. 'You don't.' I wanted to end the interaction and get back to the incident room. 'Now, if you'll excuse me . . .'

As I walked away he shouted, 'You don't remember me, do you?'

I turned round. Peered beneath the baseball cap. It was Fatima's nephew. 'Dev?'

'You ain't one of us anymore. You pretend you are but you ain't. And you ain't a proper ethnic, neither. You're a *nobody*.'

I felt anger bite. I'd dealt with variations of this day in, day out, since we came to live in the UK. First I was too different; now it seemed I wasn't ethnic enough. For a moment I contemplated stopping, reminding Dev that I was four when I arrived in the UK. Asking how the hell I could've lived in Tower Hamlets since 1982 without absorbing some Britishness. Without knowing – and loving – the streets I walked on.

But something snapped. We had people to interview and a murder to solve. I didn't have the energy to keep justifying myself. Everything else was white noise.

*

Five minutes later I was back in the canteen incident room. I poured a cup of water from the cooler and headed over to the team for morning briefing.

Dan had just got back to his desk. On the board, someone had written out the Buddhist precepts in Pali and English.

I shall abstain from causing harm – ?
I shall abstain from taking the ungiven – Linda
I shall abstain from sexual misconduct
I shall abstain from false speech
I shall abstain from all that clouds the mind

'Nice working of the old dual nationalities back there,' I said over my shoulder to Dan. I added Haniya's name to the board and circled it.

When I faced him, Dan had his poker face on.

Jeez. Didn't he know a compliment when one came his way? I continued. 'Did you manage to find the caretaker?'

'*Maya.*' His tone was urgent, and he gestured behind me with his eyes. 'You've got a visitor.'

Thursday – Steve

Steve was on his way to meet Andrea at Bow Church station, his thoughts racing. The past few days had been like something out of a horror movie. First, the split-up with Lucy. Granted that had been a possibility for a while, but he'd travelled to New York at Christmas hoping the two of them could patch things up. Start afresh. Then the delays on his flight home and Linda's death yesterday. Not just death – *murder*.

As he hurried through Tredegar Square, a police incident sign caught his attention. It was leaning up against the railings surrounding the gardens, a beacon of yellow among the greys of the sky, the bald trees, the pavement and road. 'FATAL STABBING', it said. He stopped to read the details. Female. 11.28 p.m. Last night. That was closing time. Steve wondered if any of his colleagues had still been in the Morgan Arms then.

As he was reading, a young mum trundled past with a toddler in a buggy. 'Awful, isn't it? Teenage girl, apparently.'

'Yes,' he replied. Being so close to death was unsettling. Tredegar Square was elegant. The trimmed lawns, hoovered of fallen leaves and debris. Not a dumped mattress in sight. But a metre from the yellow police sign were trails of dried blood, now crystallised and the colour of rust.

At Bow Road tube he bought a coffee from the kiosk. The station entrance was a tunnel, and the wind whipped through, sucking with it crisp packets and plastic bottles. The rain had shifted. Leaden clouds were a reminder that more snow was likely. Winter in the city was different somehow. Buildings, roofs, tarmac all blended in with the flint skies to create an impression of unrelenting grey. It was so different from the rich, peaty commons around Midhurst, and their green, yellow and coppery ferns as the flora shuffled through the seasons. Yet winter in the city had its own charm. It was as though the buildings were resting, gestating, and preparing to give birth once the spring sunshine appeared.

Warmth seeped from the paper cup into Steve's hands.

A few minutes later, Andrea arrived, her expression sombre as she walked towards him.

He regaled his run-in with the reporter at school.

'No?' She looked at him in horror. 'That woman is priceless. Thank goodness you didn't tell her anything. Neil and Shari would do their nut.'

Steve found Andrea refreshing company. After the grilling he'd got from his sister last night, then being accosted by Suzie, it was a relief to have someone to discuss the school with.

'I imagine they've arranged trauma counselling for today. That's what happened when one of the kids was killed a couple of years ago.'

'Probably.' The police had offered him specialist counselling yesterday and sent him home with a leaflet on PTSD symptoms.

Andrea began walking more quickly. 'Let's get to the sports hall. I don't know about you but I didn't sleep a wink last night. It'll be useful to have a debrief.'

Ten minutes later, Steve followed Andrea and their colleagues into the massive building, and immediately the barn acoustics hit him. Shari Ahmed was scurrying about anxiously, dodging between the groups of staff like a sleep-deprived mouse. When she spoke, the vast space swallowed her soft voice. Steve felt sorry for her. It reminded him of covering PE lessons and struggling to make himself heard.

Inside, the building looked like an aircraft hangar, except without the planes. It was a huge empty space, built using breeze blocks round a metal structure, with unpainted internal walls. At his job interview, during the tour of the site, Steve had learned it was an old rag trade warehouse, riddled with damp and dry rot when the school acquired it, and they'd rebuilt it.

On the surface, Neil Sanderson, the bursar, looked as if he was bearing up better than Shari, but his baby-blue shirt was a size too small and hugged his rounded belly. Several shaving nicks dotted his chin and neck. Four other people accompanied Shari and Neil, two men and two women. In the freezing space, they stood, hunched and uncomfortable, blowing on their hands and shifting to keep warm.

'Wonder who they are,' Steve whispered in Andrea's direction.

'Either from the LEA or counsellors. I'm sure the black woman is a counsellor. I've seen her before somewhere.'

Over the next fifteen minutes, the remaining staff drifted into the hall, each person visibly lost within the awfulness of Linda's murder. Faces showed the strain of trying to zip up their shock and contain their grief. Today, silence replaced Moira's questions. Rozina arrived, flanked by two colleagues. In little make-up, a black *hijab* framed her pretty face.

'No Allen then,' mumbled Andrea.

'I was just thinking about him.'

'I bet everyone is. It's disgraceful. Everyone will know he came to the pub. Moira will have made sure of it.' She looked round. 'Can't see Rich either, can you?'

'Is that the caretaker?' Steve shook his head. He didn't know what to make of their absences.

In the middle of the giant space, someone had laid out chairs and set up a microphone in front of them.

Neil cleared his throat. 'Take a seat, please,' he said, herding the staff in with his arms. They filed along the rows of chairs in a daze, muttering and whispering. Once everyone was seated, Neil spoke again.

'Morning. As you may have noticed, the crime scene area has been expanded overnight. DI Rahman has authorised us to use this part of the school site.' He pulled himself up straight, stroked his belly, and took a breath. 'Mrs Ahmed and I met with the school governors last night and the LEA. We are all keen to get the staff and pupils back on track as quickly as we can, while acknowledging Mrs Gibson's passing.' As he exhaled, relief loosened his facial muscles and posture. 'We have to allow the police to do *their* jobs, and Mrs Ahmed and I will focus on the staff.' He tugged at the collar of his shirt. 'With that in mind, we are going to do some debriefing work this morning, led by an expert in trauma counselling, Dr Judith Middleton. This will enable you all to air your thoughts and feelings about what happened, and get some guidance, should you want it. We will shortly be relocating to a neutral venue. We have arranged for coaches to transport us all up to the Travelodge at Stratford, and we will be spending the day in their conference room. Mrs Ahmed, did you want to say anything?'

Shari got up and approached the microphone. 'Apologies for getting you all to come here first. Mr Sanderson and I only managed to arrange the Travelodge late last night. Before we leave for Stratford, I would like to introduce the people who will be with us today.' She gestured to the four people on her left. 'Dr Middleton is meeting us at the hotel. Immediately on my left is Carmel Sunday. Some of you may remember Carmel from the session she ran for us when Akhil Haque was attacked in the park last summer. Next is Angie Singh, then Michael Brown and Alan Day. They're all counsellors specialising in trauma and grief.' She raised her gaze and scanned from one side of the seats to the other. 'Please now head out to the coaches.'

Trauma counselling. Andrea had been right. Steve gulped. What the hell was that going to dredge up for everyone? And for him?

Mile End High School, 1995 – Maya

'She's what?' I can't help squealing. 'Where?' Mum never comes to school. I feel a flush of excitement. Perhaps Dad's come back.

'She's come to collect you,' says the deputy head, Mr Hamilton, in his calm voice.

It's the first lesson after lunch, Biology. Mrs Day was telling us about evolution and genetic drift. Mr Hamilton's sudden appearance at the classroom door gave us all a shock. He exchanged a few hushed words with Mrs Day, and then made a bee-line in my direction.

'She's in reception,' he tells me.

I grab up my bag and coat in my excitement, sending my folder and pen cascading to the floor.

'With Jasmina.'

Jaz? Why would she come with Mum to collect me from school? She's at university.

Something's happened.

He mumbles to Mrs Day but I'm out of the door before him and tearing down the corridor. The overhead lights shine into my eyes, and behind me I hear him shouting at me not to run.

In reception Mum and Jasmina are at the front desk. Mum's holding a plastic cup.

'What's happened?' I'm hoping for a clue on her face.

'We need to get to the hospital. It's your brother.' Mum speaks in Sylheti. Places the empty cup on the desk.

'What's happened to him?'

She doesn't answer.

'Jaz?' I turn to my sister. 'What's happened to Sab?' I speak in English so Mum won't understand and silence me.

My sister pauses, and a deep frown pulls at her brow as she thinks what to say. 'He and Uddin have been attacked.'

'*Again?*'

'Hurry up, you two. We haven't got time for chatting.' Mum chivvies us over to the school entrance and car park, where a black cab is waiting. Despite being seventeen, I've never been in a minicab, let alone a proper taxi. It's exciting, flying down the streets the bus normally crawls along, buildings and signs and people whizzing past the window. But my sister's words keep circling in my head, and before I know it, we are speeding along the Stepney backstreets towards Whitechapel and the Royal London.

Once inside the hospital, Jaz asks at reception where Sabbir has been taken, and we trundle up to intensive care in the metal lift, fear beating inside our ribs. A nurse escorts us over to a bed where a body is hooked up to various machines via tubes and leads. I peer at the bump beneath white sheets, desperate to recognise my brother, while at the same time scared of what I might find.

'Sabbir?' I turn to the nurse. 'Can he hear me?'

She places her hand on my shoulder and I know it's bad news, otherwise she'd say.

I feel my lip tremble as I look at him. 'Sabs?' I wipe my nose on my sleeve. The swelling on his face has pushed his eyes closed. His left eye is so puffy that it's squished his face on one side. All I can see is a mass of blood and purple-black bruising. On his forehead a gash has been stitched, and a bandage wrapped round his head. His mouth and lips are clotted with blood, and a tube is attached to his nose. Multi-coloured lights flash in various patterns on a large screen, and machinery beeps and dings. Another tube is attached to the back of his hand, and secured in place by a large strip of plaster. The other end leads to a large colourless bag of fluid, which hangs on a hook, attached to a metal stand on wheels.

'Mrs Rahman?' says the nurse. 'Your son is —'

'Mum doesn't speak English.' Jaz looks as worried as me. 'D'you want to tell me and I'll translate?'

The nurse frowns. 'Well . . . I . . .' She looks from Mum to my sister. 'Your brother has sustained some very serious injuries to multiple organs, including his brain, and he's been stabbed in his side. At the moment he's in a coma.' She pauses, waiting for Jasmina to translate for Mum. 'The other boy didn't make it.'

Uddin's dead.

I'm clinging to Jasmina's arm, looking imploringly at the nurse. 'Is Sabbir going to die too? He *can't* die.' I remember the time he took me to school, on my first day in year seven. How he stepped up when Dad left. How he'd always helped other people.

'We don't know.' The nurse hesitates. She looks at Mum and back at us. 'Some coma patients remain in a persistent vegetative state. Others slip away. A few make a full recovery. It's early days, and how your brother responds in the next twenty-four to forty-eight hours will be a good indicator of what progress we can expect.'

'Does he know we're here?' The words emerge from my throat, barely a whisper.

'We think so. You can talk to him, and touch him – but mind the tubes.' She pointed at the back of his hand.

I fold onto my knees on the shiny ward floor. Grab hold of Sabbir's fingers. 'Sab. It's us. Me, Mum and Jaz.' I look up at the nurse, whose serious face now bears a look of encouragement.

She's nodding, willing me on. 'Talk to him. Tell him what you've been doing at school. Anything. Just your voice is enough.'

My mind goes blank. All I can remember is evolution and genetic drift. What do I say? 'We're all here . . .'

And then I stop.

Nothing comes.

The machine beeps rhythmically, and lights flash on the graphs in various colours.

The nurse's words pop back into my mind. She was warning us.

Preparing us for the worst. I feel a lump form in my throat. Try to swallow. But tears are making my throat hurt. Sabbir's life can't be over. He's twenty-two.

'Sabs?' It's a gurgle, merged with tears and snot. I wipe my nose with the back of my hand. 'You're going to get better. You're going to be fine.'

'Can we call anyone for you? Your father?' The nurse is facing Jasmina.

'Thank you, no. He's not around anymore.' The sentence rolls off Jasmina's tongue. It's the one we always use.

'Oh, I'm so sorry,' the nurse says, clasping her hand over her mouth.

I can see from the woman's face she thinks Jasmina means he's dead. It's what everyone thinks when we say that.

'The police are on their way. They'll need to speak to your mother. Is there anyone who can help? An aunt or uncle? We need to tell your mother some things which aren't very . . . which . . . Is there an adult who can translate?'

Jaz shook her head. '*I'm* an adult. We don't have any family here. It's just us.'

The tremble I hear in my sister's voice echoes through my heart, and I grab her hand. Close my eyes for a moment. Lost to the wish that Dad were here. He would know what to do. What to *say*. If Dad were here, he'd make everything okay.

A few minutes later two uniformed police officers arrive and begin asking questions and telling us what happened. A feeling envelopes me, squashing my chest like someone has their hand round my lungs.

'Your brother and his friend were attacked by eight men from the British Nationalist Party on the way back to work,' one of the officers tells us. 'Neither of them stood much of a chance, I'm afraid. These youths had iron bars, chains and dogs.' He pauses while we take in the news. 'Your brother was very brave. He stepped in to help his friend when one of the men took a bottle to his . . . After that, the men started on your brother.' He gestures to the cuts, the swelling and the bruises on Sabbir's face. 'Unfortunately, by the time the ambulance crew arrived, the other boy was dead. His skull was . . .' He stops again. 'Your brother was very lucky. He could easily have been killed. I know this isn't the first time he's been set on. It takes a lot of courage to help someone else when it puts you in danger.'

Jaz relays the information to Mum, who stands, rooted to the spot, transfixed, shaking her head. She's mumbling to herself in Sylheti, repeating the same few words over and over. 'Where's your father? Why isn't your father here?'

And for a moment something scratches at me. I wish he was here too. But Mum is bugging me and I'm feeling . . . I don't know quite what. Ever since we came to the UK, we've had to continually feel round the Braille of her moods; to be strong for *her* every day; to pretend we don't mind when often all we wanted was for her to —

'When you're ready to leave,' the police officer continues, 'we will need to escort you home. A rally is gathering outside the hospital. Asian and Black members of the community are making a peaceful protest. They want the government to do more to combat racial violence.'

'That's good, isn't it?' Hope shines in Jaz's eyes.

'Theoretically – but unfortunately a group of neo-Nazis have got wind of their action, and are also congregating. They've come armed with bottles and stones and are pelting the protesters and the police. The riot police are on their way.'

Fear grips me like a clamp. I'm still kneeling on the floor by Sabbir's bed, stroking his hand. These attacks are horrible. And crazy.

'I'm not going home. I want to stay here.' I look at the police officers, the nurse, my sister. 'Our brother needs us. We are all he's got.' I wipe away the tears with my sleeve. 'Sabs, *please* wake up. We need you. *I* need you.'

The police officer speaks again. 'We're very sorry, Mrs Rahman, but . . .' He stops and turns to Jasmina. 'Could you tell your mother that we are sorry?' He's shaking his head, as though he cannot understand how quickly things started. 'It happened within minutes. Before the police could get there. There was nothing your son and his friend could do. They were outnumbered, and these thugs were armed and looking for trouble.'

While Jaz translates for Mum, I'm still talking to Sabbir. 'You were so brave to help Uddin. You must've been terrified but you *always* help other people.' I stroke his hand.

Jaz and Mum are quiet so I stop too, and I'm racking my brain for what to do.

Then Mum drops to the floor, and like discarded clothes, her body folds on top of itself. Her glasses crunch as her face smashes on the hard surface. Tears become sobs, and then something wrenches a low moan from her throat, as though pain has woven its gauze round her and pulled tight. And momentarily I'm back in our flat in Brick Lane the day Dad left. The garbled words between them. The package on the doorstep. The mother who's met the agony of loss too many times.

'Mum?' I'm beside her now, my arms round her shuddering body, trying to hold her grief. Her hair and cheek are sticky with blood, and it's seeping into an eye.

I gently lift the broken glasses from her ears. Dab at the blood with my finger. 'One of us needs to get her home,' I say to Jasmina and see recognition in my sister's eyes, the clatter of memories for both of us, the fear that what happened when Dad left is going to happen all over again.

Except it's different now.

With Sabbir in a coma, and Jasmina away at university, I realise it's *me* who is going to have to help Mum. It's me who's going to have to look after her until she's strong again. And while my heart is connected irrevocably to hers, part of me feels utterly terrified at the prospect.

Thursday – Maya

DCI Briscall stood in front of me in the incident room, arms folded over his chest. 'I've just seen the news broadcasts. I would appreciate it if you didn't contradict me to the media —'

'Actually, Ian,' I put my hand up to silence him, then lowered it, 'I *had* no choice. It's not helpful to tell the media we are about to make an arrest. If anyone has information, they'll assume it's irrelevant and won't come forward.' Given we hadn't seen him all day yesterday, I wasn't in the mood to be lectured, and it was bothering me that Haniya's name kept coming up.

'I'm aware that your brother's death is very recent and it would be easy to get . . .' He stopped himself. 'It's important that we focus on the correct outcomes, and that is solving the murder of Linda Gibson.'

I absorbed the subtext of Briscall's words while I considered what to say. 'We've identified our main lines of enquiry. We are securing evidence, evaluating it and trying to identify suspects. *One* of our tasks is to investigate whether Linda's death may not be the first.' I pointed to the precepts on the board. 'We are receiving intelligence constantly, and we rely on it coming —'

'Haniya's death was tragic but we need to allocate resources to ongoing investigations.' Briscall must have seen her name on the board. 'I can see why her suicide might be important to you but you need to concentrate on Linda Gibson.'

I felt my body tighten at the possible implications of his remarks. 'I can assure you that my priorities are firmly focused on finding whoever strangled Linda Gibson. There's no evidence that Haniya Patel's death is related to Linda's, and there was never anything suspicious about it. But, because it's still so recent, local people are inevitably going to react more strongly to Linda's murder, and connect the two.' I drew breath. 'I've written her name up there *not* because I want to investigate her death, but because lots of people are mentioning it and I need to think about why that is.'

Round us the room had gone silent. Phone calls had paused abruptly, and everyone was still, telephone receivers suspended, breath held, wondering what was going on.

'Now, if you don't mind . . .' I shifted my attention to the team. 'Apologies, everyone. Back to work, please.' I checked the clock. 'Morning briefing will be in five minutes.'

When we gathered in the briefing area, Briscall was nowhere to be seen. On the board, next to the precepts, Dan had summarised the recent developments:

1. *Allen obsessed with Linda*
2. *Mrs Allen left him & now AWOL*
3. *Linda's baby*
4. *Precept: second of five. Coincidence?*
5. *Suspects*

He began the updates. 'The technicians are still working on Linda's devices to establish what she's been deleting. I've been looking into Linda's family background. More on that once Maya and I have re-interviewed her sister. Shen is helping Alexej trawl through all suspicious deaths with links to Buddhism.' He flicked through the updates. 'We know that Rich Griffiths wasn't in the staffroom on Wednesday when Linda was murdered. He sorted out the power cut, saw the heating engineers off-site and went to the kebab shop. After that, he couldn't get back into the school.' Rich's name was on the board as a suspect. 'I've just spoken to him.

He denies having anything to do with Linda's murder, and insists that she was alive when he left her. He's due in shortly to make a formal statement.'

'His alibi for part of that period is dead so he needs to come up with another one,' I said. 'Otherwise it's just his word against ours. And why is he always in a different place from the rest of the staff? Outside the school yesterday, and again today when his colleagues are doing trauma counselling?'

'Said he didn't fancy it,' Dan explained. 'Seems to see himself as a bit of a law unto himself.'

'Alexej, find out if anyone saw Linda alive after the caretaker was with her. Perhaps the heating engineers saw her?'

'Will do.' He clicked out of his email and began his own updates. 'The family liaison officer rang just before you arrived, and Linda's husband is well enough to be interviewed. I've been going through Linda's social media accounts. Nothing out of the ordinary or useful at the moment. Thinking about number two,' he pointed at the board, 'if Allen's obsessed with Linda, that gives his missus a motive. She could have gained access to the school yesterday.'

It was a distinct possibility. 'Can you prioritise the location of Ruth Allen? Someone's got to know where she is. Mobile phone location, bank card, ANPR. Just find her.'

'Sure.'

'Thanks. And can you ask Sanderson and Ahmed what they know of Allen's feelings towards Linda? Allen gave the impression it was common knowledge but he might have been downplaying it.'

'No problem.'

Dan was tapping the photographs on the board. 'When we questioned the two deputy heads, I got the impression Ahmed was less keen on Allen. I reckon she's the best person to target for information on him, and she seems pretty wishy-washy. But let's put a bit of pressure on them *both*.' He shifted his attention to the wodge of printouts on his desk. 'These are Linda's bank statements from Barclays.' He held them out for me to see. 'She spends one hundred and fifty pounds a week on food from Waitrose, has her hair done at Toni & Guy every six weeks and her account balance is thirty grand.' Dan flicked through the printouts. '*And* the average price of houses in Tredegar Square is one-point-five million.'

I ran my finger down the columns of figures. 'They're clearly not hard up. But picking over the lifestyle choices of someone who's just died feels a bit distasteful.' I imagined the police in Sylhet doing this after the fire at Sabbir's flat.

He shrugged. 'It's all part of the job, isn't it?'

'To an extent, but I don't see that where she shops is relevant. And we don't *all* have low-maintenance crew cuts.'

'Ooh, snarky,' he joked, jabbing me with his elbow. 'I shall ignore that comment, Inspector.' He returned to the statements.

'And Peter is still alive. It's their joint accounts we're combing through as well as Linda's.'

'Maya . . .'

'Okay, okay. You're right.' I clicked out of HOLMES. 'Still no sign of the deleted files. It's so frustrating.' I picked up my mug. 'D'you want a cuppa? I'm —'

'You *beauty.*' Dan leaped up and fist-pumped the air, then made thick strokes on the paper with a pink highlighter. 'We've got the dates. She's paid in a grand a month, in cash, into her personal account for the last eleven months. Where would she have got that sort of money from?' Dan flicked through the pages. 'And here. Look. A lump sum of ten grand, deposited a year ago.'

I felt excitement lift me. Linda's finances had finally given us a lead. 'Cash isn't easy to trace but someone has to know how Linda acquired this money.'

'There's *always* a trail. We just have to find it.' He grabbed up the phone. 'I'll see what her bank knows about the payments.'

On the next table, Alexej was scanning copies of Linda's phone records. 'The data analysts have highlighted various number patterns. Nothing of any real interest.' He handed me the sheets.

'Husband, sister, the three senior managers, friends.' I skimmed the rows of numbers. 'The cleaner. Quite a few to the GP. Can you find out what they were about? And how are we doing with the cleaner?'

'Still no answer. I'll keep trying.' Alexej opened a new browser. 'I've got into Linda's cloud storage. She's deleted scores of text messages.'

'From?'

'Her husband and sister. Roger Allen. Neil Sanderson. Ruth Allen. And a few other unidentified numbers.'

'Why would she delete texts from her sister and husband?' It didn't make sense. 'In fact, why would she delete texts at all?'

'What's the point of keeping them?' Dan seemed genuinely perplexed. 'I delete mine. They clog up the phone.'

I rolled her eyes. '*You* might, but I don't know anyone else who does. On top of what we know about her bank accounts, it suggests she could be hiding something or being blackmailed.' I tapped my pen on the table. 'Plus, whoever has been deleting her texts seems to have forgotten her cloud storage.'

'All Linda's devices are linked to the same account but they aren't *all* set to backup to it.' Alexej spun round in his chair. 'How hopeful are they of recovering the other files?'

Dan made a zero gesture with his thumb and forefinger.

'The thing is,' Alexej said, 'anyone with access to her devices could have done the deleting. We are still waiting to find out from the technicians who installed the PermErase software, and who was logged into it when the deletions occurred. Her home devices have the same programme.' He continued clicking through the contents of her cloud. 'Here we are. Some of her photographs.' He passed me the iPad.

I scrolled through. 'This must be her sister. It looks like the woman in the photo in the Gibsons' kitchen. Anything strike you as unusual?'

'No. That's exactly it. They're *completely* ordinary photographs for someone who has no children. There's one image of a man.' Alexej pointed out the image. 'Going on his physical characteristics, I'd *guess* he's related to Linda.'

'He looks like he's in his twenties here, and facially he's similar to Linda and her sister. It's hard to tell as they're much older.'

Dan joined us. 'Judging by his clothes, the photograph must've been taken a long time ago. Could be a cousin or a nephew. Someone who died? Did she have any other siblings?'

'Not that we've learned. I wonder who he is. It's strange to keep such an old photo.' It was unsettling. 'A while back I attended a course on dysfunctional families. It was to do with a case. The psychologist told us that memento-keeping can be an indicator of unresolved feelings.'

Alexej returned his attention to the iPad. 'Is it normal for someone with a heart condition to be hiking across the countryside? Several photographs show Linda and Peter out walking. In some of the images Peter looks perky and healthy. In others, his colouring is distinctly grey.'

Dan looked over. 'My old man had heart problems. How he felt varied from one day to another. The doctor told him to keep fit and active. It's possible Peter's health has deteriorated in the last few months. We've asked the Gibsons' GP for details on Peter's heart condition.' He began a new message in his email.

I was still studying the man's image. 'We need to know who this man is and what his relationship was to Linda. Her sister must know. Dan, let's get over to Bow and see what her husband's got to say, and Muswell Hill to interview her sister Alice after that.'

Thursday – Maya

Dan and I were zig-zagging through the backstreets from Limehouse to Bow.

'It feels like we've been waiting to talk to Linda's husband for ages, but it's only twenty-four hours since she was killed.' Our warm breath fogged up the windscreen and I switched on the de-mister.

'It's the time-warp of investigations.' He was engrossed with his phone. 'Plus the GP put him off limits. It was frustrating.'

Five minutes later we arrived in tree-lined Tredegar Square in Bow, where the Gibsons lived. I knew the neighbourhood as an old school friend of mine lived here with her husband and children.

'Very nice,' said Dan when we arrived, eyeing the park in the centre, black metal railings round its circumference. 'Love the yellow brick.' He had turned to the houses, admiring the five-storey properties, the Audis, BMWs and Range Rovers. 'Is this what a head teacher's salary gets you in London?' He chuckled, casting his eye round the adjacent terraces of townhouses. 'In urban Sydney property prices have sky-rocketed too. Outside Sydney, you'd get a wine estate for the bucks these must cost.'

'I doubt Tredegar Square is representative.' I heard the irritation in my voice. 'Or the Gibsons, for that matter. There's her husband's income, don't forget. And, if they've lived here a while, these houses were probably quite cheap when they first bought. This area hasn't always been so posh.' Dan's comments were interesting, but for some reason I felt the need to defend Linda and her husband from the implied suggestion of luxury. 'Plus, at their age, they may have inherited.'

'My point is, living here, how can she fully appreciate the lives of her students?' His shoulders lifted in a shrug. 'Not one house is derelict. Not a satellite dish or rotten window frame in sight. D'you reckon they all sign an agreement when they move in?' He chuckled.

My impatience pricked. 'Round the corner, behind the pub, are two massive tower blocks. And the road behind us is walkwayed social housing. It's *London*.'

Dan pulled an *if you say so* face. 'No priors at this address, just in case you were wondering.'

I gave him a thumbs up and climbed the concrete steps to the crimson front door and rang the bell. The original glazing had been replaced with blue, green and red stained glass set into lead.

The door opened and a friendly face greeted us. 'Come in.' Janet McKenzie, the family liaison officer.

I introduced Dan.

'Mr Gibson's in the front room.' She lowered her voice. 'He's been given some more Valium this morning. His memory seems a bit unreliable but he's keen to speak to you. Got quite agitated last night when his GP said he couldn't.'

The house got no sun in the front rooms and felt chilly. Mr Gibson was sitting in an armchair in the almost-dark when we entered the lounge. The air smelled musty. Beside him, a table lamp threw a dim light on his drawn face. On the table by his chair sat an untouched mug of tea and a plate of biscuits. I was reminded of Mum's nursing home up the road, arriving on a visit, heart in my throat, no idea whether she would recognise me – or even still be alive.

Janet's voice pulled me back into the room. 'Mr Gibson, the police are here to speak to you.' And to me, she whispered, 'He won't let me draw the curtains. Perhaps you can try? I'll put the kettle on.'

I stood in front of Peter, waiting to see if he would look up. 'I'm sorry for your loss.'

In the corner, a grandfather clock counted out the moments.

He stared ahead, his eyes lowered.

'I'm DI Rahman. How are you feeling?'

He was still looking into the middle distance, gaze loose, barely aware we were there. He grunted at first and then slowly looked at me. How frail he was. And vulnerable. His eyes had the same opaque film I was used to seeing in Mum's, as though life was blurring at the edges, or the harshness of the world needed to be softened, filtered. How cruel life could be. A man with heart problems, forced to retire on medical grounds, clearly intelligent, and now his wife was dead and his world had changed with just one knock at the door.

'We had so many plans.' His voice broke the silence. It was soft but it cut through the weight of the room like an invisible knife. He was studying his hands, turning them over and examining each surface as if they might yield the secrets of his wife's death or give him some clues as to how to proceed from now.

While he was gathering his thoughts, I took in the room. It hosted two busy lives. The walls and surfaces were covered with teaching-related items: to the right of a sash window, awards and certificates hung proudly. Photographs adorned the space above the fireplace. Smiling faces told the story of a happy couple who enjoyed their life together. All the scenes lacked was children and grandchildren. That wasn't unusual these days, but it reminded me of what we knew about Linda – there was no sign here of the baby she'd carried or the man we'd found in her photographs. The room brimmed with memories that, until a few hours ago, would have been a source of pleasure. With his wife dead, and a heart condition, I suddenly felt scared for Peter Gibson.

'I'm sorry to intrude on your grief,' I said gently. 'We will do everything we can to find the person responsible for your wife's death. Are you okay to answer some —'

'*Perfectly.*' The word was buoyed up by anger.

I collected my thoughts; needed to tread carefully. Perching on the sofa, I leaned towards Peter in the adjacent armchair. 'How was your wife when she left for work yesterday morning?'

'Fine.' The word rose in tone, defiantly, as he uttered it through a tight jaw. He took a deep breath in, as if he needed to inhale some hope. 'Linda was a very upbeat person and was looking forward to the new term. We had a lovely Christmas. Nice week in Scotland . . .' His gaze slid sideways as he spoke. His voice wasn't angry now, just weary – as though the life had been crushed out of him and he didn't have the energy to understand anything new.

'Were you here all day yesterday?'

'Until I went to hospital.'

I got up and walked over to the pictures, looking at each one in turn. It was always strange looking at other people's family photographs, and even more so when one of them had just died. To see them so full of life, so joyful, nurturing hopes and dreams, yet now to be facing a funeral. I had seen many of the images on Linda's desk at school, smiling with her husband, looking carefree and happy.

'How long have you been married?'

'Nine years.' His shaky finger pointed at the framed photographs dotted round the room and on the mantelpiece. 'It was second time for us both. Second time lucky, I always said.'

I got an overwhelming sense from Peter Gibson that loneliness tormented him. I remembered how Mum had ground to a halt after Dad left, to the point she could barely function.

'Did your wife express any concerns to you over the last few days? Or over the holidays?'

'No. About what?'

It was often a tricky question when someone died. As if it was inconceivable anything might have been going on in their life that wasn't anything other than lovely and perfect.

'Anything. School? Family? Friends?' The woman outside the school, Sinead, came into my mind. 'Haniya Patel?'

'No. *Nothing.*' The last word was clipped.

'What about in the past? Were there any people she'd had fallings out with, people she didn't get on with or who didn't like her? I know it's painful to think in these terms but we need to find whoever killed your wife as quickly as possible.'

'As I'm sure the staff at Mile End High have told you, Linda was a popular, respected person.' His fingers pulled at each other.

'How about friends. Any difficulties there?'

'None that she mentioned to me. I'm sorry . . .' His voice started to tremble. He stopped talking and faced away from me. With a shaky hand he picked up his mug of tea, the tremors causing spills, and forced a sip.

I waited. Hated having to ask about things that upset him. I mentally scrolled through what the most important questions were, and which could be answered by records and other people.

Mr Gibson picked up the leather-bound photograph frame that was on the table beside his mug. 'This was our wedding day. It was the happiest of my life.' He traced his finger over Linda's image and handed it to me. 'Are you married?'

The question surprised me. 'I'm not, no.'

The photograph had been taken in a beautiful piazza with a circular stone fountain behind. I recognised Piazza Navona.

'We went to Rome during autumn half term, 2009. It's Linda's favourite city.'

In the image, Linda and Peter were beaming at each other while onlookers threw rice and pasta at them. Behind the couple, window boxes around the piazza brimmed with end-of-summer lobelia in purple, blue and pink.

I recognised love when I saw it. Felt a tug in my chest as I took in the happiness of the couple in the photograph and the palpable pain of the man in front of me.

'It's a lovely picture. Rome is glorious in the autumn.' I placed the frame back on the coffee table.

He was nodding profusely, as if this barely covered it and he wanted to add emphasis. 'I'd loved Linda for a long time, you see. Even when I was married to my first wife. Oh, I didn't do anything about it and it was the result of my marital unhappiness not the cause of it. But life took care of things for us. Eventually we both separated from our partners and shortly after that we got together.'

'I gather you were a teacher also?'

He pointed at the carriage clock on the mantelpiece. 'For nearly forty years.' His voice was full of pride. 'Started off at Stepney Boys' School, just up the road from Linda. Was a Maths teacher for over thirty-five of them, and then took over a bursar position recently on the advice of my doctor and union rep. Looked after the business side of the school.' He sighed. 'I found it rather dull, but unfortunately they found me capable. I knew I'd never escape after that. Retired last year after a minor heart attack; the clock was my retirement present from the staff.'

'And how are you enjoying retirement?' I asked, somehow knowing what his answer was going to be while at the same time sensing it was important.

Peter Gibson shook his head at my question. 'I've had to get used to it for my health. But, to be honest, I'm bored stiff here on my own. Linda tells me off for calling her and I know she's busy. I miss the stimulation and variety of the school day. Stepney Boys was a busy place. No one day was like another. Unlike now,' he gestured to the room, the house, his life, 'where every – day – is – the – same.'

What a small world. 'My brother went to Stepney Boys from 1982.' It was out of my mouth before I could catch it.

'What was his name?'

'Sabbir Rahman. You probably won't remember him.'

Mr Gibson gave a tiny laugh. 'Those lads kept me on my toes.' His harrowed expression melted as he surfed happy memories, and he nodded as he mentally touched each one. 'What's your brother doing now?'

The question launched a crushing blow in my stomach, almost making my knees buckle. 'He's . . .' *Why* had I mentioned him? 'He's not with us any . . .' I heard the croak in my voice; forced myself to name the objects on the mantelpiece while the wave of emotion passed, relieved Peter was silent. I hadn't meant to talk about myself, and impose my grief on his.

'I was thinking about what you said about retirement, Mr Gibson.' Dan's words were a relief. He'd been standing against the wall of the lounge and edged closer to Peter's chair. 'Lots of people find it difficult to adjust at first. Especially after a job like teaching.'

I took a deep breath. Stood up straight. I'd be alright in a minute.

Peter shook his head gently. 'A lot of people complain about teaching. It's not for everyone but I loved it. And so did Linda.' He paused. 'It was something we had in common.'

'How did you meet?' asked Dan.

'At a teachers' conference about twenty years ago. Both married to other people, like I said.' He paused. 'We bumped into each other at various events over the years. First I got divorced and then she did.'

'Whoever said true love was dead, eh?' Dan paused; looked over at me. 'A few more questions. Where were you yesterday between twelve and one?'

'Here. Same as every day.' He let out a frustrated sigh.

'Anyone come round?'

'No.'

'Anyone unhappy about you two getting together? Disgruntled exes? Bitter children?'

He shook his head. 'All water under the bridge by then.'

'In my experience, water can often collect beside the bridge and become stagnant.'

'Not in our case, I assure you.' It was said in a deep, headmasterly voice, as if he was shocked at the suggestion of imperfection. And – was there a reproach in his answer?

'How about *your* ex-wife and *Linda's* ex-husband? Where are they now?'

'My wife re-married, someone much more suitable; Linda's husband went to Spain and joined some sort of Buddhist order.'

Dan and I caught each other's eye. This was the first hint of a link with Buddhism. 'And are you in contact with your ex-wife?'

'Oh, yes. We have children. There's no acrimony. We weren't very close when we were married so there's not much feeling now, one way or the other. We're co-parents of grown-up children.'

'And Linda's first husband?'

'Michael. I think he has a Buddhist name now. As far as I know he and Linda lost contact. A similar situation. No bad feeling, just not the right person. Linda and I often talked about whether it would've worked had we got together earlier and not married our first partners...'

My phone buzzed in my pocket. I fished it out and read the message.

'Is Linda's ex-husband still in Spain?' asked Dan.

'I think he came back a couple of years ago. I'm sure Linda said a mutual friend told her he's part of that Buddhist Centre in Bethnal Green.'

'Thanks.' He made a note in his phone. 'Could I ask what you know about your wife's computer habits?'

I was keeping my eye and ear on the interview while I read the case updates.

Peter was frowning, as if Dan had asked about Linda's gynaecological history. '*Computer habits?*'

'Yes. Do you know if your wife deleted things after she'd attended to them? E-mails, documents, photographs?'

'Not that I know of. It doesn't sound like Linda. I would have thought she was too busy. Photos, perhaps. We used to take a lot of snaps. I can't keep up with new technology. Linda would delete the duplicates and poor shots, and copy the ones she wanted to keep onto disks for backup.'

'Other than photographs, you don't recall her deleting files from her computers? Or think this is something she would have done?'

Peter sat up in his chair, his eyes more alert now. He surveyed the room, as if he needed prompts to think of what she might have deleted. 'Unless my wife had a secret life I knew nothing about, I think it's unlikely.'

'Do you think that's possible?'

For a moment the room stood still.

'No, I don't.'

'Something else we have to ask is who was unhappy about what at the school? Linda may have confided things in you she may not have mentioned to her colleagues.'

'You mean you want the *gossip*, Sergeant?'

I wasn't sure if Peter was joking.

'Er . . . yes, please.' Dan's face softened. 'Any feuds, sources of bad feeling between anyone, we would appreciate you letting us know.'

I was typing an email, wondering what Peter was going to tell us.

'All schools have problems,' Peter said. 'Linda's was no different. There were tensions between staff. The usual nonsense about timetables, class sizes, form groups. This often led to resentment or jealousy. Schools are pressure cookers and teachers work long hours. These factors play out in the staffroom. Linda managed the staff well. She was good at listening to all sides and not telling people how to feel.' He let out an admiring sigh. 'Much more sympathetic than I would have been.'

Dan was listening.

'She got on with Shari. Found Neil a bit of a bully.'

'How about Roger Allen?'

'There was some issue with him. Linda never told me what it was but I got the impression he'd been causing problems ever since she took up her post... Ah . . .' He sat up, as though something had occurred to him. 'There was something bothering her a while back about the caretaker and the school's social worker, Asad Farhan. Can't remember exactly. Something about computers.'

I cleared my throat to interrupt. 'How're we doing here?' I needed to ask Peter about the information Alexej had just given me but Farhan's name caught my attention from a previous case. 'I wanted to ask what you know about Farhan.'

'Linda couldn't stand him, and I think the feeling was mutual.'

I saw my own concern reflected in Dan's face.

'Mr Gibson, did your wife do any part-time work?'

He snorted. Shook his head. 'When would she have had time?'

'Did anyone owe you or Linda money?'

'Not that I'm aware of. Certainly not me. What's this about?'

'Your wife's bank accounts show monthly deposits and withdrawals of large amounts of cash. Do you know anything about these?'

Thursday – Maya

Peter Gibson cradled the mug of sweet tea and stared at Linda's photograph. 'I can't take it in,' he said. Ashen alarm covered his features. 'It's so unlike her. Monthly payments and withdrawals?'

I heard him swallow.

'I can understand it's a shock if you didn't know.' He seemed genuinely surprised but we needed to check. 'Are you sure you didn't know anything about it?'

His forehead creased into a frown. 'I'm absolutely sure.'

My gut feeling was that he was telling the truth. A look round the house would help me to get more of a sense of Linda's life. I asked him.

'If you wish.' He waved his hand in the air as if it was of no interest to him.

'Sergeant, could you discuss with Mr Gibson whether he's arranged for anyone to come and stay?'

On homicide training, they drummed into us that the key to a person's death was in how they lived. Their home can often yield information that an interview cannot. I preferred to be up front about it rather than pretend I needed the toilet, then do it on the sly. I began at the stairs in the hallway. The jumble sale of items on the bottom few steps. Upstairs there wasn't a scrap of magnolia or wood chip. The bathroom had been freshly painted in eggshell and an ornate silver mirror hung on the main wall. Lily of the Valley toiletries clustered round the taps of a sumptuous oval bath, and on the hand basin.

Inside the medicine cabinet above the hand basin, there were a few moisturisers, a bottle of nail varnish and some cotton wool pads. In a mug there was some men's wet shaving equipment. It was one of the emptiest bathroom cabinets I'd ever seen.

Next to the bathroom was the main bedroom. Here, glorious sash windows looked out over a lawn and summer house. In the distance, the arm of a giant construction crane lay in repose. A metal-framed bed faced a chimney breast, at the bottom of which nestled a black, Victorian fireplace. Each side of the bed, cabinets were covered with personal items. Linda's reading glasses were keeping her place inside a paperback, next to a tube of hand cream; the fly fishing magazine was presumably Peter's. They still slept together then. On the bed, two double sets of pillows looked untouched. So, where had Peter spent last night? And how on earth was he going to get back into their bed with Linda's belongings there, waiting for her? There were days when working a murder investigation made me feel like a professional snooper, voyeur and stalker, trawling through the murky undergrowth of a person's life to piece together the mystery of their death.

In the spare room next door, suits and blazers – presumably Peter's old work clothes – filled a wardrobe, the remnants of a career that was over. Now he'd have Linda's clothes to face too. On the floor above was the Gibsons' office. Without their two desktop PCs and Linda's laptop – all with the police technicians – the room felt strange. Once home to two busy lives, it now resembled a showroom office, full of shabby-chic furniture and empty surfaces. Two desks, beautifully sanded and waxed, abutted a table with a large printer. A plush two-seater sofa lay alongside a coffee table. The walls displayed Peter and Linda's university and teaching qualifications, all in matching silver frames. Next to these was a photograph of Linda receiving an award or prize, Peter, by her side, glowing with pride. I tried to visualise the man downstairs in here with Linda, one of them working while the other reclined on the sofa and read a book. It was difficult when he looked so crushed.

Next to the study was a guest room. I popped my head round the door. It, too, was untouched, unless someone had plumped the pillows first thing this morning. So, Peter *had* sat up all night.

Back on the ground floor now, I followed the sound of a boiling kettle along the hall into the kitchen. As I entered the room I brushed a notice board and knocked off a couple of leaflets that were pinned to it. I picked them up. One was a card for a local taxi company, with the name 'Saiful' scribbled on it. A Neighbourhood Watch leaflet, a heating engineer, Peter's Freedom Pass. Another card, Clean Fast, had an office number and a mobile. I used my phone to take a picture of the cleaner's business cards and the taxi firm's. At the top of the board a photograph caught my attention. The Gibsons posed with another couple in glorious mountainous scenery, next to a shimmering turquoise lake. I could practically smell the cool, alpine water. All four of them were clinking aperitif glasses in a toast. It looked like Lake Garda or Como.

The family liaison officer was pouring tea into two mugs. 'You want a tea, love?'

'No, thanks. Janet, did he sleep in that chair last night?'

She screwed up her nose. 'I couldn't get him to go to bed. I tried. Said he couldn't face it without Linda.' Her eyes moistened as she told me this. It didn't matter how long you did this job for. Aspects of it always got to you.

'Can you try and get him into the spare room tonight? It's all made up in there. Sitting up all night with a heart condition isn't going to do him any good.'

'I'll have a go.'

After the bright white upstairs, the living room felt oppressive and dark, and I was itching to open the curtains to the daylight. Dan and Peter stopped talking.

'How are we doing?' The question was meant for Dan.

'Mr Gibson was telling me about Linda's *siblings*.'

I clocked his use of the plural.

'Sister in Muswell Hill. I've got her address.' He waved a scrap of paper. 'And a brother she's not been in contact with for many years.' Dan's speech was excited. 'I've shown Mr Gibson the image we found and he says he *thinks* it's Linda's brother.'

'It's actually quite common to be estranged from a sibling.' I was thinking aloud. 'Did you never meet him, Mr Gibson?' I was wondering why he wasn't sure about the photograph.

'Never.' It was a clipped reply.

'Did Linda tell you what happened with her brother?'

'All she said was that she never wanted to see him again. I left it at that.'

Linda certainly had secrets, and Peter seemed only too happy to go along with them. 'And you never asked why?'

'No. I took the view that if she wanted to tell me, she would.' Was there a defiance to his expression? Or perhaps it was fear.

'She never talked about where he lived?'

'No. She never mentioned him and neither did I.' He tapped his fingers on the arm of his chair. 'When can my wife's body be released? I'd like to make funeral arrangements.'

'We aren't sure yet. The post-mortem was conducted this morning. It won't be until the report's been checked. I'll ask one of my officers to let you know.' I waited for him to settle, aware he seemed keen to change the subject. 'One final thing. The pathologist found a C-section scar on Linda's abdomen. I assume you knew she had a baby?'

'Yes, of course I did. But it was years ago.'

'What happened to the baby?' Around the room there wasn't one photograph of a child. Linda could be a grandmother by now.

'All I know is that my wife was very young, and she gave the baby up for adoption. I didn't ask questions. It doesn't always *do* to pry.'

His comment felt heavy. Important, somehow. I waited. Watched him, wondering what it took to love someone who had so many ghosts in their past. Except the cash deposits and withdrawals we'd discovered *weren't* in the past. They were going on now.

Peter was rubbing his temples, eyes closed. Finally, he spoke. 'Look.

I realised the pregnancy had been traumatic for her, so I pretended to have forgotten I knew.'

'If you don't mind me saying, Mr Gibson,' Dan spoke gently, 'your wife had quite a few skeletons clunking about in her closet.' He paused. 'Didn't you mind?'

Annoyance flashed across Peter's face before he quashed it. 'Don't we all have secrets, Detective?' His tone mirrored Dan's.

I waited to see what Dan would say.

'Of course. But when people are murdered it's our job to sift through those secrets and figure out whether any could have got them killed.'

Thursday – Maya

Back outside in Tredegar Square, Dan and I headed back to the car.

'Could you live with all that secrecy?' Dan kicked at some leaves on the pavement. 'It'd drive me nuts.'

'I'm not sure.' I zapped the central locking open. 'I've been trying to decide. Presumably he didn't learn about everything in one go. I think that once you've accepted one secret, the next either prompts a freak-out or it becomes a pattern. Sounds like secrets became the norm for the Gibsons; like things people tiptoe round yet pretend they haven't seen.' Mum came into my mind and it occurred to me that I had no idea how she felt when she learned about Dad's affairs, or how she navigated their existence for so many years.

We were back on Mile End Road, bumper to bumper on the dual carriageway, heading for Muswell Hill.

'Alexej's following up Peter's comments about Neil,' Dan said. 'And making enquiries about the computers he mentioned. I wonder if they're linked to the money Linda's been receiving?' He was keying into his phone. 'I'm onto the London Buddhist Centre about Linda's first husband. It's a bit of a coincidence that she was married to a man who becomes a Buddhist and her death is linked to Buddhist ethics.'

An ambulance sped past, followed by an emergency motorcycle. 'The payments are on my mind too. Perhaps someone was blackmailing her?'

Dan shrugged. 'It's possible. There are a lot of people lurking in her past who she's lost contact with. By the way, while you were talking to Peter, I looked up the figures on religion. They're completely different from Australia. In Tower Hamlets and Newham, Islam is on the increase . . . but Buddhism's become much more mainstream. Like Australia, people are being turned off by the guilt of Christianity and the sexual abuse in the Catholic Church.'

His information confirmed my suspicions. 'I'm extremely concerned that we've got a school which needs to re-open tomorrow. The parents are anxious, and the national news channels are broadcasting every detail and development into people's phones and homes. And, at the moment, all we've got is a stack of questions and no answers.'

Limehouse Police Station, 2005 – Maya

In the CID office, the faces around me look as wrung out as I feel. Colleagues are gathered round desks, bleary-eyed from the long shifts of the last six days. Empty tea mugs litter the window sills, and the room reeks of takeaway leftovers and sandwiches. Everyone has rung home to say we've found her.

Alive.

On the board, the girl, Elena Rinkis, stares back at us, eyes like stone, marks all over her arms and neck. And next to her are the mug shots of the gang members who have kept her in enforced prostitution for the last six months. And the Albanian man and his girlfriend who'd organised her transit from Riga to London.

'Well done, everyone.' Detective Inspector Briscall is debriefing us. His voice is the usual monotone. 'We've all worked tirelessly. The final piece of intelligence, which came to my attention, clinched it.'

His smug grin niggles at me. '*I* discovered the gang's location, not *him*,' I hiss at Dougie, one of my DC colleagues.

'Forget it. Taking credit for others' work is his forte.'

We're standing at the back of the room, far enough away for Briscall to be out of earshot.

'Elena's family in Latvia have been informed that she is safe. Her mother had no idea what her daughter had sunk to.'

'*Sunk to?*' The words are out of my mouth before I can stop them, their jagged shape altering the room. I'm on my tiptoes. 'That's a bit harsh, sir. Elena thought she was coming here to study and work in a restaurant.'

Dougie jabs me with his elbow. 'It's not worth it, Maya,' he whispers. 'The guy's a prick.'

Everyone's staring at me. I can feel my ears getting hot.

Around the room people begin muttering.

'Did you say something, *Detective Constable* Rahman?' Briscall pulls himself up to his full height, rocking back on his heels, eyes blazing.

He'd heard.

'You said, "what her daughter had *sunk* to". Elena was forced into prostitution. She didn't *choose* it. None of the girls did. She's *sixteen*. She chose what she thought was a better life.' I heard the reproach in my voice.

'You're splitting hairs. We're all tired.'

'Yeah, pipe down, Bangla.' I turn to see DS Paige grinning, one of the older team members and my direct report. 'We aren't all immigrant lovers.'

A few jeers go up and I feel a rush of nausea. Briscall's looking smug.

And then I realise what's clinging to me: while we are all sleep-deprived and hungry, and in need of a shower, Elena Rinkis is fighting for her life in intensive care and one of our colleagues is undergoing surgery to remove a bullet from his shoulder.

'With respect, sir, I'm not splitting hairs.' My temples are beginning to throb. 'If the media pick up on that term, it diminishes the trafficking and imprisonment crimes of Oseku and his girlfriend. We are told in training we need to use language that condemns the actions of people like him.'

'Thank you, DC Rahman, for using your university education to tell me how to do my job.' His laugh sounds hollow. He tightens his tie. Looks round the room, hoping to garner support from his male colleagues.

I trace his gaze. See concern mirrored on many of my colleagues' faces, sneers on those of a few.

A finger jabs me in the shoulder.

'He's not worth it,' hisses Dougie into the back of my hair. 'He's a sexist shite.'

Dougie's right. But Briscall's comments prompt a fist of anger in my chest.

Briscall ends the de-briefing and the team pile over to the pub to celebrate the end of the investigation.

'C'mon, I'll buy you a drink.' Dougie's behind me.

I shake my head resolutely. 'I'm going home. There's nothing to celebrate until Elena and Mike are out of hospital. I'll see you tomorrow.'

Dougie rolls his eyes at me and follows the guys as they tail over to the pub.

A few minutes later, the room's empty and I'm at my desk, shutting down my computer. I've got the telephone receiver lodged between my ear and shoulder, on hold to the Royal London Hospital at Whitechapel to find out how Elena and Mike are.

'A *word*.'

I jump.

Briscall's standing right behind me.

I wriggle out of his way. The phone cord stretches and the base unit crashes to the floor, pulling with it my keyboard and pot of pens.

'I do *not* appreciate you trying to show me up. I shall be having a word with DS Paige, but any more behaviour like that and it'll be a disciplinary. You'd do well to remember that I'm a detective inspector. You've been in CID a matter of weeks.'

I've made my point about Elena and Mike and I'm not prepared to apologise.

'Did you hear me?'

'Yessir.'

'If you want to get on in the police force, you need to understand it isn't a place for little girls who can't keep their emotions in check.'

'Everything alright here?' The Scottish accent makes me jump. It's Dougie, striding across the room, overcoat on, his face tense with concern. He sees the phone and the stationery on the floor. Glances from me to Briscall and back again.

'DI Briscall was just telling me he regretted his choice of phrase earlier.'

Briscall shifts from one foot to another, and I see his fist clench.

It's tempting to repeat what he said to me, but I can't rely on other people to step in all the time. I'm going to have to deal with idiots like Briscall and Paige myself.

I scowl at Briscall, my resolve unyielding. 'I think we should all go home, don't you?'

'What was that about?' Dougie barks as soon as we get into the lift.

'He wasn't apologising. He was telling me off.'

Concern was still written over Dougie's face. 'Be careful, Maya. Men like him nurse grudges. He'd finish your career in a heartbeat rather than lose face.'

Thursday – Maya

An hour later, Dan and I were arriving in Muswell Hill. Duke's Avenue was a winding road which led down the hill from the roundabout to Alexandra Park.

'Woah, that's some mast. What is it?' He shifted in his seat to get a better look.

'It's Alexandra Palace. Where the BBC made their first public TV broadcast.'

'Blimey.' He was straight onto his phone browser.

'It's burned down twice. Ages ago, and then in the eighties. The locals call it Ally Pally. They have some great gigs there. My brother and I went to see a band there the night before my Maths GCSE exam. He helped me sneak out.' It was a bittersweet memory. 'Sabbir had just accepted that he was gay but he was scared of people knowing. Before he committed suicide, he'd finally decided to come out . . .'

'I'm so sorry. It can't be easy, with Haniya's death so recent too.'

'Thanks.' The satnav interrupted my reminiscing. 'Here we are. This is their place.'

We pulled up at a red brick terraced house. It had neatly trimmed rose bushes in the front garden. Vintage black and white tiles offered a slippery approach to the front door. Here ceramic pots huddled, their geranium inhabitants waiting for the warmth of spring. The doorbell sounded but no lights were visible on the ground floor or upstairs.

'The curtains are drawn over that window,' I said. 'Looks like Alice is in bed. Let's give her a minute to get to the door.'

Dan stepped over to the other side of the road, and began scrutinising all the houses, looking up and down the hill, standing on tip-toes.

'That looks dodgy.' I joined him on the icy pavement. 'Someone'll think you're casing the street and call the cops.'

'Very funny. The house is smaller than Linda's place in Bow but they're not a million miles apart.'

'Muswell Hill is trendy and expensive, but the demographics are very different. It's more families than hipsters. The crime patterns differ from Bow, too, especially violent crime. But like most of London, you've got posh streets jostling alongside social housing.'

'Are those tower blocks on the other side of the Palace?' He was standing on someone's front wall now.

'That's Broadwater Farm housing estate. It's where the Tottenham race riots happened in the eighties. It was an awful time. My family had only been here for a couple of years.'

A face peered round the curtains in the first-floor window of Alice's house.

I held up my hand and smiled. 'There she is.'

The woman who answered the door bore a striking resemblance to Linda, perhaps a few years older.

'Alice Stephens?'

Her eye sockets were swollen and dark, as though she'd smeared soot round them. Her eyes were bloodshot from crying. 'That's me.' Alice stood on the doorstep in her dressing gown, clinging to the door, as if she had no idea what to do next, no reference points.

'DI Rahman and DS Maguire. It's about your sister. Could we come in?'

The request seemed to jolt Alice out of her stupor. She gestured for us to enter. 'I was in bed. Sorry.' She rubbed her eyes and tucked her bobbed hair behind her ears.

Poor woman. She had a gentle manner and it looked like the news of her sister's death had plunged her into shock.

Alice was walking ahead of us into the house and along a hall. The floor had similar black and white tiles to the ones outside.

Stripped wooden bannisters led upstairs. We followed her into the lounge.

'I couldn't get up this morning. Barely slept. Trying to take everything in. Poor Linda.'

The curtains were still closed in the front room. Alice shuffled over to an armchair and sank into it. She switched on a table lamp, fidgeted, then got up and opened the curtains.

I waited for her to settle and took the opportunity to look round the room. Around us, floor-to-ceiling shelves lined the walls, crammed with books, giving the lounge the atmosphere of a library. The room bore the hallmarks of a late night. Photograph albums were stacked on the coffee table, and individual images had been placed on the glass surface. I sidled closer, hunting for a photograph – like Linda's – of their brother. An almost-finished bottle of red wine stood next to a single glass with a mouthful left in it. If Alice had been drowning her sorrows, she'd been doing it alone.

'What happened to my sister?' She was sitting bolt upright, her hands raised to her face, fingers flat to her cheeks. 'Did she suffer much, do you know?'

I relayed as much as I was allowed.

'Oh, Jesus.' Her body slumped and she grabbed hold of the mantelpiece. 'Strangled?'

'I'm afraid so.'

She steadied herself. 'What did you say about Pali?'

'It's an ancient Indian language that was used in Buddhist texts. From two thousand five hundred years ago.'

'Hold on. Are you saying Linda's death is linked with Buddhism?' Her hands went to her mouth. 'Oh my God. You do know her first husband is a Buddhist?' She was staring at me intently, her eyes wide with alarm. 'He was getting serious about it when they were together. When they split up he had the ceremony thing where you go on a three-month retreat. What's it called?'

'Ordination,' said Dan.

'Peter told us about your sister's ex-husband,' I said gently. 'At the moment we don't understand the role of Buddhism in your sister's death.'

Alice was nodding. Blinking fast. She seemed to be thinking, trying to take in what she was hearing. 'How is Peter? He's going to be devastated. He adored Linda.'

'He's bearing up.' I wanted to shift topic. 'Do you have an address for your brother? I gather he and your sister were estranged?'

Alice's gasp slapped the air. '*Tom?*'

'Yes. We need to interview him. Just a few routine questions.'

She looked as if the request had punched her in the face. She was shaking as she pulled at the dry skin round her nails, twisting and rolling the bits she picked off.

'I'm sorry. I feel a bit dizzy.' She was trembling. 'I think I need to sit down. Could you give me a second?'

I gestured to Dan to fetch some water for Alice. 'I appreciate how distressing this must be for you.' I waited, using the time to clarify what I wanted to ask.

A few moments later Dan returned with a glass and handed it to Alice.

'Thanks.' She took a few sips and balanced the tumbler on her knee, dazed. She was gently rocking the top half of her body, as though needing to soothe herself.

'Whenever we mention your brother, everyone seems to freeze,' Dan said, his voice low. 'Peter's reaction was the same. Can you tell us why?'

The glass slipped from Alice's hand and fell to the floor, smashing into hundreds of tiny pieces on the parquet. Water splashed up her bare legs and over Dan's trousers, and slicked, uncontrolled, across the floor. The crash seemed to rouse Alice.

'Crikey. I don't know what . . .' She jumped to her feet, staring at the mess. Shards of glass lay like islands in the water.

A few moments later, Dan returned with some kitchen roll and a dustpan and brush. While Alice mopped up the water, he swept up the pieces of glass. I took out the iPad from my bag and waited for her to sit back down.

When she did, she was patting her neck and chest, and fanning herself with a magazine. Her previously wan cheeks were flushed with heat.

I held out the iPad with a copy of the image from Linda's cloud storage. 'Is this your brother in the photograph, Mrs Stephens?'

She looked up. Reached for the image and studied it, taking in each pixel. Her nod was gentle. 'Yes. That's Tom. It's an old picture from before the . . .' She dabbed at her eyes and plunged her nose into a soggy tissue. 'He would've been around nineteen then. Maybe twenty.'

'A picture from before the what?' Dan asked.

'Oh, nothing. Just that it was a long time ago.'

'What was?'

'The photograph. It's such an old shot. Dad must've taken it.'

The soles of Dan's shoes scratched on the hard floor as he walked up and down the room. 'I can't help noticing that *you* don't have any pictures of your brother either. Are you also no longer in touch with him?'

'Neither of us is.' She gulped. '*Was.*'

Dan faced Alice. 'My wife's family were furious when she married a cop. For people from Aboriginal communities, it's the ultimate betrayal.'

Alice's head was lowered but she was listening.

'Her family turned on her. Especially the older generation.'

'I'm sorry. I . . .' Alice muttered.

'It was as though they'd got together and decided to push her out.'

'DS Maguire —'

'My point is that all families have secrets, don't they? And all families have rules. Bring shame on the family, or break those rules, and you're out. Isn't that right, Mrs Stephens?'

Tears fell from her cheeks onto the floor.

'The mention of your brother has obviously shaken you. Tell us what's going on, please?'

Alice closed her eyes and sat back in her chair.

A minute passed.

Then another.

I was itching to chivvy a response out of her but knew we had to sit tight.

Finally, Alice opened her eyes again and sat forwards. 'Tom and Linda were never close.' Her tone of voice was more business-like now. 'None of us were. Tom isn't nor...' She moved to reach for the glass of water, forgetting that she'd dropped it.

'We need to know if your brother might've been involved in your sister's death.' I spoke quietly. 'We've got her school shut down until tomorrow, and at the moment I can't guarantee that there won't be any more murders.'

Alice was wagging her head, staring into the distance again.

Please don't go silent on us again, I thought. 'It will come out sooner or later, so the more you can tell us, the quicker we can find the person who did this to your sister – and everyone can start to grieve.'

'It's impossible my brother was involved in Linda's death.' Alice spoke slowly at first and then more determinedly. 'Tom's in prison.' She let the words drop from her mouth as though she was no longer able to keep them in. She twiddled a soggy piece of kitchen roll in her fingers. 'He's been inside for nine years. There were witnesses . . . a court case . . . We all knew it was going to happen sooner or later.'

It made sense now.

Alice got up and crept over to the sitting-room window. The glass squeaked as she rubbed at a mark. When she turned to face us, tears streaked her cheeks and she wiped her nose on her dressing-gown sleeve.

'What did he do to your sister?' Dan asked.

'Tom has always bullied Linda. What am I saying? It was more than that. He *abused* her. Verbally and physically. Has done since we were kids.'

'Did your parents know?' My skin ran hot.

Alice was leaning against the window frame, examining the floor. Tears dropped from her eyes. Large shiny blobs, onto shaking hands as she nodded her head emphatically.

'And sexually?'

'Yes. For years she protected him. Covered up for him. I don't know whether it was fear or love. Or both. And because of her fucked up loyalty towards him, and mine to her, she didn't get the support she should have.' Her words dripped with guilt and regret.

'It wasn't your responsibility, Mrs Stephens. You were kids. Did your parents do anything about it?'

She shook her head vigorously. 'I think they were in denial. Too painful for them. Linda tried to talk to them about it but they said she was lying.' A sob burst from Alice's throat. 'Linda was devastated. Confused. She couldn't understand why Mum and Dad wouldn't believe her. I guess it's what you said.' She gestured to Dan. 'About rules.'

'I'm sorry. What you're describing is common. Shock and denial. It's the rejection of something unbearable. First it's the "message" that gets rejected, then the "messenger".' He studied her face. 'Do you know how long it went on for?'

'Years, I think. After a while, Linda went into denial herself. As if it *was* her fault or she *had* imagined it. She left home as soon as she could. Began teaching. After that she refused to talk about it. Didn't want to hear anything about Tom. Mum's dead now and Dad's in a nursing home. She never forgave them.'

It made sense: Linda had become the family scapegoat.

'It's extremely difficult when you feel betrayed by the people who are supposed to keep you safe.' I was taking in what Alice had told us. I felt immense sympathy for both women and wondered how much Linda had been able to transcend the abuse, and whether Alice would ever be able to come to terms with the guilt she felt towards her sister.

Alice sniffed. 'That's *exactly* how she felt. Betrayed. As if she was worthless because they chose to protect Tom over her.'

'How did he end up in prison?' We needed to offer her support but we also had to get as much information from her as possible before she clammed up again.

'He was caught abusing a woman. There had been others, not just Linda. Finally, a girlfriend went to the police and made a complaint. She'd been recording him forcing her to have sex with him. There was other evidence. Enough for him to be charged and found guilty, and he went to prison.'

'When was this?'

'It was just before Linda and Peter got married. She gave evidence at the trial. We both did. I told her what he'd done to the woman, and she went to the police and told them everything.'

That would mean Tom might have a grudge against Alice as well as Linda.

'Can I see her?' Alice wiped her eyes. 'I'd really like to see her.'

'Of course. We need someone to formally identify the body. I didn't like to ask your brother-in-law.'

'Thank you.'

'Which prison is your brother in?'

'Highfield. In Barnet.'

'And what's his surname?'

'Sullivan. Thomas John Sullivan.'

I gestured to Dan to get on the phone to the prison. 'We will need the name of your father's nursing home.'

She chewed her lip.

'Please don't blame yourself for what your brother did to your sister. It wasn't your fault. It was your parents' responsibility to keep you all safe.'

'But I'm her big sister. I'm supposed to look out for her.'

'You were a child too. Unfortunately, people who have secrets trade on loyalty and fear. There's only so much you could have done if your parents weren't able to face the truth.' I hoped she would agree to get help. 'There are services that I can put you in touch with, if you would like? When you're ready.'

Alice wiped her eyes.

'Two final things,' said Dan. 'Did you know about your sister's pregnancy?'

'Yes.'

'Did she tell you who the father was?'

She shook her head.

'We will need you to come to the station to make a formal statement.' Dan waited. 'The last thing is, do you know if your sister ever visited your brother in prison?'

Shock spread over her face. 'Visited him? Why on *earth* would she do that?'

Thursday – Maya

I shut Alice's garden gate. 'What made you ask if Linda has visited her brother?'

Dan and I were almost at the car.

'The childhood loyalty. Colluding with him. The photograph. My wife sees it a lot in the communities she works with in Australia. Abuse by people we love doesn't necessarily stamp out the love; it can strengthen it.'

'But Linda gave evidence against her brother?'

Dan was nodding. 'Yup. It's part of the conflicting feelings. Rage, hate, love, all mixed up together. It's a toxic mixture. You wait. I'd put money on it.'

My stomach lurched with dread. 'I hope you're wrong.' I remembered Linda's caesarean scar and a horrible thought took shape in my mind. Alice had admitted the abuse had been sexual. If Dan's hunch was right . . . I turned to face him over the car roof. 'What if Linda's brother was the father of the baby?'

'That's exactly what I was thinking.'

Silence accompanied our drive along the North Circular and up the A10 to HMP Highfield in Barnet, North London. Dan was pre-occupied with his phone and I was pleased to have some time to reflect on what we had learned from Linda's husband and sister.

On arrival at the prison, we signed in and were searched. Leaving our mobiles at reception, we took our visitors' badges and were escorted along a series of security-coded corridors to see the governor. I wanted some background information on Tom Sullivan. Once I'd requested this, we were taken to the interview room that had been set up for us. A uniformed prison officer stood by the door of the room. Sullivan was already sitting at the table, seemingly unperturbed, as though he was waiting for a friendly visitor rather than a police interview.

'Mr Sullivan? I'm DI Rahman and this is DS Maguire.'

We sat down opposite him. With no windows and no natural light, the room was gloomy and cold. One of the partition walls had a fist-shaped hole pushed through it from inside and the plasterboard was leaning into the gap.

The man in front of us sat quietly, weighing us up.

I was struggling to reconcile the image I'd formed of Linda's brother with the man opposite me. He seemed so different from Alice Stephens, the inoffensive accountant who lived in Muswell Hill, and Linda, the lively, inspiring headmistress who I'd seen in the school video. The two sisters were petite and shared similar facial characteristics. Their brother was very ordinary. Small arms and short legs were swamped in scruffy jeans and a plain sweatshirt.

'We've been speaking to your sister.'

'Oh, okay.' His voice conveyed surprise, and his eyes widened a little. 'Which one?' His tone was soft, his manner almost *gentle*. In a strange – and disconcerting – way, he reminded me of Peter Gibson.

'The one that's . . .' I stopped myself. Started again. 'I'm sorry to inform you that Linda was found dead on Wednesday.'

'Gosh.' His mouth remained open as he absorbed the news. 'Why would anyone kill Linda?'

'We don't know yet.'

'How did she die?' There was still no hint of the aggression we knew he was capable of. Perhaps prison had mellowed him; time softened his depraved behaviour.

'She was strangled.'

'That's terrible. Why didn't someone tell me sooner?' His eyes narrowed a fraction, and I sensed a shimmer of annoyance. He stroked his chin, as though he were considering the information and his response. 'When's the funeral?' There it was again, beneath the controlled tone of voice and the mild-mannered gestures.

'Oh, cut the bullshit, Mr Sullivan,' Dan tore in. 'As if you *care*. We didn't tell you sooner because your sister and brother-in-law wouldn't talk about you, so we had no way of knowing where you were. And we know why *that* is, don't we?'

Sullivan pulled his jaw into a tight smile, revealing the sort of broken, yellowy-brown teeth that come with a cocaine habit. Other than that, there was no perceivable reaction. He simply continued to stare, through eyes that were dark hollows, cold and unmoved.

Finally he spoke. 'I'm not sure this is how you're meant to deliver the news to me that one of my siblings has passed away.' His words were slow and full of menace.

In that second, a sense of foreboding crept over me. Dan's remarks had clearly pushed Sullivan's buttons. I looked at his fingers. They were tobacco-stained and his crumpled clothes gave off hints of smoke. On his right hand, the inside of his first and second fingers were burned to the bone: heroin nodding. The burns were nicotine-stained scar tissue now but they made me wonder whether Linda's brother was getting drugs in prison, and whether he'd been assessed for psychopathy.

Sullivan continued to drawl. 'And anyway, I *do* care. I care about my sisters very much. Particularly Linda.' The control had returned now, yet he couldn't have looked less bothered.

I matched the quietness of his voice and leaned forwards to look him straight in his bloodshot eyes. 'We know about the abuse. The incest . . . And we also know Linda had a baby.'

His jerky laugh betrayed shock. 'Yeah, well, they always were liars, those two. And *dirty*.' He looked at Dan and winked. 'Know what I mean?'

Dan took a deep breath. 'The transcripts from your trial confirm the abuse.'

Sullivan made long, slow claps, grinning cruelly. 'You do know Linda's visited me, right? Several times. Is *that* in your records too?'

I swallowed hard. I hadn't checked. 'Of *course*.' The lie soured on my tongue. So Dan was right.

'Don't you think that's odd? Her claiming all those things about me – yet visiting me in prison? If I'm such a *terrible* person?'

He was clever.

'In my experience, there's no such thing as "odd".'

Alice had told us about Linda's conflicting feelings towards her brother, how much loyalty she'd shown him, and how this had become increasingly complicated when her parents refused to listen.

'And all the other stuff? The letters? Telling me, when she came here, how much she loved me? Begging me to forgive her for the lies she told? Does that fit with me abusing her?' Sullivan was on a roll. 'All I had to do was turn on the charm, the "tortured" act, the puppy dog eyes . . . and Linda was right here,' he pointed to the palm of his hand, 'wanting to fix me. And prepared to do anything to please me.'

I could picture Sullivan when they were growing up: a regular boy who somehow morphed from being normal into the sort of manipulative behaviour that abusers are capable of, perfecting the ability to say and do *exactly* the right thing to keep his victims under his spell. But Sullivan clearly couldn't – or didn't want to – understand what he'd done, and how it had affected his sister and whole family.

'Oh, give it a rest, buddy,' said Dan as he sat back in his chair and folded his arms.

'It's all documented, Mr Sullivan,' I said. 'What we would like to know is whether you were the father of Linda's baby?' Was this what Linda had been killed over?

Sullivan sat forwards in his seat and placed his slender forearms on the table, as though he wanted to add something important. Personal. He beckoned me closer with his hand and I got a waft of his putrid breath.

'You obviously don't know the answer to that,' he said, his voice low, 'or you wouldn't be asking me.' He cracked each knuckle slowly, enjoying the attention it created. 'After all, what would someone like *you* understand about *my* life?' And then he cleared his throat, and with all the force he could muster, spat a huge gob of saliva into my face.

Thursday – Maya

'Assault.' Simon Affrey, the prison governor, was unequivocal when I told him about the spitting.

We were in Affrey's office, so we could check the visitor records and see the letters Sullivan claimed Linda had sent him.

'I'll get his medical records checked for HIV and hepatitis, and have him re-tested.' Affrey tapped at his keyboard. 'He's certainly compromised his parole review.' He didn't look disappointed. 'And "someone like you"?' He jotted the phrase on his notepad. 'I wonder what he meant by that?'

I rubbed my face, convinced that traces of Sullivan's saliva had evaded the anti-bacterial wipes.

'Here we are. Linda Gibson. Visited four times since he's been with us. I'll get the archives checked for his correspondence, and see if there are any audio or video recordings of Mrs Gibson's visits. We have an open-plan visitors' room so I think it's unlikely.'

'Thanks. Can you tell me about his psychological profile? Has he been assessed for psychopathy?'

'He has. As soon as we got him. His diagnosis is Antisocial Personality Disorder with psychopathic traits. He's had regular psychotherapy but refuses to engage.'

'I noticed the burns on his fingers. What's his history of drug use?'

'Extensive, unfortunately. Marijuana as a teenager, then cocaine and some crack, and heroin. It's a trajectory we see all too often.'

I wanted to choose my words carefully. 'And recently?'

'We have had problems with drugs at Highfield in the past. I'm sure you know how resourceful the prison population is. But my predecessor implemented strict controls, and as far as I know,' he crossed his fingers, 'we are okay at the moment.'

'Do you know when Sullivan might last have had drugs?'

'Five years ago we had amphetamine, heroin and cocaine getting in for several days before we found the source. It was just before I was made governor.'

'Were visitors sneaking it in?' Dan moved from one foot to the other.

'Oh, we get regular attempts in clothing and underwear, shoes, even nappies. Chucked over the fence in a pigeon carcass. The most recent method is disguising gear in the watercolour paints on kiddie pictures from home.' He wagged his head in frustration, tutting. 'On this occasion, one of the staff was blackmailed by an inmate.'

Dan raised his eyebrows.

'The last thing I wanted to ask is whether anyone had informed Sullivan of his sister's death before we arrived.'

'Oh yes. One of the officers told him on Thursday, as soon as we heard from you. It's prison policy to do it promptly.'

*

In the prison car park, a thick frost lay on car roofs and bonnets. Overnight, temperatures had plummeted again. My head was reeling from the exchange with Linda's brother.

'I think we can rule him out as our killer, don't you?' My white breath billowed in the bitter air. 'Sullivan would've struggled to arrange a contract killing from prison.'

'I agree.'

'I'll update the team. D'you reckon Sullivan *was* the baby's father?' The thought made me shudder.

He shrugged. 'Without a paternity test, it's hard to know. We should be able to get a copy of the birth certificate and, hopefully, the adoption papers.' He paused. 'Are you okay?'

I felt my eyes fill up and sniffed hard. 'I will be.' Across the car park a pigeon pecked at a burger someone had dropped. 'It's all so depressing. Just as we get a lead, it either takes us nowhere or throws up more questions.' Three more pigeons piled on. 'And not *one* bloody suspect. No-one firm, anyway.'

In the car, Dan started up the engine and the radio began firing out alerts and emergency call-outs. Seconds later, our phones were going crazy, buzzing and ringing. Something had happened.

I answered a call. 'Alexej?'

Dan looked up from his mobile.

I cursed under my breath. 'The same MO?'

Dan was answering calls on the radio.

'Keep me posted.' I rang off. Banged my fist on the dashboard. 'No, no, no! Why did this have to happen? Allen's been strangled. And the killer's left another precept.'

Dan was checking the satnav. 'I take it we're going straight to Stepney? Who called it in?'

'His wife. She found him at the flat. Poor woman.'

'There's been an accident at Archway and traffic's solid on Holloway Road.' He pulled himself up to get a good view. 'I'll chuck a U-y. It's clear back that way.' He hauled the car round.

I was back on the phone to Alexej. 'Our ETA's just under an hour. Can you chase up the house-to-house team? It'll be dark in a couple of hours. I'll authorise the technicians to ring-fence mobiles through social media. We need to know who the last person was to see Allen alive.' I switched on the blues and twos. 'Right. Step on it.'

Dan pulled into the bus lane and accelerated.

'I was only at that flat a few hours ago and Allen was alive.' I cursed again. 'This changes everything. We've got two murders and we need to consider the possibility that the killer may be planning more.'

Thursday – Dan

Forty-five minutes later they were at the Allen's flat in Stepney. The cordons were in place, abutting the wooden hoardings of an enormous building site. Heavy machinery was lifting and shovelling, and an operative was breaking up concrete with a pneumatic drill.

'We all need bloody ear defenders,' Dan growled at Maya. An ambo stood by, its back doors open. Perched on the back ledge was an athletic-looking woman in trackies and sneakers, a shock blanket draped round her shoulders. 'That'll be Ruth Allen. I'll have a word with her.'

Maya was assessing the area. 'I'll find Dougie for a run-through of the scene.'

'Gotcha.' Dan surveyed the vicinity for CCTV. One camera over the entrance to the block but it looked pretty ancient. One on the other side of the street, on a lamp post. Possibly some private cameras. He went over to speak to the paramedic. 'I'm Detective Maguire. Is that Mrs Allen?'

'It is. I'm Lisa.'

Dan lowered his voice. 'Any chance you can move her away or inside the ambulance? They'll be bringing the body out soon. I don't want her to see her husband on a stretcher in a bag.'

'Sure,' Lisa said. 'She's in shock as it is. Came back to get some clothes for the children and found him in there.'

'Where *are* the kids?'

'At her sister's. She's been staying there for the last couple of days.'

'Right.' So much for her sister saying she hadn't heard from Ruth.

Ruth Allen's hair tumbled round her face and trackie hood. She was plastered with make-up and wearing the cleanest trackie daks he'd ever seen.

'I'm Detective Maguire.'

She stared into the distance, her gaze loose.

'I'm sorry for your loss.' Dan kicked at the frost on the tarmac. Without a glimmer of sun, and temperatures barely above freezing, the crystals hadn't thawed from earlier. 'We will need you to accompany us to the station to give a statement. I'll get someone to wait with you.'

The woman didn't speak. She had her fingers in her mouth and was chewing her nail, her whole body trembling.

'Can I get you anything? Call someone?'

She shook her head. 'Thanks, though.'

Dan walked towards the common approach path.

Dougie was on his way over. 'Dr Clark's inside with Maya if you want to inspect the scene.' He passed Dan a set of protective clothing. 'Manual strangulation. White card, left beside the body with writing on it. No binding of the wrists but a blindfold over his eyes.'

'Thanks.' Dan pulled on the forensic suit, the plastic shields over his boots, and followed Dougie into the apartment block.

The entrance from the street brought them into a lobby. Ahead, the door of the Allens' apartment was wide open. Warm air carried the unmistakeable stench of urine towards them. A crime scene officer was dusting for prints at the front door. Kiddie coats and a smart leather jacket were pulling a coat rack away from the wall, and shoes were everywhere. Pink bags hung from the bannisters and door handles, and someone had Blu-tacked children's crayon drawings to the hall wall. A wife had lost her husband and two kids were going to grow up without a dad.

The lounge was full of family paraphernalia. Allen was sitting in a tall armchair, dressed in grey, stained strides and a brown sweater. The carpet round the chair stank of piss. Beneath his slippered feet, a large wet patch was drying. But it was the man's neck that attracted

Dan's attention. His head was resting back, eyes covered with a bright white cloth. Unlike Linda's face and jaw, where bruising had only just been forming, Allen's neck was an ugly patchwork of angry, reddish-brown marks, where broken capillaries had leaked blood into the skin. Beneath the blindfold, similar marks peeped out. There were a few scratches round his jawline, but not many. Had he struggled less than Linda or had the killer used greater force? The V-shaped bone, which was protruding from the side of the man's neck, suggested that the killer had wrenched his head and snapped the spine beneath the skull. This wasn't just a functional killing. A disposal. It was an angry murder.

Dr Clark was with Maya at the body. 'G'day, Doc. Was he killed here?'

'I would say so.'

'Same perpetrator?' Dan was scanning his instinct for whether the murderer might be male or female.

'Certainly an identical MO from a medical point of view. Judging by the alcohol fumes when we arrived, and the empty whisky bottle, it wouldn't have taken much to overpower him. He wasn't a hefty man.'

Dan squatted beside the body, moving his arms and hands to get a feel for angles and positioning. 'Was he sitting in that chair when he was killed?' He looked at Dr Clark for the information. Unlike Linda's office, the lounge showed no signs of a struggle.

'That's my guess at the moment.' He pointed to the carpet. 'Urination can occur just prior to death. Sometimes it's bladder collapse at the *moment* of death.'

Dan was still leaning over the body, moving his arms and hands into different positions. 'Would the killer have stood here?' He faced Dr Clark. 'And pressed into the neck from the front . . .?'

'Dan,' hissed Maya. '*Cross-contamination.*'

'Or squeezed from the side?'

'DS Maguire. Please move away from the body. We don't know if it's been taped for fibres and hair.'

Dan shimmied away and jumped to a standing position. 'You were saying, Doc?'

'From a medical viewpoint, either. You might want to do your *tai chi* away from corpses in future, Sergeant.' Dr Clark gave him a stern look. 'I was about to say – all that's required is sufficient pressure, and that can be from thumbs or hands round the entire neck.' He gestured. 'The jugular veins are the most vulnerable as they're in the outer part of the neck. Pressure on the carotid arteries results in a quicker death.'

'Could a woman have managed to strangle him?' He was trying to grasp the technique. 'We had a case in the Sydney business district. The killer had been watching videos on the internet, and researching neck physiology. Practising.'

'Oh yes. If she knew what she was doing. It only takes a few moments of pressure and you're unconscious.'

'And I'm guessing anger and body weight can increase pressure?'

'That's right.'

'But presumably experience is key? Otherwise the victim can scream or scratch the attacker, or get away?' Dan wondered how a person went about preparing to strangle. Had Linda been the first? Was she practice, perhaps?

'Exactly. But if Allen was inebriated, he may well have been asleep,' Dr Clark continued. 'If his killer took him by surprise, he'd have been at a disadvantage. The toxicology results will tell us how drunk he was. I'll leave the rest to the police.'

'And the neck-jaw stuff…? Was this a more violent death than Linda's?'

'It's difficult to be sure at this stage. But it takes a lot to snap someone's hyoid bone.'

'Thanks, Doc.' Dan took in the room. Without the corpse and the police personnel, it was the epitome of family life. A purple scooter, just like the one Kiara had, was lodged under the coffee table, and crayons and a colouring book lay on its glass surface. On the mantelpiece, a family portrait took pride of place, next to school photographs of the girls at various ages.

Maya was talking to Dougie.

'Nothing on the doors or windows suggests forced entry,' Dougie explained to her. 'My officers are processing fingerprints, fibres, hair and skin. We've got some footprints in the entry lobby. There's less contamination potential here than there was at the school.'

That meant the killer either had a key, knew where one was left or Roger Allen had let the person in.

'The flat is on the ground floor. Any operational CCTV?' she asked Dougie.

'Nothing. There's one at the entrance to the block but it's been vandalised.'

Maya faced Dan. 'We've got more Buddhist ethics. I've just taken a photograph from the exhibits store. It's the third precept. This one translates as: *I shall abstain from sexual misconduct.* So, we have one murder linked to taking the ungiven and one linked to sexual misconduct.'

'Shit.' Dan was shaking his head. 'D'you think they *were* having an affair then?'

'I don't know. It's interesting that the killer's blindfolded him. "Eyes" and "seeing" don't seem to fit so well with the "sexual misconduct" precept as "hands" did with the "taking" precept. I'm sure about one thing though: with two identical deaths, the parents have every right to be concerned about more murders.'

Over at the ambo, Ruth Allen was sobbing. Lisa was by her side, holding a bottle of water and a handful of tissues.

'Her kids are similar ages to mine. They've lost their dad. They're going to be devastated.' Dan sighed heavily. 'Let's get Ruth Allen to the station and interview her.'

Back on the street, blobs of sleet were falling and Dan wondered if he'd ever get used to the cold here.

DCI Briscall was waiting for them. He got out of his car and strode towards them, his face pinched with annoyance. 'The shit has hit the fan. Some of the parents have heard about Allen's death and are at the school, demanding information and speculating about who the killer may target next.'

'I'd anticipated that. We are going to the school now to warn Shari and Neil, and take them through safety procedures.'

'We need an arrest, Maya. I've got the Deputy Assistant Commissioner breathing down my neck about targets and community confidence.'

She was pawing at the slush on the pavement with her foot. 'Why don't I leave that to you while we get on with finding our murderer?'

'I mean it, Maya. We need results. Otherwise I'll be forced to get the school closed.'

Thursday

The precept says:

kamesu micchacara veramani sikkhapadam samadiyami
I shall abstain from sexual misconduct

What a fool you made of yourself. Yet she never cared about you. It might not have been adultery in literal terms but that's exactly what it was. Perhaps you saw your feelings as harmless. Didn't you ever consider how your wife and children felt?

To make matters worse, you went along with her ideas and supported her decisions . . . all because of your obsession.

A Buddhist would call them selfish cravings and neurotic fantasies. A Buddhist would say that you should exercise self-restraint.

Thursday – Maya

While Dan went to the school to advise Neil Sanderson and Shari Ahmed on safety procedures, I was heading to Bethnal Green to interview Linda Gibson's ex-husband, Vajrasiddhi. The London Buddhist Centre had given us contact details for him.

When I arrived, I discovered the 'men's Buddhist community' meant a shared, four-storey, terraced house in a popular side street.

'Mr . . . sorry, what did you say your name is again?' I tried to take in the pronunciation.

'Vajra-siddhi. We don't use "Mr" or "Mrs", just the one name.' He led me into a large open-plan kitchen. His top lip and chin were covered with stubble, and speckled with ginger and white bristles. The house was freezing, and mud-brown hair peeped round a woollen beanie.

'And that's a Pali name, is it?' The room was a mish-mash of influences. It reminded me of a flat I'd shared at university. Books everywhere and cheap furniture. None of it matching, and all looking like a job-lot house clearance. In a corner, a gold Buddha statue sat proudly on a table.

'It's Sanskrit. When you're ordained you are given a name by the person who performs your private ceremony. Some are in Pali, some in Sanskrit.' He filled the kettle.

It struck me how different Vajrasiddhi was from Peter Gibson. In walking boots, jeans and a fleece, he looked as though he'd just come in from the garden or a walk. Despite being retired, Peter Gibson was always dressed for the office.

'Do Buddhist names have a significance?'

'They generally have two halves to them. They're supposed to represent qualities the person ordaining you considers you have, or are on the way to developing.'

'And what does yours mean?'

'"Vajra" means "thunderbolt" and "siddhi" means "enlightenment" or "perfection".' He laughed. 'Sounds a bit grand. All it really means is I'm a slow learner but get there in the end.' He blushed and gave a tiny laugh.

Mention of the word 'enlightenment' sent a shudder through me. Took me back to evenings in halls of residence, crammed in someone's sweaty room, discussing 'reality' and the meaning of life. And before that to Dad. He'd been interested in Sufism and Buddhism as well as Islam.

I tried to picture Linda with this man. If Vajrasiddhi's day-to-day life was about being mindful of what he was thinking and feeling, and Linda's had involved staffing, budgets, parents and exam results, it was no wonder their worlds had diverged.

A handbell rang.

Vajrasiddhi must have seen my expression. 'It's to announce meditation.' Creases formed round his eyes. He seemed nice. 'It's okay. I don't have to go. Amarata leads meditation on Thursdays. We take it in turns to teach. Unless you'd like to try a bit of meditation?'

'No, no. Thank you.' In many ways, the men's community here was similar to the mosque in Sylhet: the religious symbols, the books, the hushed speech, the required observances and rituals. How different spiritual life was, with its disregard for material things and its singular focus on . . . on *what*?

While Vajrasiddhi's ex-wife was being murdered, what was he doing? Meditating? Could we be sure he wasn't involved? I realised I'd got distracted.

'I need to ask you about your ex-wife.' I got out my notebook. 'When did you and Linda last have contact?'

'Gosh, that must've been eight or nine years ago.'

'How did your marriage end?'

'I was increasingly concerned about Linda's attitude to her work. And various other things that weren't in accord with some of my values, if I can put it that way.'

'How did the two of you meet?'

'At a yoga class when she was . . .' He stopped there, and scratched his beard growth, as though the words had fallen from his mouth before he realised what he was about to say. His eyes were darting about the room. For a moment, his jumpiness reminded me of Linda's sister, Alice, when we'd asked her about their brother.

The atmosphere in the kitchen had shifted in one incomplete sentence.

'You met at a yoga class when Linda was . . .?' I prompted.

He seemed to recover. 'Yes, at a local class. We were both into yoga then.' He got up and walked over to the sink, drew a glass of water and drained it. Came back, wiping his mouth on the back of his hand. 'We got together when we were young. I wanted to get more involved in Buddhism. Linda was ambitious at school. Her concerns were material and practical, mine spiritual.'

'Was there any bad feeling?'

'A little, yes.' He looked down at the floor. 'One of the main principles of Buddhism is impermanence. That everything is in a state of flux. Linda liked to try and control things in life. Shoo away bad stuff, make the good stuff last. It caused problems in the end.'

'Who was the one with the bad feeling?'

He was examining his hands, tracing the lines on his skin. 'Actually, me.' He let out a gasp and covered his face with a splayed hand.

'Because . . .?'

'I was disappointed Linda didn't share my view of the world.' He spoke into his hand in embarrassment. 'I suppose I took it personally. Plus, I thought her priorities were wrong.' He stopped there. His manner had changed as we'd begun to talk about Linda. Twitchy. Uncomfortable. As though he was ashamed. 'Eventually I realised *I* was the one who was wrong. People are on their own journeys in life.'

'Did you finish it, then, or did she?'

'Linda did.' He sucked in an enormous breath, as if needing it to sustain him. 'She said she wanted a divorce.' He opened his hands. Resigned.

'What happened after that?'

'I went to a men's Buddhist community in Spain, and Linda and I lost contact. We hadn't had children so after the house was sold, and the divorce finalised, there was no need for us to keep in touch.'

'And the bad feeling?' I couldn't help admiring his honesty. If this was what Buddhism did for you, it was appealing.

'I worked on it. Felt very uncomfortable about it. Like I said, I'm a slow learner.'

'And now?'

'I've wished Linda well for a number of years. I wrote her a letter a year or so after we got divorced. I never heard from her. But she was married by then. Probably water under the bridge.'

That phrase again. It made me suspicious. Had he moved on? Could he have travelled to Bow and Stepney and strangled Linda and Roger? It seemed unlikely. I needed to ask him about the incest and baby, but still wasn't sure if we needed to consider him a suspect.

'Did Linda talk to you about her brother?'

'All she told me was they hadn't got on when they were kids. Said he'd never been nice to her but she never elaborated. I got the impression Linda had been badly affected by whatever happened but she wouldn't tell me.'

'And what made you come back from Spain?'

'Living in the mountains was what I needed at the time. The silence. The isolation. The rain. But I missed the UK and eventually yearned for home. I came back for a visit and decided to stay. I was able to get accommodation at the London Buddhist Centre in exchange for some teaching. This house belongs to the Order.'

I scanned the shared kitchen. Blobs of Blu-tack on the walls. The eco-friendly washing up liquid. Charity shop crockery. What would he make of Linda's plush house in Tredegar Square and her expensive toiletries?

'Where were you at lunchtime on Wednesday?'

'Here.'

'Can anyone confirm that?'

'I was leading a meditation class in the shrine room upstairs with around twenty-five people. It started at one o'clock.'

That would be easy to check. 'And Thursday morning?'

'The same. Teaching here.'

Discussion of Pali and Sanskrit reminded me of the precepts the killer had left. Vajrasiddhi would know what they meant. I took out my phone and swiped at my photo gallery, scrolled through and found a close-up of both phrases.

'Can you tell me a bit about these?'

'They're guidance for members of the Buddhist community.' He got up. 'All Buddhists, not just Order members.' He fetched a book from the table.

While I had my phone out, I typed a brief email to the team, asking for someone to verify with the Buddhist centre whether Vajrasiddhi was teaching when Linda was killed.

He sat back down and handed me a page of text. 'The precepts encourage Buddhists to avoid causing harm; taking what's not been given to us; causing sexual harm; use of false speech; and anything that clouds the mind.'

I was absorbing what he was saying, and trying to imagine how it might apply to Linda and Roger. My face must have communicated confusion.

'Has this got something to do with Linda's death?'

I told him about the card the killer had left.

'Ah.' He took his beanie off and was rubbing his head, clearly rattled by the news. 'Not taking the ungiven is about not manipulating and exploiting people, and giving rather than taking.'

'Do you have any idea who might want to do Linda harm? And what the words might imply in this context?'

He walked across to the window. 'I'll need to have a think. The words mean what I've said, but why someone might apply them to Linda, I honestly don't know. As for candidates, I've no idea, I'm afraid. I haven't been close to Linda for many years now.'

In my coat pocket my phone vibrated.

'My sense of Linda was that she was well-meaning. This is all an immense blow. Can you leave it with me? If I think of anything that might be useful, I'll let you know.'

I fished in my pocket for my contact details, handed him my card and then swiped my phone to read a message from Shen.

Vajrasiddhi was not at the house all day on Wednesday. Left around 9, returned eve.

Thursday – Dan

Close up, and under the bright lights of the interview suite, Ruth Allen was the epitome of devastation. Dark furrows lay beneath pained eyes, and her greasy skin was clogged with make-up, as though she hadn't slept well for months.

'I'm sorry for your loss,' Dan said.

She was staring ahead, eyes drifting, gently massaging her temples. She must've heard a blur of condolences in the last few hours, none of which would bring Roger back.

'Can you take me through what you found when you arrived home this morning?'

'The kids needed more clothes.' Her voice was quiet, deeper than Dan expected, and she was trembling. Her toned shoulders were hunched, and her arms were clamped to her body. 'We've been staying at my sister's. I rang the flat buzzer. Roger didn't answer. I assumed he was at work so I let myself in. The place stank of cigarette smoke and booze. The door into the lounge was open and that's when I saw him. In that chair . . . with that *thing* over his eyes.' A large shiny tear snaked down her left cheek, leaving a mark on her skin. She sniffed, retrieved a tissue from her trackie sleeve and blew her nose loudly into it. 'Poor Roger. He must've drunk himself into a stupor. He didn't deserve this.'

So far they'd only heard her husband's side of the Linda story. 'Where were you on Wednesday between midday and one p.m.?'

'I was at the flat with the kids all day; they hadn't gone back to school and Roger was staying in a bed and breakfast. We'd had an argument late into the night on Tuesday and I didn't sleep well.' She placed the palm of her hand on her forehead, as though trying to push her thoughts into place.

'Are you okay? Do you need anything?'

'Some water, please. I've got a pounding head.'

Dan got up and headed for the water cooler at the side of the room. 'Can anyone verify that you were at home all day?'

'The neighbours? My sister came round just after lunch, when she finished work.'

Dan handed Ruth a cup of water. 'How did you feel about Linda Gibson?'

Ruth let her head drop forwards. Dan got the impression she was tired of talking about her.

'She was a nice lady. I met her several times. She and her husband were a lovely couple.' Her manner changed now. 'But there was some weird *thing* between Roger and her. Not on her side, I don't think. *His.* It was like he was obsessed with her. Started when she got the head teacher post. He was furious with her. It seemed to shift from hate to . . . a kind of obsession. I honestly think he was in love with her. Or something like that.' She looked directly at Dan and he saw the pain bulge in her eyes. She ferreted in her bag and took out a battered strip of paracetamol, popped a couple of tablets and took a swig of water.

Dan waited until she swallowed. 'I have to ask – did you kill Mrs Gibson?'

'Of course not.' She looked shocked at the question. 'Roger's obsession wasn't an easy thing to live with but it wasn't her fault. And they weren't having an affair. Bumping off Linda wouldn't have stopped my husband's feelings, would it?'

Dan didn't react. 'If *you* didn't, did your husband kill her?'

'I very much doubt it. Roger wouldn't hurt a fly. And definitely not Linda.'

'We'll need your fingerprints and a DNA sample.'

'That's fine.'

Dan wondered how Aroona would feel if he had an obsession with a colleague. Ruth had given them the run-around the last twenty-four hours but it couldn't have been easy to have lived with a husband who'd been in love with another woman for several years.

'Do you have any idea who might want to kill your husband? Had he fallen out with anyone recently or mentioned that someone was giving him a hard time?'

She was shaking her head now, genuinely perplexed. 'Roger could be outspoken but I'm not aware of him falling out with anyone. He was often ruffling feathers at the school because he couldn't stand all the bullshit. I called him the school's Cassandra: the one who issued warnings that everyone dismissed.' Her gaze fell to her hands. 'But there may have been more school stuff going on than he told me. I noticed he was drinking and smoking more, but I said months ago I didn't want to hear about Linda or the school, and he stopped mentioning them.'

'I see.' Dan considered her information. It fit with the overall picture. 'On Wednesday, your husband phoned in sick. Where was he? When we called round to your apartment, you told us he wasn't there.'

'When I told him I wanted a divorce, he stormed out of the flat around two a.m. My guess is he bought a bottle of whisky and drank it. When your officers came round, I rang to tell him but his mobile went straight to voicemail. His charger was at the flat so his battery may have died or he might have switched his phone off.' She closed her eyes briefly. 'When my sister arrived, I decided to give us both some space and went home with her. I gather he came back to the flat at some point between then and . . . Today was the first time I've seen him since we had that stupid row . . .' She burst into a flood of tears, and used her hand to shield her eyes.

Dan tugged a handful of tissues from the box on the table and passed them to her. Her body was wracked with sobs. One thing was obvious: they weren't for show. These were genuine tears of grief and regret.

Ruth blew her nose. 'I can't take back the things I said. Telling him I wanted a divorce. I couldn't take it anymore. But I feel bad . . . you know . . . and worried I've somehow contributed to him ending up dead.'

'There's no reason for you to think that, Mrs Allen.'

'Do *you* think Roger killed Linda?'

'We don't know at the moment. But it's extremely important you tell us if you can think of anyone who had it in for Roger.'

'Okay.'

'Your husband told us that he had clashed with Linda professionally. Do you know what that was about?'

She shook her head.

'He also intimated that colleagues at the school wanted Linda out of the way. Does that ring a bell?'

She shook her head again.

But for a fleeting moment, Dan wondered if he saw a flicker of fear in her face.

When Dan arrived back in the incident room, PC Li was waiting for him at his desk. She had the BBC website open.

'Sarge, the mayor of Tower Hamlets has just appeared live on BBC News, talking about Mile End High School. The technicians have recorded it for you.'

'Okay. Let's see what he's got to say.' He settled in front of his monitor and opened the link in his email, showing a presenter in the BBC news studio.

'Following developments in the police investigation at Mile End High School, our reporter, Parvinder Sethi, is with Mayor Hayes at the Town Hall in the docklands. What's the latest over there, Parvinder?'

'Yes. The mayor, David Hayes, has been explaining his concerns. Mayor, let me hand over to you . . .'

'Thanks, Parvinder. The death of Roger Allen this morning has thrown our community into turmoil following yesterday's tragic news that head teacher, Linda Gibson, had been murdered. Both were

166

well-respected staff members who dedicated their lives to serving the community. Crime, and fear of crime, are key concerns for Tower Hamlets residents. Until a year ago I was a governor at Mile End High School, and I'm sad to see this wonderful school in a state of such instability after so successfully avoiding being taken into special measures. Since it opened, the school has welcomed students from around the world. As mayor, I am committed to improving community cohesion within the borough, and my cabinet and I know that safe schools are essential if we want to meet the challenges posed by our increasing population. With the tragic suicide of Haniya Patel, these two dreadful murders, and the safeguarding concerns raised at the 2016 OFSTED inspection, I believe Mile End High School should be closed temporarily. The school is *vital* to our community but a short closure would allow the LEA and governing body to put the right staff in place to get it stable again. And I would urge you to join me in calling for this to happen. Thank you.'

'Worrying news there from the mayor —'

Dan switched it off.

A two-minute statement on television and the atmosphere in the MIT office was like someone had pricked a balloon.

He dialled Maya's mobile. She had to know – but she wasn't going to be happy.

Thursday – Maya

'That's good news. Thanks for letting me know.' My words sounded hollow.

Simon Affrey, the prison governor, had rung to confirm that Sullivan's records didn't have him as positive for HIV or hepatitis, and he'd been re-tested after spitting at me. I should have felt relieved but, after the events of the day, it was hard to summon much feeling other than exhaustion.

I arrived home with my head banging. The whole way home, I'd been imagining the hot bath I was going to climb into. The aromatherapy candles and silence. But, as I put my key in the lock, heavy metal music came thudding through the door and along the hall once I got inside. I popped my head into the kitchen. Dougie was at the cooker, stirring saucepans, his sleeves rolled up. Coriander and okra and other bags of ingredients swarmed over the worktops, and the smell of spices wafted round the room.

'Hey.' My heart sank. My plans for an evening of quiet and solitude had disappeared in the turn of a key.

He jumped at my voice over the music and the pleasure on his face made me feel guilty.

I dumped my coat and keys, and gave him a kiss; pointed at the speakers that he'd connected to his iPhone. 'Could you turn it down a bit?'

The stillness and quiet of the canal beckoned through the French windows. I slid the doors open and stood on the threshold. The night air smelled of sleet, and sludge had gathered in the corners of the balcony. Each day the view over the lock and Canary Wharf was subtly different. Tonight the sky was cloudless, and the moon was reflecting on the water.

In the kitchen the music went off.

'Good day?' I asked, pleased not to have to shout.

'Uh-huh. I saw your update on Sky news.'

I told him about the mayor's TV interview.

'Has he got a point about the school closing?'

'There's no evidence the kids are in danger and arguably there's less risk if the staff are in one place. Certainly less than if we close the school at short notice.' I stepped out onto the balcony and leaned over the rail. In the dark, a semi-translucent blanket of blue hung over East London. Above me, stars floated, demure and knowing. In my head, a mish-mash of the day's conversations were re-playing, layering on top of each other.

'I'm sure you've done a risk evaluation. You always do.' Dougie popped his head out. 'But I don't get why you're so insistent it should stay open. If it closes for a few days 'til you catch Linda and Roger's killer, what's the big deal? The kids and teachers will get a few days off.'

'The school's got fourteen hundred pupils. If a quarter of them are left to their own devices, that's a lot of kids. Even if it's ten per cent, that's one hundred and forty kids, some of whom will be eleven, twelve and thirteen years old.'

'Maybe it's because I'm from Glasgow but if that'd been *my* school, at that age, I'd have had a bloody ball. At the arcades —

'With paedophiles and drug dealers?'

'At my mates' then.'

'And if they were locked out too?'

'Out on my bike?'

'All day?' I pointed at the patio doors. 'In the sleet and snow? And when you're hungry?'

He shrugged. 'Maybe you're right. I don't know.'

'Anyway – it's different for boys. Although boys get murdered too.' I went back inside and over to the fridge, fetched two beers and passed one to Dougie. 'Briscall doesn't care about the school or the kids. Bangs on about wanting Linda's murder solved like he's the only person who cares.'

'The guy's a prize dick. We sussed that ten years ago.'

'That's what irks me. He's got no idea what it took Linda to raise standards after Mile End High was told it needed to improve.' The conversation was winding me up all over again. 'Anyway, let's change the subject.' I told him about Fatima's nephew, Dev, confronting me at the school earlier. 'He was furious because I didn't recognise him at first. It didn't seem to occur to him that he was at primary school when I saw him last.'

'Thing is, you've lived here for thirty years. You're bound to have absorbed British customs, just as I've picked up English ones. When I go back to Glasgow, the people I grew up with rip the shit out of me for my English accent and my poncey food.' He gestured to our supper and we both laughed at the irony of a six-foot-three Glaswegian man cooking curry for a Bangladeshi female.

I took a swig of beer; cast round the kitchen for cultural signifiers. On the fridge, my teenage niece, Sadia, had stuck a selfie of her with her school pals. On one wall there was a black and white print of Sabbir, Jaz and I, before we left Bangladesh. I'd had it enlarged and made copies for each of us. Me, all gappy teeth and mop hair; Jasmina, poised and demure; Sabbir, looking aloof and cool. Another photograph showed Jasmina and Rubel's wedding. My gaze drifted to the door, where an IKEA frame held a photograph of me in my police uniform, lined up next to my peers.

'I remember that being taken. You were behind me and kept poking me.'

Dougie chuckled affectionately. 'I spent several years trying to poke you, if I remember correctly. Not that you noticed.' He wiped his hand on a tea towel and pointed at the images of me with Jasmina and Sabbir. 'We're all different from our siblings. It doesn't make *you* any more or less Bangladeshi, or *me* more or less Scottish. Your sister married someone who was much more into Islam than her. But she was just as westernised as you before she and Rubel got together. I've known you guys for years, don't forget. You've both changed and so have I. We take on new layers.'

Trying to ignore how unnerved I felt by Dougie having read my mind, I inspected the photographs more closely, as though they might yield answers to the questions that were swirling in my head. Jasmina beamed proudly from under her burnt-orange *hijab* and peach-coloured *saree*. Dougie was right. She had changed since meeting Rubel.

'When you first joined the force, you were reeling from your mum's reaction to you wanting to be a police officer. You were adamant, but she wanted you to get married and hoped you'd all go back to Bangladesh.'

A belly laugh made its way out of my mouth. I remembered the numerous occasions when Jasmina and I had talked about getting married. We'd both said we didn't want to. Then she'd met Rubel, who had just come over to London from Pakistan. I remembered how overwhelming I had found their wedding, with all the rituals and expense.

'I suppose over the years I *have* felt less Bangladeshi.'

'But that's not a bad thing. Maya, don't let it bother you when people accuse you of not being "one of us". Life's too short for all that "us and them" shit. All it means is that some people feel threatened by others who are different from them. It's bollocks.'

I thought for a moment. 'I suppose it bothers me because it implies I can't understand their experiences and feelings anymore, and I don't think that's true.'

'Doesn't it depend who "us" is? If that young lad, Dev, was born in the UK, maybe *he* feels *he* doesn't fit in? Perhaps he was projecting his own crap onto you? Don't know about you but I find I notice change in others much more than I do in myself.' He took the lid off one of the pans and tasted it. 'Nearly ready. Alternatively, it could be because you're a cop and a female. That's always been Briscall's problem with you. That and the fact he's a bloody racist.'

I took place mats out of the drawer and laid the table. Cutlery. Water glasses. Pepper and salt.

'Thing is, I chose to work in Tower Hamlets because it's where I've lived since we arrived in the UK. You'd think I'd have got my head round all this by now.'

'Hold up. Why should you? The whole world can't get its head round cultural and religious differences.' He switched the cooker off. 'Do you remember in training when we all had to share why we'd joined the police? You said you wanted to use your background to help people in the community. We were all so impressed. I just wanted a job. To get out of Glasgow for good.'

Dougie was probably right.

'I know you don't like me saying this but you can't solve the world's problems on your own. Sabbir's, your mum's, your dad's . . .' Dougie opened two more beers.

'Who said I was doing *that*?'

'Aren't you? I'm not knocking the fact you care, Maya. Just . . . I *worry* for you. You can't take on the world.' His eyes were light blue now and were locked on mine. 'Why won't you move in with me? Let me look after you? You never give me a proper answer.'

'You *know* why.'

Dougie walked over to me. 'I know your dad left, and I get that's huge. But you can't be an island forever. I'm not going to disappear on you. *Or* cheat on you. We've been together for years and nothing's gone wrong yet, has it?'

'No, but people change. *Stuff* changes.'

'I'm not your —'

'*Don't*. Please.'

His hands clasped my face. His mouth sought my lips.

*

172

An hour later, Dougie and I were back in the kitchen. Dougie had re-heated the curry and was spooning it onto plates.

On the worktop, my mobile beeped in my bag, returning my attention to the case.

'I'd better check . . .' I scrolled through the messages for what was urgent. Among updates from Alexej, there were two missed calls from the Patel's landline. I dialled into my voicemail and listened to the message Haniya's mother had left. Her voice shook with fear, and she repeated over and over that she needed to speak to me urgently.

Mile End High School, 1991 – Maya

The bell goes and noise erupts. Chairs screech on the hard floor and within minutes the classroom is deserted, except for me. Even Fatima has gone ahead.

I pack my school bag slowly: heavy text books at the bottom, then exercise books, and my pencil case and ruler at the side.

On the ground floor, the cleaner has begun her rounds, sloshing the mop over the linoleum. Jasmina is leaning against the lockers, checking her watch, her face scrunched in irritation.

'Come *on*,' she urges, as soon as she thinks I can hear.

When we reach the school gates, the last few children are leaving with their mums and dads, all squeals and giggles.

'I can't see her, can you?' I'm scanning the playground, the pavement, the road.

'We'd better hang on. She might just be late.' Jasmina doesn't believe that any more than I do. She plonks her bag on the pavement and wriggles up onto the wall. I copy and clamber up next to her, feeling the cold bricks on the back of my legs.

Someone's clunking a chain. 'You alright, girls?' It's Mr Green, the caretaker. He's padlocking the gates.

'Yes, thanks,' Jasmina replies dismissively over her shoulder. I want to get away from him too.

'Let's walk,' I say. 'I'm freezing.' I jump down from the wall and swing my bag onto my shoulder. A magpie bobs on the fence, pecking, hopping, watching.

We retrace the route we always take to school, in case Mum's on her way, and chat about lessons, teachers, PE, both reluctant to mention what's really bothering us.

The flat's in complete darkness when we arrive. Jasmina fetches the key from under the mat and lets us in.

'Mum?' I yell. 'Are you home?' But there are no cooking smells, no music. Instead, all that greets us is silence and the cold.

'*Mum!*' I shout again, dump my school bag down and switch on the hall light.

The lounge door is on my right. That's where we found her last time. I hover, my fingers on the handle, feeling sick. Then push it open. And from the doorway, I see her, in a ball on the carpet beside the sofa. From the table lamp above, weak rays of light splash onto her motionless features. Eyes closed, she's clasping something in her fingers.

'Oh, *Mum*. It's okay.' I spring over and slide down beside her, and pull her frozen mass into my arms. 'In here, Jaz,' I shout.

A few moments later, she's kneeling next to me. 'I've got it,' Jasmina whispers, and she prises the photograph from Mum's grasp. 'It's okay. It's going to be okay.' And gently Mum begins to rock in my arms, lost to the chaos of grief.

Outside, the street lights come on and darkness closes in; garden gates click, car doors slam and neighbours return home from work. Upstairs they're cooking and the smell of onions makes my mouth water; next door, the TV blares out the news and the twins are screaming. While day shifts into evening and night for those around us, we are suspended in time, on the floor with Mum, in the cold and the dark. And while *we* are waiting for Sabbir to come home, Mum's still caught in the cobwebs of her loss, waiting for Dad.

'Shall I see what we can have for tea?' I whisper to Jasmina. That's what we did last time.

So we put her to bed, with the photo of home: of Mum and Dad, and the three of us, on the balcony of our Sylhet flat. And we camp on the floor in Mum's room, doing our homework while we eat stale bread and sardines from the tin.

And I'm scared to think about later. Or tomorrow. Or what will happen if she never manages to free herself.

Friday – Maya

'I've rung Haniya's mother several times,' I said to Dan over the desk. 'Keep getting their voicemail.' Last night's message had got me worried. 'I wonder what she wanted to discuss at nine o'clock at night?'

'All you can do is keep trying or wait 'til she rings back.'

Today the pupils were due back at Mile End High School. The MIT unit had moved back to its permanent base at Limehouse police station and was about to commence briefing. Dan, who had been using my desk while I was on leave, was gathering his belongings.

'She sounded as though she was making the call secretly and was worried about being overheard.' I could still hear the fear in the woman's voice. I thought back to when Haniya's death was reported. Mr Patel had insisted the police dealt only with him. I tapped my notepad with my pen.

'Sounds like she wants to talk to you without her husband knowing.'

'I agree.' Haniya had been frightened of her dad, and given his wife was scared of him too, could he have killed Linda and Roger? I scanned my list of tasks for the morning. 'I'll drive over to Shadwell after briefing. See if I can catch her. Can you speak to the mayor?'

'Yup.' Dan was stacking text books on top of folders and printouts. On a coaster by the monitor was a mug that had been printed with a beach photo.

'This yours?' I held it out for him. The image was of a woman on the sand with her arms round two smiling girls. 'Is that your family?'

'Uh-huh.' He stuffed the mug in his coat pocket.

'You must miss them?'

'I do.'

'Are they planning to join you?' I felt like I was prying but we'd been thrust together and knew nothing about each other.

'I honestly don't know.' He stopped what he was doing.

I felt his sadness.

'We're trying to figure it out but Sharna's at kindie and Kiara started school last year. My wife, Aroona, works as an advocate for people in the Aboriginal communities who are dealing with addiction, incest and abuse. Some of them are her relatives and ancestors. Things are finally beginning to change in Australia and her job is at a critical stage. She doesn't feel she can leave . . .' He broke off.

I was wondering what it must be like to be working on the other side of the world from your family. 'Oh, gosh, that must be hard . . .'

'On her pay and mine, we barely scrape by. This post – the whole fast-track thing – was meant to be a way out. A new life for all of us. But . . . Oh, I dunno. It's complicated.' He shook his head and went back to bundling his belongings into a rucksack.

While the server processed my log in, I cradled my hands round my coffee and scanned the suspect list. We knew from Peter that Linda hadn't found Neil easy, and that Rich and Farhan may have been in cahoots.

Alexej came over. 'Morning. The post-mortem report is on file for Linda Gibson. Cause of death is . . .' He consulted the report. 'Hypoxia due to venous occlusion arising from manual strangulation. The multiple forearm scars are from shallow incisions and probably occurred during her teens and twenties.'

'Thanks,' I said.

'She's definitely carried a baby to full term and the birth certificate doesn't list a father.'

'In Alice Stephens' testimony, she claims not to know what happened to the baby. Can you check adoption registers?'

'Will do. I —'

'I don't think Linda's baby should be a main line of enquiry,' Dan interrupted. 'It's too distal.'

'I wasn't suggesting it should be. But we cannot assume it's irrelevant until we've established that.'

'We need to prioritise. Enquiry lines that may reveal the killer's ID have to be more important, surely?'

'What if her murder's linked to her pregnancy?'

'I'm not suggesting we don't follow it up. Just delegate it to one of the analysts or the PCs. And find out what Mrs Patel wanted, but for goodness' sake don't start re-investigating Haniya's death. You said it yourself: her suicide wasn't suspicious and I don't think it's linked to the deaths of Linda and Roger.'

Dan's curtness grated but I could see it had churned him up, talking about his family, and I didn't want an argument. While I *didn't* miss the unethical aspects of our old team colleague, I missed DS Barnes' laid-back manner. No-one knew whether his suspension was going to turn into early retirement or whether he'd be back at his desk one day.

'Okay. Let's review our lines of enquiry. Alexej, what were you about to say?'

'I called the taxi company to check the journeys taken by the Gibsons. Spoke to the guy whose name you had, Saiful, and the controller. Saiful's a driver. Most of the journeys were to the Royal London Hospital. Sometimes with Linda, most frequently just Peter.'

With his heart condition, that figured. 'What about the cleaner?'

'Still trying her. The ring tone on her mobile suggests she's on the continent. I'm waiting for the owner of the company to call me back.'

'Thanks.'

Dan's belongings were now safely stowed in a rucksack, and, as we talked, he'd been fiddling with his iPad and the projector. Suddenly a bright light shone onto the wall in front of us, in the centre of which were two images: one of Linda Gibson, smiling confidently behind her desk, and Roger Allen, in his office.

'With Allen now dead, our suspect pool has changed,' I said. 'Based on your interview, Dan, I would suggest we rule out Allen's wife.

179

Next, I can't see what motive Vajrasiddhi could have for killing either Linda or Roger, but we need to investigate Asad Farhan further, the school's social worker, and Neil Sanderson. It could be that Linda and Roger knew too much about something going on at the school. Or perhaps someone needed them out of the way. Is someone's job at risk, for example?'

Dan shifted names around on the suspect board.

'Any developments on Rich Griffiths?'

'Yes. I spoke to one of the heating engineers.' He flicked through his notebook. 'Bloke called Alan Cardwell. He confirms that he and his colleague left with Rich, and Linda was alive. She was asking them why the heating had stopped working.'

'That rules Rich out then. We've now got one murder at the school and one at the victim's home. That doesn't help us deduce whether the motivation for the murders is professional or personal.' I was still mesmerised by the images of Linda and Roger.

Dan clicked the projector on to the next image: the five precepts. 'We still don't know what "I shall abstain from taking the ungiven" and "I shall abstain from sexual misconduct" mean to our killer. And at the moment the only person with a connection to Buddhism is Linda's ex-husband.'

I remembered what Dan had said about Buddhism being on the increase in the UK. 'Although it's fair to say that lots of people might have dallied with it. Perhaps the killer is using it as a red herring?' I was organising our priorities. 'The interview, forensic and CCTV data are going to be key. Dan, can you re-interview Neil and the caretaker, and find out from the mayor what prompted his TV appearance? Alexej, you continue to investigate who has connections with Buddhism. I shall see what I can find out about the Patels, and pay Farhan a visit.'

Twenty minutes later, I was on the doorstep of the Patel's flat on the third floor of a concrete block. Metal security bars clung to their front door, and an alarm box sat to the side of a top window. Over the window, the word 'SLUT', which had been sprayed on the bricks in black aerosol, had been scrubbed to a pale grey.

With the burglar chain in place, Bashira Patel peered round the door, her face taut with anguish. She unlatched the chain, leaned over the step and checked the walkway in both directions. '*Quickly.* Come in.' She pulled me inside, her voice a frightened whisper. 'Tariq won't be long.' Her eyes were bloodshot and swollen, and for a moment they reminded me of Linda's, squeezed from their sockets as her breath was taken.

I followed Bashira into the tiny kitchen. It was spotless.

'That man from the school. The Somalian one.' Her words were a gabble. 'He's been round here.'

'Asad Farhan?'

She nodded.

'What did he want?'

'He —'

The sound of a key in the front door made Bashira freeze. Cold air blasted down the hall, and she was momentarily immobile, her eyes wide with fright. Then frantic activity began, straightening her *hijab*, muttering under her breath in Punjabi. She started babbling and tidying the already tidy room.

'He will be very angry. You must go.'

This wasn't the same anxiety that had greeted me. I grabbed a business card from my pocket. Made sure Bashira saw, and slid it into a drawer by the sink. 'Call me. Text. E-mail. *Anytime.*'

Moments later, Tariq Patel was in the doorway, his face consumed with fury. He had a newspaper tucked under his arm.

'I was in the neighbourhood.' I needed to take the lead while Bashira composed herself. 'You've probably seen the news so I dropped by to see how you are.'

He grunted. Barked something at his wife, who moved towards the kettle and filled it. Flicked it on to boil.

'I was away over Christmas and Mrs Gibson's death —'

181

'Please leave us alone.' He kicked at the chair leg. 'We don't want any more interference . . . the media . . . my wife . . .' His voice petered out.

'Mr Patel, you're probably aware that Linda Gibson was murdered on Wednesday. We are pursuing a number of lines of enquiry. Could you tell me where you were between twelve noon and one-thirty p.m.?'

'We pray five times a day. I was here. For *salat al-zuhr*.'

'And Roger Allen was murdered yesterday. Could you tell me where you were between nine and ten a.m.?'

'Here. Having breakfast.'

'Can anyone confirm those times for us?' I made sure I didn't look at Bashira as I didn't want to give him an excuse to be angry with her.

'Why do I need to confirm anything? Am I suspected of something?'

'Routine enquiries at this stage, that's all.'

'After all the judgements we've been subjected to. The harassment. I want you to *leave*.' He shook the newspaper at me, anger burning in his eyes. 'Just get out. And tell that journalist to stop bothering us and making up her lies.'

Friday – Steve

The kids were due back today so Neil and Shari had scheduled a staff meeting for 9 a.m. A three-line whip had gone out to *all* staff on the payroll, including part-timers and support staff. On the first day of teaching in January, excitement and apprehension usually produced an adrenaline-fuelled atmosphere among the staff: they were halfway through the academic year and winter would soon ease into spring. But today, as they filed into the senior hall, everyone was subdued as they tried to take in the news that Roger Allen was also dead.

The air smelled musty from where the room hadn't been used for a few weeks. Rows of seats had been placed in a crescent shape round the stage. In the large space, sounds echoed, and chairs screeched on the hard floor.

At the front of the hall, Shari and Neil stood together. He checked his shirt was tucked into his trousers and cleared his throat.

'Here we go,' said Steve.

'Morning everyone.' Neil surveyed the room. His Adam's apple bobbed as he swallowed. 'We hope you all found yesterday's sessions with Dr Middleton useful.' He paused, and placed a notepad on the lectern in front of him. The sheen on his forehead caught the overhead lights. 'Most of you will know from the news that our deputy head, Roger Allen, was found dead yesterday.'

A heavy silence hung over the hall. They all knew, but it was a shock to hear it said aloud.

'The students arrive at eleven o'clock today. We've put the start time back so we can all feel prepared for the day ahead.' Neil kept his voice steady and spoke slowly, but his pitch was higher than usual and his armpits and face were damp with sweat. 'Today isn't going to be easy for any of us. When the students arrive, we will begin with a single period of form time and then launch into two lessons. Lunch will be at one. Afternoon lessons will run normally and the day will finish at four.' He wiped his forehead with a handkerchief. 'All parents have been sent a letter explaining exactly what has happened and what the plans are. Some are keeping their children at home for the time-being . . .' Muttering rippled round the room, and Neil carried on quickly. 'But we hope it doesn't prompt a mass exodus or a boycotting of the school.' He shifted from foot to foot as he spoke.

In front of us, a woman stood up and asked, in an agitated tone, 'How many more deaths are there going to be? And why isn't the school closed?'

Steve recognised one of the school's receptionists.

'Oh *God*,' Andrea hissed.

'Brenda, we've consulted with the police, the LEA and our governors. Having handed the school back to us after Mrs Gibson's death, the police advise that it will be much easier to keep staff and pupils safe in one building than scattered in fourteen hundred homes.' He looked at Brenda for a few moments. 'Mrs Ahmed and I agree.' He returned his focus to the staff. 'As I said, we know that the next few days are not going to be easy. None of us have faced a situation like this before —'

'It's easy for you to say that we're safe but a lot of people are worried about who's going to be next.'

'I agree.' Moira was on her feet now, looking round at everyone for allegiance. 'Brenda is only saying what we're all thinking. And where is Asad Farhan? We were all told we *had* to be here.'

Neil paled. He signalled to Shari who was clutching leaflets, which she began handing down the rows.

'It would be those two, wouldn't it?' Andrea said. 'Neil's blood pressure must be through the roof.'

A man stood up. 'You know what teenagers are like. What do we say if one of the kids asks us *how* they were killed?'

Neil was quick to respond. 'Shoful, the police have said it's important we don't go into *any* details. Mrs Ahmed is giving out —'

'Can I have everyone's attention?' Shari's voice was shrill. She stomped back to the front of the room. 'Brenda, Moira, Shoful, sit down, please.' Her face was pinched with irritation and her voice was unusually strident. 'In just over an hour we will have fourteen hundred pupils in school and we have to be ready for them. It's likely the students *will* ask questions, so the purpose of this briefing is to equip you with what to say, otherwise we may as well all give in and close the school now.' She flapped the leaflets in the air and began scuttling down the rows. 'I'm giving you all a printed statement, which you can use in response to any questions.'

While Shari scuttled about, Neil faced the staff again and Steve's confidence dropped through the floor when he realised that the bursar was just as lost in the awfulness of the murders as everyone else.

Friday – Steve

Briefing over, Steve and his colleagues trundled off to greet their form groups. Steve felt torn. He was relieved to be out of the senior hall but he had no idea what the day had in store for him.

The bell for registration rang just as he reached his classroom. At the front of his planner he'd placed the slip of paper that Shari had provided, with the statement they were to give in response to any questions. He knew students could act up with an inexperienced teacher, especially when they were anxious. The media hadn't mentioned it was new boy Steve who'd found the head teacher, dead, but he knew it was only a matter of time. What the hell would he say if he was asked about that? Argh. Butterflies. The psychology teacher he was covering for, Zoe Smart, had a year-twelve form group. He was excited about being their tutor . . . as long as he could manage them.

Within minutes the students filed in, some in groups, shouting, others in pairs, laughing.

'Morning, sir,' said a chubby boy with mischievous brown eyes, which were half-obscured by black hair. He rolled through the door with three pals, chatting and pushing each other, in no hurry, and apparently oblivious to the teeming rain outside.

Four girls arrived in a splash of colour, giggling and dizzy. Their brightly coloured *hijabs* were in cerise, canary yellow, rose pink and fuchsia. They shuffled over to a cluster of chairs and sat down, nudging each other when they noticed the opposite sex.

At the entrance to the classroom a couple of boys were messing round with some girls going into the adjacent room. They swaggered and flicked their hands in mock gangster gestures. The hormone years, Steve called them. When love entered the classroom, learning and manners took a back seat. Thank goodness his first placement school had been up the road in East Ham. He had a feeling he was going to find these students very different from the ones in sleepy Sussex.

'In you come, guys, please. Take your seats and let's get started.' He walked towards the door to shepherd the stragglers in. Bitterly cold outside, the room wasn't warm and condensation clouded the windows.

'Chill, sir,' said one boy, with an even more exaggerated swagger as he entered the room. He made a point of going over to the girls who'd just come in, rather than going to sit down. 'Urgh, stinks in here.' He checked over his shoulder to see if Steve was looking. 'Like smelly socks. You farted, Khaleda?'

The girls tittered. Squirmed.

Steve struggled to keep his face straight. He checked his register to figure out who Khaleda was. There she was: Khaleda Hussein. He wouldn't ask the boy's name. He'd learn it soon enough.

More students arrived. Two more girls, one taller than the other and clutching a purple folder and matching mobile phone. The other was a jangle of bangles. They were followed by another gaggle of boys. Steve recognised them from the bus the day before.

Apart from the boy who was flirting, all the students were now seated.

Steve did a quick head check. That was twenty-one so far.

'Sanchez, bro, sir's waiting to start,' said a male voice.

Sanchez looked up from the girls and faced Steve, feigning surprise.

Steve checked his register. 'Mr *Owusu*. How nice of you to join us. That's four minutes of mine you've just wasted. Care to make it up at lunchtime?'

'How d'you know my name, sir?' He shot straight over to where his friends were.

'Secret.' Steve tapped his nose. '*Here*, please, Sanchez. And that's another minute.' He pointed to the desks. 'Next time, come in and sit down straightaway.'

Sanchez paused for a few more seconds, muttered under his breath and sloped over to the empty table, sucking his teeth as he went.

Steve noticed his exaggeratedly slow pace and let it go for now. He stood up straight and surveyed the room. 'I am Mr Rowe.' He pointed to the board and then stopped, realising he looked like an air hostess, indicating the fire exits and toilets. 'I'm your form tutor while Mrs Smart is on maternity leave. I will also have the pleasure of teaching those of you taking AS Psychology.'

A ripple of nervous excitement went round the room and Steve felt his shoulders drop a little and his stomach muscles relax.

Up the hall he heard Shari's voice.

'Jehangir's got caught,' one of the girls whispered before Steve could see who it was.

A minute later Shari appeared at the door of Steve's classroom, red in the face and flustered, and with a student in tow.

'I found a straggler, *smoking*,' she said. She ushered the boy into Steve's classroom.

He entered, shimmering with indignation and anger. Heckling broke out.

Shari stood facing the class, feet apart, head tilted back and arms folded.

Steve hadn't absorbed before how short she looked in the black *jilbab* on her dumpy frame. Now he understood why her nickname was Pingu.

She waited until the boys stopped their comments. 'Jehangir, lunchtime, my office.' Point made, she looked at Steve. 'Have you got everything you need?'

'Yes, thanks, Mrs Ahmed.' He arched an eyebrow. And then to Jehangir he said, 'Have a seat next to Sanchez.'

'Have a good morning, everyone,' Shari said to the class, and left.

Steve handed out paper and sat on the edge of his desk, facing the class. He checked his watch. 'I would like you each to write down three goals for this term. I'll give you two minutes.' He hoped the task would give students the opportunity to air their feelings and concerns.

Immediately the class burst into chatter.

Steve checked his register. Out of a form group of twenty-five, everyone had come in except three people. One was a girl called Damla, whose parents were keeping her at home because of the murders. Ayesha Hutchinson was absent. No-one seemed to know where she was, or at least they weren't letting on. And an Irish student, Maria, was unwell.

Suddenly a voice piped up. 'Sir, is it true you found Mrs Gibson's body?'

The room stood still.

Steve looked up as he heard Linda's name. His heart sank with dread, and panic fluttered in his chest.

It was Jehangir.

Steve tried to keep his voice calm. 'We've been asked not to discuss what happened,' he said in the boy's direction, aware of the eyes of all the other students on him as he answered.

He'd been dreading this question. Shit, what was that sentence they'd been asked to use? 'What has happened is tragic but the police are doing everything they can to find out what took place.' What was the last bit? Something about letting the police . . .? Steve's mind had gone blank. All he could hear was his own breathing and someone sniffing and the clock ticking.

Jehangir piped up again. 'On Facebook, someone said Mr Allen and Mrs Gibson were . . . you know . . .' He wriggled in a mock-embrace pose and made 'ooh' noises.

'Enough, thank you, Jehangir. Would you like to go and repeat what you've just said to Mrs Ahmed?' He saw the boy's bravado drop at the mention of Shari. The kids didn't mean to be disrespectful when they made jokes; it was just their way of coping. Steve tried to exhale without it being too obvious a sigh of relief. And not for the first time, he found himself wondering how the hell they were all going to get through the day, not to mention the next few weeks.

Friday – Maya

When I left the Patel's flat, an uneasy feeling took hold of me. It was difficult to know whether Bashira was in physical danger but it was clear that we needed to talk to the two of them separately. I was leaving Shadwell when Dan rang.

'You'll never guess what.' Dan had been to speak to the mayor of Tower Hamlets. 'David Hayes is a mate of Briscall's. And you remember Briscall said he knew two of the governors at Mile End High? Hayes is one of them. Well, he *was* until he took up his mayor post.'

'Why doesn't that surprise me?'

'The news teams contacted the town hall after Allen's body was found. Hayes denies that Briscall primed him on what to say, but Briscall's name is in the visitors' book at the town hall for Thursday afternoon.'

'Is it? The sneaky —'

'And Hayes isn't prepared to retract his suggestion about the school because he's concerned it will affect his reputation.'

Half an hour later I arrived at Mile End High School to interview Asad Farhan. As much as I was reluctant to spend any more time than necessary with the educational social worker, who I'd had the unfortunate pleasure of dealing with in the past, Roger's death meant investigations into Linda's background had to take a back seat to revisiting the school and its staff – and Bashira Patel's apparent terror at Farhan's latest visit to her flat meant he was number one on my list.

The top floor of the school was a different world. Gone were the swanky corridors and glitzy display boards, the rows of shiny lockers. Here, the air smelled of dust rather than polish. Broken desks and chairs were stacked, higgledy-piggledy, against a wall to the left of the lift. Discarded computer monitors and printers lay with their innards trailing on the floor. This was where the school housed its pupil exclusion room. Run by Farhan, it was where pupils were sent who'd been excluded from lessons, either for a few hours, to cool down and reflect, or for a pre-agreed amount of time.

Farhan was a respected figure in the Somali community, and active in the local mosque. He also had form with the police – and me personally. The rumours had been circling for years: Farhan hushed things up and put pressure on others to do the same. A fixer. A cultural and religious mediator. At his previous school in Tower Hamlets, a pupil, Alison Cooper, had made a serious sexual allegation about a male teacher. Farhan *suggested* to Alison that she might like to withdraw her complaint to avoid negative consequences. The girl refused and told her parents what he'd said. He vehemently denied it, said the girl was imagining things and the police were discriminating against him. The case was dropped, and the following year he appeared at Mile End High. Sure, he could have been the victim but I strongly suspected he hadn't been.

I shivered now as I recalled Farhan's words and manner back then when he warned me off. How he'd hissed into my face that it was none of my business, and that I'd regret it if I continued to interfere. How he'd laughed when I told him it was my job, and that I had no intention of butting out. How he'd crowed when the girl and her family had moved away.

Today the door to the exclusion room was open. Four students were engrossed in something, three with their backs to me and their heads down. One boy was engaged in a discussion with Farhan. Another staff member was helping him, a man, in jeans and trendy long-sleeved T-shirt, presumably one of the teaching assistants or learning mentors. I knocked on the open door, and cleared my throat.

Farhan's face fell when he saw me. For a moment I thought I saw fear flash across his craggy features.

'I know my colleagues have interviewed you but now it's my turn.'

'Sergeant Rahman.' The contemptuous sneer was unmistakeable. He'd always had a hefty build but he'd put on a couple of stone since I last saw him.

'It's Detective Inspector. Could we go somewhere private, please?'

Farhan muttered something to his colleague. 'Come this way,' he snapped at me, and led me next door to his office, where he unlocked the door. He deposited the metal key bundle on his desk and let out a loud sigh of irritation. 'How can I help?' He made his way round to the other side of the table to sit down. Stared straight at me, his mouth set at an unpleasant angle.

In the room every surface was covered with folders and papers and pieces of computer equipment.

'Do you usually lock the door to your room?'

'I don't see that's any concern of yours. There a law against locking doors?'

'I was checking the interview records and noticed that quite a few people haven't been too complimentary about you.'

He snorted. 'Do you really think I care what people think?' He banged the space bar of his keyboard to wake up his computer.

'Where were you yesterday morning between nine and ten a.m.?'

'At the debriefing in Stratford.'

'Anyone vouch for that?'

'Various colleagues, I'm sure.'

'How did you get on with Linda?'

He gave a disdainful sniff. 'She kept interfering with things she knew nothing about and she was incapable of making up her mind and sticking to it.'

'So, did you want her out of the way?'

'Don't be ridiculous.'

'Someone did.'

'Evidently. But it wasn't me, I can assure you.' He picked up his keys. 'Allen was much more of a thorn in my side than Linda ever was. Took it upon himself to be the school's conscience.'

I recalled Ruth calling her husband 'Cassandra'. 'I've also been hearing rumours about you and the caretaker – something to do with computers. Anything you want to tell me?'

'*Rumours?*' His eyes hardened and he glowered at me.

'Yes. It wouldn't be anything to do with that jumble sale of office equipment you've got in the corridor?'

'We have an approved contractor who collects that.' He eyed the clock. 'Now – is that it? It's been nice to catch up but I've got a lot to do before the event I'm chairing at the mosque this evening.'

I approached the desk and leaned towards him. 'I will be keeping a very close eye on you. And if I find any evidence that you were involved with *either* death, I will not rest until you are brought to justice.' I forced myself to hold his gaze for several beats. Finally turning away, I took in the debris on Farhan's desk. An ancient phone off its hook. An ashtray, brimming with butts, peeping out from behind a dried-out spider plant.

And a notepad, with an almost illegible scrawl upon it: the name 'Tariq Patel'.

Friday – Maya

Peter Gibson had toothpaste on his cheek when he answered the door. His greying hair was dishevelled, as if he'd either not brushed it that morning or had been lying down.

'Just a quick visit. Could I come in?'

He stood back and held the door open. 'I was making something to eat.' He padded along the hall in his slippers towards the kitchen at the rear of the house. From behind, I noticed he'd pulled a jumper over the same clothes as the day before.

Ahead of us the microwave gave a ding.

Peter went straight over to it, retrieved a steaming plastic container, and placed it on the worktop.

'I came to see how you're doing.'

'Stupid thing is we've got plenty of meals in the freezer,' he said, and I wasn't sure whether he'd heard me. 'Linda made them for me. Low cholesterol, no salt.' He was grappling with the film, trying to prise it away from the hot plastic container. 'Darn thing.' He took a knife from the drawer. 'But I just can't bring myself to eat them.' He pointed at the floppy plastic dish. 'The dietician won't be happy with me.' As he sawed at the plastic, the large serrated knife looked precarious in his trembling hands.

I studied his face for a few moments, trying not to be too obvious. His features ached with anguish. There were lines and furrows in his face, and dark bags round his eyes. 'I'm sure it won't hurt to have a couple. After that you might feel like one of Linda's.'

He jabbed with the knife and it pierced the film. Sauce spurted up at him, flicking red splats all over his beige jumper. He flung the knife on the worktop and covered his eyes, as if it was all too much.

He pushed the plastic container away from the edge of the worktop and dabbed at the tomato sauce with a tea towel. 'I wasn't hungry anyway.' Then, as if to explain, 'The house is so quiet. I can't bear it. It's just not the same without Linda. Is there any progress with finding . . . ?'

'We're still pursuing enquiries at the moment. But you've probably seen it on the news – there's been another murder and many of the details are similar. Roger Allen.'

'*Allen?*'

'I'm afraid so.'

'That's terrible.' Peter's hand went out to steady him and he thumped down at the kitchen table.

'It means that Linda's murder is no longer an isolated incident.' I was studying his reaction. I needed to ask him about the Buddhist precept that was left at his wife's body. 'There's a possibility the killer may believe that Linda took something that wasn't hers. Can you think what that might mean? We haven't been able to recover the files she deleted yet.'

'No, no . . . I . . .' He rubbed his chin. 'Is this to do with the money you mentioned?'

'We don't know whether it could be something as literal as that or something more symbolic. Does it ring any bells?' I was interested that he'd made that connection.

My phone vibrated.

'Why don't you dig into your pasta? It's probably cooled down now.'

'I'll have something later. I don't know why I put it on, really.'

'Excuse me a moment.'

The text was from Dan. Some of the parents, who had heard about the murder of Roger Allen, had now formed a demonstration outside the school. They were marching with placards and loud hailers, demanding the school remain closed on Monday if the killer wasn't found. To top it all, Suzie James was broadcasting the whole thing on the internet, via Facebook Live, to several thousand of the newspaper's followers.

Friday – Steve

After an extra day off, the year thirteens burst into the room, fizzing with energy. The media and police presence at the school had given them plenty to talk about. In the corridor, a hip-hop track was playing through a phone loudspeaker. Some students curtailed their conversations as they approached the classroom entrance, while others wanted an audience.

'Yo, miss,' a lanky boy said breezily. 'You've changed since last term.' His eyes danced with mischief as he laughed at his own joke.

Steve gave a curt nod. 'In you come, please.'

The hip-hop was silenced, and the students tumbled into the classroom.

He'd met his year twelves earlier and had just about recovered. Now it was time to begin a new module with the A2 students. He'd taught this unit, on the psychology of relationships, at Midhurst High School and was aware that the sections on cultural differences might prompt questions about arranged marriage and Haniya Patel's suicide, particularly since the tragedy was still so recent for everyone.

Once he'd taken the register, he paired the students up and asked them to think about how relationships differ between cultures. Chatting and giggling immediately broke out.

'Once you've identified a difference, come and write it on the board.' He waved the marker in the air and placed it on his desk at the front of the classroom. Steve cast his eye round the room, watching and listening.

'Sir, d'you mean, like, *sexual* relationships?' asked one of the boys, looking over at the girls, grinning.

Steve was used to questions like these. '*All* relationships, Amir.'

Outside, rain blistered on the window panes and dark was enveloping the playground and streets. This was the graveyard slot, especially in the winter.

Farzana pushed her chair back, adjusted the *hijab* round her face and shuffled over to the board, ballet pumps sliding like slippers on the hard floor surface. On the board she wrote LOVE and next to it drew a heart.

'Woo-oo,' came an eager voice from the back of the room. A broad grin stretched across Hasan's good-natured features. His head wobbled, his obvious excitement concealing bloodshot eyes.

Steve managed to stop himself from laughing. For a moment, he wondered whether Hasan had been smoking weed. But as the boy moved, Steve caught a glimpse of a uniform or overall peeping out of his coat. He logged into the school's data management system on his laptop and clicked on Hasan's record. His hunch was wrong: Hasan worked long shifts in his father's restaurant, seven days a week, and often came to school on no sleep at all. That explained the red eyes, poor kid. Often fell asleep in class and rarely had time to do his homework.

For now, thankfully, Hasan was awake and inspired.

Other students came up to the front and added terms to the board.

CHOICE.
DIVORCE.
WORK.
FAMILY.
RITUALS.

'Any we've missed?' Steve asked.

'I know,' said Shuab, climbing out of his seat and almost

knocking it backwards. He sauntered over to the board and wrote HOMOSEXUALITY.

There was an intake of breath around the room, as always happened when someone mentioned sexuality.

'Good. Shamila? What were you and Clare talking about?'

Shamila wrinkled her nose and referred to her notepad. 'Clare was talking about her boyfriend, sir.'

'I bet Shamila hasn't got a boyfriend,' said a voice with a strong Eastern European accent. 'She's waiting for her arranged marriage.' There was a sneer to the words. Steve recognised Lukas from his register, a Ukrainian boy. There was something defiant in the boy's body language. Arms folded, sitting back in his seat. 'Are you married, sir?'

Steve knew he was being tested. 'I'm not, no,' he said, glossing over the topic. 'What about — ?'

'Are you gay, sir?'

The whole class fixed their attention on Steve.

'*That's* a bit too personal, thanks, Lukas.' He shot the boy a warning glance, then asked students who hadn't written on the board to comment on something another pair had offered. 'Ayo, how do you think the role of the family differs in relationships?'

The boy jumped as he heard his name. His eyes travelled the room for moral support. 'Er . . . Well, my parents want my sisters to get married.' He scanned the faces of his peers. 'It's different for me and my brother, though.'

'How do your sisters feel about that?'

'One of them doesn't mind. The other wants to go to university. My parents, they ain't happy.'

'Must be difficult. Thank you.' Steve felt a flutter of pride. It wasn't easy for the kids to talk about their home life to a virtual stranger. 'Who can say something about choice? And lack of it?'

Amina thrust her arm in the air. She was perched on the edge of her seat, her petite height and frame making her look much younger than the others. 'With arranged marriages you can say whether you want to marry the person. I'm Somalian. My sister didn't like the first man my family chose for her. The man she married was the second one.'

'And have things worked out well?' Steve asked.

'She's really happy. The first guy was much older than her. She wanted to marry someone who was a similar age. They got to know each other and by the time they got married they were in love. People often look down on arranged marriages but they aren't all bad.'

Steve eyed the room. 'Anyone else got any experiences to share of arranged marriages?'

'What about that girl? The one from here?'

From the accent Steve guessed it was Lukas again.

'She wasn't given a choice, was she? The one that . . . y'know.'

The boy drew his forefinger across his throat in a cutting gesture. Everyone in the room stared at him in horror.

'*Lukas.*' Amina was on her feet.

Lukas feigned wide-eyed innocence. 'Hey. Don't shoot the messenger. We should be able to talk about it. It's relevant to our course, isn't it, sir?'

The atmosphere in the classroom was tight. Absolute silence. The year thirteen students had their eyes peeled on him.

'It's important to distinguish between arranged marriages and forced marriages, so that . . . ' He stopped right there. Who the hell was he to pontificate based on the few text book chapters he'd read, and a handful of cross-cultural studies?

Tension shimmered in the air.

'Sir?' Amina's voice brought him back into the classroom.

'It *is* relevant to what we're studying. *If* it is true that Haniya was not given any choice regarding her marriage, that's been illegal in this country since 2014 and can result in a jail term of seven years.'

Shock skittered round the clusters of tables.

'Come on, guys,' continued Lukas. 'We all know Haniya's parents were forcing her. It's just no-one wants to call it. She changed completely when she came back from Pakistan.'

'That's enough, Lukas. I cannot discuss the specifics of Haniya's situation, not least because I don't know much about them.'

Outside, rain battered the windows and the street lights still hadn't come on. Life *was* messy, he wanted to say. Forced marriages *were* wrong.

But he couldn't.

This was a shock. Lukas was right: everyone *had* referred to Haniya's marriage as arranged. Had it been forced? He sank down onto his chair. Somehow, he had to get himself together and move the discussion on.

'How about another controversial topic on our list?' He gestured to the board. 'Homosexuality.' He faked a laugh, knowing it sounded hollow. He wanted the class to know he was struggling, but he cared and was doing his best.

The group burst into laughter. Nervous, slightly hysterical but appreciative laughter.

'Sir, in the UK, homosexuality is accepted.' The comment came from Hasan. 'But among Muslims it isn't. Not for men or women. If you're gay, you have to keep it a secret.'

They spent the next few minutes discussing homosexuality and Steve drew the lesson to a close. 'That was a lively discussion, wasn't it?' He tried to lighten his voice. 'Who's glad they chose A-level psychology then?' Exhaustion seeped over him. He sat down at his desk, relieved to have the seat beneath him, realising that he was trembling.

Then a voice blurted, 'Sir, you know Mr Allen? The deputy head?'

Steve looked up. What the hell was Lukas going to say now?

He had his mobile in his hand. 'We live in the same block as them. My brother saw the cops arriving yesterday and everything.' Lukas' eyes glinted with excitement.

Fortunately, the bell went and the students began to file out before he could carry on.

Friday – Maya

Something wasn't right. Instead of the usual cacophony of noise in the MIT office, there was complete silence. And no movement. Had something happened?

Across the room, Dan had his hands round Alexej's neck. The team looked on in horror, Dan's face tight with concentration, his arms contorting at angles as he grunted.

'What the hell are you doing?' I sprinted over.

Dan pulled himself round to face me. His face was flushed with exertion. 'Thanks, mate.' He tapped Alexej's arm, and he got straight to his feet. 'S'alright. Don't spit the dummy. I was checking angles and resistance. Alexej's fourteen kilos heavier than me. It was easy to overpower him.'

For a second, I genuinely hadn't known what he was doing. He clearly went in for method acting.

'Dr Clark is right. A woman could definitely have killed Gibson and Allen.' He strode towards the white board and pointed. 'Ruth Allen, for example. She certainly had a motive.' He circled Ruth's name on the suspect board.

Five minutes later, we had just started talking about Bashira Patel's phone call when Alexej interrupted. 'You're going to want to see this, boss.' He opened the browser on his monitor. 'The media alerts have just flagged up an article on the *Stepney Gazette*'s website.'

We gathered round his screen and read the text. Suzie James had repeated details of the victims and the crimes. Then:

With two of Mile End High School's senior managers dead, parents and community members do not feel their voice is being heard. They claim the remaining two deputies aren't capable of safeguarding the children and staff. School governor Talcott Lawrence, whose daughter is a year nine pupil, told us that the parents have taken matters into their own hands and set up an online petition, demanding that the school be closed if the police don't make an arrest by 2 p.m. today. The petition has been live since last night and has already amassed over a thousand signatures.

I felt my stomach tighten. 'Open the link.'

Alexej clicked on it. 'Twelve hundred signatures already.'

'Shit.'

'Don't you think they've got a point?' It was Dan.

'I completely understand that they're worried but sending fourteen hundred kids home at two p.m. is *not* viable. Many parents will not be contactable at such short notice and it could leave their children on the streets and at serious risk.' The office clock showed 12 noon.

Dan was shaking his head disapprovingly, nursing an 'if you're sure' expression. 'If we don't meet that deadline, the school will *have* to be closed. If we keep it open, and another member of staff is killed — '

'What about if we close the school and one of the kids is abducted by a paedophile or murdered?'

The signature counter went up.

'Given Roger was murdered at home, there's no guarantee that shutting the school will keep anyone safer. The parent group clearly look up to Talcott Lawrence and have elected him as their spokesman. I'm going to speak to him to see what I can agree.'

Alexej began flicking through his notepad. 'Lawrence is an interesting chap. His parents were part of the Windrush generation from the West Indies. He was telling me about it. Looks after the daughter on his own. His wife died a year ago.'

'I didn't know about his wife.' I called up Lawrence's number from the database and began dialling. 'Two secs. Then let's take stock.'

Dan grabbed a board marker and began writing furiously.

I rang off. 'I'm meeting Lawrence in twenty minutes. That gives us ten minutes to assess our knowledge gaps. Let's get cracking.'

'How do we evaluate the role of the precepts?' Alexej asked. 'Are we looking for a Buddhist or someone who believes the world should operate according to its principles?'

'That's important. Next.'

'Where does Linda Gibson's brother fit into things? And has anything been recovered from Linda's computers?' Dan was ranking the points on the board.

'Yes.'

'Could there be two killers?'

'Thanks, Alexej. Given the similar MO, it seems likely that the same person killed both people.'

'Have the students all been ruled out?' Dan asked. 'Exams have such high stakes. Shari was telling me.'

'Uniform have interviewed and ruled out all pupils with grievances against the school. They've also interviewed everyone who's responded to the social media requests and so far no-one saw anything on Wednesday or yesterday. *Or* they're not saying.'

'*If* the killer has another target in mind, how do we identify possible victims?' Alexej asked.

I felt my stomach contract. 'The problem is that we don't know the killer's motive, or whether the precept order is a coincidence, so we have to consider it a possibility that they're planning more murders. Linda and Roger were both on the school management team. I suggest our hypothesis is that the killer is targeting senior staff. That leaves Neil and Shari. Anyone disagree?'

Dan and Alexej shook their heads.

I wrote it on the board. 'This is the plan: Dan, can you chase the technicians for progress on Linda's deleted files, and Dougie for forensic data from both crime scenes? Alexej, could you and Shen monitor progress on the social media ring-fencing and establish who else is connected with Buddhism?'

Shen jumped into a free seat.

'Let's meet back here at one-thirty p.m. sharp. Keep me posted.' I grabbed up my bag and car keys. I was waiting for the lift when my mobile rang. It was Bashira Patel.

Friday – Maya

'Suzie James has been round to the Patels', scaring the hell out of them.' I was on the hands-free in the car, updating Dan on what Haniya's mother had told me. 'She went over to Shadwell, caught Mr Patel when he was doing his morning prayers, and told the pair of them that people believe Haniya's suicide is linked to the two murders.'

The chunter of traffic muffled the cursing that came through the loud speaker. Ahead, there was a snarl-up of lorries on the main road, so I nipped down Southern Grove, alongside Tower Hamlets cemetery.

'*And* Asad Farhan has been threatening them. Telling them they'll regret it if they say anything about how he dealt with Haniya's marriage.'

Dan would speak to Suzie, he said. And I was on my way to meet Talcott Lawrence.

When I arrived fifteen minutes later, Talcott was waiting for me. Wearing a navy blue anorak, woolly hat and scarf, he was sheltering from the wind and sleet under the porch, just inside the school gates. Since Linda's murder on Wednesday, I'd been determined that closure of the school wasn't necessary or in the public interest. But I knew I had to search my conscience. Did I want Mile End to stay open out of a misplaced sense of loyalty and nostalgia? With 1,400 students in total, what I needed to know was how many parents genuinely *believed* their children were at risk.

As I was parking, I saw two figures at the side entrance of the school, off the car park. It looked as though they were deep in conversation.

It was Neil Sanderson and Asad Farhan. Seconds later, they both dashed back inside and I hurried round to meet Talcott Lawrence.

Talcott offered me his hand to shake, and gestured to the shelter of the porch. 'I've spoken to all the parents,' he told me, his manner matter-of-fact. 'With another death, they're understandably concerned. But almost all those who think the school should be shut have been whipped up into a frenzy by that journalist with the dreadlocks. She's asking them if they're worried there's a serial killer, and roping anyone she can find into signing the petition. When they realised school closure would mean having to arrange childcare for several days, their conviction withered.'

Hope soared.

'They've agreed to put the petition on hold and take stock at two p.m. on Tuesday. I've discussed the issue with my fellow governors, and the education authority has appointed a temporary head, to start immediately. We believe that should reassure the parents and provide some security.'

I felt relief wash over me. We *had* to have identified the perpetrator by then. 'Oh, thank you.'

He shrugged. 'You're welcome. The school's a big asset to this area. I intend to see it stays that way. I want my daughter to be safe, like all the other parents, but it doesn't need to be closed. Mr Allen wasn't killed anywhere on the property. And there's no indication that the students are at risk. My daughter would be far more vulnerable being left with a neighbour all day while I'm at work.'

I had never forgotten the times, after Dad left, when the school had to close early and Jasmina and I'd had to find somewhere to wait until Sabbir picked us up; how we'd had to pretend we weren't scared and that we hadn't noticed the stench of piss at the bus shelters or got chilblains in those draughty community centres.

'Can I give you a lift? I'm heading back to the office but I'll happily drop you off?'

'That's very kind, but I've got to pick up Katie's new school shoes from Stratford. I promised her some for the new term. I'm not up on girl's fashions . . .' A pained sigh left his mouth. 'That was always something she did with her . . .' He stopped, as though he couldn't bear to finish the sentence. 'Now Katie chooses them and I pay for them.'

'I'm so sorry about your wife,' I said quickly, not wanting him to have to elaborate if it was going to cause further distress.

'Thank you.' He took out a handkerchief and blew his nose.

'One of my officers said your family came over on the Windrush.'

'That's right. In 1948. I was born in Poplar. Never moved from Tower Hamlets. It's changed a lot. When my parents' generation arrived, the area was much more Jewish, particularly Brick Lane.'

'It was kind of you to come and meet me when you've got so much on. Thank you.'

He opened his hands apologetically. 'It's not as unselfish as you might think. I'm just looking out for my daughter.' The strain showed on his face. 'She misses her mother terribly. I do my best, but it's not the same. And I have to work.' He checked his watch, and then mumbled, 'Sometimes I think it would have been better if she'd lost me instead.'

'I'm sure that's not true.' It was difficult to know what to say that wouldn't sound trite.

He gave a disbelieving shrug. Cleared his throat. 'Bad things happen to good people all the time. And vice versa. My wife always said —'

The vibration of my phone cut his sentence.

Lawrence put up his hand to indicate he was off, and headed for a row of cars by the road.

Friday – Steve

After school, Steve and Andrea piled into the late matinée at the Genesis cinema in Mile End Road. Relieved to have some distraction, and the chance to let off steam, an old Hitchcock was just the ticket. Afterwards, in the Bay of Bengal restaurant just up the road from the cinema, they studied the menu and giggled at the peppermint green table-cloths and green walls.

Steve loaded lime pickle and mango chutney onto a poppadum and told Andrea about Lukas.

'I taught Lukas in year eleven,' Andrea said. 'He's a prize stirrer and always the first to get the gossip. Spent more time in that unit Asad Farhan runs than any other student I know.'

'What is Farhan's job?' Steve mumbled through a mouthful of poppadum and lime pickle. He fanned his mouth and took a gulp of beer.

'He's the school's educational social worker. Very much an elder in the Somali community but loathed by many of the school staff. He's some sort of coordinator for Somali mosques and business networks across the UK.' Andrea lowered her voice. 'It's just a shame that he's a crap social worker for the school. It was one of Linda's initiatives to have a minority ethnic person to liaise between students, parents and the school. The rumour was that she did it so she could distance herself from sensitive issues. Farhan only started last academic year. Before that there was an English woman doing the job but she crossed swords with Neil Sanderson.'

'So, in that role, Farhan could have intervened with Haniya's marriage arrangements if he'd wanted to?'

'We've had similar situations at the school. He never intervenes.'

'Surely that means he's breaking the law? Or the school is?'

'Both, probably. About twelve months ago a girl got pregnant. This girl wasn't Muslim. She was Catholic. She wanted to have an abortion but her parents insisted she have the baby adopted. Rozina let slip that Linda was furious but Farhan did nothing then either. He says people shouldn't interfere in other people's cultures.' Andrea looked at the empty poppadum plate. 'Are you ready to order?'

'Yup.' Steve spun round to catch the attention of one of the waiters. He did a double take when he saw who was sitting at a table at the rear of the restaurant, heads together, deep in conversation. 'Have you seen Neil and Shari behind us? Shari does not look happy.'

Andrea shifted in her seat to get a look. 'She certainly doesn't, you're right. Wonder what's going on there. I know they're pals, but . . .'

Steve shrugged. 'Let's pretend we haven't seen them, shall we?' He took another swig of beer. 'Lukas brought up the subject of Haniya's suicide today. He said that everyone knows it was a forced marriage but no-one will admit it. It really threw me. At my induction, Neil categorically told me that it was a regular arranged marriage.'

Andrea was keeping her voice low. 'Linda took a lot of time trying to understand how the whole thing worked. She talked to the staff, the students, the governors, the education authority, parents and inter-faith community groups. She was strongly opposed to forced marriages and anything involving coercion. Rumour was she, Asad and Sanderson fell out after the girl I was telling you about left school to have her baby just before her GCSEs. Haniya was never going to get support while Farhan was in post.'

Once they'd ordered, they began chatting about the film.

Suddenly, Shari's voice got louder, and she stood up at the table, threw down her napkin, and yelled, 'You've *got* to tell the police.

Either *you* tell them or I will.' She picked up her coat and bag and marched towards the exit.

Steve and Andrea both fixed their attention on the tablecloth.

Shari yanked the door open and stormed out, her coat and bag over her arm.

'Shit. What's that about then?'

Andrea pulled a *don't ask me* face. 'Tell the police what? God, I hope they didn't bump off —'

'Sssh,' said Steve, using all his willpower not to look over his shoulder at Neil, who, moments later, followed Shari out of the restaurant.

Friday – Maya

'Jeez.' I did a double take. 'When I said to dress *casually* . . .' The vision that greeted me at Bethnal Green tube station was full on Aussie outback: neckerchief, waxed cotton cattle coat, and bush cowboy hat.

'Strewth, Sheila.' Dan hammed up his accent, and gave a dry chuckle. It was hard not to laugh.

We crossed over the road and headed towards the London Buddhist Centre.

'What is this full moon *puja* thing you're dragging me to?' he asked.

'Vajrasiddhi suggested it. I thought it might help us understand the role of Buddhism in Linda and Roger's deaths.' A disenchanted Muslim, and a lapsed Catholic, we were credible candidates to be interested in Buddhism. I assessed my scruffy jeans, ankle boots and long coat. 'You might not blend into the background but no-one will suspect you're a British cop.'

Once we arrived at the Buddhist Centre, we were surrounded by people hugging each other, even the men. A rough head count told me there were about a hundred people in the room.

'Don't get any ideas, alright?' Dan hissed through his teeth. 'Physical intimacy is *not* part of my contract.'

Realising everyone had taken off their coats and shoes, we did the same. A bell sounded, like the one at Vajrasiddhi's house, and we all filed into a large room with a laminate floor and a massive gold Buddha statue. Quickly people laid out meditation cushions, which they kneeled astride and sat on. Others arranged chairs. We followed suit, and placed two seats at the back of the room. Within minutes everyone's attention was on a male Order member who stood at the front of the shrine room.

'Welcome, everyone,' he said. 'I'm Amarabodhi. Let's salute the shrine.' He then led a series of chants in call and response. The first part was in Pali. After that, he recited the precepts.

'I shall abstain from causing harm,' said Amarabodhi, his expression sombre, 'and will purify myself with kind actions.'

We repeated it.

'I shall abstain from taking the ungiven and will purify myself with generous actions.' His voice got louder, and the energy in the room shifted as everyone focused their minds on the attitudes and behaviours they should strive for.

'I shall abstain from sexual misconduct and will purify myself with simplicity and contentment,' he said, and so did we.

Amid the heady atmosphere of the chanting, it was unsettling to be repeating the words on the cards that had been left at the crime scenes for Linda and Roger.

'I shall abstain from false speech and will purify myself with truthful communication.' Amarabodhi's voice was strident.

Of course, if there was going to be another murder, lying was the next precept.

'I shall abstain from all that clouds the mind . . .' said Amarabodhi.

So, if there was another murder, and the killer was following the sequence of the precepts, it would be an encouragement to tell the truth.

'. . . and will purify myself with mindfulness,' said Amarabodhi.

As the *puja* progressed through several more stages, it was hard not to be swept along, but my mind was flitting about, preoccupied with the case. After half an hour, the chanting stopped and, one by one, people got up and made their way to the front of the shrine room where they kneeled down before the Buddha, lit a tea-light or piece of incense, and sat or stood in silence for several minutes. Some of the men stretched out flat on the floor.

'Submission,' Dan whispered.

That word, the incense and the atmosphere all made me feel . . . I wasn't sure what. A fevered intensity simmered beneath the calm in the room. Was this why people were suspicious about Buddhist rituals? Did they expect some kind of sacrifice?

Once the *puja* was over, everyone sat quietly for a few minutes and then stacked away their chairs and cushions, and made their way out in a respectful silence. Dan and I followed. Across the room I caught sight of Vajrasiddhi, and waved.

He came over. 'Did you enjoy the *puja*?'

'It was certainly . . . different.' I was trying to figure out how I felt. I introduced Dan. 'Do the precepts have negative and positive aspects?'

'Yes. The negative formulation advises on what we should abstain from, and the positive is what we should strive for.'

Dan was listening. 'Why did you tell DI Rahman you were at your accommodation Wednesday, when you were out all day?' He spoke softly.

'I explained that. I got the days mixed up.' He looked at me.

'And you went to Brighton to . . .?' Dan asked.

'Visit an old teacher of mine. There were some personal issues I wanted to discuss.' It was the same answer he'd given when I asked him.

Something occurred to me. 'When you were telling me about meeting Linda at a yoga class, you said it was when she was . . . *something*. You didn't finish your sentence and then dismissed it as being "a long time ago". Was Linda pregnant when you met her?'

From Vajrasiddhi's face, it was obvious that he didn't always find it easy to be truthful either. Perhaps Dan was right in being suspicious?

Friday – Steve

Steve flung back the duvet. He'd been in bed for what seemed like five minutes when the flat buzzer went. He decided to ignore it. But it went a second time. He rolled out of bed and stood up. Made his way to the hall and the intercom.

'Hello?'

'It's DI Rahman.'

Of course. He'd left a message saying he needed to speak to her. It had gone completely out of his mind.

'Come up. It's the second floor.' He buzzed her in. Panicked. He couldn't speak to the police in his boxer shorts. He ran down the hall, grabbed up his jeans and top, and pulled them on. He was still trying to compose himself when he opened the door.

'Sorry to call late.'

'That's okay.' Steve was trying to flatten his hair, aware that four minutes ago he'd been fast asleep. She looked different from the last time he'd seen her, at the school just after Linda had been murdered. And the male officer was . . . actually, what the hell was he wearing?

Inside the flat, Steve led the detectives into the lounge.

'We got your message . . .' said the woman.

For a moment Steve's mind went blank. Then it came back to him. 'I feel like a complete grass telling you this, but I was in a restaurant this evening with a colleague and we overheard Mrs Ahmed and Mr Sanderson having an argument.' He relayed what had happened.

'"Either you tell them or I will"?' The female cop looked at her colleague.

'That's what she said.'

'And then she left?'

'Yes. It's just . . . it was all very odd. Mrs Ahmed was not happy at all and it didn't sound like it was something minor. I got the impression it was something they both knew about, and which *he* wanted kept quiet.'

'You've done the right thing. People often don't pass on information to the police because they don't want to look like busybodies or grasses.'

'Please don't mention that it was me who —'

'We will handle it carefully, don't worry.'

'There's something else . . . One of the students blurted out that Haniya Patel's marriage had been forced. This surprised me as I was told it was arranged.' He explained about the module he was teaching on cultural differences in relationships.

'What else did this student say?'

'That everyone knew it was forced but no-one wanted to say.'

'I see.' She seemed surprised too. 'It *was* investigated thoroughly at the time of her suicide but there wasn't any evidence to prove her parents were forcing her. The law is extremely complex, and it's often difficult to prove there's been a lack of consent, or that pressure and threats have been used.'

That made sense. Lukas was probably just stirring. What was the other thing he'd mentioned? He'd better tell her that too. 'One of the year thirteens also mentioned that his family live in the same block as Mr Allen. His brother saw the police arrive and . . . Oh, that was it really.'

She had her gaze fixed on him. It scared him a bit. They were eyes that missed nothing.

Steve felt ridiculous now, wasting their time. Why on earth had he rung them? It was a Friday night and he was half-pissed. 'I just want the murders solved. If I'm honest, it's partly self-interest. Because I found Linda, and I'm new, I'm worried that people think I did it. Or that someone might . . . Oh, I dunno.' He was being neurotic.

The woman considered his comments. 'Of course. Thank you for letting us know. And don't worry, you're safe here. We have no reason to suspect that you're in any danger.'

He saw the two officers out. Fat chance he had of getting back to sleep now. It was all very well for DI Rahman to say that he was safe at home, but Roger Allen hadn't been.

Saturday – Maya

I keyed Dan's accommodation address into my satnav. When I pulled up, he was sitting on a wall outside a dilapidated block of flats. On the exterior of the building, cracked pebble dash was coming away, and cheap UPVC window frames were a mottled grey. A ground-floor window had been boarded up and graffiti-sprayed.

He got into the car, doing up his tie. 'Y'alright?'

Hip-hop was booming out of an open flat window, making the car vibrate.

'You look rough.'

'Cheers.'

'Is this where you're living?'

'Uh-huh.' He peeled back the skin on a banana and took a bite. 'The graffiti wasn't me though.' His phone buzzed. 'Sorry, I need to get this.' He placed the banana on his lap. 'Hold on, hold on, don't cry.' His voice softened and he shielded the speaker with his hand. 'What's the matter?'

I thought about the warm bath I'd just had, and the fresh porridge. I had no idea Dan didn't have a comfortable flat somewhere. On top of being separated from his family, living here couldn't be easy.

'Oh, darling. They're itchy, are they?'

The voice on the other end of the phone was distraught.

'Has Mummy put calamine on them? . . . Okay, try not to scratch. I'm at work at the moment so I'll call you later.' He rang off and continued eating the banana.

Ruth Allen was towel-drying her hair when we arrived at her sister's flat in Limehouse. Wearing no make-up and a fluffy dressing gown, she looked ten years younger.

'Sorry. The kids and I went to Roger's parents in Hinckley and I only got your messages last night.'

'Your husband mentioned a couple of things about Mile End High School that we need to investigate further,' I said. 'Could we ask you a few questions about this, please?'

'I'll tell you what I can.' She led us into the lounge and gestured to the three-piece suite. It was a small area and joined an open-plan kitchen-diner.

'He mentioned Linda's initiatives and said that his management colleagues went along with her publically but, behind her back, weren't happy. He even hinted that staff at the school wanted Linda out of the way. Did he tell you anything about this?'

Ruth stopped drying her hair and sat on one of the dining chairs. 'Roger tried to keep things cordial with Neil Sanderson, but I know he never trusted him, and I know he told Linda not to. The other person he didn't like was Asad Farhan. Farhan isn't management but Roger always said he acts like he is. "Bad news" was how my husband described him. Said the school should never have appointed him but no-one listened.'

I jotted Neil and Farhan's names on my notepad. 'In what way is he bad news?'

'Have you seen how he runs the exclusion unit on the fourth floor? With all that junk up there? He's the only staff member who locks his office. Roger said that not even Neil locks his door.'

'Going back to Mrs Gibson, your husband obviously didn't agree with some of Linda's methods. Did you get the impression this was a personality clash or a —'

'Despite his crush, or whatever it was, Roger wasn't stupid. He found Linda's attitude exasperating and irresponsible. He said that the issues that she refused to acknowledge made her a liability. Some serious safeguarding failures were identified at the 2016 OFSTED inspection and the school was told it needed to improve to avoid being taken into special measures.' She towelled more water from her long hair. 'In 2017, the inspectors were satisfied that those improvements had been made and rated Mile End High as "good".'

'What sort of safeguarding failures?' I knew but wanted to check what Roger had understood.

'Roger said that schools, workplaces and prisons are radicalisation risks. For years he told the governors that Mile End needed to educate everyone – the kids and staff – about radicalisation, homophobia and illegal cultural practices.' She stopped. 'And *properly*. Not pay lip-service.' She dumped the towel on the carpet.

'Was your husband satisfied with the new inspection rating, Mrs Allen?' Dan pulled the blind slats apart to get a look over the Thames.

'No. Not completely.' Her manner was jittery.

'What did he still have concerns about?' He let the blinds swing back into position.

'The school updated their policies and staff handbook. Carried out compulsory training for all staff, governors and students, and installed sensitivity controls on their IT systems . . .'

Her words reminded me of my interview with Roger, and the way he'd talked about Linda's stream of initiatives. 'But?'

'Roger didn't feel that any of it was sufficiently rigorous. He warned Linda. He told her someone was going to get hurt. She just . . .' Ruth waved her hand in a dismissive gesture.

Dan was hovering, as though he had something to say. 'Changing the subject slightly, do you know the entry-code to the school, Mrs Allen?'

'Yes. I don't advertise it, of course, but I'd often go in and meet Roger from work. Drag him away from that bloody place.' Beneath her words lay sadness, but there was an anger to them too, and I could see they'd confirmed something for Dan.

'Moving on, before Christmas, what was your husband's understanding of the factors contributing to Haniya Patel's suicide?' I was thinking about what the teacher had told us last night.

Ruth gulped. 'He said she was unhappy because her parents wanted her to marry a Pakistani man and she didn't want to. Something about a boy from a local school.'

'You see, the police investigated and didn't find any evidence to prove that her parents were forcing her.' This was on public record so I wasn't breaching confidentiality. 'But we understand the kids may have known she was being forced. Did Roger know anything about that?'

She began to nod. 'The students liked Roger. They confided in him. He knew what they were saying and he told Linda. He said that they *had* to investigate the rumours and bring in the Forced Marriage Unit, if necessary. But . . .' Ruth looked away and I had a feeling I knew what she was going to say. 'She asked Farhan to deal with it.' She was shaking her head in disbelief. 'Roger raised it again at their management meeting, but Neil said he was being alarmist and unhelpful.' She wiped her eyes with the back of her hand. 'It's a shame no-one listened to him. Perhaps if they had, they all might still be alive, and my kids wouldn't have to grow up without their dad.'

Saturday – Dan

In the tiny Bow café, the milk steamer roared on the cappuccino machine. Dan and Maya had stopped for a sandwich and were in a corner so they could discuss developments in the case.

'We've got Ruth Allen's testimony and Steve Rowe's.' Maya sipped her drink and began drawing up a chart in her notepad. 'Ruth's supports the idea of Neil and Asad Farhan being dodgy.'

'Yeah, but it's only *her* version of what Roger felt. We need direct evidence.' Dan was irritated he couldn't get any reception or 4G on his phone in the rear of the café.

'I know that but pretty much everything is circumstantial at the moment and we still need to consider it.' She continued to jot notes. 'And Ruth's provides further support for the hypothesis that Haniya's marriage may have been forced and the school may have covered it up.'

'Based on some gossip among the students? Come on. You know what kids are like for making stuff up.' He tutted and tucked his phone in his pocket.

'That's why I referred to it as a *hypothesis*. Of course it all needs investigating and corroborating.' She watched him take his phone out again and check the signal. 'Alexej is going to try to speak to Shari today. Can you interview Neil? Find out what Shari meant by "Either you tell them or I will".'

'Yup.' Dan was worried about Kiara. He hated being away from the girls, especially when they were sick.

'That leaves Farhan – who I want to interview myself.' Maya was jabbering away. 'Neil, Shari and Farhan all work full-time. What with shopping and family commitments, it's going to be harder to catch everyone given it's the weekend.' She tapped her biro on the table.

The repetitive noise irritated him. Her questions and hypothesising. The screech of the coffee machine, and the clatter of crockery and furniture in the enclosed space. At a table nearby, a young family were enjoying their weekend. The mum had her arms round a toddler and the dad was talking to a boy. The scene made him think of Aroona. Would she agree to bringing the girls over?

'Hello-o, Earth calling DS Maguire.' Maya was staring at him.

'Sorry. Miles away.'

'I gathered. *And* cranky. What's up?'

'Oh, nothing. Just . . . stuff.'

She sighed. 'I rang the laboratory this morning. They're still processing the forensics. With so many possible suspects, we need something that puts one of them at one of the crime scenes.' She was circling names. 'I've asked Dougie to chase the results. Especially the fibres, hair and skin.' She sat back in her seat. 'I'm still not sure whether we are after a man or a woman. Are you?'

'No. I was looking at Ruth Allen just now. I remember when I interviewed her the first time and she was in her gym gear. She looked pretty strong. Roger was killed in his seat and Linda was petite.' He took Maya's pen and drew an arrow by her name. 'She's clearly upset about her husband's death, and the school safeguarding failures, but she could've done it, I reckon. She has motives for killing them both. She had the opportunity. She knows how to get into the school and she knows all about the various white-washes. She could've picked those precepts. *I shall abstain from sexual misconduct.* Who's more likely to be upset about that than Ruth Allen?'

Saturday – Maya

'Damn.' Neil's mobile had been going straight to voicemail all day. I left another message and hung up. The Sanderson's au pair had told Dan that Neil and his wife had gone away for the weekend. Not only was he *incommunicado*, we also wouldn't be able to track his phone if it was switched off. I rang Alexej on the hands-free. 'How'd you get on with Shari?'

'I kept it vague about who'd said what. Told her that some of the restaurant staff overheard their row and saw her leave, then contacted us because of the investigation at the school; that we are speaking to both her *and* Neil. She downplayed it. Said it was nothing, and that they'd simply had a tiff.'

'What about?'

'She faltered a bit when I pushed her to tell me, but finally said it was about when to tell the year tens and elevens that the school has dropped modern foreign language A-levels for 2019. She said Neil kept delaying the announcement and it annoyed her. I've checked this out and it *is* true. Funding cuts. Why they were arguing over that on a Friday night, I have no idea. I asked her whether she was sure that's what the row was about. Other than calling her a liar, I couldn't do much more.'

'D'you think she was telling the truth?'

'Nope. She was cooking when I called round, and the children were in and out of the kitchen, but she seemed extremely agitated and knocked milk from one of the children's bottles all over her *jilbab*. She also asked if we had *already* spoken to Neil about the argument.'

'No doubt she'll be straight on the phone to him then, warning him and telling him what she told us.' It was another dead end. 'Thanks, Alexej.' Perhaps I could get some sense out of Farhan.

I knew where Farhan lived and twenty minutes later was ringing the doorbell of his three-storey house in Whitechapel, wondering how his family coped with the constant drone of traffic on Commercial Road. It was an arterial road, connecting the City of London with Canary Wharf, and was rammed with lorries, taxis, buses and cars, day and night.

A tall man opened the front door. His curly hair was completely white and he was wearing a khaki shirt with a pen in the pocket. He peered at me over the top of glasses, which sat halfway down his nose.

I showed my warrant. 'I'm DI Rahman. Can I speak to Mr Farhan, please?'

His face clouded over when he saw the Met's insignia and I noticed wariness in his eyes. 'Me Farhan.'

'I mean *Asad* Farhan. From Mile End High School.' Was this Asad's father?

He frowned, and shouted over his shoulder into the house in what sounded like Somali.

A few moments later I heard a young woman approach, calling back along the hall as she walked. She ducked under the arm of the older man and the first thing I noticed was her warm smile.

'My grandad doesn't speak English.' She was tall, like her grandfather, and wore a black *jilbab*. 'Asad's not here, I'm afraid. I'm his wife, Jamilah. Is this to do with the murders?'

I introduced myself. 'Yes. Where can I find him?'

'He's chairing a national conference at the Somali mosque in Sparkbrook.'

'Where's that?'

'Birmingham. There's a big Somali community living round

Stratford Road. He's on the Somali Elders Council of the UK, so he's always doing these events.'

This was a blow. 'When's he back?'

'They finish on Sunday evening, so either late Sunday or early Monday. If it's late, he often stays over and drives home at five a.m. and goes to work. If it's urgent, you can call him but I doubt he'll answer. Or I can call him but I doubt he'll pick up for me either. He's in a world of his own when he goes to these things.'

'What's the conference about?' I knew Farhan was very involved with the Somali community.

'It's to help people from Somalia to find employment and form business networks. They're running skill-sharing workshops. Practice interviews. Speakers.'

I was running through my options. If I drove up to Birmingham and hauled him away from his event, he'd most likely refuse to comment. If I got a message to him that we needed to speak to him first thing on Monday, he might be more cooperative.

'Could you call your husband, please, and tell him he needs to be at Mile End High School, ready to be interviewed, at nine a.m. on Monday? If he's not there, I shall arrest him and take him to the police station for interview there. I'll get the same message to him myself.'

Alarm danced in Jamilah's eyes. 'Is he a suspect?'

'Could you get the message to him, please. Tell him he's lucky I'm not driving up to Birmingham now.' I knew the prospect of being cautioned in front of his peers would rattle Farhan and felt confident that Jamilah would tell him what I'd said. I handed her my business card.

She nodded, and I felt a dart of guilt knowing that my visit had brought anxiety to her weekend.

As I returned along Commerical Road to the car, I rang the team, hoping I'd made the right decision. A cooperative Farhan was better than a pissed off and unhelpful one – as long as he turned up on Monday.

Saturday – Maya

From Mile End, I cut down Burdett Road, eager to get home. Other than the interview with Ruth Allen, it had been a frustrating day with questions piling up and few answers.

When I arrived home, I pulled into the car park beneath the flats. In one of the visitors' spaces, nestled in between a gleaming BMW and a rusty Mini, was a black Range Rover that I recognised. My sister's registration plate was easy to spot. She and my niece, who were getting out of the car, were a flash of blue and pink in the dingy underground space.

'Hey. Wasn't expecting to see you two,' I shouted over as I locked the car, delighted at their surprise appearance. 'Everything okay?' My sister's job keeps her as busy as mine, and it was rare to see her in the daytime.

The bitter canal air whipped round the car park, sending a can tumbling over the concrete. I tucked my scarf round my neck and scurried over to their vehicle to give them both a hug.

'Mum's sent me.' Jasmina wrinkled her nose apologetically.

'That's alright.' I felt my stomach lurch but we both knew the score. We'd looked after Mum for years. Spent our whole lives having to conceal or reveal information at her behest. 'Is she okay?' For a moment, I was back at school the day Mum and Jasmina came to collect me when Sabbir was attacked.

'Can we come in for a cuppa? Sadia had a netball match at Ben Johnson Road.'

Sadia grinned, flashing her braces, then laughed self-consciously behind her hand, tiny nails painted in fuchsia varnish. She was so like Mum. Her features, her eyes. And in her grey and black sports kit, with a vibrant pink bag over her shoulder, she radiated youthful energy and excitement.

'Come in. I'll put the kettle on.'

'Sure? You look shattered.'

'I am. But it's lovely to see you both.'

We took the lift from the car park to the third floor. A welcome whoosh of warm air greeted us as I opened the flat door.

'I'd forgotten what stunning views you get up here,' said Jasmina, looking over at the French windows in the lounge. 'You can see Canary Wharf. The canal's frozen over. Look, Sadia.' She moved towards the doors. 'Reminds me of our old apartment in Bangladesh.'

'It's why I chose the flat. The balconies along the waterfront are gorgeous in the summer. Can be quite noisy, though. And, from the towpath, it's a voyeur's paradise.'

In the kitchen, I gestured to the table and filled the kettle. Last night's washing up was stacked in the sink, and Dougie's phone was on charge on the worktop.

'How are you, Sadia? You were choosing your GCSE subjects last time I saw you. I remember us talking about Biology and Chemistry. What did you opt for?'

'All the sciences, Maths, English and Spanish. I want to be a crime scene investigator.' Sadia had made herself comfortable at the table, and was busy with her phone, thumbs tapping at high speed. 'I'm going to be fifteen next birthday. Will you come to my party, Auntie Maya?'

'If you want me to, but surely you don't want boring old adults getting in the way?' I laughed and felt my spirits lifting. Her joy and innocence were just the tonic I needed.

'Don't encourage her,' said Jaz. 'The party is still under discussion.' She tapped the side of her nose and said in a mock whisper, 'Her dad's not thrilled about the make-up and nail varnish, and is threatening to embargo the whole thing.'

I chuckled, enjoying the familiar, easy relationship Jaz and I had. Despite her being married, and a mother, the shared references were precious. 'Do you want to choose some music, Sadia? My CDs are over there.' I pointed to the racks. 'What's Mum's message then? To call her back? To go and see her?' The dread surfaced again, like an old adversary, sandwiched between concern and resentment. I opened the fridge and pointed to a bottle of wine. 'Or would you prefer tea?'

Jasmina draped her long coat over the back of a kitchen chair. Taller than me, and in her navy and white *shalwar kameez,* with scarf draped casually, she looked so elegant. Hair pinned up, unlike my scraggy mess, long earrings, and heeled shoes to my boots, you'd never think we were sisters. I possessed one set of *shalwar kameez,* which I'd worn at Sabbir's funeral, and once before that to please Mum for a wedding a decade ago. But what struck me most was that I'd never noticed the shadows round Jasmina's eyes so markedly before. The long hours in court, and evenings spent reading documents, were catching up with her.

Sadia raised her gaze from mountains of CDs. 'Go on, Mum, have a glass of wine. Dad's got a council meeting tonight so he won't notice.'

Jaz and I met each other's glances and giggled about a teenager telling us what to do.

'A glass of wine would be lovely. Thanks.' She gave a hearty laugh. 'Rubel knows I drink. I have no intention of hiding it from him.' She pulled out a chair and slid onto it, folding the material of her beautifully ironed trousers as she crossed her legs. 'Shall we get Mum out of the way? Then we can relax.'

I handed her two glasses and the bottle, and fetched some crisps from the cupboard. 'Go on, then.' I checked the fridge again. 'Sadia, what would you like to drink?'

She was fine, thumbing away on her phone again, distracted from the CDs by message alerts.

'I know we've suspected for a long time,' Jaz continued, 'but she's officially been diagnosed with dementia. They've done the assessments. She's okay at the residential home for the time being.' She glugged out the wine and passed me a glass. 'But her awareness is getting increasingly erratic.'

'I'll get over there as soon as I can. I've been receiving a lot more calls from her. She seems to forget she's rung. I admit, I don't always phone her back straightaway, but often she forgets when I have and calls me again the next day.'

Jasmina was nodding. 'We've been getting the same. She'll have a long conversation with Rubel and forget all about it. Part of the dementia, the consultant says.' She sipped her wine and grabbed a handful of crisps. 'The other thing is she keeps mentioning Dad.'

'*Dad?*' That was a bash over the head. 'But none of us have seen him since he went out for candles during the —'

'Power cut.' She was shaking her head. 'Took me a while to get my head round it too. I have no idea whether she's imagining it, dreaming it, or what. But she's said a few times now that he's been in to see her.'

'*Shit.*' My hand was over my mouth as soon as the word was out. 'Sorry, Sadia.' I knew how fiercely protective my brother-in-law was of his daughter. Last thing I wanted was for her to go back home and start swearing.

'I have heard swear words before, you know.' Sadia was back at the table now. 'This *is* Tower Hamlets and I am nearly fifteen.' Her expression was so earnest, it was hard not to laugh.

'Been to see her? What else has she said? Has anyone else seen him?'

'Steady on, Detective.' Jasmina laughed.

'Sorry . . . habit.' My thoughts were swirling. 'It's been *twenty-eight years.*' I was on my feet. I had to think. 'I'm serious. What exactly did she say?'

'If you stop pacing and sit down, I'll tell you.' She gestured to the chair I'd been sitting on. 'Each time she's said she's woken up and he's "been there", whatever that means. I've tried to press her for details but that's all she says. And that he disappears as suddenly as he arrives.'

'That'll be right. Sounds like Dad.'

Jaz was staring at me. The joke released our tension and we were soon laughing together, my sister's infectious giggle making me snort.

'You're the cop. Go and ask her. The staff haven't seen anyone. No-one using Dad's name has signed the visitors' book, and they have security staff monitoring the CCTV. Nothing unusual.'

'That doesn't mean much. You know what Dad's like. If he wanted to get in and see Mum, he'd manage it.'

'That's the thing. I *don't* know what he's like. Do you? I mean, *really*? We were kids when he left.'

Suddenly hip-hop blasted into the silence of the kitchen.

'Argh. *Sadia.*' On top of the news about Dad, the assault of the noise made me snap. The idea he may be alive and in East London somewhere was inconceivable. 'I can't take this in. Can you? If it is Dad, why choose now to put in an appearance? And where has he been all this time?' I thumped down on my chair. Topped up our wine glasses. 'The package on the door step the night of the power cut . . .? The candles . . .?'

'And the *bagels.* Come on. It had to be Dad. Who else would bring back bagels?' Longing shone in Jasmina's eyes. 'We never found out, did we? Mum couldn't cope with Dad leaving so she forbade us from talking about it.'

'I've never understood why she told us a neighbour left those bloody candles. I always believed Dad came back and put that package there. He left anyway but cared enough about us to go out and get candles and bagels, and bring them back. Rang the bell to let us know they were there. Why did Mum want us to believe he had left us without any light?'

Jasmina shrugged. 'Sabbir didn't know either. Mum's always refused to talk about where Dad went and whether she knew he was leaving. I assumed she was angry with him and wanted us to be.'

In Jasmina's eyes I saw the same pain as I'd felt all my life. Our childhood confidences had come back to life. We were both back in our tiny flat in Brick Lane. To 1990 and the agony of every hour and day after Dad left, trapped in the wilderness of not knowing what happened, because Mum felt scared and ashamed. But, at the same time, talking about Sabbir and Dad made me feel closer to them and reminded me why I'd wanted to be a cop all those years ago. I was *determined* to solve the murders at the school.

I felt queasy. I'd knocked back two glasses of wine on an empty stomach, and my head was starting to turn. 'I really need to eat something. I'm going to put some pasta on. Would you like to stay for tea?'

Sadia wheeled round, eyes blazing with excitement. 'Oh, Mum, please can we?' She leaned forwards imploringly. 'I'll even change the music. And I can paint your nails if you like, Auntie Maya?' She produced a pencil case, and, from that, a bottle of nail varnish.

Jasmina laughed. 'Thank you. Some food would be lovely.' Then added, 'I'm very tempted, for old time's sake, to ask: what's for tea?'

We both chorused, 'Rice and curry,' and, drunk on shared memories, giggled like hysterical teenagers while Sadia pretended not to notice.

I rummaged through the fridge, and produced a red pepper, some black olives and a fresh block of parmesan. 'No curry, I'm afraid. How does pasta with tomatoes, olives and tuna sound?' I lined up all the ingredients on the worktop and began to chop. It was a relief to have something to take my mind off Mum and Dad. 'How's the law going? And how is my councillor brother-in-law?'

Jasmina and I chatted amiably and prepared the food, while Sadia listened in, fiddling constantly with her phone, and acting as our DJ. We took our supper into the lounge and ate on our laps. Squeals and laughter filled the room, and all three of us poked and scolded each other playfully. After we'd eaten, Sadia painted my nails, and I groaned when I realised I didn't have any nail varnish remover in the flat.

Before we knew it, the lounge clock said 9 p.m.

'Is that time right?' Jasmina looked at her watch and got up. 'We need to go. Rubel will be home. He's been in Pakistan all week so I've hardly seen him. Get your things, Sadia, please.'

Not needing to drive, and reeling from shock, I'd drunk more than

Jaz. I accompanied them down in the lift and safely into the car. It had been a delightful evening.

She was about to drive off, when Jasmina lowered the window. 'That was so lovely. Why don't we do this more often?'

Her question hit me in the solar plexus. 'Yes,' I said, 'let's do that.' And as I stood and watched the tail lights of the Range Rover disappear into the night, I realised that I'd assumed Jaz had been making a suggestion, but perhaps she had simply been asking a question.

Sunday – Maya

The following morning it was a relief to escape the walls of the flat; to shut the front door behind me and breathe the canal air; to feel the crunch of the towpath beneath my feet. I watched the mallards glide and turn through the murky water, pecking at the weeds on the surface. From Ben Johnson Lock, I turned east through Mile End Park. As I strode, the feelings of the last thirty years, which were still wriggling from last night's conversations with Jasmina, bedded back down. At Mile End, I passed under the yellow arch of the Green Bridge, and weaved through the backstreets. Soon, I found myself in the graveyard at Bow Church. It was a spot I knew well, one Dad had brought Jasmina and I to when we were small. 'An island of tranquillity' was how he referred to the church, because it was situated, literally, in the middle of the road, with traffic flowing round it.

I sat now under the yew tree, on my favourite bench, with its damp wooden slats underneath me. My breath was white in the chilly air. It was the same bench Jasmina and I had huddled on so many times with Dad. We would bookend his huge form and snuggle into the softness of his body, feeling safe in sturdy arms. Dad had enjoyed soaking up life here, observing the subtle changes. He wouldn't recognise it now though. Instead, if he were here, he would chat to us about the tiny, Anglican Bow Church, with its colourful history, and the Catholic Church of Our Lady and St Catherine of Siena that stood opposite. He would make up stories about the projects being hatched in Bow Arts Trust next door, and who was getting married at Bromley Public

Hall and Registry Office. The rows of red hireable bikes at the tube station would make him chuckle. I could imagine Dad saying, 'Girls, we're sitting at the intersection of religion, bureaucracy, culture and politics.' Then he'd salute the magnificent statue of Gladstone, laugh in that deep, throaty way of his, and get out his Golden Virginia and roll a cigarette.

Suddenly, I had the urge to go inside the church. I got up and wandered towards its large oak doors. In the foyer, the sign said, 'Welcome! Looking for peace?' Next to the racks of leaflets about coffee mornings and discussion groups, several bookshelves offered second-hand paperbacks for sale. Although this was an Anglican church, I had a feeling if I went into the Catholic church over the road, the Buddhist Centre in Bethnal Green, or the mosque at Whitechapel, similar things would be on offer. As I stood here, I understood why religion could be so appealing, not just to those who were lost and lonely, but to anyone whose equilibrium had been disturbed by the eddy of life.

Like Haniya.

Her name had been rubbed off the board back at the police station, but I couldn't shake her from my mind, particularly after hearing from Steve Rowe and Ruth Allen that the Patels may have been forcing Haniya to marry the man they'd chosen. How desperate and alone she must have felt to have seen no option other than ending her life. What was going wrong if parents ended up hurting their children or pushing them to suicide rather than protecting them?

The clunk of the church door interrupted my musings. It was the vicar, Angela Kelly.

'Hello,' came her friendly voice. 'Don't let me disturb you.' We'd often met at community events and Angela knew I was in the police.

'Oh, don't worry. I need to get going. Just enjoying a quiet moment. I used to come here with my dad sometimes.'

'I came back for my purse. Sally needed some change for the coffees and teas, and I must've left it behind. I can put the kettle on if you fancy a quick cuppa?'

A current of melancholy tugged at me. The vicar, Angela, was a similar age to me but the concern in her gesture reminded me of Mum and Jasmina. For a moment I felt tears begin to form in my eyes, and a fist of emotion in my throat.

'That's very tempting but I think if I start talking I may never move from here.'

'I was very sad to hear about Linda. She and Peter attended services sometimes and I knew her a little.' Angela disappeared into the kitchen and came back clutching a red purse. 'I don't think she found the school easy but it was obvious she cared a lot. She came to discuss sensitive issues with me many times. She was troubled by the cultural tensions, and wanted to do the right thing. We talked about Haniya twice.'

'I didn't know that.' I paused. 'Did she talk about it as an arranged marriage?'

'Linda said that Haniya's family had arranged a marriage for her and Haniya was unhappy about it, as she'd been seeing a Catholic boy behind her parents' backs. Linda said she'd been reassured that it wasn't a forced marriage, but she'd found it hard to get the facts, and was being pressured at the school to drop the matter.'

'I see.'

'We spent some time talking about it. She didn't want to involve the FMU if it was arranged, as it could make her look interfering and judgemental, and alienate the Muslim community. She was in a difficult position. When Haniya committed suicide, Linda came to see me again. She felt terribly guilty. She said she'd been wrong to let someone else deal with Haniya's situation, and had let her down.'

This was news. It put the head teacher's decisions in a fresh light.

'Linda said repeatedly that Haniya might not be dead if the school had intervened more.'

So Linda had wanted to support Haniya but hadn't known what to do and had caved in to – whom? The Patels? Asad Farhan? Neil Sanderson?

'You wouldn't think human nature would shock me anymore, but it does. Haniya. Linda. Roger. The school. It makes me sad that we often cause each other harm, even when we mean well.'

I felt like a kid when someone asks what's wrong, and you feel the lump in your throat, and you want to say, *everything,* and blurt it all out in the hope they will magically make everything alright again. In addition to the two murders, what bothered me most was the abuse Linda had suffered at the hands of her brother, and the desperation that Haniya had experienced – and how both sets of parents had refused to acknowledge their daughters' feelings. It was heart-breaking to think how different their lives might have been if only someone had stepped in to help.

Empathy spread over Angela's face. 'In my experience, people *do* mean well.' She sat next to me on the pew. 'They genuinely want to keep their loved ones safe. But all of us can do the wrong thing for what we think is the right reason.' She paused. 'I wonder if perhaps it's when we're scared or unhappy? Self-preservation, probably.'

'And when we're convinced we're right.' Talking about Linda and Haniya brought other conversations to mind, as though a door had been opened and memories and ideas were flooding in: the sexual abuse that Dan mentioned, which the Catholic Church had hushed up; the incest he'd told me about in the Aboriginal communities; the honour killings that were still happening. Perhaps hurting each other was an inevitable part of being human? I thought of Tom Sullivan. Would he *always* have been an abuser or had the drugs sent him nasty? Perhaps there'd been another trigger.

'Are you sure you don't want that cuppa? It's no trouble.'

Angela's voice brought me back to the church. 'Thank you, no. I really do need to get moving.'

*

Instead of going home, I decided to go into the office. The revelations about Haniya's marriage were niggling more and more. Was it possible the police investigation had missed a cover-up? Yet again, my instinct told me that Haniya's suicide and the murders were linked. I'd collected my car and was halfway to Limehouse when my phone rang. When I saw whose number it was I couldn't answer quickly enough.

'I've just picked up your messages,' Neil Sanderson's voice boomed through the Bluetooth. 'Family time, sorry. How can I help?'

I asked him about the argument with Shari on Friday evening.

'Yes, it wasn't very discreet of us. Shari likes to deal with things promptly and I put them off.' He repeated what Shari had told Alexej. 'The students are going to be furious that they can't do language A-levels but the government don't care. It was a silly thing to argue over but it's not been an easy time lately and I think some of the tension spilled over. Nothing to worry about, I assure you.'

'And you'll be in school tomorrow, should we need to speak further?'

'Regular as clockwork,' he purred smugly.

Ten minutes later, I swiped myself into the police station. In the MIT room, I printed out the five Buddhist precepts and placed them on the desk in front of me.

I shall abstain from causing harm (?)
I shall abstain from taking the ungiven (Linda)
I shall abstain from sexual misconduct (Roger)
I shall abstain from false speech
I shall abstain from all that clouds the mind

Without Briscall and Dan in the office, insisting Haniya's suicide wasn't linked to the murders, I was able to sift through each precept again in peace. My thoughts fell on the two after Roger's. If the killer had more targets planned, and the precepts represented the way they saw their victims, who might they consider guilty of false speech, and who of a clouded mind? I got up and stood in front of the board of mugshots, examining one face after another. There were a dozen people to whom at least one of the precepts could apply. Was our hypothesis still correct, and the killer was targeting the school's management team? I clicked on the recording of Mayor Hayes and jotted notes as I re-watched him speak on the BBC news.

Fear of crime
Community cohesion
The increasing population
Safe schools
OFSTED concerns about safeguarding

Roger had mentioned the OFSTED inspection before Linda took up her post. He must've known about the more recent concerns. On the Mile End High School website I located the OFSTED reports. There it was: assessed in 2016 as 'requiring improvement' and one step away from special measures. Some safeguarding and child protection failures. Improvements needed to training on the risks and warning signs of extremism, radicalisation and forced marriage.

Neil and Shari had mentioned the main challenges facing the school. I pulled up their statements. Neil cited language and literacy issues and Shari talked about tensions among the staff over recruitment, and the effect religious views had on social events. Even though the school had been rated as 'good' in 2017, why hadn't they told me about the safeguarding failures the year before? It was so depressing. How could the school I'd adored have changed so much? Or had my immature eyes simply not computed the implications of the problems I'd seen as a pupil? And then there was Haniya, whose suicide seemed to symbolise everything that Linda, Roger, the mayor, Neil, Shari, Peter Gibson and the inspectors had raised. Tomorrow, at 2 p.m., the parents' petition would go live again, and with the national and local media behind their campaign, as well as the mayor, closure would be imminent. If there was a shred of evidence linking Haniya's death to the recent two, I was *going* to find it.

I pulled up the Patel case files and stacked them on the edge of my desk. I trawled through every report, statement and interview. But three hours later, disappointment began to seep into the gaps where confidence had been. There was nothing here. Or at least, I couldn't see it for looking.

I was ready to go home. To leave work behind, just for an evening.

After Jasmina's bombshell last night, Dad was preying on my mind. I would dig out the box of photographs and have another read of the notes I'd made on all our attempts to trace him . . . before we'd decided to give up.

Monday – Steve

Steve had been in his teaching room since 7.30 a.m. Through the blinds, it still wasn't fully light. His attempts to get the freezing classroom warm had fogged up the windows. He sat with his coat and scarf done up, updating his register and planning lessons. Outside somewhere, two pigeons scuffled and cooed.

The door opened.

'Morning, sir.' The young girl shuffled in, her ballet pumps dragging on the floor. She brought with her a heavy energy.

Steve looked up from his spreadsheet. 'It's Maria, isn't it? Are you feeling better?' Her greeting seemed downbeat but she'd been absent on Friday so Steve didn't know what she was usually like.

She grunted something unintelligible.

'I got your message about not being well.' Steve hadn't liked to ask her friends too many questions as they were still getting to know him, and he didn't want to pry into the girls' private matters.

'Bit better, sir.' Her gaze was downcast and her voice sounded flat.

'That doesn't sound very good. Are you sure?'

'Yeah, sir.' She gave a weak nod. 'What did I miss in psychology last week? Was there any homework?'

Steve told her.

'I'll do it now.'

Steve watched her creep over to a table. Something wasn't right. She was a slim girl but her body seemed stiff. When she sat down, she coughed to conceal what he was fairly sure was a cry of pain.

Her facial features contorted briefly. When she leaned over to get her books from her bag on the floor, the groan was unmissable.

'Maria?' He tried to keep the alarm out of his voice. 'What's the matter?'

'I'm fine.' Her reply came a bit too quickly. 'Just walked a bit far yesterday.' Shiny tears had gathered in her eyes. She sniffed and rubbed her nose.

'Walked? The girls said you were in bed with the flu.'

She blushed and put her hand to her head. Her eyes closed for a few seconds while she thought how to answer. 'Oh, yeah, I was.' She paused. 'I got up a bit later and went out for a walk. I forgot.' She busied herself with getting her folder and textbook out of her bag, and trying to focus her attention on what she'd missed in class.

Steve continued to sit at the computer, pretending to work but unable to concentrate. Over the top of the monitor he watched Maria. He saw her take some tablets out of her handbag and push two out of the plastic strip. She popped them into her mouth and washed them down with a couple of swigs of water.

'You got a headache?' He was trying not to push her too hard as he was aware she could get up and walk out.

'A bit. It's this flu.'

'Are you sure you should be here? And not at home, resting?'

'No. *Definitely* not.' Her hand rose to her mouth, as though she realised she had given too much emphasis to her words, given something important away. She spoke more quietly now. 'I don't want to miss any more school. I'll get behind.'

'As long as you're okay.' Steve was trying to think of what to say. Suddenly all the suggestions from teacher training deserted him. 'Did the girls not pick you up this morning? I thought they stopped for you on the way to school?'

'I was . . . um . . . late.'

'But you're the first one here?'

'Oh yeah.'

'Where are they then?'

'Dunno.' She shrugged. It was a small, instinctive movement and it made her wince. 'Maybe they took a different route?'

'You're being a bit vague. Is everything okay? You seem to be stiff and in pain.' He pointed at the bottle of water she'd drunk from.

'Course. Just a bit achey.'

A few minutes later she stood up to walk across the room to the printer, and as she did so her woolly scarf fell away from her neck. Steve still had his eye on her and the movement caught his attention. As she shuffled, the girl's scarf unravelled further. Underneath, she was wearing a round-necked jumper. Her neck was mottled with red-brown bruising, like someone had been hauling her around, and there were angry weals on her skin.

'How did you get —'

The girl grabbed at her scarf. 'Oh, it's nothing.' She wound it back round her. 'Really, it's just . . .' She faced away, pulling her hair round onto her neck to further conceal what Steve had seen. 'Is there any more paper for the printer? It's run out.'

Steve got out of his seat and walked over to her. She was pulling at her scarf, and trying to put her coat back on, but in her haste it kept falling away at the neck. The closer he got, the more he saw.

'You're covered in bruises. We need to get you some medical help.'

'I'm fine. Honestly. It was just a silly fall.'

Steve was certain something was wrong. 'I could see how stiff you were when you came in. What's happened?' He was in front of her now.

'I'm fine. I'll be okay in a couple of days. I fell over when I was walking. It's so dark in the afternoons. I just want to forget about it and get on with my school work.' She added, 'Otherwise I won't get to university.'

Steve was taking her words in. 'Has someone been hitting you? Those bruises . . . and you can't walk properly. Was this why you didn't come into school on Friday?'

Eventually she nodded and stared at the floor. She was fidgeting, and pawing at the carpet with her shoe.

'It's my own fault.'

'What is?'

She was dabbing at her eyes and sniffing.

'I'm sure the school nurse would see you if you wanted to go over now. Would you like me to come with you?'

'She won't understand.' Maria must've seen Steve frown. 'Mum says I've brought shame on my family.'

Steve's heart sank. He got up and shut the classroom door. 'I can help you. But you need to tell me what's been going on.'

'My dad will go mad if he finds out. It's this boy. He's Turkish. Someone told my mum I've been seeing him after school sometimes. She wants me to marry a boy from Ireland so we can all go back and live in Donegal.'

'And what happened? Did your mum do this to you?'

Tears streaked down her pasty face and dripped onto her grey and white scarf. 'Please don't say anything to anyone. It'll just get me in more trouble. She said it was to stop my dad getting his hands on me. If she didn't make me see sense, he would.'

This was way more than Steve knew how to cope with. But he had to keep her talking. 'What has she done, Maria? This is serious.'

She took her coat off and peeled back her scarf to reveal large red hacks and lumps on her neck. She pushed her neckline down and showed him the marks that continued down her shoulder and arm.

Steve felt himself go cold all over. 'It's okay. Pull your top back up. We need to get you to a doctor.'

'No. I can't. My mum'll kill me if I tell anyone.' She shot over to where her books and folder were, and grabbed up her bag and coat. 'She said if I told anyone, she would . . . I've got to go. This was a mistake.' She dashed over to the door, yanked it open and fled the room, sobbing.

Monday – Steve

Steve tailed Maria out of the classroom and along the main corridor on the ground floor, calling after her. If she went home, it was likely she'd get into more trouble with her parents, especially if they asked her why she wasn't at school and she told them she'd spilled the beans. But Steve was unable to persuade her to stop, and with registration imminent, he couldn't follow her further than the school gates. He'd tell the head of sixth form. Refer it on to her. But when he arrived at her office, she wasn't there. Probably visiting form tutors. He would ask the head's PA, Rozina, to inform the head of sixth.

But Rozina wasn't in her room when he got there either. Steve called out a few times. No-one was around, and Linda Gibson's office was still locked. He checked his watch. He'd leave Rozina a note. He searched her desk for a pen and a piece of paper. Typical. She was a neat freak. His own desk was a jumble of pens and Post-its and notes scribbled on bits of paper – but here everything had been put away. Leaning over the desk from the front, Steve pulled out one of her drawers. It was cack-handed and he had to half lie over her desk and grope round in the drawer to find a pen and a pad. He felt like a burglar or a thief. If someone came in, they'd wonder what the hell he was doing. He rummaged a bit more. Finally, his hand felt paper. A pad. Good. He pulled it out of the drawer and yanked his body upright again. Except, when he looked at it, it wasn't a pad. It was a slim paperback, entitled *Introducing the Dharma*, with an image of Buddha sitting cross-legged on the front. What on earth was a book on Buddhism doing in Rozina's desk? With her tunic and *hijab*, he'd assumed she was Muslim.

He opened the book. As he fanned the pages, a leaf of paper fell out onto the desk. It was an A5 piece of card, a flyer for a meditation class at the London Buddhist Centre in Bethnal Green.

Monday – Maya

'I'm pleased you got the message.' As arranged, I was back in Asad Farhan's dingy office at 9 a.m. After Steve and Ruth's testimonies, and a two-day wait while Farhan was in Birmingham, my patience was on the thin side. 'Could you explain what the school did to investigate whether Haniya Patel's marriage was forced?'

'Who?' The muscle under his eye twitched.

I repeated her name and met his gaze, every bit as hostile as his was to me.

'Oh, *her*. The silly girl who caused an innocent driver to crash as he drove home from his night shift?'

His words made me furious. In essence, what he said was true. A car driver *had* seen Haniya fall from the bridge and had crashed his car as a result. But Farhan failed to acknowledge the poor girl had been driven to suicide. The *imam*'s words came into my mind from before Sabbir's funeral, reminding us that suicide is a major sin in Islam, and anyone committing it will be in the fire of Hell forever.

'Now we've established who I'm talking about, perhaps you could answer the question. You worked closely with Mrs Gibson.'

'No idea, I'm afraid.'

I remembered some of the comments at the time of Haniya's death. Letters to the newspaper, articles online. Claiming she'd been selfish to take her own life; caused distress to her family and friends; killed the car driver, and caused suffering for his family too. Why were we so lacking in compassion towards people who were desperate?

'How can you have no idea? Mrs Gibson consulted you about it and passed the matter over to you to deal with. I'm sure you are familiar with section one-two-one of the Anti-Social Behaviour, Crime and Policing Act, 2014, so I'll repeat my question: what did the school do to investigate whether Haniya Patel's marriage was forced?'

He shot me a filthy look and sucked his teeth. 'Has that hysterical secretary of Linda's been telling tales again?' His voice was quieter now, but coloured with fury. For a moment he reminded me of Tom Sullivan. The two of them had the same hateful manner.

I flinched. 'I seem to remember that you called Alison Cooper "hysterical" when she reported that a member of staff had sexually assaulted her?'

'Those allegations were dropped.'

'Because you frightened her into dropping them. Mile End High was your second chance. Your *last* chance.' I gestured to his desk and the room and the power the stacks of files gave him. 'It's going to be different this time. Failure to comply with legislation on forced marriages carries a maximum jail term of seven years.'

He was on his feet now, eyes burning. 'What would you know about our culture? Call yourself a Bangladeshi? A Muslim? Being born somewhere doesn't mean a thing.' He waved his hand at me dismissively.

I felt the hairs prickle on the back of my neck. How dare he? 'Unfortunately you aren't in the position to give me orders. See this?' I flashed my warrant. 'You can either answer my questions or come to the station with me under arrest. Now, what do you know about Haniya?'

He rubbed his hand across the beard growth on his chin, exhaled a protest, then said, begrudgingly, 'Haniya had got in with a crowd of girls who were a bad influence. Been cavorting with a Polish boy after school when she was supposed to be studying. Announced she wanted to marry him. Her parents had arranged a husband in Lahore for her.' Farhan slumped down in his chair and paused for a few moments, as though he was thinking what to tell me. His jaw clenched on gum as he chewed.

The police had known Haniya had a non-Muslim boyfriend. I'd check the files when I was back at the station, but from memory I was pretty sure they'd wanted to interview him and not been able to locate him.

Farhan cleared his throat. 'They took her over to Pakistan to meet the man they'd chosen but the stupid girl caused a scene, and his family withdrew the offer. Her parents were very upset and they had a dreadful row. She went to the bridge and killed herself. All unnecessary hysterics. A silly phase. I'm quite sure she would have grown out of it and realised that what her parents wanted was best, and that marrying a Catholic wasn't right.'

A silly phase.

His expression hit me in the middle of my chest. What patronising sentiments they were. They implied Haniya was fickle and didn't know her own mind. She was naïve and misguided. It reminded me of how I'd felt each time Mum had used that expression when I said I wanted to join the police, and how disappointed she'd been when I said I didn't want to move back to Bangladesh and get married. And how her disappointment always brought a veil of something crashing down, as though I was to blame for how *she* felt. For not wanting what *she* wanted.

My thoughts shifted back to Haniya. 'You talk as though she was given a choice. Without full consent, which is freely given, it's a forced marriage. Same where there are threats and coercion.'

Farhan tutted.

'She must've felt desperate to have taken her life in the way she did. Doesn't that mean *anything* to you?'

'In the eyes of Islam, suicide is a sin. She may think she's escaped suffering but she hasn't. And what about the suffering she's caused her parents?'

The forensic data showed there had been no doubt Haniya had intended to kill herself. The police technicians had found that 'most successful suicide methods' featured regularly in her internet search history. But it was pointless trying to convince Farhan to empathise with Haniya's predicament, or to believe forced marriages were wrong, so I changed tack.

'Why do you assume Rozina is involved with all this?'

He groaned and rolled his eyes. 'She got it into her head that Linda should've insisted that Haniya's parents stop the marriage plans. Stormed in here screaming at me about it.'

'What was Linda's view?'

Farhan groaned again. 'Linda was a young head teacher. She had a lot of good ideas and she was ambitious. She realised early into her appointment that the key to her success here was getting the minority ethnic community on her side. And that meant not condemning things she didn't understand.' His face was furious. 'She discussed her concerns with me. Neil Sanderson was worried about Linda jeopardising the progress the school has made, particularly after being told by OFSTED that we needed to improve. I gather he persuaded her to leave Haniya's parents to me.'

'How do you get on with Neil? I saw the two of you deep in conversation on Friday, in the school car park. What were you talking about?'

'I can't remember. We have lots of conversations.'

'I'm sure.' I mirrored the contempt in his expression. 'So, you're the school's hatchet man?' I remembered what the vicar said: Linda *had* wanted to help Haniya, but she'd been talked out of taking any action. Vajrasiddhi had referred to Linda as ambitious. If she'd colluded with Farhan and Sanderson, whose interests was she protecting?

Farhan reached for his cigarettes behind the plant, then checked himself.

'What did you agree with Haniya's parents?'

'There weren't many options.'

'There were two: they force Haniya or they don't.'

He shrugged. 'It's not as simple as that. As the police discovered when they investigated.'

'There's much more evidence now that the school may have ignored the law and done nothing.'

'If you prove it, be my guest,' he said sneeringly. 'I did it *our* way. Tariq said Haniya had brought shame on the family and needed to be removed from unhelpful influences. She refused to stop seeing this Catholic boy, and her father wanted her to have a Pakistani husband in order to continue traditions and help family business. We agreed he would deal with the situation himself. I wouldn't want anyone telling me how to raise my daughter so I left him to it.'

This was all a horrible, tragic mess.

Then a voice popped up: if Haniya had gone to Pakistan, got married and settled down happily, who was to say the marriage would have been a bad decision, even if she hadn't consented to it? Could anyone have foreseen that she might kill herself? *Should* they have?

It was impossible not to think about Sabbir. Had any of us contemplated he'd take his life? Hadn't we all tried to help but eventually buried our heads in the sand and hoped desperately, blindly, naively, he'd shake off his ghosts and find a way to be happy? Suddenly a wave of guilt crashed over me, carrying with it the force of years and years of suppressed grief and anguish.

I couldn't breathe. I had to get out of this office. Mumbling excuses, I charged towards the door. The teacher, Steve Rowe, was on his way in.

'Inspector? It's Rozina. I need to —'

I pushed past him. Had to get some air. As I stumbled forwards, all I could think about was if Haniya and Sabbir had received the support they needed, they might not have felt that death was their only solution.

I spotted the sign to a ladies' toilet. Staggered in. I grabbed hold of the hand basin for support. Splashed cold water on my face, revived by its coolness. And then I remembered that the teacher had mentioned Rozina, and I'd got the impression there was something he had wanted to tell me.

Monday – Steve

Steve cleared his throat loudly and repeated what he'd said. 'It's about Maria O'Connor in my form.' He felt like an idiot as he stood in front of the cluttered desk in Asad Farhan's office, waiting for him to look up from his keyboard.

He must've heard Steve, surely?

'She was absent on Friday and has come into school this morning covered in bruises. Says her mother hit her to make her stop her going out with a Turkish boy.'

'Uh-huh.' Farhan's face was an angry red.

'She's just run out of my classroom in tears. I can't find the head of sixth form. I'm worried if she goes home, her father will —'

'These silly girls. They cause so much trouble.' Farhan chewed on his gum. Still didn't look up.

What did he say? 'Maria's hasn't *caused* any trouble. She's *in* trouble. She needs help.' Steve moved closer to the desk. The man's attitude was bugging him. He peered over Farhan's monitor. 'Are you listening? Her mother has beaten her all over. She's covered with bruises, can hardly walk, and is scared to go to the nurse in case she gets into more trouble. It's physical assault.'

'Okay. Leave it with me,' he drawled, resentfully, and picked up a pencil. 'Maria O'Connor in twelve-S?' He scribbled on a scrap of paper and chucked the pencil on the desk. It hardly inspired confidence. 'It's almost registration time. Hadn't you better attend to your form?' And for the first time in five minutes he actually met Steve's gaze.

This was pointless. Why the hell was Farhan the school's educational social worker if he wasn't interested in student welfare? It was hard to believe that he was as involved with youth initiatives, as Andrea had mentioned. Steve left the room with anger pricking in his chest. It was Farhan's job to mediate between families, children and the school, but he hadn't shown the slightest concern for Maria. He'd have to get hold of the head of sixth form. Any minute Maria might arrive home in desperation, and walk into another round of beatings with her mother. Or perhaps, this time, her father?

He sprinted along the corridor, hurled himself round the corner and collided with the female detective he'd seen leaving Farhan's office a few minutes earlier, sending her flying to the ground like a collapsed umbrella.

'Shit. Sorry. Let me . . .' He bent down to pull her up. 'Are you okay?'

On the ground she didn't look like a police officer. She seemed so small.

'Fine,' she said, sounding far from it. 'Asad Farhan doesn't seem to have a good effect on anyone.' She was gathering her legs from under her and was on her feet now. She was bent over and rubbing her knee. 'Did you say something about Rozina back there?'

'Yes. I've got to register my form in about five minutes. Could we walk back to the ground floor and talk?'

She rubbed her knee again, wincing.

Idiot. 'Sorry. Can you walk?'

'I'll be fine in a minute.' She limped forwards a few steps, stiff and in pain. Then placed her weight more confidently. 'Rozina? Is that who you were discussing with Farhan?'

'Yes. No. Sorry. I went to talk to Farhan about an Irish student in my form whose mother beat her up.' He explained. 'I couldn't find the head of sixth who we refer pastoral issues to, so I went to find Rozina – who also wasn't in her office. Because the bell was about to go for registration, I wanted to leave her a note but there weren't any pens on her desk. Long story short, I opened one of her drawers to get a pen and some paper, and found a book on Buddhism with —'

'Is it *her* book?' She'd stopped walking.

'I think so. Inside the book was a flyer for meditation classes. Rozina had written her name on the back of the leaflet.'

'Did you put the book back in her desk?' She was staring at him.

'Yes. Why?'

Monday – Maya

The tear-smudged face opposite me in the interview room didn't look like that of a killer. Rozina, Linda's PA, was immaculately dressed, just as she had been the last time I saw her. A moss-green *hijab* clung to her elegant features and complimented her pale green eyes. From a distance, the smoky-kohl eyeliner and heavy mascara made her eyes look darker. She was hunched in her chair, like a frightened child. She covered her mouth with soggy toilet roll and as tears fell onto her lap, she wiped her eyes.

I presented Rozina with the Buddhism book from her desk. 'Is this yours?'

She blushed. Stared at the book on the table in front of her. 'Yes.'

'Are you a Buddhist?' I gestured to her clothes and *hijab*. 'I assumed you're Muslim.'

Under the harsh lights of the interview room, Rozina looked first at Dan then me, her face full of questions. She swallowed. 'Why do you want to know?'

'Could you answer, please?'

On the wall, a plastic clock ticked out the seconds in the small space.

She nodded. A small one at first then more decisive. 'But no-one must know. Apostasy is a big thing in my...' she flicked a glance at me, '...in *our* culture. As you know, the majority of Bangladeshis are Muslim.'

I understood what Rozina was saying. It *was* a huge thing for a

Muslim man or woman to renounce their adherence to Allah and Islam, and to defect to another religion.

'Do your parents know about this? Any of the people in your community?'

Her eyes changed. Terrified now, she shook her head. 'Only my mum. She said not to tell Dad yet as he'll go crazy. Probably send me back to Bangladesh.' She clutched at her rib cage as though needing to contain her fears. 'You can't tell anyone. *Please?*'

We had to tread carefully. Whatever reasons Rozina had for turning her back on Islam, they could put her life in danger if people within her community found out she no longer considered herself a Muslim.

'I'm hoping there will be no need. Can you tell us why you decided you wanted to be a Buddhist?'

Rozina's gaze was fixed on her hands now. She was pulling at the skin round her nails, picking and prodding and chewing bits off. 'Many Muslim girls have marriages arranged for them. The girls who have come over here to live, and especially those who've been born here, are often sent home to marry. A lot of our parents want us to have traditional lives and don't want us choosing to marry a non-Muslim man.' She stopped here and took a deep breath. 'Sometimes our parents consult us on who they think we should marry and sometimes . . . well . . .'

'Have your parents arranged a marriage for you?' I asked.

'My dad's busy arranging my little sister's marriage. She's going back to Sylhet in a couple of months to get married. She's met the man they've chosen, and likes him. And that's fine – because it's what she wants. But it *isn't* what I want. My life is here in the UK. I like my job and my friends and my freedom. And I want to choose who I marry and what religion I follow.'

I understood what Rozina was saying, but unless it involved the school in some way, she was unlikely to be involved in the murders of Linda and Roger, and that meant her religion was of no concern to the police. We had to tread carefully, though, and hope she'd tell us about Haniya.

Dan must've picked up on this, too. 'Rozina, how did you feel about Mrs Gibson?'

'Linda?' Rozina looked startled. She shielded her mouth again. 'I liked her. She was kind to me. I've been her PA for nearly four years now, since she joined the school.'

'Any tensions?'

Rozina was pulling at her hands again, twisting her fingers round each other.

'Rozina? Any tensions between you and Mrs Gibson? It's important you tell us if there were.'

She nodded, as though she was weighing up what she thought was relevant, how much she was prepared to disclose. Intelligence danced in her eyes but also something heavier and more burdensome.

The atmosphere in the small room had changed suddenly. The air had folded in on itself. As Rozina thought about what to say, I could feel each beat of my heart. Each breath in and out of my lungs.

'I don't want to be disloyal to Linda. Especially now she's dead. It's just . . .' She covered her face. Shook her head.

I opened my mouth to speak and closed it again.

Dan softened his voice. 'Telling the truth isn't being disloyal, Rozina. If it helps us to find out how Mrs Gibson died, surely that's being loyal?'

She shrugged. 'You know the girl who killed herself before Christmas? Haniya Patel?' She repeated what we knew, her eyes brimming over with tears. They splatted onto her hands and her tunic.

The box on the table was empty so I delved in my bag on the floor for tissues, and handed Rozina a fresh packet.

She blew her nose and sniffed loudly. 'I begged Linda to investigate whether Haniya's family were coercing her, and to help Haniya to get a protection order if her parents wouldn't back off. But Linda said she couldn't interfere with the decisions of Haniya's family, that it wasn't her place to condemn cultural practices that she didn't fully understand.'

Those were the exact words Asad Farhan had used.

Dan and I exchanged looks.

This was a minefield. It was further proof that this shiny, successful school had failed to discharge its duties. Linda had clearly been in a delicate situation and it might have been difficult for her to have confronted Haniya's parents but, with the new laws against forced marriages, she could've handed the issue over to the Forced Marriage Unit. And, as a head teacher, she should've been used to dealing with sensitive issues every day.

'Linda had worked hard to gain the trust of the Muslim community,' she said, 'and didn't want to jeopardise their faith in her and do anything to reverse the progress the school had made. She said Farhan assured her it was a standard arranged marriage – but he would, wouldn't he?'

'Why were you angry about this?'

'In Buddhism we're encouraged to be mindful. To try to see things clearly and impartially, and to tell the truth. Linda knew forced marriages often had dreadful consequences. I took some documents to her desk once and she had the Karma Nirvana website open, the one that campaigns against forced marriages. Sadly, she was more interested in keeping the Muslim community happy than doing the right thing for Haniya. We all know each other round here. Haniya's younger than me but I've known her sisters for years. Linda basically ... caused ... Haniya's death.' She spluttered through tears. 'And unless ... someone does something ... it's going to happen ... again.'

I waited to see if she wanted to add anything.

'Someone *had* to do something to stop what was going on.'

Her words hit me. Was *Rozina* ...?

'Someone had to do *what*?'

Implications hung in the interview room and time slowed down.

Dan repeated the question. 'Rozina? Someone had to do what?'

I was holding my breath.

'Confront her. Make her realise. I told her if she didn't protect girls whose parents were forcing them into marriages, I'd report her to the police.'

'How did she respond?' It struck me how courageous Rozina was, not just to shift away from Islam but to challenge Linda on the school's stance on forced marriages.

'She tried to minimise the situation. Said they were arranged marriages, not forced ones. I printed out a fact sheet for her on the 2014 law. When she saw the bit about a seven-year jail sentence, she panicked.'

'It can't have been news to her, surely?'

'I don't think it was. But mention of the police completely freaked her out. Linda begged me not to report her. Said she'd lose everything. That Peter was ill and couldn't work. Eventually she said she'd tell Farhan to get Haniya's parents to call off the wedding. But Farhan had other ideas and she changed her mind. Haniya's father threatened Haniya and she went to the bridge and . . . If only someone had helped her, she might still be alive.'

So, Rozina wasn't our murderer and Haniya had died needlessly. And something clicked into place in the back of my mind. 'You must've been the person closest to Linda in the school. Can you think who might want to kill her? Were there any people she fell out with?'

'The stuff with Roger Allen was weird. He didn't make things easy for Linda but she always said he was harmless and well-intentioned. A "noisy fly" was how she described him. She was pretty patient with him. Way more than I would have been. Everyone saw he was in love with her. She told me once that she knew what it was like to love the wrong person. I don't know what she meant and I didn't ask.' Rozina looked perplexed. As though the woman she'd worked for was a mystery to her. 'She got on alright with Shari. Neil was different. He didn't mind Linda being the head, but often put her under pressure to do things the way *he* thought they should be done. He wanted the school to lead the way in cultural relations, and was always swanning off to conferences to advise other schools on how we do things.'

I'd been wondering about Sanderson. 'How did Linda feel about that?'

'She hid it well but it annoyed her. She felt *she* took the rap and *Neil* took the credit.' Rozina stopped speaking and fiddled with the pin on her *hijab*. I got the impression there was something else she wanted to say. 'Please don't tell Neil I told you that. He's got quite a side to him.' She looked straight at me. 'Just like Farhan.'

It occurred to me that, with Rozina's Buddhist perspective, she'd given herself a different lens, but she'd also made herself an outsider.

'Can you think of anyone who might want Linda dead?'

She shook her head.

'What about Roger Allen?'

'He was different. He was often disagreeing with his management colleagues, and issuing warnings, but they all ignored him.'

When the interview was over I saw Rozina out and mulled things over as I made my way back to the office. Her testimony had convinced me all over again that the murders of Linda and Roger were connected to Haniya's suicide and the school – but I still had nothing more than a hunch to go on. I was convinced we had missed something.

*

Back in the office, the Patel files weren't where I'd left them yesterday. I looked around the room. 'Anyone got the files on Haniya Patel?'

Alexej covered the phone receiver with his hand. 'Briscall's got them,' he whispered. 'He said he wants to see you as soon as you get back.' He mouthed, 'Sorry'.

I suppressed a groan. 'Okay, thanks. Briefing in ten minutes? I'd better see what he wants.'

Monday – Maya

The door to Briscall's office was off the main MIT room. As I approached I heard his voice. Then a female one. Superintendent Campbell was with him.

'Of course, I've had to keep tabs constantly or we won't meet targets. Her brother's suicide has affected her badly and . . .' He dropped his voice and I couldn't hear the rest of the sentence. 'So I suggest we tell DS Barnes what we've decided.' He was audible again. 'And advertise his post.'

The jumble of words hit my brain just as I put out my hand to knock on the door. Forward momentum brought my hand in contact with the wood, so I cleared my throat to disguise my clumsy knock.

'Morning, ma'am. Ian. You wanted to see me.' My brain was scrambling to make sense of their conversation.

'Come in, Maya.' He beckoned.

Was I imagining it or had Superintendent Campbell blushed slightly when she saw me?

'Fiona, I'll keep you posted on the matter we were discussing.' He shuffled a few items around on his desk as I came in.

'Could you wait a moment, ma'am? I can walk back with you? I wanted to speak to you.' I stood in front of Briscall's desk, impatient to get back to work. 'I gather you have the Haniya Patel files? May I have them?'

'I do.' He glanced at his senior colleague nervously. 'I told you last week that —'

'Haniya's death was tragic but we need to allocate resources to ongoing investigations, and that you could see why her suicide might be important to me, but I need to concentrate on Linda Gibson. Yes, sir. You did.' It wasn't easy but I made sure my voice was non-confrontational and my facial expression neutral.

He was looking straight ahead, devoid of any emotion. 'Er . . . quite. And I gather you are *still* insisting her suicide is relevant to the two strangulations, so I've confiscated the file and taken the matter out of your —'

'Wait. That's it.' I spun round, elated. 'It *is* relevant. That's what it means.'

I dashed out of Briscall's office and across the room to Alexej and Dan.

'I've got it, I've got it,' I shouted. 'The two murders *are* linked to Haniya.' Everyone was staring at me, sensing we were on the verge of a breakthrough. '"I shall abstain from taking the ungiven" refers to the fact that Linda took Haniya's decision about her future away from her, by refusing to protect her. As head teacher, she had ultimate responsibility for ensuring that the school investigated the suspicions of a forced marriage – internally first – and then referred it to the FMU, if necessary.'

'You little ripper,' said Dan. He googled the precepts; skimmed various web-pages. '"I shall abstain from sexual misconduct" doesn't just mean infidelity. Look.' He pointed to a chunk of text, written by a Buddhist Order member.

I was reading the information too. It was what Vajrasiddhi had explained. 'Yes. Look. It talks about the way that obsessive behaviour can hurt others and says that sexual misconduct stems from selfish cravings.'

Dan was on his feet, punching the air.

'The killer is telling us that they're not happy about Linda failing to protect Haniya,' I said. 'And that Allen's obsession with Linda wasn't fair on his wife and family.'

Ten minutes later, I'd collected the Patel files from Briscall and we'd all gathered for briefing. I began by taking the rest of the team through our new interpretation of the precepts. The mood in the room had lifted. We hadn't identified the killer but we were creeping closer.

'These precepts are crucial to our understanding of the murderer.'

Dan updated everyone on what Rozina and Ruth had told us, and then summarised the other key developments. 'The post-mortem's been carried out on Roger Allen. Dr Clark confirms the cause of death as hypoxia due to venous occlusion, arising from manual strangulation. Broken larynx and hyoid bones. His blood-alcohol concentration was extremely high.'

'Thanks. Still nothing in Allen's correspondence and records?'

Dan shook his head. 'Nothing that suggests a motive. Only what he told us. A few texts from his wife, clearly pissed off. Pictures of Linda. Nothing sexual.'

'And *still* no success recovering Linda's deleted files . . . argh.' I was thinking aloud in exasperation; clicked out of my email. We may have been closer to understanding the killer's motivations. But, without knowing what Linda had deleted, we were trying to solve a puzzle with half the pieces missing. I grabbed up the phone and dialled.

Monday – Maya

We couldn't wait any longer. The decision was made and so was the phone call.

The technicians were still struggling with PermErase and we needed Linda's deleted files. On a course a year ago I'd met a digital engineer who the police used frequently. The man, Talis Seglins, was Latvian. He'd proudly boasted there was nothing he couldn't recover. The thing about Talis was that his communication was exceptionally blunt. It was refreshing but made you feel you had to match his ability to sift through the sand of irrelevance and find the pearl of importance within seconds. On the other hand, you knew where you stood with Talis: time was money and money was king. Talis wasn't police personnel. He worked as an independent consultant and charged a fortune. But we needed the best in the business and if our technicians couldn't crack PermErase, Talis was our man.

Two hours later, I was sitting opposite him in a cafe in Mile End. I had no doubt his charcoal suit cost £500 but was meant to look like it was £24 in Primark. The watch looked like a crappy, knocked-off Rolex but was the genuine article. It was the best double bluff on the planet. Except for the latest iPhone that lay, gleaming, on the coffee table next to his raspberry and white chocolate muffin, fully loaded and not pretending to cost a penny less than a grand.

'PermErase is bitch,' he said, and then bit the top off his muffin.

'The killer may have more deaths planned and we have to stop him.'

He sucked a piece of dried raspberry from an incisor and eased it out with his fingernail. 'Always there is way. Trust me.' He tapped his nose.

I might not trust him, but I was quite sure Talis Seglins knew a thing or two. And fortunately, after having had to return the Patel files so soon after confiscating them, I'd been able to tap Briscall for some contingency funding. It was going to come in useful.

'I will do it by tomorrow lunchtime. I give you my word.' He placed his hand on his heart, his face very solemn.

I stood up. Part of me felt like I was commissioning a hit man.

Talis polished off his muffin, drained his coffee mug and was out of the door before I had time to give him my contact details.

Monday – Maya

That evening, when I got home, one thought tumbled over another and conversations looped in my head. While I was making dinner, an old friend, Fatima, rang to invite me to a party. The murders were all over the news, and as I couldn't discuss the investigation, we quickly fell into chatting about our time at Mile End High School.

'After every sports day, I always scoured the photos on the display boards,' she said, 'praying there wouldn't be any of me.'

I'd known she hated sport but hadn't realised the school photos bothered her so much. Fatima's comments made me think about Haniya. How had *she* felt at Mile End High, surrounded by images of smiling, happy students? With Linda boasting on the school video that everyone should feel safe? Had Haniya felt her life was represented in the school narrative of cultural harmony and success? I couldn't help wondering whether it had all contributed to her feelings of alienation, failure and desperation.

When I got to bed, I couldn't relax. I lay in the dark, fidgeting, while my mind picked over all our unanswered questions. One of these was why the murderer had chosen strangulation as their MO. I switched the bedside lamp on; googled 'strangulation'. Pressure on the neck stopped the flow of oxygen *and* blood. If the killer was telling us, via the precepts, that they objected to the way Linda and Roger had behaved, perhaps strangulation was their way of 'snuffing out' their actions? Literally killing off their beliefs by taking oxygen and blood away from them?

After a cup of tea, I tried again to sleep but images of strangulation kept creeping into my mind. In the pre- and post-midnight hours, my thoughts returned continually to Haniya. My gut instinct *still* insisted that her death was related to both murders – except we'd not been able to get round the fact that *nothing* connected Roger to Haniya, and her death *hadn't* been suspicious. The post-mortem had stated unequivocally that it had been suicide. So who had the killer targeted for precept number one? Would they return to the first precept when they were through with the others? What was I missing?

Perhaps Briscall and Dan were right, and I was banging away at Haniya's death because of Sabbir's suicide? Perhaps the link was nothing more than the fact the second precept referred to Linda taking Haniya's decision away from her? Yet, however intangible it felt, I couldn't shift the sense that all three deaths were linked. I checked the clock on my bedside table: 3.20 a.m. If I wasn't asleep by now, I might as well get up.

I had a sudden urge to visit the bridge. To pay my respects, I told myself. But deep down, I knew I was hoping to figure out once and for all why Haniya's suicide was bothering me so much.

The flat was bitterly cold. I pulled on layers of clothes, wound my scarf round my neck several times, stuffed Sabbir's tatty volume of Michael Ondaatje poetry in my pocket and pushed my hands into gloves. It wasn't snowing but the cold shimmered. Even inside the flat, my warm breath curled in feathers in front of me.

As I began walking along the canal path to Mile End Road, in my peripheral vision I caught an outline, a shape, in the shadows where the weeds and vegetation met the wall. But as I moved, so did the light. The shape seemed to billow in the breeze and disintegrate in front of my eyes. Having lived beside the canal for ten years, I wasn't easily spooked or given to imagining things. But there was something about this shape that looked like a human figure. And I was sure I could smell Golden Virginia.

Dad's tobacco.

In a nanosecond, the smell pulled me back twenty years, and a shiver ran over my whole body. I was tired; imagining things after talking to Jaz. Dad wasn't the only person to use Golden Virginia for roll-ups, for goodness' sake. I shone my torch on the spot where the shape had been. Nothing. Only grass and weeds, and a few pieces of newspaper, tumbling in the wind. It was just a lie that had been created by the light.

Five minutes later I was on Mile End Road and walking up to the Green Bridge. I remembered its opening in 2000. The locals quickly nicknamed it the Banana Bridge on account of the yellow paint along its length. It crossed the busy Mile End Road, and linked the two parts of the eighty-acre Mile End Park. And rather than the bridge simply being a concrete walkway, it had been landscaped with grass, plants, trees and benches. Soon I was walking up the path that led from the crossroads at Mile End tube station to the top of the bridge. On a clear day the view was lovely. In the early hours of the January morning, it wasn't cloudy but the moon was a slither and the sky was as dark as a cave. Glad of my layers, I followed the street lamps up to the top of the bridge. The exact spot was marked by a few flowers and cards, a fraction of the number left at the school. Someone had tied a fluffy teddy to the railings and beneath it a tiny silver frame held a photograph of Haniya with a young man. Beneath the image were the words:

If only things could have been different.
I love you, Roman xx.

This was the Polish boy that Farhan mentioned. So, he was around.

I reminded myself why I was there: to pay respects to a girl who had died. It was the right spot to read the poem I'd read at Sabbir's funeral. Just as I'd done it for him, I wanted to do the same for Haniya and for anyone else who'd been forced into taking their lives.

When I finished, I looked down, facing west, towards the church and Stepney. Haniya had chosen the westbound side of the bridge to jump off. I turned round to check the eastbound side. Cars could

268

approach the bridge from all three directions of the crossroads at Mile End tube. Had Haniya chosen the other side so anyone driving under the bridge from Bow wouldn't see her on top? It was a horrible thought. And seemed likely given the driver had swerved to avoid her.

The police report emphasised how much time she'd spent planning her suicide: sourcing strong sailing rope to hang herself with; carefully calculating the length required so it would be a long drop rather than a suspension hanging, but not so long she'd hit the ground. With 75,000 cars passing under the bridge every day, she'd presumably chosen 4 a.m. as the time likely to have the least amount of traffic. How must she have felt when she was looking this information up? It made me feel sick. Whatever people said, this *wasn't* a cry for help. It *wasn't* hysteria or point-making. This was a conscious, considered act that she'd wanted to result in her death. If only someone had protected her, things might have been very different.

Still facing west, I tried to imagine the procedure she would have gone through. Had she looked down and seen the road below? Once her neck hit the noose she'd tied, death would've been almost instantaneous. With the noose knot positioned at the left side of her neck, under the jaw, as the forensic report described, the torque on the neck at the bottom of the drop would have dislocated the axis and severed the spinal cord in one *snap*. The only consolation was the speed of death. With blood pressure dropping to zero within a second, Haniya would've lost consciousness very quickly. Had she known all this when she jumped?

I remembered the complete unravelling I'd experienced when I received the call saying Sabbir had killed himself; when they told me he had doused himself with petrol and set himself alight. Had Haniya's parents felt remorse when they realised their actions had driven their daughter to kill herself? Or had they felt ashamed? How tragic to end your life because of what someone else thinks. And because they *insist* they know what's best for you.

A deep sadness clawed at me, tearing my insides like desperate fingers. My whole body felt weak. Haniya, Linda, Roger Allen, Sabbir,

Dad, Mum. It was impossible to separate what I felt about whom. I folded to the ground; cried out as gravel cut into my palms and knees. Tears obscured my view and streamed down my cheeks. As I sobbed on the ground, I felt a loosening of my grief, a releasing of years of loss that I couldn't begin to put into words.

I sat on the ground until no more tears came.

I re-read Roman's message. If only someone had helped her, it seemed to say. With a sinking feeling in my stomach I realised that, in various ways, Linda, Roger, Farhan, Shari and Neil, and the Patels, were *all* responsible for Haniya's death. They'd all failed to protect her and, in so doing, had extinguished any hope she may have had.

That was it.

The missing link.

In the killer's mind, Haniya's death was the first murder. The first precept, *I shall abstain from causing harm*, applied to her. As I teased out the connections, exhilaration flooded through me. But quickly, panic set in. We now had three precepts in order. The next was: *I shall abstain from false speech*. Rozina, Roger and Peter had all held Asad Farhan in low regard. If anyone was guilty of false speech, he was. We knew the killer was targeting everyone they considered had helped to cover up wrong-doing at the school. If my hunch was right, it meant two things. Firstly, Haniya's boyfriend had a strong motive for killing Linda and Roger. Secondly, and more urgently, Farhan was going to be the killer's fourth victim if I didn't get to him first.

Tuesday

The precept says:

panatipata veramani sikkhapadam samadiyami
I shall abstain from causing harm

Poor Haniya.

You were the last straw, and were where it *all* started.

Buddhists are encouraged to avoid causing harm to all sentient beings. They see the suffering of others as their own and are encouraged to help.

You relied on others to protect you, didn't you? But the people who should have kept you safe were busy looking after their own interests. A Buddhist would argue that failing to protect those in our charge is allowing them to come to harm.

You may have taken your own life but they killed you. They *all* did. They knew about the safeguarding failures and they knew how unhappy you were – yet they looked the other way. They might as well have handed you the rope to hang yourself, put your neck in the noose and given you a shove.

You weren't the first to suffer because of their negligence but I had to make sure that you'd be the *last*. You'll understand that, won't you?

Tuesday – Steve

'Have you seen what Suzie James has put on the *Stepney Gazette*'s Facebook page?' Andrea handed Steve her phone and plonked herself down next to him in the staffroom.

On the social media site, a fluorescent yellow digital clock counted down the hours and minutes until the petition was reinstated.

'She's posted a reminder on Twitter too.'

Steve mumbled through a mouthful of bread. It was 7.30 a.m. and he was finishing a sausage sandwich he'd bought from a café, about to head off to his form room to do some preparation before morning registration.

'Oh. It's a man. I've just heard.'

Steve swallowed. 'Who is?'

'The temporary head. He's a deputy at Whitechapel Boys.'

Their colleagues were arriving, and tuning in to the conversation. The unsolved murders were still weighing on people's minds, but everyone was looking forward to paying tribute to Linda and Roger at the assembly that evening.

'Name's Richard Williams. He's coming to the memorial assembly this evening. Shari told me in the loo. Someone's bound to know him. You know what teaching's like.'

Around them, the staff chatted excitedly about what a new head would mean for Mile End High School. And *all* of them.

Steve was teaching Jehangir and Sanchez first lesson, and today the prospect resulted in his guts crunching a little less. Last night, for the first time since Linda's murder, Steve had got to sleep at a civilised hour and hadn't dreamed about Lucy, or Linda's dead body. This morning he'd woken feeling like he'd slept off a mass of fatigue, and was beginning to release his regrets. And for the first time this morning he hadn't thought about Midhurst when he was travelling to school.

'What d'you reckon will happen to Shari and Neil?' asked Tessa Black, one of the Maths teachers.

'Goodness knows. Depends what comes out in the wash, I guess.' Andrea placed her mug on the coffee table. 'Shall we check what posts have been advertised?' She pointed at the *Times Educational Supplement* on the table. 'I think it's a good thing we're getting a new head. New blood, new broom. I hope so, anyway. They'll have to replace Roger as well.'

'Yeah, who's going to apply for senior management then?' asked Moira, her beady eyes glinting under the harsh lights.

Mutterings went round the group, and they exchanged curious glances. School staff varied in their feelings about applying for senior management. Teaching commitments reduced significantly when you left the coalface of the classroom for meeting room chairs.

'*I've* decided *I'm* going to,' Andrea said, smiling and looking proud. She took a swig from her mug. 'Totted up last night. Seven years I've been here. Thought I'd give it a go. I'm not going anywhere. Why not?'

The mutterings stopped.

'*You?*'

'Yes, Moira. Me. Why don't you apply? Best man wins?'

Moira harrumphed, and flicked her curtain hair. 'You'll soon be one of *them*. Forgetting what it's like to be an ordinary teacher and —'

'You'll be fabulous, Andrea,' said Tessa. 'Moira's been chewing lemons, as usual. It'll be a good combination to have a new head from outside, and staff promoted from within the school.'

Cheers of encouragement bounced round the group.

'You kept that quiet,' Steve said, nudging Andrea.

'Sorry. I was still mulling it over this morning on the way to school.' She laughed. 'Shari told me something else in the loo…'

'What?'

Round them, their colleagues were busy discussing the new head.

'Zoe Smart has decided not to come back to school. It's not been formalised yet but —'

'How come?'

'Her husband's accepted a research post in Hong Kong. They're off to be ex-pats for a few years. Keep it under your hat but I'd guess that will mean they'll offer you her job once everything has settled down.'

'Cool. I don't know what to say.' He grinned. It would give him a bit of stability. He was pleased some of the staff had asked him to help at the memorial assembly later that evening. It seemed a sign that their suspicions were falling away and they were beginning to accept him.

Steve was checking his emails on his phone. 'There's an e-mail here from Maria O'Connor's social worker. Maria's given a statement to the police about the beating from her mother.'

'That's a relief. I taught her GCSE English. She's a nice kid.'

'She's in temporary foster care.' Steve recalled how terrified Maria had been about going home and getting another beating from her mother. 'I wonder what'll happen to the Turkish boyfriend?' Steve was relieved she was safe; pleased with how he'd handled things. But he wished Maria's future was more certain. After foster care, what would happen to her? Would this involvement from social services be enough to stop her parents from getting physical with her again the next time she stepped out of line?

Steve got up. It was time to hit the lesson plans. 'See you later,' he said to Andrea.

En route to his classroom, he passed the open doors of other forms. Was he imagining it or was there more noise than usual? Chatter and . . .? It was still early too.

Down the corridor a commotion greeted him. Yells and screaming reverberated from his form room. It wasn't the sort of shouts people make when they're scared. This was more . . . more —

'That's *disgusting*,' came a female voice.

He quickened his pace.

Inside the classroom, the kids were huddles of hair, faces and coats, clustered round one of their peers with a phone. Screaming, clapping each other on the back and shouting orders at each other.

'Urgh. *Gross*,' said Becky. Her hand was clamped over her mouth, her facial muscles clenched in disgust.

The sight of Steve prompted whispers. Scurrying. And some of them stuffed their phones away in panic, cussing under their breath, all the while trying to look normal.

'Sir, you need to see this.' Sanchez held his mobile out.

The room went silent.

Stood completely still.

Then a phone vibrated. And another pinged a Facebook notification.

Around the room, gasps and expletives burst like fireworks.

Steve hurried over to see what the kids were looking at.

Sanchez was waving his mobile in the air.

'Oh my God. The blood . . .' Becky's voice was full of horror. 'The puffy flesh. Eew. That looks like *chopped liver*.'

Steve took the phone and looked at the screen. It was a collage of images, posted on Facebook, taken in poor light and from different angles. Close-up shots of someone lying on the snow, in a pool of watery blood. The neck had been sliced open. Above and below the slit line, globules of neck tissue spilled over, shiny, and oozing with blood.

Jehangir stared at Steve. 'I know who that is, sir.'

Tuesday – Maya

An accident at Limehouse had put the A13 into gridlock. I took Dan's call on the hands-free.

We were too late.

Farhan was dead.

And gory images of his body had been shared all over the internet, in groups on Snapchat, WhatsApp and Facebook.

I slammed my left hand down on the passenger seat.

It was a blue light dash from Bow to Shadwell. As I drove, all I could think of was that if I had only realised the pattern earlier, I could have prevented a third murder. Was Haniya's boyfriend our serial killer? Until we found him, we wouldn't know.

Even in the early morning light, the tower blocks of Shadwell Park Estate were shrouded in shadows. The three-storey, pre-fabricated buildings were once the flagships of planning committees and architects but now structural decay accompanied their tatty appearance. Behind them, as each one systematically received a demolition order, cranes carried the steel frames of the replacement constructions in their longs arms.

Dan greeted me at the car with a face that would curdle milk. 'That bloody tyke posted those photos on every Facebook group he could find.' He stuffed protective clothing into my arms. 'And WhatsApped them to all his buddies. He didn't even call the police. Left that to someone else.' Anger rippled his face.

'Let's hope they didn't move the body. Who *did* call it in?' I'd never seen Dan so wound up.

'A young mum found the body on the way to the childminder with her two kids. She drops them off at seven a.m. every day and had lost their dog. Her four-year-old daughter found the terrier, licking away at Farhan's frozen blood.' He kicked at the smattering of white on the ground. 'You wait 'til I get my hands on whoever it was. It was immature and irresponsible to photograph the body and leave it. Quite apart from that little girl, the delay is going to cost us critical forensic evidence.'

'A four-year-old? Poor little girl. Where are they?'

'Gone to hospital. She had blood all over her.' Dan was right to be annoyed.

At the crime scene perimeter, the national news crews had gathered. Reporters were speaking earnestly into fluffy microphones, while gangly tripods held huge cameras steady. I did a double take when I saw that the Sky reporter, Carly, was interviewing Mr Patel.

'What's he doing here? He told me he was fed up with the media and that Farhan had been threatening them.'

'I'll nab him when they're finished,' said Dan. 'We've launched a manhunt for Roman Maleski. The tech guys have checked his social media accounts and he started using them again about a week ago. He's definitely in the area so we should have him soon.'

'Let's hope so.'

The CSIs were trying to preserve the crime scene before the snow started again. There was no chance of a thaw in this temperature. I pulled the forensic suit on.

'Do we know what Farhan was doing in Sniffers Alley.'

He laughed. 'That what it's called? We've plenty of those in Sydney too.'

'I wonder if it's a coincidence that the Patels live in Shadwell? The Limehouse side, but nevertheless . . . How long's the body been here?'

'Dr Clark suspects all night.'

'Where's our happy snapper?' I looked about.

'We haven't identified him yet. The tech guys are on it. I can't wait to give him a bollocking, believe me, not to mention find out what he saw.'

I could hear snippets of what Mr Patel was saying. Compared to the aggression he'd shown me at their flat, this was an all-out charm offensive. Was it virtue signalling or was he genuinely trying to help?

'Find out where he was from eleven p.m. last night,' I said to Dan. 'I've figured out who the first precept relates to. Haniya.' I hadn't had the chance to tell the team yet so I filled him in.

'Oh my God,' Dan yelled. 'It was under our noses all the time. And you were right.' He let out a whoop. 'For the killer, it all started with Haniya. Then Linda, Roger and Farhan. It makes perfect sense.'

'Speaking of Farhan . . . let's get this over with, shall we?'

The alley ran between a two-storey community centre with a basketball court next door, and another tower block. It was a popular cut-through. I made my way over to the common approach path. The CSIs had secured a canvas shield across the alley and over the area where Farhan's body lay. With the height of the surrounding buildings, and the weather shield, flood lights had been rigged up. Beneath the canvas, the lights were shining onto the snow, not just illuminating Farhan's body but accentuating its colours. He was lying on his side in a pool of black blood. His left cheek was flat to the soil, the other faced upwards.

I approached the body. 'Is all the blood from his neck?'

'Most of it.' Dr Clark was recording temperatures and assessing rigor. 'The wire was cranked tight with a stick. It's cut deep into the neck tissue. It's still in place. Barely visible, of course.'

At its margins, blood had seeped into the snow, altering its pure white to a watery, translucent red. His left arm lay beneath him while the right one curled around his blood-matted head. Above the ligature mark, his skin was puffy and red; below it was lighter.

I inched closer to get a better look at his throat and neck. 'Has the killer changed MO?'

'I'd say it's more of an escalation.' Dr Clark came over. 'It's a similar medical mechanism. Vascular obstruction. A ligature stops blood flow to the heart by cutting the jugular veins, and blood flow to the head by occlusion of the carotid artery. Manual strangulation obstructs the same veins and arteries, just by compression.' He pointed to the neck area. 'Reduced blood flow means reduced oxygen. It's still hypoxia.'

'I wonder why he strangled Linda and Roger manually, but used a wire for Asad?' I was thinking aloud. 'Is a wire quicker? Obviously the alley is public so there was more danger of being seen.'

'Generally, it's quicker when used with a crank. And wire like that cuts into the flesh like a knife through cake.'

'Yeuch. I —'

'Sorry to interrupt.' Dan had came over. 'The killer's used the same signature. More Buddhist ethics.' He showed me his phone. 'As we suspected, it translates as: "I shall abstain from false speech".'

'How did they know he'd be here? In this alley, last night?' Thoughts were darting.

'Perhaps the killer arranged to meet Farhan?' Dan replied.

'Maya, you might want to see this.' Dr Clark was still recording measurements on his clipboard. 'It's not obvious because he's lying on it but for the purposes of warning his relatives . . .'

'What's that?'

'His corpse has been attacked . . .'

I stared at him.

'. . . by vermin. In sub-zero temperatures like these, they're hungry. From the pattern of the teeth marks, I'd say it was foxes. They've chewed his left cheek off.'

Tuesday

The precept says:

musavada veramani sikkhapadam samadiyani
I shall abstain from false speech

You've always been a liar, haven't you? How you got away with it, I'll never understand. It was as though you lived by a different moral code to everyone else. There was the truth, and there was the one you constructed and reconstructed to suit the situation. I often wondered how you kept track of all your lies. You know what bothers me most? That you never cared about anything at all.

A Buddhist would say that skilful communication is truthful, beneficial and kind.

At least we'll be safe from you now.

Tuesday – Maya

I left the crime scene boiling with frustration. Feeling that we were on the verge of a breakthrough was meaningless when we had a third murder and still didn't have a firm suspect. We had to review our facts. First, though, I needed to advise Neil and Shari on the next level of safety precautions.

As I drove from Shadwell to Stepney, I discussed what we knew over the hands-free with Dan.

'Mr Patel says he was at home in bed all night, and his wife alibies him,' he told me.

'Very convenient.'

'So many people have motives, but other than Roman, none might want to kill all three staff members. I keep feeling that we've overlooked something.'

'The Patel files confirm that the police spoke to Linda about the marriage and she referred them to Asad Farhan. Linda is on record saying she deeply regretted Haniya's death but hadn't known how distressed she was. I need to re-interview Rozina. Didn't she tell us she'd explained to Linda precisely how unhappy Haniya was, and begged her to intervene?'

*

When I arrived at Mile End High School, Neil was in his office.

'I'll take it from here, thanks,' I said to the teacher who'd escorted me from reception. I knocked on the door and pushed it open. 'Could I have a word with you, please?' I said as I entered.

Neil looked up when he heard me. He was sitting at his desk, a spreadsheet open on his monitor. A few feet away, on a chair, with a mug of tea in his hand, was Rich, the caretaker.

'Yes, of course. I . . . Do you want to have a seat?' He indicated to Rich to hop it.

'I'll stand, thanks.' I waited for the door to close behind the caretaker, and informed him of Farhan's death. 'Late last night.' I was studying his reaction.

'*Dead?*' His hand went to his mouth briefly and then he snatched up his mobile. 'I need to —'

'Put the phone down, please.'

He lobbed it on the desk petulantly.

'Where were you last night from eleven p.m. onwards?'

'In bed 'til six a.m, and here by seven-thirty. Why?'

'Anyone verify you were at home the whole night?'

'My *wife.*' He rubbed his chin. 'Hold on. Am I a suspect?'

'Routine enquiries, that's all.' I moved on to Haniya Patel's suicide. 'What action did Linda take when she learned that Haniya was possibly facing a forced marriage?' I looked him straight in the eye.

Neil's cheeks coloured. He dropped his biro and drew breath. '*Action?*'

I noticed the annoyance in his body language and tone of voice. 'Yes.' I'd thought carefully how to phrase the question so as not to lead any particular answer.

Neil removed his glasses and began wiping them. 'She discussed it several times with Shari, Roger and myself, and she enlisted the advice of Asad Farhan and a couple of other respected individuals. We reviewed the relevant legislation and . . .' He stopped.

'And?'

He replaced his glasses.

The door opened and Shari burst in, eyes darting. 'Mark in English told me you were here.' Her voice was jumpy. She looked at Neil and, sensing she'd interrupted something, shifted her gaze to me. 'Everything alright?'

'Mr Sanderson?' I had my eyes locked on his face.

'We decided there wasn't sufficient evidence of coercion to hand the matter over to the FMU. Linda understood Haniya's feelings about Roman but we all felt it would alienate the Muslim community if we were seen to condemn a marriage that the girl's parents thought was in everyone's interests.'

'Despite the fact forced marriages have been *illegal* in this country since 2014? And carry a jail term of up to seven years?'

'Yes . . .'

'You *are* familiar with the Anti-Social Behaviour, Crime and Policing Act, I take it? So what *action* did she take?'

Shari had clearly got the drift of the conversation. She didn't speak but her watchful eyes and raised height made me wonder what she was thinking.

'We spent a long time discussing what to do. Asad assured us that it was an arranged marriage, not a forced one, and we agreed that the best course of action was to let him have one final go at persuading the family to call off the marriage if it wasn't what Haniya wanted.'

'How was that decision taken?'

'I can assure you, Inspector, that it was not as unanimous as that,' Shari spoke up. 'We did *not* agree about whether to involve the FMU and we *didn't* agree about how Haniya's marriage should be dealt with.' She glared at Neil. 'Asad was brought in and we took two votes.'

'But he wasn't part of the management team.'

'No. *That* wasn't my idea either.' I'd never heard her speak with such conviction. She must've had a change of heart since Saturday.

'Was that what you were arguing about in the restaurant on Friday?'

'Yes. Sadly, I was out-voted. I wanted the FMU involved so that the matter could be handled impartially and thoroughly. I suspected that Asad had no intention of doing that.' She fanned her cheeks and loosened her *hijab*. 'When it came to the second vote, Roger wavered at first but finally sided with Linda, Neil and Asad to let Asad deal with the situation as he saw fit.'

Neil was squirming in his seat.

'Both were a mistake in my opinion,' Shari added.

'I'm sure Haniya wasn't the first pupil here to be suspected of facing a forced marriage. Surely Linda knew about sources of support for girls in this situation?'

'Of course she did,' Neil chipped in, looking indignant. 'It's Tower Hamlets, for goodness sake.'

'Where does Rozina come into all of this?'

Shari thumped down on the other spare seat. 'Like me, Rozina wasn't sure whether Haniya's parents were arranging the marriage or forcing it. Haniya was determined that she wanted to be with the Polish boy, Roman, and was extremely distressed. Then, all of a sudden, she clammed up and refused to talk to anyone. It was when she came back from Pakistan. Rozina said she was sure the Patels had threatened Haniya, and Haniya refused to talk to her. Rozina wanted Linda to intervene and she was extremely angry Linda wouldn't.'

'Angry enough to kill Linda?'

'Of course not. I've known Rozina all her life. She's a lovely girl. Her mother is one of my best friends. We're from the same part of Sylhet. Rozina was in the staffroom with all of us having lunch. She isn't a murderer. She was extremely fond of Linda.'

'Was Rozina in the staffroom the *entire* time you were having lunch?'

Shari screwed her eyes up as she tried to think back. 'As far as I know. But the first day of term is always hectic and Roger was off sick and Linda was in her office.'

I knew it would have been recorded if anyone had left the staffroom. 'While I have you both, I need to warn you that we have now had three murders, all senior staff at the school. That means I need to advise you of the ways in which you can keep yourselves safe.' Once I'd done that, I explained what the police would do to help.

The whole time Neil glared at me, and Shari sat sniffing, dabbing her eyes with a tissue.

Once I'd finished, I put on my chirpiest voice. 'I may see you both at this evening's memorial assembly.'

'*Excellent*,' Neil parried. 'We're getting a new head, a temporary one. He's coming along this evening to meet the staff.'

'Yes, I know. I'm pleased.' The school needed someone fresh to take over from Linda. To take the school forwards so it didn't sink back towards special measures. 'I will need to report the possible protection failure regarding Haniya's marriage. Linda, Roger and Asad are dead, so that leaves you two. And anyone else who was involved.'

Shari gasped and clamped her hand over her mouth. 'Oh my goodness. Will that mean . . .?' She looked at Neil, who was glowering, his face coloured with fury.

'You will need to tell the authorities exactly what you've told me. I assume the voting was minuted?' The question was intended for Shari.

Relief spread over her face. 'Oh yes. Roger took the minutes and Rozina typed them up.'

Tuesday – Maya

Ten minutes later I'd intercepted Rozina, and taken her into a room to re-interview her. She scrunched into a ball on the seat, chewing her cheek. The make-up round her eyes had smudged and she said she wasn't feeling well.

'The day Linda was killed, when you were all having lunch, did you leave the staffroom at any point?' I asked.

'I've been asked this already. I went to the loo. Then came straight back.' The frown altered her features.

'How long were you gone?'

'How long does it take to go to the toilet? They were about to begin the afternoon training sessions. I literally went to the loo, washed my hands and came back. Someone else went at the same time. One of the science teachers. Yvonne Bray. We were chatting and came back together.' Rozina fiddled with her nose stud and set it in place.

I made a note of the name. 'And you used the toilet on the ground floor, did you?'

'Yup. It's to the left of the staffroom.'

'After you went to the loo, are you absolutely sure you didn't go anywhere else?'

'To kill Linda, do you mean? *No*. Ask Yvonne. We left the staffroom together and came back together. She told me her son had gone into anaphylactic shock on Boxing Day and they'd had to take him to hospital.'

'I also need to ask you about Haniya's boyfriend.'

'*Roman?*'

'We gather he's back in the area. Have you heard from him?'

'No.' The reply came a bit too quickly.

'Are you sure? What about Facebook?'

She shook her head. 'Don't use it much.'

'Is there anything you haven't told us about Haniya?'

She let out a deep sigh of exasperation. She rubbed her eyes and slouched forwards in her seat. 'Look. I was furious about how Haniya's marriage was dealt with. *Yes*, I thought the school should intervene, just as I did when Ella Hayes got pregnant. *Yes*, I'm disillusioned with Islam. *No*, it's not a phase or whatever other bullshit they're probably telling you. But I am not mad enough to kill someone over Islam. Not Linda or Roger or Farhan. How would me *killing* people help Haniya now she's dead? There are other things I'll do to help. The charity, Karma Nirvana, is always advertising for volunteers. If I go to prison, how can I help other people?' She raised her hands in frustration to either side of her temples. 'Linda was a good head teacher. She cared about the school, and the students and staff. It did strike me she was looking after her own interests rather than Haniya's.' She paused, and I got the sense she was weighing up whether to tell me something important. 'I had to type up the minutes. I know how they all voted. Farhan should never have been brought in on the decision. If Roger had stuck to his guns, and Linda kept her word, things could have been very different for Haniya. With Shari's vote, Neil and Farhan would have been out-numbered.' She paused. 'Linda didn't trust that creep, Farhan, any more than Shari and I. She promised me she wouldn't vote for him to deal with the Patels but she did. I was so disappointed in her.'

Tuesday – Maya

It was sod's law that when Talis' call finally came through, I was in the toilet.

'Rahman.' I lodged my mobile between my ear and my shoulder, and wiped my wet hands on my trousers. The hand dryer was blasting air into the room, so I shuffled towards the door to hear him.

He was downstairs, in reception, with the files.

I hurried to meet him in the lobby.

Two minutes later, Talis appeared from the lift, wearing another snazzy suit, his brow and cheeks tight. He nodded his greeting.

'Please come through.' I led him into a meeting room and shut the door. 'How did you get on?' I gestured to the chairs.

He sat down, clutching a document case to his chest. 'Three things.' His poker face was superior to Dan's by a mile. 'Gibson and Sanderson deleting files. Money from Sanderson to Gibson. But Sanderson corrupt.' He released his parcel and slapped a wodge of A4 paper on my desk in a plastic file. 'It's all here.' He pointed at the papers. 'You can read.' He passed over a USB. 'And backup. Some photograph too.'

I grabbed up the pack of papers. 'Thank you so much.' I patted the plastic wallet. 'Were you able to recover all her deleted files?'

'*Ja*. On every occasion was either him or her log in. No-one else.'

Then he was off his chair and speeding towards the door before I was on my feet.

'I won't bother showing you out then,' I said to the room. The man was a whirling dervish.

I spread the documents out on the table and collated them into the topics Talis had mentioned. The more I saw and read, the more I realised what had been going on. And as the threads began to join up, I sat with my head in my hands.

Poor Linda.

How much anguish she'd experienced. How much had Peter known?

Five minutes later, having skimmed the documents for the big picture, I gathered the team for an emergency briefing. Briscall leaned against the window ledge, arms folded and chin jutting.

'Gibson and Sanderson and money,' Alexej repeated. 'So, Sanderson has been siphoning off money from the school's accounts and using it to bribe Linda into turning a blind eye to forced marriages and teenage pregnancies. Didn't Rozina say he enjoyed swanning round the country giving talks about how to run a successful multi-cultural school?'

'Going on average pay for inner London deputy heads . . .' Dan ran his finger down a column on his screen, 'Sanderson will be earning around sixty-five grand, plus another ten for his extra responsibilities. That's a load of bucks to lose if the school went under.'

'And Linda's been using the money to help fund a refuge for girls who've got pregnant or whose families are forcing marriage?'

'Yup,' I said. 'Until recently, when Sanderson decides he won't make any more payments, thereby dropping Linda – who's taken on responsibilities – in the shit.'

Dan was summarising the main findings, grouped them around mugshots of the people concerned and projected them onto the wall from his iPad. 'The first payment corresponds with the date Ella Hayes got pregnant last year.'

'Perhaps it's her way of compensating?' I said. 'Atonement of sorts. If she had her own baby adopted, she's bound to be sympathetic to others in a similar position, and feel guilty about looking the other way.'

Alexej was rubbing his chin. 'Do we think that gives Sanderson a motive to kill Linda, Allen and Farhan?'

'I'd value everyone's input on that.'

Briscall tutted loudly.

'The emails between the two of them aren't pleasant.' I handed him the printouts that Talis had given me. Dan had the USB stick. 'I will send them to you all once we've finished. Basically, Sanderson wanted Linda *not* to jeopardise the school's standing or alienate the Muslim community. It's unclear whether he was thinking about his own career and interests, or the school. Linda wasn't happy about it. She said she would only keep quiet if he helped to fund a refuge to help girls like Ella and Haniya – so they could get pregnancy advice and medical treatment, and support from agencies dealing with forced marriages. When Sanderson said he couldn't afford the payments any longer, she said she'd need to go public about the refuge to secure the funding to keep it going. They had a huge row about it.'

'I'd say that's quite a motive.' Alexej sat back in his seat.

'There are numerous deleted texts from Peter encouraging Linda to consider her career, to look at the big picture, to focus on what benefits the majority . . .'

Around the room the team were nodding.

'It's Sanderson,' Briscall's voice boomed from the back of the room. 'The killer is Sanderson.'

I groaned inwardly. Typical knee-jerk reaction.

'I'm not sure it's him.' Dan shot him a silencing look.

'I *am*. We need to arrest Sanderson.' He approached the table and jabbed his forefinger at the bursar's photograph, spilling water from our cups. 'And let's get this case put to bed. We've wasted far too much time on these wild goose chases.' He made a sweeping gesture with his arm.

Everyone stared at him.

I gathered my thoughts. 'Ian, we need to rule out all other explanations before doing anything. We can't just charge into the school and arrest a staff member. It's not the Wild West.' I sucked in a deep breath. 'We need to be certain we've got the right person, and if there's insufficient evidence, the CPS won't prosecute.'

We were all tired.

I focused my attention away from Briscall.

'It's clear as day. It's Sanderson.' Briscall's voice was insistent, devoid of doubt. He was pacing across the room now.

'You've said that, Ian.' It was hard to keep the irritation from my voice. 'Can you be patient, please? You aren't the only person who wants these murders solved. Sanderson might have had a motive for killing Linda but why would he kill Roger Allen and Asad Farhan?'

'I thought you said Roger Allen was obsessed with Linda? Maybe Roger started getting heavy with Sanderson, wanting to protect her or something? And Sanderson had enough?'

'Unless Sanderson and Shari lied,' said Dan, 'they both testified that they were in the staffroom when Linda was murdered.' He faced me. 'Alright to use your computer?' Dan jumped onto my chair and was tapping at the keyboard. 'These emails *are* pretty damning of Neil Sanderson.'

'Exactly. It's him. I know it.' Briscall was like a toy you couldn't switch off.

'It's all circumstantial evidence,' I said. 'Sanderson was annoyed with Linda but that's all the emails show.'

'I say we pick him up this evening at the memorial assembly.' Briscall had stopped pacing and was standing now, facing the whole team. Hands on hips.

'And *I* say we need to go back over his statements about where he was on the occasion of all three murders, and double-check his alibis.'

Everyone's eyes were on us.

Briscall's arms were folded across a puffed out chest. He had pulled himself up to his full six foot, towering over me.

'Ian, shall we . . .?' I stopped. It wasn't worth it. 'You know what? You're the DCI, so if that's what you want to do, you go ahead, but I want it on record that I don't agree.' I focused on a point on the wall while my breathing slowed. 'Guys, we'll leave it there. Dan, can you send the whole team Talis' documents and get someone to check Sanderson's whereabouts at the time of the murders?'

My chest was tight with tension. I inched over to the water cooler, trembling. Poured out a cup of cool liquid.

Briscall's eyes were bulging. The veins on his neck protruded, swollen with annoyance. He was still now, glaring at me. 'If you won't go to the school to arrest Sanderson this evening, I will.'

Tuesday – Maya

It was mid-afternoon and we were all absorbing the revelations from Talis Seglins.

'D'you reckon it was blackmail?' I asked Dan. Determined to solve the murders, I'd pushed Briscall's outburst to the back of my mind. The knowledge that Neil Sanderson had bought Linda's silence made me furious, but given what Rozina had said about him having a 'side', and taking the credit for the school's successes, it wasn't a complete shock.

Dan looked up from the hundreds of recovered emails, his pale face full of concentration.

'And if so, did Linda *ask* for money to keep quiet about the marriages or did Sanderson *offer* it for her silence?' Thoughts rattled through my mind. Did it actually matter? Transactions had taken place, to which both were party.

He shook his head. 'No idea.' He continued to look at me, his expression pensive. 'Is Briscall really planning to go to the memorial assembly and arrest Sanderson?'

I sighed, perplexed. 'I honestly don't know. I doubt it. I can't remember when he last arrested anyone but he's more interested in targets and outcomes at the moment than solving crimes. One minute he wants an arrest, the next he wants the school closed. Now he's chasing an arrest again.' I checked the time. 'We do need to bring Sanderson in for questioning but, given the memorial assembly for Linda and Roger starts in a couple of hours, I don't want to ruin it for everyone. I was thinking about visiting Peter Gibson in a minute, before he goes to the school. If I go to the assembly too, I can give Peter a lift – make sure he gets there okay – and bring Sanderson back with me once it has finished.'

'If Briscall's not already —'

'*Exactly.* This is assuming common sense will —'

'*Inspector?* Inspector Rahman?' A uniformed officer was shouting across the room and pointing at me. 'Roman Maleski is here with his parents. He's asking to speak to you.'

Tuesday – Maya

Roman Maleski's parents looked exactly like the photographs I'd seen of them, but Roman was unrecognisable. I tried to contain my shock as Eryk and Marianna helped their emaciated son along the police station corridor. They'd both perfected the art of matching their walking speed to their son's shuffle, and they held his twig-like arms with feather-lightness, painfully aware, as was I, that a slip or a knock could snap a bone. From behind, Roman's hips protruded through his coat, square and unnatural. His shoulders weren't rounded; they were angular and the width of a young boy's.

'Rozina said you were asking about me,' Roman said when we got him seated. His voice was weak and his English had no accent.

'I'm assuming you've heard about the murders at the school?'

'Of course. It's all people are talking about.' Skin lay like clingfilm on his cheekbones, and his scalp was visible through wisps of mousey hair. 'I had nothing to do with them, if that's what you're wondering. They've only just started to allow me home.'

'Home?'

'I've been in hospital for the last six weeks.' Roman paused to gather his energy. 'I'm recovering, but I'm in a wheelchair most of the time. I can't *get* anywhere on my own. I'm not allowed to *be* alone at the moment.'

I'd guessed as much. 'Oh Roman, I'm so sorry.' This was awful.

Eryk sat beside his son. His grey eyes brimmed with concern. An ironed shirt clung to a stocky frame, and he was patting his wife's hand reassuringly.

Marianna followed his strokes with her eyes, as though they helped to keep her emotions in check. 'Roman's been through enough. It's shameful what people —'

'It's okay, Mum.' A faint smile was all he seemed to have energy for. 'I've done nothing wrong.'

'It's *not* okay, Roman.' Marianna pulled her hand free and stood up. She swiped at the air angrily and turned to face me. 'The things people said about our son. About our whole family. *Chrystus.*' She continued to mutter under her breath.

'Why couldn't people just let us be together?' Roman said. 'I still can't believe she's gone.' Months of agony had dulled the whites of his bulging eyes, and only broken blood vessels brought colour to their grey.

'Inspector, my wife and I told the police that Roman had disappeared because we wanted him to have some privacy.' Eryk's voice boomed round the small room. 'I'm an anaesthetist and I do a lot of work at private clinics. I know what it's like when journalists take long-range shots of people when they're ill. We wanted to protect our son.'

Their actions were understandable. 'We'll need to update your statements, Dr Maleski, and we'll need the details of your son's hospital to confirm where he's been. Hopefully, you won't be bothered too much after that and your son can get well.'

'It wasn't Roman's idea to lie to the police. It was *ours*. And it was he who wanted to come here today. When the police came round and —'

'*Dad.*'

Eryk and his wife had lied to uniformed officers earlier but their motives seemed clear. 'Under the circumstances, it's unlikely there will be any charges.' I turned to Roman and asked gently, 'Did someone put the teddy and the photograph on the bridge for you?'

His face softened. 'Mum helped me make the photograph and do the inscription. We chose the teddy together and my sister took them up to the bridge.' He glanced at his mother, who was leaning against the wall. 'If only things had been different,' he said. 'I'm lucky.' He gestured to his parents. 'All that's happened to me is I've lost five stone and fucked up my GCSE year. At least I'm still alive.'

And it was one of the saddest things I'd ever heard.

Tuesday – Maya

Half an hour later I was ringing the doorbell of the Gibson's house in Tredegar Square. An Asian man came to the door. He seemed familiar, although I couldn't place where from.

'DI Rahman,' I said, and showed my warrant.

'I'm Dr Khan.'

'Ah. You're the Gibsons' GP . . .'

'That's right.' His tone was friendly. 'I'm just leaving. Heading back for afternoon surgery. Peter is determined he wants to go to Linda's memorial assembly at the school this evening. I wanted to check he's fit to go.'

'Is he?'

'I think so.'

'If you're leaving, could I speak to you then? I can walk out with you. There's something I wanted to ask.'

'Sure, if it's quick. D'you want to come in for a minute? It's bitter out. I'll just finish up with Peter and collect my bag.'

I followed him into the house and along the hall to the lounge. Peter was on the sofa, rolling down his sleeve. A blood pressure machine was on the coffee table next to him, and some piano music tinkled in the background.

'How are you, Mr Gibson?' I asked. 'Just passing. Thought I'd pop in and check on you. See if you wanted a lift to the school.'

'That's very kind. Still a few dizzy spells and my memory's a bit hazy, but that's nothing new.' He buttoned up his cuffs and pulled his sweater back on. 'Alice is due any minute. We're going to discuss Linda's funeral and our eulogies. Linda wanted a cremation.'

'That's a lovely thing to do.'

'Yes. After that, Alice and I are going to the memorial assembly together.'

'I hope it goes well. I may see you there.' I was relieved to see Peter sounding more optimistic; pleased he wasn't going to the school alone. It would be a comfort for him and Alice to keep each other company.

Dr Khan and I left. A gust of wind whipped round the naked trees of Tredegar Square, sending leaves rustling over the tarmac. I pulled my woolly scarf round my neck. It was only 3 p.m. but dark had already started to close in while I was inside the house. In front of us, a dog walker was scuttling along behind a Labrador, a swathe of layers and urgency.

'There's a pub over there, Dr Khan. Can I buy you a quick coffee and pick your brain for five minutes? It's urgent or I wouldn't ask.'

The doctor pushed his sleeve up and checked his watch. 'I'll literally need to go in ten minutes, if that's long enough. Evening surgery starts at four and I've got calls to make.'

'It's over in that corner.' I pointed diagonally across the square. Over the tops of the trees a mist was starting to settle.

Once inside the Morgan Arms, I ordered two coffees and we grabbed seats at an empty table by the window. How different the place was in the daytime – fewer after-work drinks, more business lunches, mothers meeting up, and students bunking off lectures.

'I wanted to ask you about Peter.' I placed my coat and scarf on the chair next to us and sat down.

'If it's part of the investigation, fire away.' He folded his coat on top of mine and sunk into a chair.

'Peter mentioned dizziness. What's that about?'

'Something he's had for a few years.' He took a slurp of his coffee. 'We aren't sure if it's a middle ear issue or connected to his heart condition. His blood pressure is very low sometimes and he's had a number of falls. With Linda no longer around, we need to make sure he's safe in the house. Unfortunately, bereavement isn't good for cardiovascular problems.'

'In your opinion, do his health problems affect his ability to get out and about?'

'Most definitely. Recently, for example, he's been practically house-bound. But his condition has varied quite a lot over the years. At one point he was quite fit and active, and they went walking most weekends. I know he's been very anxious about leaving the house when Linda wasn't around. Scared of falling. And his heart condition means he gets tired and breathless easily. We've changed his medication and increased his morphine. Things have been much better up until recently.'

It was hard to imagine what Peter Gibson's life was going to be like if he was basically confined to the house. 'What is the morphine for?'

'Peter has inoperable lung cancer. He isn't a well man and his prognosis is not good.'

I checked the time on the clock on the pub wall. 'How long have the Gibsons been registered with you?'

'I've been their GP for five years.'

'And did you see them both regularly?'

'I saw more of Peter than Linda. He has greater needs. But I've treated Linda too. She came to see me six months ago to request counselling.'

'I don't remember seeing that on her medical records.'

'Linda was concerned about having a mental health referral on her file. She asked me to document it as something we discussed, so it's probably just one line in her records. In the end Linda decided not to go through with it and said she was feeling better.'

'And the reason for the counselling?'

'Stress. She was experiencing difficulty sleeping, irritability, emotionality.'

'Did she say what was causing her stress symptoms? Work or personal?'

'She said it was a combination of the two. She was having difficulty with a member of staff at the school and she wasn't finding it easy having Peter at home all day. Couples quite often find this when one retires before the other. I know Peter didn't find it easy either. They were a lovely couple. Extremely fond of each other.' He let out a wistful sigh as he said this, and drained the last of his coffee. 'Linda was Peter's life. He's going to need a lot of support to move on from this.' He checked his watch. 'Right. I'd better get going.'

'Thank you.'

He picked up his coat and left.

I sat back in my chair. It was bothering me that no-one at the school had hinted at Linda suffering from stress. Given their behaviour, Roger Allen, Neil Sanderson or Asad Farhan could be the colleague she was having trouble with. I fished my mobile out of my coat pocket and rang the office; asked Alexej to review Linda's health records for any mention of stress or insomnia. He had news: he'd finally managed to get through to the cleaner, Cathleen O'Doherty, whose business card I had seen at the Gibsons'. She'd been abroad on holiday and had just got home. She'd had her phone off to avoid roaming charges.

'Text me her address and tell her I'm on my way. It's extremely important.' The knots were finally beginning to unravel.

Tuesday – Maya

The Gibsons' cleaner didn't live far from my flat on Regent's Canal. On the other side of Ben Johnson Road, walkwayed social housing stood in pebble-dashed blocks, next to balconied, glass-fronted duplex apartments. I don't know what I'd been expecting but the woman who answered the door was no more than five-feet tall, and had a scrubbed, pink face and a shiny complexion. A weary air surrounded her.

'Cathleen O'Doherty?'

'Yes?' She was peering round the door, anxiously checking to see if anyone had seen me arrive.

'DI Rahman. Could I come in?' I noticed the woman's edginess. 'There's no need to be alarmed. You aren't in any trouble.'

She patted her chest and opened the door fully, standing back to allow me to enter the flat. She had a tabard over her clothes. 'I saw the ambulance the other day. Is Peter okay? I was just off to Menorca.'

Cathleen led me down the hall into the kitchen. Bijou didn't cover it. The room had a cooker, cabinets, fridge and table and chairs crammed into a space the size of a car.

'I gather you used to work for the Gibsons?'

'Almost four years. It was all legal. I pay tax and everything.'

'I'm not here about tax, Mrs O'Doherty.'

'Call me Cathleen, would you now?'

'Could you tell me why you left?'

With each passing beat, Cathleen blinked, all the time staring ahead. She clasped her hand over her mouth and sank into a foldaway chair, putting her hand out to the table to steady her as she sat.

'Is it to do with her death? I don't want to get into any trouble.'

Here was a woman approaching sixty, who looked as though she either suffered high blood pressure, diabetes or both.

'We think it may be. You won't be in trouble. But it *is* important. Why did you leave them?'

Cathleen studied every millimetre of the tablecloth. 'It was about that poor girl, the one who killed herself before Christmas. Haniya Patel. It wasn't right.' With her hand, she marked her forehead, chest, left shoulder and the right one, muttering under her breath. She stood up, filled a glass on the drainer from the tap and sipped it, her back to me. 'I tried to do their cleaning when Mrs Gibson wasn't there but during the school holidays it wasn't possible. The sound travels like anything in those houses as they've got so many staircases. I kept hearing them arguing about the school. I think they often forgot I was there.'

'What were they saying about the school?'

'Linda felt sorry for Haniya. She wanted the school to help Haniya stand up to her parents. Something about not trusting one of her colleagues to deal with it.'

'What else?'

'Peter was a lovely man and he adored Linda. But he thought she should stay out of the business with Haniya's family. He kept encouraging Linda to leave it to whoever this person was at the school. Kept going on about how much they had to lose now he was retired, and telling her not to rock the boat.' Cathleen was shaking her head, eyes full of anguish. 'If only someone had helped that poor girl.' She paused. 'Oh Jesus, Mary and Joseph, what am I saying?' She fanned her face with her hand and made the sign of the cross again. 'The first time I heard it, I ignored it; told myself it wasn't my business. But we had a young girl in our church whose father was . . .' she whispered '. . . *you know* . . .' Cathleen pointed at her crotch. Blotches were creeping up her neck and into her cheeks. She began fanning herself again with her hand. 'And the priest told us all afterwards that it wasn't right to look the other way.'

'Did you tell someone or speak to Linda?'

She put her hand on her forehead, as if to check she was okay. 'I told my Bill. He told me to mind my own business.'

'So, what did you do?'

'I just left.' Her voice was shaky, her eyes wide with alarm. 'Was that wrong of me?' She cleared her throat. Coughed. Began gasping for breath and wheezing.

'Do you need anything? Can I —'

'My inhaler . . .' She pointed to her handbag on the counter.

I grabbed it up and passed it over, and seconds later she'd dispensed her puffs and the coughing subsided. 'We've all got that girl's blood on our hands, haven't we?' Her lips were pursed as she was picturing what she remembered, and as the implications of her behaviour were slowly dawning. 'One thing's sure: Peter doted on Linda. With her gone, what's he got to live for?'

Tuesday – Maya

Dan was striding across the MIT office towards me, brandishing a printout. His pale face was flushed. 'Peter Gibson's medical records have arrived. The doctors have increased the amount of morphine he was taking —'

'Wait a minute. Dr Khan just told me the same thing.'

'Shit. What if he's been stockpiling it at home?'

'He said Alice was due over but I have a really bad feeling about this. That's a man with a heart condition and emphysema, who's just lost his wife. Which means . . .' I recalled the cleaner's face when she mentioned Peter not wanting to live without Linda. The GP's comments were similar.

'Alexej, get an ambulance to the Gibsons' house in Bow. We'll meet them round there *now*. I really hope I'm wrong.'

Tuesday – Steve

Piano music wafted round the senior hall. To the right of the stage, Gary Wilks, the head of music, sat behind a grand piano while a uniformed student proudly turned pages for him. On either side of the stage, two giant boards had been erected. On one, photographs of Linda clustered round an A3 image of her. Pinned to the board were a mass of cards, letters, notes, mementos. On the other was a large image of Roger, and similar personal items. White fairy lights hung from the top of both boards. A couple of bar stools stood next to a microphone stand in the centre of the stage.

'Alright, sir?' said the school's head boy, Fayzul, who was greeting guests with his female counterpart.

Bronagh handed him a programme.

'Well done, guys. The hall looks stunning.' He scoured the room for Maria O'Connor, hoping she'd come along this evening.

The large space was rammed with what must've been two thousand people. It was a kaleidoscope of colour. Over the last two days the staff and pupils had been decorating it in honour of Linda and Roger. Tributes and bouquets lined the hall. Shari and Neil had invited the families of both staff members; all current staff, students and parents; the board of governors; plus anyone previously connected with the school while Linda and Roger had worked there.

Steve looked for Andrea. She was chatting to a couple of students, and he headed over to sit with her.

All around, people were in clusters, talking about Linda and

Roger and the school, and all the things that the two of them had contributed. What they remembered. Funny lessons, disastrous and spectacular school plays, skiing trips, assemblies ruined by technology failures, parent – teacher fundraising quizzes. It was exactly as a memorial gathering should be.

Neil let Shari go up the steps to the stage first and then followed. As usual she was fussing with her *hijab*. The audience stopped chatting and looked up. Neil cleared his throat and wiggled his pink tie upwards to ensure it was tight.

'Evening everyone. Thank you so much for coming. If you could take your seats, please.'

Once everyone was settled, Neil began. 'We've gathered to honour the lives and contributions of our two colleagues, Mrs Gibson and Mr Allen. Due to his health, we aren't sure whether Linda's husband, Peter, will be joining us but he's very kindly helped us with some of Linda's preferences, for example, the Mozart that Mr Wilks was playing so beautifully when we all arrived. Mr Allen's wife and family are here this evening. We've arranged this event in conjunction with their two families. Both have requested we don't make things too solemn.' He looked at Shari for moral support. 'Following the awful news this morning about the death of our social worker, Asad Farhan, we will be holding a memorial for him next week, but have decided to go ahead with tonight's event given all the hard work and planning that's gone into it. Mrs Ahmed?'

'Yes. The last week hasn't been easy for *any* of us. But one thing we know is how important the school was to both our colleagues. And judging by the number of people asking to give tributes this evening, I'd say they were important to a lot of you too. Mr Sanderson and I will leave our pieces until the end. I'll hand over now to Talcott Lawrence, one of our longstanding governors, who's going to introduce each person.'

A man approached the microphone. He was wearing a cream suit and must've been feeling the chill in the hall as he still had his overcoat and scarf on top.

Steve recognised him as one of the parents who'd gathered at the school earlier in the week.

'Yes, hello.' He looked out into the audience. 'You won't believe me when I say I didn't set the running order – but we're going to start off with my daughter Katie from year nine.'

A slight, dark-haired student got up. She looked at the front row several times, as though needing reassurance from friends sitting there, before saying in a small voice, 'I'm going to read a poem for Mrs Gibson.' Her hands shook as she took a scruffy piece of paper out of her pocket. 'Mrs Gibson was very kind to me when my mother died.' She read the first few words and hesitated, her voice going quiet, her eyes glassy. She looked at the front row again and seemed to gain confidence. She stopped looking at the paper and launched into a recital of *Funeral Blues,* by W. H. Auden.

There wasn't a wriggle or a cough in the room. Apart from Katie – silence.

Steve let the words wash over him. He knew them by heart.

At the end of the poem, the room froze for a few moments until the screeching feedback of the microphone brought the audience back to the school hall. On stage now was a woman in her late sixties. She wore a small leather bag across her blazer, and had a patterned scarf tied round her head.

'Beautifully delivered,' Talcott said, hugging his daughter. 'Now we have Shirley Wyndham, one of our receptionists.'

She tapped the microphone. 'Can you hear me?' She looked up nervously. The feedback had stopped. 'I'd simply like to say a few words about how grateful I am to Mrs Gibson for giving me a chance to re-enter the workforce. Many employers wouldn't give me the time of day when they heard I was undergoing chemotherapy. I told Mrs Gibson I didn't want sympathy or special treatment. This job has enabled me to feel like a human being again. I've finished treatment now and am waiting for the next round of results from my oncologist.' She patted her head and a weak smile found its way onto her face. 'This morning I found a few strands of hair growing back on my scalp. It's white, but that's okay. So, fingers crossed, I'm going to make it. I regret that Mrs Gibson won't be here to share it with me. Thank you.'

She wiped her face with a tissue, and stared into the audience, wide-eyed. There wasn't a movement or noise in the room and for a few moments Shirley Wyndham was held in time and space, and collective affection.

'Sorry to interrupt,' a man's booming voice burst through the silence from the back of the room, accompanied by loud footsteps on the hardwood floor. A large-framed man strode down the centre of the hall to the front of the audience where Neil and Shari were sitting, his coat flapping outwards. A uniformed officer followed him through the gap in the chairs, practically running to keep up with him.

'Mr Sanderson?' the man asked.

'Ye-es,' said Neil in a shaky voice.

'Neil Sanderson, I'm Detective Chief Inspector Ian Briscall. I am arresting you for the murders of Linda Gibson, Roger Allen and Asad Farhan.'

'What's going on?' Neil was startled. He surveyed the room, as if it was a practical joke or a mistake, and he was waiting for someone to own up. 'I don't —'

'You do not have to say anything. But it may harm your defence if you do not mention . . .'

The whole room fell silent. All eyes were on the school bursar as the detective read him his rights, and as they witnessed the words they'd heard so many times on television.

'Come with me, please, Mr Sanderson.'

The officer with him took hold of Neil's arm and led him out towards the hall exit, leaving a stunned audience in their wake.

'Neil?' said Andrea. '*Neil's* the murderer?'

Steve spun round to see if everyone was as shocked as he and Andrea were. At the front of the hall Shari Ahmed's attention moved between Talcott Lawrence and the door. Everyone was facing the front of the room. Steve caught a movement at the side of the hall and recognised the reporter, Suzie James, standing next to the caretaker. On her iPhone, she was videoing Neil Sanderson's arrest.

Tuesday – Maya

In Tredegar Square, Dan and I dashed along the icy pavement to the Gibson's house. Morphine was metabolised quickly. If Peter had given himself an overdose, we had minutes to save him before he went into respiratory arrest.

The square was in darkness except for the faint glow of a few street lamps in the mist. I took the steps to the front door two at a time, yelling, 'Mr Gibson.' Jabbed my finger on the bell and clacked the letter box, shouting his name through it. Panic was rising in my voice. I pushed the bell again and thumped on the door knocker. '*Mr Gibson.*' I groped in my coat pocket for my phone to check an ambulance was on its way.

Someone from a neighbouring property flung open a window and stuck their head out. 'Hey. I'm trying to get my kids to sleep.'

'Police,' I yelled. 'Has anyone got keys to the Gibsons'? It's an emergency.' I beat my fists on the door panel.

Dan was behind me. 'Move out the way.' He pulled me back from the steps, and aimed a powerful kick at the lock area of the door. With a splintering crack from the frame, the door burst inwards and bashed on the hall wall. Dan fell to the ground halfway over the doorstep, clutching his ankle. 'Go in,' he shouted. 'I'll follow you. I'll check upstairs and you check the lounge.'

I jumped over him and entered the house. 'Mr Gibson?' I couldn't hear anything from the lounge and went in. I heard Dan's feet up the stairs, and his shouts to Peter. Perhaps we'd got it wrong? Perhaps

Peter had gone to the school for the memorial assembly and we'd just kicked his door in? I slid my hand up and down the wall, groping the surface for the light switch. Finally, my fingers made contact and the ceiling lights came on.

There he was.

'Fuck.' I squinted as the bright light hit my retinas.

Peter was in the same chair as earlier, his eyes closed. His arms rested either side of his frail body. In his lap lay the photograph he'd shown me. Next to him, on the coffee table, was an empty syringe. Drops of clear liquid spotted the wood. The empty phial had dropped onto the carpet.

'Where are the bloody paramedics?' I yelled. '*Dan*. He's in here.'

It was too late.

We were too late.

I launched myself at the man's legs, and as I fell to the carpet, my legs folded beneath me and I skidded towards him on my knees. He couldn't die.

'Peter? Stay with us, Peter. Help's on its way.'

It was as if, all at once, he was Peter Gibson . . . but also Sabbir, Linda, Haniya, Roger, Farhan. All dead.

'Peter?' I clung to his legs, sobbing, jigging his legs to rouse him. 'You can't die. You can't.' Tears blurred my vision, hair in my face and mouth.

What was that?

Had he moved or was it me?

'Wh-e-re . . .?' It was a croak.

I raised my head. 'Thank Christ.' I sat back on my heels, kneeling. 'Mr Gibson? It's DI Rahman. Help's on its way.'

'. . . dizzy . . . where . . .?' His voice was weak, his speech slow, slurred. His heart could fail any moment.

'In here. In the lounge,' I yelled.

Dan had arrived now. 'The paramedics are here. Maya? They can take over.'

A young man in a high-visibility jacket dashed over from the door. Followed by another paramedic, an older woman.

'Move away, please,' he said.

The paramedic reached for Peter's wrist to take his pulse.

I picked up the phial and handed it to him so he could see what Peter had taken. 'He's been prescribed morphine for pain. He's got lung cancer and cardiac disease.'

The paramedic snapped open a new syringe and phial, and injected Peter.

Peter was stirring now. 'If I . . .' His voice was raspy, barely audible. He tried to raise his hand. 'If . . . I . . . my heart . . . no resuscitation.'

I took his hand. 'It's okay, Peter. We've heard you.' I placed his hand on the arm of the chair and moved away.

An urgent cry caught my attention. Peter's face was agitated and he was trying to raise his arm again. 'Just remembered . . . Linda's office . . . I rang her . . . heard someone . . . there was someone in her office.'

'Move away, Inspector, please.' The paramedic placed her hand on my shoulder and wheeled a stretcher in place. 'We need to get him to hospital.'

The significance of Peter's words settled in my mind.

Five minutes later, the waiting ambulance was leaving Tredegar Square. A uniformed officer was on-board to record everything Peter said. We had to hope he might remember who the person was.

For a few moments I stood next to Dan in the darkness, dazed. Watched as the ambulance tore round the corner of Tredegar Square, lights flashing in the mist, its siren announcing another tragedy to the early evening sky.

Emotions circled.

Relief.

Sadness.

Then a wave of doubt.

'Did we do the right thing?' I said to Dan. 'Would it have been better for him to have died at home?'

'We did the *only* thing. Preservation of life.'

In the dark, I let the tears wash my face. 'Maybe we've simply prolonged his suffering?'

'We are police officers. We didn't have a choice. We suspected his life was in danger and we acted on that.'

I faced him. 'Thank you.'

'See all these perfect houses? No-one knows what goes on behind the doors of other people's lives.'

It was so true. 'Talking of doors . . . is your ankle okay?'

'Nothing a couple of Panadeines won't cure.' Then, in a stupid voice, 'Hey. Me macho Aussie man, remember?'

I think we both appreciated his attempt at humour.

A few minutes later, Dan and I followed the ambulance to the Royal London to wait until we could speak to Peter about the person who was in Linda's office. The urgency of Peter's comment suggested it was important. In the A&E unit, we sat in the waiting area, watching life and death arrive on a trolley. We bought cups of tea from the drinks machine, which we didn't want or drink, and waited for news.

As I raked through the events of the last few days, I remembered my visit to the Green Bridge. 'I've never asked you what you think about arranged marriages,' I said to Dan. The question came blurting out. I was feeding change into the snack machine.

Dan's eyebrows rose as he considered the question. 'Something I've learned from Aroona is that customs exist for good reasons.' He got up and walked over to a table of magazines. 'In many cultures the extended family and community are the key focus. Some arrange marriages to enhance business relations. It makes sense. The bit I don't agree with is forcing your kids to do something they don't want to.'

*

Four hours later, and with a crick in my neck from falling asleep on the plastic seats, the A&E doctor finally agreed for us to speak to Peter Gibson for a few minutes.

On the ward he was linked up to a flashing heart monitor, which was beeping loudly. An intravenous drip ran into the back of his hand. An oxygen mask was helping him breathe.

'Glad to see you're feeling a bit better,' I spoke clearly. 'You gave us quite a fright.'

He blinked. Inhaled. Exhaled.

'Can you remember who you overheard in Linda's office the day she was killed?'

He pulled the oxygen mask away from his mouth and rested it under his chin. He tried to swallow a few times, as if his mouth was stuck together. He started to cough. Cupped the mask back over his nose. Removed it again. 'The person was . . .'

Dan and I were leaning over to catch Peter's words.

'Was it a man or a woman?'

He started coughing again.

'Peter?'

He was barely a bump under the sheets. The heart monitor gave out a series of beeps, and an alarm sounded.

No, no, he couldn't die.

Within seconds a nurse arrived and two doctors.

The nurse began pulling the curtains round his bed and chivvied us backwards. 'I'm sorry, Detective Inspector. You need to leave now.'

Tuesday

You never stood a chance, did you, Peter?

My issue with you was that I knew you were encouraging Linda to abdicate from her responsibilities. You didn't want her to jeopardise the school's progress and her career. And, of course, you hoped you'd get more of her time and attention for yourself, didn't you?

The precept says:

> *suramereya majja pamadatthana veramani*
> *sikkhapadam samadiyani*
> I shall abstain from all that clouds the mind

Except . . . this one's got nothing to do with you. No, precept number five is still to come – but you've caused a helpful distraction.

I hoped you would.

After all, I knew you'd never want to live without your beloved Linda. Shall I tell you who I've saved the fifth precept for? No. That'll spoil it. Let's see if you can figure it out.

Tuesday – Steve

As the police led Neil Sanderson away, all eyes were on the procession to the door. Staff, pupils and parents were all peering round each other to get a view of the spectacle.

Steve climbed over a couple of seats and shot over to the wall by the stage where Suzie James was still filming. 'Would you stop that, please? It's intrusive.' He stood in front of her, blocking her view.

'Lighten up, college boy. It's a public event.'

'Actually, it's a private event, on invitation. Covering the assembly is one thing, filming distressing events for gossip and titillation is another. Now switch your camera off.'

'It's okay, I got the best bit. Who'd have thought it, eh? The school bursar?'

'Please think about what you're going to do with that film,' Steve hissed at the journalist. 'These are people's lives.'

On stage, a man tapped the microphone in preparation to speak.

'And that's *exactly* what our readers are interested in.' Suzie placed her phone in her pocket, a look of glee plastered to her shiny face.

'Can I have your attention, everyone, please? I'm Richard Williams, the school's acting head. This was an unanticipated and upsetting disruption to the evening. Nobody knows what's happened but I would suggest we end the evening here, and reconvene on another occasion to pay tribute to Mrs Gibson and Mr Allen in the way they deserve. Thank you for coming, and I wish you all a safe journey home.'

Around the hall were dazed faces. Others were asking what was going on, and had Neil really killed Linda, Roger and Farhan? Confusion flew round the room as the excitement and anticipation of a wonderful evening had ground to a halt. What an anti-climax.

Steve spied Suzie James, sloping out of the side door. What a bitch. Instead of being able to write a heartening piece about the memorial evening, and how much Linda and Roger had meant to everyone, she was now going to stir up more gossip and speculation for the school by, no doubt, reporting every detail of Neil Sanderson's arrest.

Andrea had come over. She saw who Steve was watching. 'I wonder how it must feel to prey on other people's misery to sell stories. She's going to love all this. She was the same when Haniya Patel died – sniffing round the staff, trying to get them to talk to her about the suicide, to dish the dirt. It was a horrible time for the family, and Linda. She made it worse for everyone. It wasn't factual reporting. It was a feeding frenzy.'

'Oh, he's off too, look.' Over at the side door, Steve saw the caretaker glance back at the room and slip out. People were streaming out through the main exit, keen to escape. The whole evening seemed unreal.

Andrea let out a heavy sigh of relief. 'Oh well. At least it's all over now.'

Tuesday – Maya

When Dan and I arrived back at the MIT office, the optimism of earlier had evaporated. The breakthroughs we'd hoped for had come to a crashing standstill. Briscall had arrested Neil Sanderson despite the fact that no-one except him believed the bursar was guilty. One piece of information offered a glimmer of hope: Peter had overheard Linda talking to someone in her office before she was murdered.

Alexej heard our approach and looked up from his laptop. 'The Suzie James arrest video has had nearly two million hits on YouTube already, and she's put it on the newspaper's website and social media accounts.'

'I'm tempted to pretend I haven't heard that piece of information,' I said. 'We'd better get it taken down though.'

'I'll get onto it. Rowe called in. Said something about one of his students . . .'

I stood still. When we called round at his flat, Rowe mentioned that a student of his had seen the police where Allen lived.

'It sounded like he was phoning from the pub, and I think he was a bit pissed . . .'

'Hang on. Rowe is a bit naïve but he's not an idiot . . .'

Across the office, a landline was ringing. Shen answered the call. 'It's the hospital,' she yelled over to me. 'Shall I put them through?'

Oh no. Peter Gibson. My stomach lurched with dread. I picked up the receiver.

'DI Rahman.' The ward sister's words sank in. 'Thanks for letting us know.' I hung up. 'Peter Gibson's alive. He's had another heart attack but he's stable and speaking. He's sure the person he heard in Linda's room was a man. He asked the nurse to call us.'

Excitement lit up Dan's face.

'Peter heard him speak. Couldn't distinguish the actual words, but *definitely* heard a male voice.'

'But he doesn't know who it was?' He looked from me to Alexej.

I shook my head. 'Peter got the impression Linda knew the person. Something about the way she greeted him. The nurse said she'd let us know if he remembers anything more.'

Dan was reviewing possible male suspects.

Neil Sanderson

Vajrasiddhi

Tariq Patel

Rich Griffiths, the caretaker.

Next to the list of suspects he'd abbreviated the five precepts.

'Wait a minute.' I faced Dan and Alexej, and pointed at the board. 'The first precept advocates no harm to any living thing. Unless they've somehow got shunted away from Buddhist values, whoever killed Linda and Roger and Farhan can't be a Buddhist. Either that or we're looking for someone who isn't religious at all.'

Shen and I were sitting side by side, watching the video Suzie James had taken of Sanderson being arrested. On-screen, I saw Sanderson's face fall; behind him, Rozina's expression was shocked, and Talcott Lawrence grabbed the lectern, looking unsure of what to do next.

'I know him,' Shen said, pointing at the screen. 'That's Mr Lawrence.'

'He's a governor at the school. So?'

'He used to go to the Buddhist Centre in Bethnal Green with his wife. I don't know him much but I know his wife. She's Chinese. Like me she's a Buddhist.' She blushed. '*Was.*'

My pulse began to race. 'Then what happened?'

'He stopped coming just before she died. She told me he was very angry about her illness. His daughter is Katie. She's half Chinese, half Jamaican.'

I remembered what Talcott had said about Mile End High School being an asset to the area, and how he *intended* to make sure it stayed that way. How he'd been concerned about his daughter yet was adamant the school didn't need to be shut. I'd assumed it was because he recognised the risks of a short-notice closure.

Then I remembered that, before the ward sister called, Alexej had mentioned Steve Rowe saying something about one of his students. I pulled up Steve's contact details. Dialled his number.

Fortunately, he answered.

'It's DI Rahman here. What's the name of the student who told you his family lived in the same block as Roger Allen?'

He told me.

'Alexej, get onto Shari Ahmed. Or someone from the school. Not the caretaker. Get the flat number for Lukas Shadrova's family and nip round there. It's the Allen's block. Find out from Lukas' brother exactly what he saw on Thursday morning, when Roger Allen was killed. Who arrived and left, and when. Even after we ring-fenced mobiles in the area, when we did the interviews and house-to-house, no-one reported seeing anything. Double-check the witness statements for anyone seeing Lawrence near the school Wednesday lunchtime, the Allens' flat on Thursday, and Shadwell Monday night.'

Lawrence had said he lived in Limehouse. 'Dan, come on, let's pay Talcott Lawrence a visit.'

Ten minutes later we parked behind an over-flowing skip in the Limehouse backstreet, outside a mansion block covered in scaffolding and boards. The building had three entrances, and housed around fifty flats. We'd obtained Lawrence's address and I rang the buzzer of their ground-floor flat.

Hip-hop blasted through the intercom, its bass practically vibrating in my chest. A young girl's voice answered.

'It's the police,' I said. 'We need to speak to your father. Can we come in please?'

The girl was giggling with a friend and echoing the words of the rapper in time to the music. 'Hold on. I'll get him.'

Through the intercom I heard muffled discussions in the flat. A few minutes later she returned. 'He was here a minute ago but you've just missed him. My friend says he nipped out to get a newspaper.'

Dan dashed out onto the street, quickly disappearing in the mist. 'Is that Katie?' I tried to sound casual.

'It's just my dad who calls me that. My real name's Chun.'

'Not to worry. Thanks.' Lawrence had done a runner. We'd lost him.

'Over here,' came Dan's voice.

Except for a few tired street lamps, the road was in darkness. How the hell were we going to find Lawrence in a mass of moving shapes and shadows?

'He bolted down that passage.' Dan pointed to a narrow opening between a boarded-up shop and the end of their apartment building. 'I caught his rear view just as I came out. He's got a bag with him.' A ripped mattress leaned up against the wall, half its innards tumbling onto a pavement of broken glass.

Years ago I had a school friend who lived over the street. We used to cut through the alleys to the main road. One ran alongside each end of the mansion block. Back then, they were genuinely used for access; nowadays it was drug dealers, pimps and fly-tipping.

'You follow him from this side of the flats and I'll head him off from the other end. We need back-up to meet us from the high street direction.'

Dan was already in pursuit.

When I got to the alley opening, I saw how neglected and overgrown it was. The ground was uneven, and littered with Rizla packets and rusty lager cans. A couple of crumbling car tyres leaned against the chain-link fence. As I ran, bare tree branches clawed at my face and hair. I stumbled over rubbish and debris, and fell against the wall. My heart was pounding against my rib cage, and the smell of piss filled my nostrils. Ahead, an orange street lamp illuminated the path beneath the fog. The brick wall had become rusted metal railings. A dumped armchair lay next to an old syringe, broken springs poking through mouldy upholstery. I clambered over it, straining my ears for sounds ahead, but there was nothing other than my breathing and the thump of my feet as I landed on the solid ground. I staggered round a corner back into complete darkness. On a nearby roof, a cluster of pigeons cooed and flapped their wings.

I waited for my eyes to readjust.

In the distance, a faint torchlight was bobbing in the night air. A cry of pain rang out, followed by a crashing sound and a thud. Was it Dan or Lawrence? Or was someone else picking their way along the rubbish-strewn passage beside the flats? I swiped my phone into life, hoping the screen would give a flicker of light. In front of me were steps down. At the foot of the slope, on the ground, was Talcott Lawrence. He lay, clutching his shoulder, groaning, his lanky frame curled into a ball. His cream suit peeped out from the sleeves of his dark anorak.

Around us, sirens wrapped themselves round the dank air.

We finally had him.

Tuesday – Maya

Back at the police station, Talcott Lawrence's clothes had been taken for forensic analysis. He was in the medical room being checked for fractures and Dan and I were waiting outside.

Alexej had returned from Stepney and was updating us on what the Shadrova family had told him. 'Lukas' younger brother, Alik, has given a witness statement. He bust his ankle recently so he was home alone, with his foot in a cast. Boredom drove him to peer out of the window. He saw Talcott Lawrence arrive at the entrance to the flats where the Allens live around ten-fifteen a.m., followed by Ruth Allen, and the police soon after.'

'Bingo.' Dan punched the air.

The door opened.

'He's all yours,' the doctor said as he left the room. 'No breaks just a lot of bruising and some nasty scratches on his neck.'

'Thanks, Doc.'

Five minutes later, in the interview suite, Lawrence sat in a sweatshirt and tracksuit bottoms. On his neck, a couple of gouges looked puffy and angry.

'Where were you on Wednesday last week, between twelve noon and one p.m.?' I studied his body language.

He didn't consider the question for long. 'I had a business meeting in Poplar with some of my colleagues.'

'Who was there?' I picked up my pen and started a fresh page in my pad, as though I believed him.

'I'll need to check the minutes.'

'How about Thursday?' I asked. 'Where were you between nine and eleven a.m.?'

'I was with Katie until I dropped her at school at eleven a.m.'

'She'd confirm that if we asked her, would she?'

'Of course, but I'd prefer it if you didn't. I don't want her upset unnecessarily.'

'Actually, we won't need to do that,' I said gently. 'Because we have a witness who saw you entering the flats where the Allens live on Thursday morning around ten-fifteen a.m., and leaving approximately fifteen minutes later.'

Lawrence muttered to himself. Wriggled in his seat and winced with pain. 'That's not possible. I was nowhere near the Allens' place.'

'Their testimony *proves* you were at Roger Allen's flat minutes before he was murdered.'

'Oh, that's right. I must have forgotten. I popped round to check Allen was okay. I knew he'd been drinking heavily recently and it was unusual to be absent from school on the first day of term. I was worried about him. I didn't stay long and he was fine when I left.'

'You didn't go round there to kill him?'

'No, I did *not*.'

'And Linda?'

'What about her?' He flicked at the table with his finger.

'We believe you went to the school and strangled her.'

'Why on earth would I do that?'

'You tell *us*.'

'There's nothing to tell because I didn't do it.'

'How about Monday night? Where were you between eleven p.m. and midnight?'

'At home with my daughter, of course.'

'When you leave your daughter at home, do you take your phone with you? So she can contact you?'

324

'Usually.'

'You took it with you last night, didn't you?'

'I don't recall.' His gaze was still lowered, and was shifting from side to side.

'You see, we've used cell site data and tracked the position of your mobile to Shadwell at 11.28 p.m. last night.'

'So what?'

'You just said that you were at home all evening.'

He shrugged.

'You see, we believe you were in Shadwell, strangling Asad Farhan with a piece of wire.'

He jumped in his seat, bashing the table, and clutched his shoulder in pain. 'I most certainly was *not*,' he shouted.

'We believe you killed Linda and Roger and Asad.'

He shook his head vehemently. 'No, no, no. I had nothing to do with any of their deaths.'

I wanted Lawrence to realise that we had enough evidence to charge him. I also wanted to understand his motivations, and how other aspects of his behaviour had fed into his actions.

'Tell me about the board of governors. Is that a way of keeping tabs on what's going on at the school?'

'That's a rather cynical view,' Lawrence responded, his tone indignant. 'When Linda took over as head, there was a chance to turn Mile End High into a place that parents would trust. I've tried to make the most of that opportunity. It hasn't been easy.'

'Why not?'

'It requires a particular kind of head teacher to take over a school on the verge of going into special measures. It was obvious that Linda didn't have the right experience. And in a community like this, with so many potential influences on our children, it's important to guard against ones that are unhelpful. My daughter, Katie, is in year nine. She's at a vulnerable age. With her mother dead, she has only me to protect her. I promised Su I would keep Katie safe and I intend to.'

I was absorbing what he was saying. 'What sort of influences are you worried about?'

'Take a look around. That dreadful hip-hop music they all listen to. Schoolchildren on drugs. Students getting stabbed. Allegations against teachers. Linda Gibson's pregnancy advice unit. Safeguarding failures. The worst is the pressure to turn a blind eye to potentially illegal behaviour just so we don't upset anyone.'

I knew Lawrence wasn't Muslim. 'Is that why you got so involved with the plans for the new mosque at Whitechapel?'

'Someone's got to monitor what's going on, and bring reason to bear when necessary.'

A sinking feeling was developing in my stomach as I tried to understand his objections. 'I gather your wife was a committed Buddhist? And you went to the London Buddhist Centre together?'

He sat back. 'It's no secret. Like many Chinese, Su had been Buddhist all her life. My parents' Christianity does nothing for me and I found Buddhism appealing. Except since . . .' He broke off. His words hung in the air.

Now was the time to ask him about the precepts.

'*I shall abstain from taking the ungiven.* Do you think that's what Linda did with Haniya?' Was I imagining it or did he flinch slightly?

'No . . . I . . .'

'Didn't you think that Linda took Haniya's decision away from her? Took her *life*, even?'

'No.'

'So, you were happy with how Linda dealt with Haniya's marriage?'

'*No*, I wasn't. But that doesn't mean that —'

'*I shall abstain from sexual misconduct.* Didn't you disapprove of Roger's obsession with Linda?'

'No.'

'*I shall abstain from false speech.* I'm sure you know why Farhan left his previous school. Imagine if it'd been Katie who'd got pregnant at Mile End High . . .'

That got his attention.

'Didn't you object to all Farhan's lies?'

'*No. Yes.*' He slapped his forehead with the palm of his hand, as though he wasn't sure anymore. 'I did object to his lies but . . .' He stopped, almost as if he knew his denials were pointless.

I leaned forwards in my seat. 'Shall I tell you what I think? I think you were protecting your daughter from the evil you saw at the school. Am I correct?'

Lawrence's face hardened. 'I don't know what you're talking about.'

'You had the means, motive and opportunity to kill all three people. You've admitted you went to see Allen the morning he died. Your phone places you in Shadwell last night when Farhan died.'

'All circumstantial.'

'That's not all we have, Mr Lawrence. The crime scene forensics are being processed and we've obtained a warrant to search your home.'

'You can't —'

'Actually, we can.' Dan sat back in his seat. He was tight as a rack next to me. 'Listen to yourself, would you? You're looking at a good stretch of time in prison, so why don't you cooperate and maybe the judge will take that into account? Huh?' Dan eyeballed Lawrence. 'Why don't you tell us about the five precepts? Starting with Haniya Patel and *I shall abstain from causing harm.*'

Lawrence released a long sigh and covered his face with one hand. 'They thought they were protecting the interests of the students by letting that snake, Farhan, handle things with Haniya's family. But they were simply looking after their own interests. They thought that condemning forced marriages would alienate many Muslim families. Utilitarianism is fine if you're talking about opening hours for a library, but when it puts the life of even *one* person in jeopardy, it isn't fine.' His face glimmered, as though it all made perfect sense.

'Why did that bother you?'

'I cannot have my daughter endangered like that. Linda, Roger, Neil, Shari and Asad, they all had their hands round the rope that Haniya hanged herself with.'

'So Haniya was the first precept? The final straw for you and where it all began?'

'Yes. Haniya's suicide symbolised everything that's wrong with the school.'

'And Linda?' asked Dan.

'She of *all* people should have helped Haniya. And Ella Hayes. As head, she could have overruled the vote and brought in the Forced Marriage Unit. What if my daughter gets in with a crowd who . . .?' He wagged his head, the disbelief and·fear too much for him.

'So, you killed Linda to protect your daughter?'

'No. But someone with a background like Linda's shouldn't have been in charge of children.'

Dan and I exchanged looks.

'What about her background?' he asked.

'Secrets don't stay secret round here. However divided our community is, it's still close-knit, and someone *always* knows something. You just have to ask the right person. I knew about the refuge she ran.' He slumped in his seat. 'You don't have to be a genius to realise she was over-compensating for her own mistakes and for ignoring the rot that lies at the core of the school.' He looked up now, in the madness of his grief, oblivious of how his actions might seem to others. 'When the head teacher post was advertised, I made it my business to research all the applicants. One of my Chamber of Commerce friends had been a clerk when Linda gave evidence against her brother. He was sworn to secrecy, of course, but . . . there's always a price, isn't there?' Lawrence fixed his gaze on mine.

Dan wasn't finished. 'So, you killed her? You used the entry-code system to let yourself in at lunchtime on Wednesday and you strangled her?'

Lawrence let out a long sigh.

'What do you reckon we'll find at your home? White cloth? Card?'

Lawrence rubbed his face.

'Tell us the truth. You killed Linda, didn't you?' Dan placed both hands palm-down on the table.

'Alright. I did.' His voice sounded weary. 'I had to. Linda had to be stopped.'

We'd finally got him to confess.

'So, Linda was the second precept and Roger Allen the third.' I heard the heaviness in Dan's voice. 'Tell us about Roger. Why did you kill him?'

Lawrence scoffed. 'The man was a liability. Oh, he had scruples and insight – but his infatuation with Linda eclipsed both. He agreed with everything she suggested.' Lawrence rolled his eyes. 'It made no difference that they weren't having an affair. His attention wasn't on the right things. His wife, his girls . . .' He looked up. 'Buddha taught that we should practise stillness, simplicity and contentment instead of indulging our selfish cravings.' Lawrence pushed up his sleeve to check his watch. Concern spread over his features. 'I need to check on Katie. She'll be —'

'We've got that in hand. She's with one of our officers.'

He relaxed.

'What about Farhan? You gave him the fourth precept.'

As he had before, he covered his eyes and shook his head gently. 'I've never met a man so utterly corrupt. Roger was a besotted fool. Neil was ambitious. Linda was misguided. But Asad simply didn't care. He would say whatever was necessary.' His eyes ached with sadness. 'Su always recited, *I shall abstain from false speech.*'

'Katie told one of our officers that you dropped her at your neighbour's on Wednesday morning, just after eight, and that your neighbour took her to school, not you.'

'Well, there you are.' Lawrence sunk in his chair at the mention of his daughter.

'It can't have been easy. Your wife passing away?'

He closed his eyes, as though the pain was too much. 'Su had a series of strokes and her condition grew progressively worse.' His voice was quiet. Defeated. 'For the last year she was bed-ridden and fed by a tube into her stomach. It was extremely distressing for all of us, and meant twenty-four hour nursing care for my wife. Eventually, she developed a chest infection and double pneumonia. We lost her a year ago next week.' He put his hand on the back of his chair, his grief raw.

'I'm sorry to hear that.' I waited for a moment, and fetched Lawrence a cup of water from the cooler. 'What about Peter?'

'Peter's always been weak. I wasn't surprised when he killed himself.' Talcott's voice had an edge. 'I can't say I'm sorry. I knew he wanted Linda to stay out of Haniya's marriage – we got chatting at the school play a few months ago. He didn't want Linda rocking the boat and jeopardising her career. But, with his wife gone, his connection with the school disappeared and he wasn't a risk to anyone else, so he was none of my business.'

I noted the past tense and threw Dan a glance.

'Did you think Peter was dead?' Dan asked.

'Isn't he? I saw the news reports.'

'No, he's fine.' It was as though grief and fear had blinded him to quite how distorted his logic had become. 'There's something else, though. If you didn't have Peter lined up for the fifth precept, who did you have in mind?'

Lawrence frowned. 'Neil Sanderson, of course. The last precept says: *I shall abstain from all that clouds the mind*. It's about mindfulness, and avoiding things that cloud our thinking. Without a clear mind, it's easy to break the other precepts. Sanderson was the worst of them all. He was drunk on greed, ambition and power. I knew he was blackmailing Linda and putting pressure on her to defer to Farhan, yet he had the cheek to take the credit for the school's successes and pretend to be Mr Nice Guy.'

The interview room door opened. Alexej entered, carrying a note that he handed to me. Officers had completed the search of the Lawrences' flat.

Alexej placed three bagged exhibits on the table in front of me.

'I believe these are yours, Mr Lawrence.' I slid the items over to him. 'The wire is the same as the one used to kill Asad Farhan last night. The crime scene fibres have been fast-tracked so we'll soon know whether they match these.'

His arms remained on his lap. Through broken eyes, he stared at the items that officers had found in the wardrobe in his bedroom: white cloth, a pack of card and wire. He tilted his head forwards and placed both hands over his face. Then, very gently, his tightly-wound features softened and he began to sob.

*

One hour later, after a full confession, Lawrence had given a DNA sample and had his fingerprints taken. Dan and I had concluded our interviews and handed Lawrence to the custody sergeant for charging.

When I dragged my body into the lift, to return to the main MIT office, mixed feelings weighed on my heart and pulled my priorities in opposite directions. Staff and pupils at Mile End High School were safe now. They would get a new permanent head teacher, and new managers to replace Roger, Neil and Shari. In time the school would recover. But Peter? Linda's sister, Alice? The Allen family? Katie Lawrence? What would the future hold for them?

The lift arrived at the third floor.

Dan had gone ahead to begin processing the paperwork.

I took a deep breath and pushed open the double doors into the MIT department. People were darting across the room, shouting questions. The place was in pandemonium. Had a new case come in?

Amid the hubbub, Dan must've spotted me and came charging over, weaving round colleagues and waving his arm in the air. 'The CPS refused to allow Briscall to charge Neil Sanderson with murder. He's still downstairs, understandably annoyed at being hauled off in front of his peers. I'm about to interview him about the payments to Linda. After that the fraud guys want to speak to him about the money he was siphoning off from the school, and the Forced Marriage

Unit are going to be investigating everyone who colluded with the cover-up over Haniya.' He let out a loud whoop.

I tried not to grin. 'Thanks, Dan. Where's Briscall?'

'He scarpered soon after he heard that Suzie James' video had gone viral.'

A small laugh fluttered in my stomach. He'd brought about his own downfall after all. It was a shame it had taken so long.

'There's more. By the time the video that Suzie James uploaded got taken down, it'd had millions of hits.'

I chuckled. 'She takes not giving a shit to a whole new level. She'll pitch up at the next murder case, you watch. Actually, I never thought I'd feel appreciation for her but that video has done me a favour. Where's Alexej?'

'Speaking to social services about Katie Lawrence.'

*

Half an hour later, I pulled my coat on and switched off the lights. Exhaustion weighed my body down but I wanted to stop off at the hospital to see how Peter Gibson was. On my way to the lift, I looked over at Briscall's office. Where the blinds were normally down and the door shut, it was now wide open, the blinds up and the lights off.

'Got a call from Superintendent Campbell, apparently,' said a familiar voice. Dougie was striding towards me, a huge grin plastered on his face. 'The arrest video pinged into her inbox and she was *not* happy. When Sanderson's solicitor announced that his client's making a complaint, Campbell arrived here and told Briscall to go on immediate leave.' He waved a bunch of forensic reports that he'd brought over. 'We all heard it.'

Sylhet felt like ages ago. It had been a long investigation.

'C'mon,' said Dougie. 'I'll buy you a drink. Dan and Alexej are already over there. With PC Li.'

332

Wednesday – Maya

The smell of fried breakfasts greeted me as I entered the lobby of Woodside residential home. Exhausted and hungry, I felt queasy as I signed the visitors' book. I popped my head round the door of the nursing staff's office, and collected a flower vase.

Stashed in my bag was a bunch of orange roses, and a selection of photographs. Despite my preparations, dread fluttered its wings, as it always did when I visited Mum. Would she recognise me today? The dementia waxed and waned, cruel and unforgiving, chomping at her personality and memory. Today, there was the issue of Sabbir's funeral to raise again.

It was after 8 a.m. when I arrived. Mum was already dressed, sitting in a chair in her room, hands folded in her lap as if she was waiting for something. From somewhere, Asian music weaved through the air. Her eyes were closed, and the skin looked soft over her cheekbones.

'Mum?' I whispered, not wanting to startle her. 'It's me.' It felt strange talking to her in Sylheti.

She didn't stir. My heart sank, for a brief moment wondering if she had slipped away. I kneeled down on the carpet at her side and clasped her frail, age-spotted hand in mine.

'Mum?' I stroked the baggy skin, relieved to feel a weak but regular rhythm in her wrist.

Her eyes opened. Beneath the milky film, which age had drawn over her once deep green eyes, there was a flicker of recognition.

'I've brought you some flowers.' I tried not to notice that she looked like a child in an adult's chair. Guilt twisted in my stomach. I could visit her more, cook her some meals and bring them in, come and read to her.

'Maya?' Her weak voice was lined with pleasure. I'd never heard it before. Recognition raised the corners of her mouth. 'It's been ages.' Her tired eyes were wide now.

I felt a jab of pain on seeing my mother so diminished, so utterly crushed by life and disease. I tried to let the pain settle so I could feel the warmth I'd forgotten I felt. But I knew it would never settle, and the best I could do was reach beneath it.

'Sorry, Mum, work's been crazy and —'

'Did you bury him?' Grief leaked through each syllable.

The voice on the radio began talking in Sylheti.

My breath caught in my throat. She *had* taken in our conversation last time. 'Yes. I thought we could do a little ritual or a prayer, if you'd like? I've brought Sabbir's favourite poem. And a picture of the swamp hens you both love.'

'You should have fetched him home. Back to his family. Where he belongs.'

I was expecting this. Had rehearsed my reply. 'I know you're disappointed, Mum, but it was what *he* wanted.'

'He didn't know what he wanted, poor boy. He was so confused.'

How could I move her on without upsetting her? 'No, Mum. He stated in his will if anything happened to him, he did *not* want to be brought back to the UK. He hated it here, remember? He never recovered from the attacks...' I hesitated, 'This recent stuff was the last straw.'

I'd planned what to say to Mum to avoid mentioning the abuse Sabbir had got when he finally came out as gay.

'Why did he have to take his life? My poor boy.'

Although it was my mother in front of me, I had to assume some emotional distance otherwise I couldn't cope and nor would she. Jaz and I'd had years of feeling responsible for Mum, years of looking after her. And despite my police training, none of it made any difference on the inside. They just gave me masks and techniques. Beneath those, I was biting back tears. 'He was *desperately* unhappy. Whether we understand his decision, it was what he wanted.' I held her hand between both of mine. 'He didn't want to live anymore.'

Mum rocked gently. Pulled her hand away and tugged a tissue from her cardigan sleeve. 'It's wrong,' she muttered under her breath. 'To take your life like that. Leave everyone behind you suffering and feeling guilty.'

I'd spent days and nights after Sabbir died turning this exact issue over in my mind. Hours on the phone with Jaz. Repeating myself to Dougie, boring him silly.

'Right or wrong, when you've felt as desperate as he did, and for so long, perhaps all you can think of is finding a release.'

Mum blew her nose and dabbed at her eyes.

'Shall I put your flowers in a vase for you? I got your favourite.' I peeled back the cellophane and showed Mum the bunch, knowing what she'd say.

'Thank you, dear. I remember the ones we used to get in Bangladesh . . .'

I arranged the stems. 'Is that one of the nurse's phones?' I pointed at the music source, a scratched iPhone.

'I thought you brought it?' Her face fogged over. 'One of the girls puts it on for me in the morning.'

She was confused again. Getting people mixed up. The radio was nice company for her, and a link with home.

The question popped out before I knew it. 'Are you pleased we came to live here, Mum? Or do you wish we'd stayed in Bangladesh?' I hadn't realised until now that it was the question I'd been desperate to ask for years – but had been too scared to.

Mum drifted and I wasn't sure if I was going to lose her.

I fished out the photographs from my bag and waited.

But then she spoke. 'At this time of year, when it's bitterly cold, I long for the summer monsoons. To feel the rain on my face.' She closed her eyes and put a hand on her cheek. 'To smell the rain

335

on the soil. Proper rain, not cold, thin, London rain. So green and lush. Where we grew up, we were surrounded by acres of pineapple plantations, and orange groves and tea terraces.'

'I brought some of the old photos, if you'd like to look at them?' I pulled over a table-on-wheels and spread out the pictures like a deck of cards.

Mum's bony hand reached out to an image of her and Dad, with us three children, in our old apartment in Sylhet, on the wooden veranda overlooking the Surma River. On Dad's face a languid, enigmatic expression made his features glow. I was on his lap, and he had one arm round Sabbir and Jaz, and with the other, he was stroking Mum's hair.

'Have you seen your father?'

The question struck like a dart.

'Why d'you ask that?' I didn't mean to snap.

She shrugged and stared into space. 'Just wondered.'

'Why? Why ask after all this time? No-one's seen him for nearly thirty years.'

Even the word 'father' made me feel shaky. As though it brought a presence to the room that hadn't been there for a very long time.

Mum traced her finger over the surface of the image. '*I've* seen him. A few weeks ago.' An energy had overtaken her face and eyes. 'He was so handsome.' She beamed as she said it and it was the saddest thing I'd ever seen.

'What d'you mean?' Was she imagining things? She had before.

'He came here.'

It was exactly as Jasmina had said. I felt sick. Hang on. Did I believe her? 'Mum?'

'What? Oh, I don't know, dear. Maybe I dreamed it. I get so confused. What did you ask me?'

I'd been so worried we were going to fall out over Sabbir's funeral. Little did I know she was going to mention Dad. 'You asked if I'd seen Dad.'

'Did I?' She was getting tired.

I placed the family photograph in Mum's lap. 'Shall I read the poem?' I found the page, and seeing the words that I virtually knew off by heart, I felt the tangled beginnings of understanding; of how scared my mother had been when we came to live in London, and how difficult it had been for her to adapt. How she'd clung to her language, and beliefs, not out of laziness but fear.

Taking Mum's hand in mine, I saw the words of the poem with fresh eyes. About the boy who waits for the hug he craves from his oblivious father. And I realised: perhaps that's what happens when people hurt others. As they shuffle along the path of life, they're simply doing the best they can.

Acknowledgements

Many of the ideas in this novel have been going round in my head since I started teaching in Tower Hamlets in 2002, and living in Newham soon after that. Both were diverse, vibrant places to work and live, and they prompted lots of questions about cultural dislocation and contemporary urban life.

When I left teaching in 2011, I decided to use fiction to explore some of the questions I had, and I combined these with my interest in the psychology of violence. I used the academic part of my MA dissertation to research how I could use imagination and empathy to write about cultures from the 'outside'. I used the creative part of my dissertation to begin the story. *Turn a Blind Eye* is the novel that's emerged as a result. The events and characters in it are fictionalised versions, and amalgamations, of ones I've experienced. I've also folded in things I've read and heard about in the news.

Many real-life events have inspired the book, including: the Tottenham race riots in 1985, and the murders of Cynthia Jarrett and PC Keith Blakelock; the BNP attacks on Bangladeshi students from Tower Hamlets College in the 1990s, many of whom suffered life-threatening injuries and died; the alleged murder in 2003 of seventeen-year-old British Pakistani, Shafilea Ahmed. In addition, since visiting Australia twice, I've wondered what can be learned from penal transportation and the experiences of the Aboriginal communities.

Turn a Blind Eye would not have been the book it is without the input and encouragement of numerous people from the writing community on- and off-line, and many non-writing friends. I am hugely grateful to my agent, Adam Gauntlett, and editor, Clio Cornish, who both loved the book from the outset. Both have helped me to shape and sharpen the story immeasurably. Thanks to: Stav Sherez for being a sounding board when I was hatching plans for the book; Anya Lipska and Eva Dolan, for their encouragement; to Abdul Wahid, Zack Miah, Razia Begum, Amina Chowdhury, Shoful Islam, Oksana Kovalenko and Amal Kutub for helping me with my research. To the many people I've accosted on the streets of East London in the rain and sunshine over the last four years; Bill Weaver, Elizabeth Haynes, Lisa Cutts, Caroline Mitchell and Rebecca Bradley for help with police procedures (all inaccuracies and flights of imagination are mine); Juliet Mushens, who supervised my dissertation; Sarah Hilary and Sophie Hannah for answering questions for my dissertation; David Mark for information on journalism and reporting; Emma Kavanagh, Claire McGowan, Sarah Pinborough, Rachel Amphlett. Thanks, also, to my Aussie pals for help with Maguire's language, and Zoe Valentine for reading for me.

Thanks are due to people who have read chapters, synopses, blurbs, and early drafts of the book: Lynne Milford, Louise Mangos, Debi Alper, Caroline Slater, Yvonne Johnston, Josephine Jarman Wiltshire, Pam McIlroy and Joanne Bartley. To Dave Sivers for beta reading for me, and Anne Hamilton for giving me feedback on two consecutive drafts.

To everyone else who's encouraged me – or simply listened – when I've burbled about writing: thank you. When I was growing up, reading and writing were my saviour. They still are.

If you are interested in the poem that Maya reads at Sabbir's funeral, again at the Green Bridge and at the end with her mother, it is *Bearhug* by Michael Ondaatje.

Vicky

Keep reading for an exclusive extract from

OUT OF THE ASHES

the next DI Maya Rahman novel – coming soon.

Friday 5th April, 2019, Brick Lane, East London
– Rosa

Rosa stood at the door of her newsagent's, staring out at the street she'd known since she was four. Above her, the drone of the fan heater filled the void in her head which grief had hollowed out. The tired contraption – one of Józef's purchases – made little impact on the chilly air in the shop behind her. These days she barely registered the crumbling plaster of the walls, nor the black mildew which clung to corners and crevices like an ugly rash. Her wrists and knuckles were giving her gyp again, now so gnarled by arthritis that the shop lock was stiff, drawers heavy, and she was beginning to drop things.

Across the street, activity caught her attention. She peered over the dusty window display to get a better look. A shiny red sign was going up on the premises opposite, where Rosenberg's jewellers used to be. Glass so tinted it was almost black. A fancy new bar by the looks of it, slap bang next-door to Mr Hamid's curry house. He wasn't going to be happy. Although these days, Brick Lane was barely recognisable from when she'd grown up and they were *all* struggling to make a living. It was so unsettling. Every fibre of her being was exhausted by the continual need to make decisions; to think about whether to follow her compatriots out of the East End and into the London suburbs.

Rosa did up her baggy cardigan. The loose waistband on her skirt should have told her to eat. Today was Friday, after all. But without Józef, the Sabbath meal wasn't the same, and except for the rare occasions when she had visitors, she didn't bother with the rituals anymore. What was the point of lighting candles when there was only one of you? She'd steam a plate of yesterday's chicken and potatoes. That would do her. She didn't have to go far to get home, just upstairs to the flat, even if it was still freezing at this time of year.

Through the shop window she noticed that the lights were out and the shutters down at the new soup place over the road, run by the Lithuanian couple. The ugly neon sign, with its air of Margate or Blackpool, wasn't flashing for once. That was odd. Not like them at all. They were usually open all hours of the day and night, selling their fancy five-quid soups to whoever could afford them. She had no objection to people earning a living, but her parents would be turning in their graves. For several years after the war, when the Feldmans had arrived from Warsaw, they'd survived on the food and handouts from the soup kitchen in Brune Street. It was extraordinary to think that what had been humble subsistence for many families was now a fad-food. So many of the newcomers had too much money, that's what it was. She'd been over for a spy at the menu, of course, when they were shut. Couldn't find a single thing she fancied and didn't know what most of it was, let alone how to pronounce it. Keen-war, or something, a girl with a nose-stud and pink hair had told Rosa.

She sighed. She missed her old neighbours. *Those* were Sabbath meals to look forward to. Mrs Blum from the bagel shop over the road – what was now the soup shop – would make the challah. Rosa could smell it now: rich, eggy and sweet. It had been ages since she'd felt one of those in her hands, soft and warm, in its pretty braid shape. The Altmans would bring the wine, and dear Mr Altman was always happy to fix any wobbly furniture. The Posners would bring candles and offer to mend shoes. And the Rosenbergs, the jewellers, always came with freshly-made kugel. But now they'd all died or moved away.

Except Rosa.

And there was that feeling again, a gnawing emptiness, a sense that life had moved on without her.

The sound of voices jolted her back into the present.

Yelling.

And music.

Outside in the street a thumping bass beat started up. Tremors vibrated through the shop, and a booming noise invaded the silence of her thoughts. Yobbos, probably, spitting everywhere and pumping out music from one of those dreadful sound-systems. They'd pass in a minute.

But they didn't.

The music got louder and louder, and – oh, typical – the group seemed to have stopped outside Rosa's shop. All guffaws, swearing, floppy hair and hoodies. More voices, shouting and cheering, and one by one, more people were joining them. What on *earth* was going on? On a Friday afternoon, from lunchtime onwards, she was used to the steady trickle of people down Brick Lane, getting ready for a night on the tiles and a curry, but it was unusual to see so many people together. She edged over to the corner of the shop window to get a better view. The music had changed and a handful of them were dancing, if jabbing a finger in the air and screaming counted as dancing these days. Teenagers, by the look of them. Some younger. She wasn't very good at judging age, and they all wore such similar clothes, but she'd put money on some of them not being a day over ten.

Rosa squashed her nose against the pane of glass. She couldn't believe what she was seeing. She used to know all the kids round here; knew their families by name, but none of this lot looked familiar. There were at least ten of them, dancing in the street, throwing themselves about like acrobats, bending, leaping, twirling each other around. For a moment, Rosa was transported back to the tea room dances she and Józef used to go to before Agnieszka and Tomasz were born. They'd save for weeks, get dolled up in their best clothes. *Oh, how much fun they'd been.*

Outside, the street hummed with a similar joy. An innocence. This new style of dancing wasn't her thing, of course, but they weren't doing any harm, were they? There were more than twenty of them now, maybe thirty. And someone was lighting sparklers and passing them round for the kids. She *adored* sparklers. Before she knew it, her fingers pulled the handle and she was outside, the bell dinging as the door shut behind her. The sulphurous smell set light to her dulled senses and she felt irritation shake itself from her shoulders. She was a kid again, at bonfires and street parties in the summer, with people passing sparklers round. Rosa cleared her throat. Coughed. Her lungs weren't good these days, weakened by years of a poorly heated flat, the crumbling plaster of the damp shop walls, and Józef's cigarette smoke.

She joined the throng of passers-by who were huddled, mesmerised by the dancing. Was it some kind of student gathering? She was puzzled. Who was in charge? She couldn't see any organisers or anyone giving instructions, and had no idea where the music was coming from. People were merging with the group of their own accord and encouraging others to do the same.

The music brought a smile to Rosa's cold lips. Her heel began to tap and she was lost to nostalgia. It was such a relief to forget the pain and drudgery of the last year. Was that Lulu and 'Shout?' Her heart leaped. Many a time she and Józef had danced to that tune. Her mind was flooded with memories of all the occasions when they'd danced together, his warm hand in the small of her back, guiding her forwards, the other clasping hers, keeping her safe. She felt a lump in her throat. They were glorious memories but tainted now by the agony of loss. It had only been a year. She still missed him so much.

A waltz kicked in, floaty and dramatic. Initially, it had been youngsters dancing but now it was people of all ages, lured over by the infectious atmosphere of Brick Lane on a chilly April afternoon. Hearing the waltz start, a Sikh man checked his turban and clasped the hands of a silvery-haired woman in a navy-blue trench coat. She was about Rosa's age. She was giggling, and had a small flat bag diagonally across her body, her head tilted back, carefree and stunned, as though she hadn't had so much fun in ages. Perhaps she was a widow too?

Rosa's hips started to sway, and she was tempted to go over and join in. *What was she thinking?* She was being silly. She couldn't. Who would mind the shop while she was cavorting in the street?

Another crowd of youths arrived, hee-hawing and smoking, head-to-toe in sweatshirts, drainpipe jeans and baseball shoes. Didn't they feel the cold? In tow were several more young boys. Why weren't they all at school?

Elvis' crooning tones wafted down the street and once again Rosa's spirits soared. The teenagers looked so funny, impersonating the rock 'n' roll moves of 'All Shook Up'. She sniggered. It was the most fun she'd had on a Friday afternoon since ...

Józef would have enjoyed this. 'Come on, Rosa,' he would have said in his calm, decisive voice, and he'd have locked the shop, led her out into the street and begun whirling her around with that boyish grin of his.

A quick head count told her there were about fifty people dancing now and a good twenty more hanging around. The street whiffed of whacky-backy. Rosa had forgotten her nagging joints and aching legs; the grimy shelves with mounting dust; the delivery boxes she couldn't carry; the cans that had gone out of date. For a few sweet moments, she'd stopped feeling sick to death of the damn shop, of book-keeping and worrying and making decisions. She didn't care about any of it anymore. All she wanted was –

A loud splitting sound tore through the air, followed by a series of cracks and bangs. Huge orange flames burst out of one of the top floor windows of the shop opposite, and billowed upwards, followed by swirling streams of black smoke. Then flames burst from another window on the same floor, and acrid fumes filled the street. Burning timber peeled away from the windows and fell on the crowd below.

Screams pierced the clouds of grey as embers rained down on people's hair, faces and clothes.

Shouting.

People were running for cover, desperately trying to shield their faces from the falling debris.

'Help, *help,*' came a cry from the ground in front of her. Someone was clutching their arm and screaming.

The air was cloying. Putrid. Flames flapped and licked at the outside masonry, and one after the other windows blew out. Swathes of grey were creeping round the front door of the shop and a blanket of smoke obscured large parts of the building.

Screaming, as people were plunged into blind terror, realising that they could die.

Through the haze, people were coughing, retching and staggering, scarves and hands clasped over their mouths, desperate to escape the blaze.

Rosa was paralysed by sounds from years ago, of the bombs and blasts in the Warsaw Ghetto; of the homes and synagogues which were blown up and burnt to the ground.

But this wasn't Poland and it wasn't the war. She had to escape; had to ring 999 and get the fire brigade. As the blaze ripped through the roof, smoke continued to spiral upwards into the sky. Rosa stumbled blindly towards the blue door of her shop, to the step and doorway, arms groping ahead for something to grab. The fumes snagged at her throat and caught her chest, making her wheeze. She was gasping for air so much she was retching. Finally, her hands made contact with the handle. She used all her weight to heave the door open and stumbled inside, pushing it shut behind her as quickly as she could. She sucked in a lungful of air. It was like breathing through needles. She had … to get … to … the back … room … and … the phone. Stands and magazine racks flashed past her as she lurched towards the till, gasping for breath and snatching for a hold. She hauled her way round the counter, head spinning, and grabbed the phone receiver from the wall. Her eyes were streaming.

Keep blinking, she told herself.

Breathe.

You've been in this situation before and you made it out.

She tried to calm herself; to rub away the tears that the fumes had produced; to steady her shaking hands and press the buttons. What should she say? Had there been a bomb? Was it terrorists? Just say fire. *Fire.* FIRE.

Rosa felt her head starting to spin. Lights flashed and she went floppy. Her mind slipped sideways and everything stopped.

DI MAYA RAHMAN RETURNS IN

OUT OF THE ASHES

A terrible accident – or a fire set to kill?

A flash mob is interrupted by a huge explosion, and DI Maya Rahman is called to the scene. Fire is raging through Brick Lane – and it's soon clear that it was a deliberate act of violence.

The discovery of two charred bodies in the burnt-out shell of a building turns an arson attack into a double-murder investigation. And, with witnesses too caught up in the chaos to have seen a thing, Maya is without a single lead.

There are many possible motives. Money? Terrorism? Revenge? And when reports of a second, even more horrifying crime arrive, Maya knows she doesn't have long to find answers – before all of East London goes up in flames…

COMING SOON FROM VICKY NEWHAM – AVAILABLE TO PRE-ORDER NOW

Q&A with Vicky Newham

1. Why did you choose to write a Bangladeshi detective? Given your own background, how did you go about creating the character of Maya?

When I was teaching in East London, a lot of my students were Bangladeshi. In order to help them gain as much as possible from their education, I tried to learn about their lives: the challenges they faced; their cultural norms; their fears and aspirations; their world-view. Much was different from my own background but, beneath those differences, their hopes and fears were exactly the same as mine. As the plot grew for my novel, set in and around the area where I worked, it was a no-brainer to have a female Bangladeshi as my main character. I could write the story from (partially) her viewpoint. All I had to do was flesh out the details of her age, family and relationships. I made her the senior detective as it enabled me to explore gender in what's still a male-dominated world.

2. Tell us about Maya.

Maya and her family arrived in the UK in 1982. Like many Bangladeshis, they left Sylhet after the Liberation War and settled in Brick Lane, hoping for a better life. Maya was four, the youngest of three children. Her whole family have adapted to life in Tower

Hamlets in different ways, as you'll see from the novel. These experiences motivated Maya's decision to join the police. *Turn a Blind Eye* gives the reader a good idea of who Maya is and there's plenty more to come. I wanted her to be human and relatable. She has flaws and ghosts, as we all do, but she has a happy relationship and isn't an alcoholic!

3. Do you have a personal connection to the area?

Yes. I used to teach A-level and GCSE Psychology in a Tower Hamlets school, and at the time I lived in Newham (the adjoining borough). Given my surname, it was weird when I had to phone the council! I loved living in East London, and used to cycle from East Ham to Stepney every day to get to school. I'm still in touch with lots of people there, which is useful for the books.

4. There are a lot of timely social issues at the heart of *Turn a Blind Eye*. Can you tell us a bit about them and why you wanted to use a crime novel to explore them?

Pick up any paper or switch on the news and inequality, immigration, identity and cultural differences will come into one of the stories. As a teacher, a psychologist, and an ex-East London resident, I saw how these issues affected people's lives day-in, day-out. I found it simultaneously heartbreaking and inspiring, and it literally kept me awake at night. In the book, I wanted to explore the things I experienced and try to make sense of what's going on in the world. However, I was keen for these to be in the background in the way they are in a lot of Scandinavian crime fiction and the TV drama, *Hinterland*. In *Turn a Blind Eye*, the focus is on the puzzle that lies at the heart of the story, the characters, their lives and experiences. The reader sees the characters dealing with inequality, for example, while they go about their lives, trying to make the best of them. Crime fiction is ideal for this.

5. Can you tell us a bit about the research that went into the book?

A lot of it took place inadvertently while I was living and teaching in East London. I stored all sorts of questions in my head and kept notebooks of details. The beginning of the novel started life as my MA dissertation piece, so when I began to plot it, I had to read up on writing outside one's own culture. I was keen for the book to feel believable so I spent months walking round the locations, talking to people and taking thousands of photographs. I also wrote numerous scenes there, in cafés and parks, on benches, buses and station platforms, so I could bring the setting and people to life on the page. It was helpful also to be able to consult people I know who still live there. In addition, I listen to East London radio a lot and continually scan the local papers. For Maya's colleague, Dan, Australian crime fiction and dramas are useful. I have Sydney radio and television on to catch vocabulary, accent, and news stories (my neighbours must wonder what I'm doing), and have been there twice, so that helps. In fact, Dan's character stems from those trips, and from my interest in penal transportation and the experiences of Aboriginal Australians. I hoped his ethnicity would give him an interesting lens through which to view Britain.

6. Tell us a bit about yourself?

I live on the south coast of England in the pretty seaside town of Whitstable. I love it there. It's slower-paced than the city, and the vibe is like going back in time. People are friendly and chat in the street, and I swim in the sea in the summer. I still teach and tutor a bit of psychology. If you follow my Twitter feed, you'll know that I have a crazy cockerpoo (dog), who is great fun. I'm still passionate about education and learning, and I've written since I was a child. My writing is very psychological as that's my background and the way my brain works.

7. What would you like people to 'get' from the book?

I'm hoping they'll find a gripping story. It's a contemporary police procedural with a puzzle at its heart, with a few extra bits! In addition to a recognisable investigation, there's an exploration of the psychology of violence. I'm also hoping the book offers a window into what it's like to live and work in East London from the point of view of a Bangladeshi female and her Australian male colleague.

You can find out more about the DI Maya Rahman series at http:// vickynewham.com/.

Vicky is on Twitter as @VickyNewham and on Facebook at https:// www.facebook.com/VickyNewhamAuthor/

Join the conversation with #TurnaBlindEye

ONE PLACE. MANY STORIES

Bold, innovative and
empowering publishing.

FOLLOW US ON:

@HQStories